I0653928

Star Divers
Dungeons of Bane

By Stephen Landry

Published by Level Up in the United Kingdom in 2019

Cover by Claire Wood

ISBN: 978-1-83919-295-1

www.levelup.pub

For Tori

ACCESS

NAME: BREQ

Age: 17	Class: Scout
Level: 30	Health: 100
Status: Alive	Stamina: 100
Mana: 100	

Load out: M7-7 kinetic Rifle, Sabre (melee), Short grip energy pistol, smoke grenades

Checking for necessary update files...

Initializing...

Player environment meets necessary requirements.

Retina scan / Identity confirmed.

Dive 100%

Loading player data...

Year 2074

1.
A Boy in a Star

LOCATION: ALPHA CENTAURI A
ENVIRONMENT: INHOSPITABLE
RESOURCES: NONE

> **Quick Lore**
> Alpha Centauri A, Alpha Centauri B and Proxima
> Centauri make up the Alpha Centauri Star system.

— Quest —
Orbital Decay
Expected Difficulty: Expert
Rewards: Artefact

It was more than a few hours since I had dropped in and I felt like I was getting close to finding the artefact.

If you ask me how I come to be standing inside the decaying shell of an old-world starship, plummeting into a star with my arm bleeding and poison running through my veins, it might be a little hard for me to explain. We could start with why I was risking my life, or I could jump straight to why I was outside my armour and armed with only my rifle and a knife, or maybe it would be easier to talk about how I got this gash on my hand. Truth is, I'm not really sure about the gash or the bleeding arm and I think the poison is my own fault for not having come properly prepared. Not that I care to admit that. Maybe it's the absence of nausea or the lack of headaches and muscle strain but when I'm playing *Bane* I can feel the game guiding me. Like a sixth sense that awakens when I dive. Something about this world makes me feel more alive than the one I come from. Alive enough to push past the pain.

I've been a Corpse Diver for almost two years, since right before I turned sixteen, just old enough to play. Since being emancipated this has been my full-time job. My career. Becoming a Corpse Diver is kind of like joining the army, only the risk of perma-death is a lot lower. Not that it didn't happen…sometimes things in the game have repercussions in the real world. Both mind and body.

I was rescued by the game. Picked from the streets of South Boston in the New England Recovery zone where I joined the corporation my father worked for before both he and my mother had passed away. After their death the corporation had left me on my own and left to my own devices I learned to survive for a year until I found my way back to them.

I wasn't really bleeding inside a starship trapped in an orbital decay. No, my real body was back at Keen Industries Industrial complex strapped safe and sound inside a full dive pod. Probably being monitored by some tech in a lab coat doing a study on virtual immersion and said side effects.

This was my second solo mission. The first for which I had hijacked one of our shuttles and the first I'd seriously screwed up. Normally, missions I go on are fetch quests, low level hunts for artefacts and courier missions. For this one, I'd gone after an artefact on the edge of the 'Cold Zone'.

Artefacts, or echoes, are remnants left behind by player character deaths. Guarded by Hollows, ghostlike figures that can kill a player with their touch, artefacts are rare to find and worth a great deal. The echoes left behind farther from the Spire can have rewards that are rare, while if a player dies close to the core worlds the echo rewards will be common. Not only do players pay us to chase their echoes but many companies both in-game and in the real pay out large sums for rare artefacts. The artefacts themselves could be anything. Most of the time they come as weapons, gems, or some kind of unique apparel.

Nel, my hovering robotic companion, had picked up this bounty several days ago and informed me first about it this morning. It was high risk, high reward. I'm sure if I had asked the others they would have said 'no'. Of course, had I told them it would have meant a smaller cut for me. Artefacts can be traded for real world money but we were under contract from Keen Industries. In return for service they give us food, shelter and a small allowance. Death means restarting at Level 1, rebuilding your avatar, losing all your equipment, powers, upgrades etc. Being a Corpse Diver is a dangerous job, the kind that most players stay away from.

We were deep inside the shell of an old world seed ship called the *Lockhead*. Looked like it had been derelict for some time before making its way this close to Alpha Centauri A. They were on the wrong side of the system but that was all a part of *Bane*'s lore. Humanity had fled Earth sometime in the late twenty-first century after discovering what they called a 'world gate' near the edge of our solar system. They found themselves stranded. Because of a malfunction in the world gate, once they passed through they could never return back. Not to mention it was unknown whether the gate would bring them back to Earth at all. The colonists believed that while they had been trapped inside the gate the malfunction had caused them to diverge from Earth's timeline by over thirty-thousand years.

Emerging from their time capsule, it wasn't long before they discovered one habitable world and set up a basecamp, built over the top of alien ruins. They called it the Spire. Human and alien technology merged as new technologies developed, allowing us to extend our reach across the landscape and towards the stars. It was at the Spire humanity discovered an alien species called the Brosechels, aka Chels for short. That time of discovery soon led to an age of rebellion as colonists abandoned the Spire and sought shelter elsewhere. The discovery of a second world gate led to the discovery of a third and fourth and so on until 76 quadrants had been identified. The game itself picks up three hundred years later. Humanity, aided by the Chels in an effort for both species to survive, are mapping out all 76 quadrants or levels and christened a newly discovered number 77 the 'Cold Zone'.

Many things about *Bane* made the world feel post-apocalyptic. For one, all our worlds were in ruins. There were guardians to keep the peace but most of the zones were filled with pirates (also called raiders or marauders) and smugglers. Backwater worlds traded with the Spire which acted as the Hub of the entire game.

Alpha Centauri was as far away from the Spire as I could go without being stranded and I had to use a hack to get my dropship as far as I had. It was somewhere just between the fifth and sixth quadrant. I was good at the game but I wasn't the best. So far *Bane* had a player count around four million but sometimes it felt like everyone on the planet was playing.

I wasn't here to play games. This quest was off the record and I wouldn't have a team coming to back me up anytime soon. I was getting tired of basic fetch quests and fighting low level monsters. I needed to start making a name for myself if I was going to continue levelling up.

'Are you really going to quit?' asked Nel. Nel was neither a man nor woman but would take on the persona of a female more often than not. At the moment she sounded like she was in shock at the idea.

'Where did you hear that?'

'Cass was telling me about it.'

'I thought you weren't supposed to spill secrets?'

'I was never asked to keep it secret,' Nel responded.

'I've thought about it, I don't want to live as an indentured servant forever, there is more out there, more to this world and the real world that I want,' I replied focusing ahead.

'Are you planning to apply for a position with another cruiser?'

'No, I want my own,' I replied and felt happy at the thought.

'With the amount of allowance you gain from bounties that would take you three hundred and forty-seven years of saving…and that does not account for any inflation or…'

'Enough, I know,' I said, cutting Nel off before she went on about how having my own starship and crew and running my own guild was next to impossible. 'A kid can dream.'

'Dreams are useless; if you plan on selling the artefact from this bounty yourself you will have to acquire approximately forty-seven more similar jobs should this artefact itself be estimated at a value of two million credits,' Nel said.

'Thanks, so you'll come give me a hand on those right?'

'I am programmed to serve you so long as you are a Corpse Diver.' Nel hesitated, 'the fact that they let you join before you even reached level ten is a miracle and I find that I wish you to survive and succeed.'

For an artificial intelligence the response was solid enough. I knew Nel didn't want me to leave…telling me the odds was her way of convincing me to give up frantic quests like this. The two of us had been together since the beginning. Everyone else would have said owning my starship was just a pipe dream as well…well, maybe not my best friend Damien. Luckily for me it wouldn't take forty-seven more quests. Unknown to Nel, the black market was alive and well inside the Spire and artefacts could be sold for double sometimes triple the amount they would via corporations and merchant guilds.

'This is going to be great: drop in, grab the artefact and get out before the starship crashes into the sun,' I said. No one was listening except Nel who also, might I add, had the personality matrix of a child. Meaning she was either playful or dead serious all of the time. Sometimes both.

'I told you the odds of your being successful were three hundred thousand to one,' Nel was following close behind me.

If I managed to grab the artefact and escape, Nel would most likely have to carry whatever it was I found. This thought amused me and holding my side, I pushed on. I was dragging myself along the hallway…It was easy to forget I was losing health. My bleeding resistance was low. We were running out of time. I was running out of time. Nel had a tracker built in that allowed her to sense the location of the echo. My guess, it was similar to the same sense, acting as a radar, that allowed her to track teammates and call for aid no matter how far out we were. Some called it the ansible and it was the only way inside the game to send and receive messages instantaneously from light years away.

'They are going to kill you if we aren't back in a few hours,' Nel said.

'I know, that's why we're not going back empty handed.'

'What's the excuse this time? Another joyride across the rings of Minerva?'

'Something like that, that's pretty good, do you still have any images left over from our last side quest in that region?' I wanted to laugh but my ribs were killing me. So far, I hadn't run into any creatures or Hollows and that wasn't a good sign. 'It's not possible the echo is gone?'

'No, echoes take days, sometimes weeks to dissipate,' Nel confirmed. I knew that but the farther down the rabbit hole we crawled the harder it would be for us to reach our shuttle on the side of the hull. My health had already dropped to about 8. I had maybe two stims I could use that would give me a boost of 10 HP each, but those would have to wait.

'We can turn back now if you are too tired,' said Nel.

'Just think of all the EXP and credits we'll lose.'

Nel cut me off. 'That YOU will lose, I am an artificial construct, I gain no pleasure from E X P or credits.'

In my head, I was thinking of something to say in response. I had already joked about oil changes, getting Nel's gunmetal grey body polished, tune-ups and adding some chrome, but usually my smart remarks fell on deaf ears. Everything Nel needed was paid for and supplied by the corporation and subtracted from what we - the Corpse Divers - made.

'This is still better than trying to beat the main story quest,' I said. The main storyline was hidden. *Bane* was an open world MMORPG with survival elements. There were side quests, quests made by players, etc., but the main quest...the one that progressed the world as a whole, was still being put together piece by piece. Every so often, some lucky player managed to stumble across a scripted event that progressed the world in some small way, but for the most part we were all playing the game as a second life.

'Will this be your second or third strike?' Nel asked.

'Not sure, I think I've had more than three already,' I said. Three strikes and the company let you go, but with so few players willing to put their characters on the line divers were becoming harder and harder to replace. I also had friends that had covered for me more than once. Damien one of them. The higher your level the more valuable you were.

```
Location Discovered: Hall of Immortals
Environment: Hospitable
Resources: Artefact
```

I walked inside the 'Hall of Immortals'. Now this was different. Ships are separated out into distinct parts but the actual layers aren't given specific location names. I smiled and moved myself away from the wall. The room that stood before us was a great hall with a tall ceiling. The walls themselves were grey and covered in metal plating like most of the ship but several runes were carved all around in intricate designs across the top and bottom. The runes seemed to almost point in the direction of what looked like a fallen paladin, a high-level soldier wearing an astronaut suit. At the time of his arrival the ship's environment must have been haywire. From where I had been standing I could see dried blood across the ground. There had been another body dragged away.

'Nel!' I shouted, 'stand back we aren't alone down here,' I snapped up right holding my rifle forward. The problem with tracking echoes was that you never knew exactly how the person died. Sure, some might say something about the cause of death in the bounty or while they are giving you a description of the quest, but for the most part it is a mystery until you are right there in person. I glanced at my heads-up display. Nothing had changed.

My health was displayed on a small red bar across the bottom of my vision, just above a blue line for my stamina and a green bar for powers (which were currently greyed out since I hadn't been blessed with anything useful quite yet). The user interface was minimal. Just enough information we didn't have to do a circular motion or gesture with our hands all the time to check our stats. The hand gesturing was mostly for building skills or casting simple abilities such as hacking. The minimal interface also made for a better more immersive experience.

'Do you want me to contact the others?' Nel asked.

'No, not yet, I don't want to drag anyone else into this.'

'What about Damien?' Nel asked again.

Damien had been my best friend since I made peace with my parents passing. I was starving on the streets when he walked past me holding a bottle of water. I attacked him for it and after he nearly knocked me out he shared some with me. Damien helped me find shelter for the night and the night after. Meeting together he even convinced me to sign up for *Bane*. Damien was almost two years older than I was and had his own hover bike; loving parents; a home and a job (he worked as a Corpse Diver and went to school and hoped to study engineering). When he saw what my situation was he talked to some of the people at his work and they came and offered me the chance to work for them. That was how I made my return back to the company. It was a separate division from that in which my father worked but it still felt like I had returned in some way. Damien took me under his wing and introduced me to the rest of what became my team: Aiden, Brand, Shiru, Pierce, Eli, and Cass.

'No, do not contact Damien,' I said, 'I'll handle this.'

We were traversing the lowest part of the ship. It would take anyone several hours to reach us regardless, unless they could teleport to my exact location.

A spider-like creature emerged into the Hall of Immortals but ignored me, I was hidden in its blind spot. My heads-up display gave me a variety of information about it.

I was ready to fire on the creature before giving it a second thought. Aiming down my sight. Unlike most players, who utilized the game's auto-aim feature, I relied on my own skills. Damien had taught me that. Showed me how to be capable on my own. He told me those were the skills that would make me a valuable player.

```
Arachnid
Level: 35
Hostile
```

It was five levels stronger than me. I should have expected that going in. A creature's health was never displayed unless for some unusual circumstance. It was well known that most creatures level 1 -10 had a health in the hundred range (like that of players) while creatures 11-20 had up to a thousand health or so. Creatures above 20 were in the several thousands range. One creature I had faced during an event almost a year prior had a health close to fifty thousand. It took dozens of players to take the thing down. I knew this quest was expert level and I hadn't done anything solo like this in a while. Not that I did much solo at all. A part of being in a guild meant I almost always worked together with a team.

So far I was lucky. The Arachnid hadn't spotted me. It likely had a health close to two-three thousand. Five thousand if it was a queen. Guess it was a good thing Damien had told me to build my stealth level up as much as possible and also a good thing I wasn't wearing any bulky, loud armour. If I got a critical hit with my first shot my stealth would double the impact. I could probably knock a few hundred HP off in one or two attacks. Worst case scenario I was glad for what I had on. The black mesh I was wearing was an Environmental Protection Suit. It would heat up in cold temperatures, cool down in heat, even create a small shield around me for a second if something tried to fire at me. The shield had a cool down of 5 seconds but most of the time that would be enough to get a clean shot off at whatever was trying to kill me. The suit was also capable of helping me survive in the vacuum of space for 2 minutes and 30 seconds exactly.

I drew my rifle and aimed but couldn't stop shaking.

So much for being capable.

I couldn't get a clean shot.

I could feel something was amiss.

The Arachnid turned towards me and I felt paralyzed.

Nel had a small handgun attachment and fired.

The Arachnid took five points of damage but that hardly mattered.

'Shall we retreat back to the shuttle now?'

'No!' I was more determined than ever to retrieve the artefact.

'Our odds of survival are now two million three hundred and ten thousand to one, and let me add that if you break me the corporation will be very upset with you.'

I thought about telling Nel to shut up but that wouldn't have mattered. The Arachnid was already moving towards us. I charged my shot and fired at what was probably an eye, watching closely as the creature's health dropped. I could make a quick guess based on the impact of my shot. I had hit it in a critical area. Encouragingly, the creature's health dropped by about a quarter. Charged shots tripled my rifle's damage, but I had to wait another ten seconds before firing; alternatively I could switch to rapid fire and try and take the Arachnid down quickly using small bursts.

Click. I changed the mode on my rifle and fired three small bursts of energy at the spider. Barely a scratch. I prepared myself for its incoming attack as Nel rushed front of me to knock the creature backwards. I rolled to get an angle and fired again, switching back to charged shots.

For five minutes we danced. The Arachnid stabbing down at me with sharp points at the end of long ebony limbs and me dodging what were undoubtedly fatal attacks. I could see the red stain on one of the legs where it had killed the player character. Every time, no matter the whether the odds were for or against me it didn't matter. Knowing what was at stake, the fact I could lose my entire progression, years of work. I was afraid yes, Sad for the player that died yes but focused on myself, my own survival. That fear, floating anxiety, every time I faced down a creature, if I wanted to survive I had to let loose and focus on combat.

As often as I safely could, I fired back and the spider grew weaker, until Nel got the final shot: a critical shot on the Arachnid's abdomen. I was rewarded with half the EXP.

'Almost level thirty-one,' I said proudly looking at the corpse of the Arachnid, studying it, hoping maybe it had dropped some extra loot. Nothing. I moved back towards my main objective.

Laying on the ground beside the dead astronaut was an **artefact weapon** disguised as an M1 Garand, a World War II service rifle used by American soldiers. I picked it up and looked it over. I recognized the weapon as my father had a replica of one that he kept on display in his office. My great-great-grandfather had served in the Second World War. My father would tell me it was important that we honoured our past as we looked towards a brighter future. It would have been nicer had the world not started falling apart earlier.

A number of lines had been etched onto the side of the rifle along with a pair of eyes scratched just along the barrel.

'Almost don't want to sell it,' I said, slinging the artefact over my shoulder.

'Sir, we have a situation,' Nel said.

'What now? We've got the artefact.'

'We are entering the point of no return, the *Lockhead*'s hull is starting to fracture and in less than fifteen minutes the atmosphere inside the ship will no longer be hospitable.'

'Okay, that is a problem, can you get us out of here?'

'No sir, we're going to have to steer the starship away from Alpha Centauri's orbit or we will collapse under the star's gravity,'

I had the feeling that Nel was smiling, or at least looking to tell me 'I told you so,' to some extent.

'Lead me to the bridge control,' I ordered.

Two minutes later I was standing in front of a holographic interface.

```
┌─────────────────────────────────────┐
│              HACK                    │
│       60% Chance success.            │
└─────────────────────────────────────┘
```

I drew a circle with my hand and activated one of the few abilities I had. I could see a pattern of numbers before me. Another sixty seconds and I had control of the ship.

'Twelve minutes until death,' Nel said floating behind me.

'You could help, you're a machine: can't you just talk to the *Lockhead?*'

'Negative, *Lockhead* uses old technology that is incompatible with AI,' Nel answered.

'Fine, fine, I got this,' I felt calm and placed my hands on the controls, slowly turning the gigantic starship to the left...

'Other way,' said Nel.

I began turning the controls back towards the right, firing the ship's boosters and burning up what power was left in the ion drive.

'Sir, we have an incoming message,' said Nel.

'Not now!' I shouted trying to concentrate on steering the two of us to safety.

'Sir, it is a message from Damien.'

'I'll call him after we aren't falling into a star.'

'Sir, the message is marked urgent,'

'Nel, calculate the odds of our survival should I stop what I'm doing to read my messages,' I was studying our position

13

through a holographic display as we slowly began to spin away from the star. Nel was silent.

I let go of the *Lockhead's* control.

'That should buy us some time, too bad I can't salvage the whole ship,' I said looking towards Nel.

Nel was silent.

'Nel, let's head back to the shuttle for extraction. We'll store the artefact and head back to the Spire. I need to logout to eat some dinner, please don't tell any of the others about what we found.'

Nel was silent.

'Call the shuttle to meet us at the closest airlock. Nel?'

Nel's silence broke...

'Damien is dead.'

2.
The Spire

LOCATION: ALPHA -1 STAR SYSTEM
ENVIRONMENT: THREE HOSPITABLE WORLDS
RESOURCES: IRON ORE, GOLD, OXYGEN,
MERCHANTS GUILD, BANK

Quick Lore

Alpha-1 is located near the Kettle Nebula inside the Serpent Cloud and has three hospitable worlds (Apus, Orithyia, and Lyra) with small settlements. Each settlement is run by a mayor and owned by different players or companies. The Corpse Divers have a hub on Apus where their cruiser, the *Ibanez*, floats in orbit.

— Quest —
Funeral for a Friend
Expected Difficulty: None
Rewards: None

The walk back to the shuttle was silent. Neither Nel nor I said a word to one another as I strapped myself in and programmed a course back to the planet Apus where the other Corpse Divers would be waiting for me. I already had a call from Cass asking me where the hell I had been. I lied and said I went to explore Alpha-3 Euthenia in quadrant 2, a low-level dungeon where newer players went to grind. When I first started it was a requirement to spend several days a week levelling up your character and traversing different environments. In the beginning it was a blast. The game world felt fluid and the enemies were overwhelming. Each kill was a rush. I can still remember having chills the first time I slayed a Wraith boss. I would have to hack the shuttle's navigation and history before I logged out but that was easy. Hacking was one of the few skills I had that I was actually good at.

It would be another twenty minutes before the shuttle was close to Apus in Alpha-1...I had to speak to Damien. Nel had to be lying.

```
Logout
```

There was no one waiting for me outside my pod. No interns, no doctors, not even security marching up and down the halls. I unstrapped myself and pushed my headgear to the side. 'How did Damien die?' I wondered aloud, standing up, ready to ask him where it was he had gotten himself killed.

Next to me was an empty pod with a 'Do Not Use' sign taped on the front of it. I walked down the hall. I felt alone as I felt the cold air brush against my cheeks. I was wearing normal clothes...a graphic tee and some cargo pants. Nothing warm, even though the weather outside was changing. Anyway, Keen Industries were supposed to deliver me a jacket with their logo, so I didn't see the point in buying anything new. Each of us were given what we needed and even assigned specific pods to use. They were ours, paid for by the corporation as another incentive for us to hand over everything we found in the game. Technically they didn't have to pay for us to have our own pods but as much as they made selling artefacts it was cheaper for them than having players not able to login from broken dives at home.

16

Damien played for the love of the game. He didn't need it like I did. He had a loving family, a home to go back to while I stayed in the shelter at the complex with several of the others, sleeping on a dirty cot. Sometimes I crashed at his place. He had his own personal pod too…maybe he had stayed home. Corporate were always doing maintenance on the pods, so maybe he had tried to come to work and couldn't. No. It was rare if ever he would use his pod at home for anything other than personal gaming.

As I continued to wander through the complex my mind began to fill with terrible ideas. Nel couldn't have been serious. Damien couldn't be dead. Not really. He was already level 52 and had just purchased his own personal fighter with a bonus he made during *Operation Two to Tango*.

'SIR!' I yelled, finally spotting someone.

'Kid? What are you doing wandering around here?' said the attendant. It was a security officer. I could see he had a small fire-arm attached to his hip and he was wearing a bulletproof jacket over a t-shirt and name tag.

'Do you know if Damien Walker came in today?' I asked.

The security officer looked at me and down at the floor. 'You're on his team aren't you,' he said at last. His eyes looked hollow.

'Yes sir, I'm a Corpse Diver, zeta-one-nine,' I told him my in-game profession and call sign, as if that would mean something to him.

'I'm sorry,' the officer said, 'it was heart failure about half an hour ago.'

You can only imagine my reaction.

Damien was gone.

My best friend's funeral was held a few days later. His mother blamed the game: calling for a ban on the pods. Damien wasn't the first to experience heart failure while playing during a full dive and he wouldn't be the last. Sometimes even with pain dampeners set on the lowest setting and the game's feature that made death feel like a dream there were situations where the user's body reacted in negative way. All of that was off the record though. Just rumours I had read on the net. Nothing was certain. The doctors said Damien had some kind of undiagnosed heart condition, that it was an accident. There was no way to prove whether the game was actually the cause of death and with millions of players the loss of a few meant nothing. We also all had contracts. Not to mention the game-world was a way of life for many, myself included. Most were grateful for VR. There was less crime and the pods were a turning out to be a beneficial way to measure one's health.

Sometimes I don't know how I keep going. I don't know why I get up every day. Face my demons. I don't know how I eat, how I drink, I don't know how I keep moving forward despite having lost so much in what feels like such little time. I get up. I dive into the game. I lose myself despite no guarantee anything will ever get better. Life moves forward with or without me. At least in some little way I am achieving the impossible. Building my stats, helping my team. I am a part of something bigger than I am. Damien was just like my brother. He was there for me since the beginning and unlike others he never turned his back on me.

I didn't speak at his funeral. I wish I had but I couldn't. I wasn't family and other than the life we had inside the game we barely saw each other anymore. His parents knew me as the boy from the streets. Not that they looked down on me. They were nice. His father shook my hand, his mother hugged me. They were the first adults who had shown me any kind of care or comfort since I lost my own family. Damien's father said I looked good in a suit. It was a rental. I had paid for it out of my own pocket using the small allowance I had saved. The sleeves were too short. The only other clothes I owned had been hand-me-downs and graphic tees I borrowed from other members of my guild. I couldn't think of the right words to say. I ended up standing there in the back beside three other members of our team Cass, Aiden, and Brand. We were the only ones that came…or at least that we recognized. After the funeral, when Damien's body was being lowered into the ground a woman came up beside me.

'Meet me at the Spire in three hours I have some information to trade,' she whispered into my ear.

It had been three days since I logged in.

Access

I woke up from stasis inside the shuttle. We were back in Alpha-1 orbiting the planet Apus. The shuttle was already inside the hangar of our main ship, a cruiser called the *Ibanez*.

Nel had done exactly as I asked. The artefact was safe. Only now I felt guilty holding it. Cass was suited up by the time I made it through the shuttle door bay. Cass was beautiful. She was a year older than me. Slightly taller than I was with short, bright red hair. Her avatar had pointed, elf-like ears. I think she use to play fantasy games a lot when she was younger. She didn't look happy to see me as she stood staring at the M1 Garand I had swung over my back.

'Are you trying to get yourself killed!' she shouted moving closer to me.

I didn't say anything as I tried to move past her. Losing Damien was enough.

'We just lost our best pilot, one of our best paladins and you were off running around the edge of the quadrants hustling!' she continued to shout.

I wanted to scream, I wanted to shout that I had no idea what Damien was up to or what I could have done to make things different. We were all trying to get by…ALL of us. I've always liked exploring and after being stuck for so long in the outside world all I wanted to do was play again. I felt like I could lose myself for days inside the game.

'This was my chance to prove myself,' I finally said.

'Prove what? Damien, the others, me! We love you like a little brother, we don't care if you're running around but you hacked your way into a system that was off limits and almost got yourself killed,' Cass stopped. She was nearly in tears.

I glanced over at Nel who seemed to shrug in the air and turn away.

'You hacked her didn't you,' I asked.

'Damn straight, I was trying to find out if she knew anything about Damien,' Cass was crying.

'I'm sorry,' I said.

'I can't stand not knowing what happened, I can't understand, everyone is treating his death like it was just an accident but there isn't even an echo…it's like he didn't exist,' she said resting her head against the wall.

'What do you mean there isn't an echo?'

'There's nothing. It's like Damien never played the game, we've been searching everywhere. Aiden and Brand have been playing non-stop since it happened.'

'Why didn't you tell me this at the funeral?'

'We didn't want to upset you, we knew the two of you were close. You were more like family than the rest of us,' Cass sighed.

I moved closer and placed my arms around her.

'If his body is out there, we will find it,' I said, not telling her I was about to grab Nel and hijack another ship, a Frigate, from the hanger and make my way to the Spire.

> **Quick Lore**
> Starships in Bane are crucial to the gameplay itself. Most starships are system based but the larger ships have to be equipped with quantum drives or STL (space time light drives). The STL drives manipulate dark matter and create a pocket in time around the starship that allows it to traverse light years. It is the only way to travel from one system to next without the use of a warp gate, which are few and far between.

Class	Minimum Crew	Maximum Crew
Drone	0	1
Small Fighter	1	2
Shuttle	1 – 2	8
Escorts	2 – 3	8
Scouts	2 – 3	8
Interceptors	1 – 4	8
Frigate	2 – 10	20
Tanker	2 – 10	20
Destroyer	10 – 30	40 – 100
Cruiser	20 – 75	200
Transport	20 – 100	200 – 250
Battle Cruiser	40 – 100	200 – 300
Assault Transport	50 – 100	200
Prison Transport	50 – 100	300

Battleship	200	500
Carrier	300	1000
Dreadnaught	500	2000
Monarch	600	3000
Spartan	600 – 700	3500
Supercarrier	1000	5000
Titan	10,000	50,000
Orbital Carrier	100,000	500,000
Orbital Research	10,000	500,000

Cass let me go. I told her I needed to be alone.

We took the frigate because it was faster than the shuttle. Normally a frigate had to be manned by at least two people but Nel, besides being an AI that could carry a ton of gear, was also a great co-pilot. The carrier had several hangars and ships were always coming and going as different teams came and went. I took one of the older models, a PY-775, built to haul rovers and cargo. It was brown and square and looked like it had been designed in the 1970s. It wasn't my first choice but it would get the two of us where we needed to be with more than enough time to spare.

'Maybe you should tell the others?' Nel said it like a question.

'Tell them what? I'm going to some secret meeting with someone that I met in the real world at a funeral for my best friend,' I was holding back my anger, my tears.

'Yes...' Nel was silent.

'If whatever I learn turns out to be useful I'll let them in, but I don't want to drag them into whatever this is.'

'You are worried it is a trap?'

'Yes, we have our fair share of enemies and it could be another company looking to gather information from us.'

'Another reason we should not be traveling alone.'

'Okay, your sister, Tel, the *Ibanez* AI. Can you ask her to monitor us, that way if it is a trap they can jump to our location and provide support.'

'We are not allowed to fight inside the Spire.'

'Correction, we can fight all we want inside the Spire as long as the guardians don't find out or catch us. They can't catch stealth kills or people being taken prisoner.'

'You give cause for great concern.'

'I know,' I said smiling. Damien would be proud.

A minute later auto-pilot was on and we were approaching the Spire.

```
Location Discovered: The Spire
Environment: Hospitable
Resources: Everything
```

The Spire was everything the city of the future should be. There in the centre was a large citadel where the Chel resided and talked to the elders that were in charge of humanity as a whole. Mostly these leaders were NPCs, though there were a few actual players that had joined the Chel's elite as members of a group called the FTC. The citadel was surrounded by several temples and places for mediation and training along with several buildings that were residences for player characters. While *Bane* wasn't necessarily play-to-win, having money meant having real estate. Besides player homes there were also offices, holo hotels, and of course merchants. Every merchant guild had a shop somewhere in the Spire. Even several pirate organizations had offices that would enlist new recruits.

The Spire was always night. They called it the night-eternal. There were clubs filled with music and even drugs that made players feel 'different'. The only thing that wasn't allowed inside the Spire was murder, unless it was inside an arena or outside the Spire's safe zone. If two players went into combat AI enforcers called 'guardians' would appear and stop the fighting by killing the players involved. I had never seen a guardian myself, but I had heard stories. They were supposed to be large, mech-like machines with giant rifles and blades. It was rumoured their hit points numbered in the hundred thousand. To this day no one had actually taken out a guardian and there had only been one raid attempted that ended badly for everyone involved.

We landed at the Pier. A hangar set up over a toxic river.

Landing inside the Pier was like floating inside an enormous cavern. The catacombs they called it. Besides a few blue lights it was pitch-black and so large our own lights barely made a dent. We landed on a platform meant for supply freighters. We could see shipping containers on our left-hand side that had just been unloaded and strapped to the back of a giant wall.

'Ready for pressure release.' Nel said as my ears popped. There was a loud bang as clamps closed over our frigate's engine and the door to exit the bridge began to open. The air outside was cold so I grabbed a small black jacket with fur around the collar and placed it over my mesh armour. The vents were still hissing when we walked outside and were greeted by another floating robot. Nel paid for our parking, taking it out of the allowance I was given by Keen Industries. It was four times the amount it should have been.

'Okay,' I said, with any luck, I would make a small fortune from the rifle.

'Thanking you,' the floating robot said before freezing. I licked my upper lip waiting for it to move or respond expecting it to say more. Another few seconds passed, and it turned around heading towards another ship. A destroyer had been following behind us in the dark the entire time. The destroyer was barely visible with its all black stealth paint job. It belonged to a guild known as the Crimson Kings.

Outside the safe zone was a wasteland inhabited by mutated creatures that adapted to live in the radiation poisoned deadlands. A normal player could technically survive in the wasteland if they had the right gear…first and foremost being a rebreather and radiation meds. The wasteland itself had its own fair share of dungeons that could be looted. Merchants in the city sold many of the found items as souvenirs. Outside the Pier I, I paused and bought a necklace from one of the street venders. I'd spotted the item, which looked like a shark's tooth. Found in one of the dungeons southwest of the Spire it was said to bring luck and I felt I'd exhausted what little luck I had in the battle with the spider.

Nel and I left the Pier after marking our ship's location as a waypoint on our shared map and went straight towards the centre of the city on a hover cycle we had brought along. Nel flew beside me while I drove into town towards a shop called the Upsilon.

The Upsilon was run by a player who went by the name Gorge. His avatar was half cybernetic human and half 'Orc'. He was bulky and looked like a grey Terminator with sharp pointed teeth and a dark grey beard but all in all he was a fairly nice guy so long as you didn't get on his bad side. I still had half an hour before I was supposed to meet the woman from Damien's funeral, not that I knew how or even if she would contact me. The only thing I had to go on was that she said to meet in the Spire and I wasn't about to waste the trip. Among his many skills Gorge was also a weapons dealer in the black market. The Upsilon itself sold weapons from all over the system, including artefacts such as the one I had brought with me.

At first glance Gorge wasn't sure what to think.

'Looks old, like an antique. Does it actually fire or is it an ornament?' he asked.

'I don't know, I haven't tried using it in combat,' I answered.

He held it in his hands examining the M1 Garand, aiming down the sights at the wall. A red line of sight appeared, and he fired.

The rifle blew a small chunk of the wall apart. I ducked down and screamed, 'WHAT ABOUT THE GUARDIANS!'

Gorge laughed, 'didn't aim it at anyone, not worried; it fires just fine.'

'How much do you think it's worth?'

'I could give you two point five million credits for it now,' he smiled.

When Gorge smiled I knew he was low balling me.

'Three million,' I smiled in return. I wasn't the greatest at negotiating and probably could have made five or six. I could have even said I had another offer, but I wasn't thinking about credits. I was looking at the time in the lower left hand corner of my heads up…a digital clock only I could see as I waited to see what would happen next.

Gorge swiped his finger left and circled the air.

'Deal, transferring credits to your account now,' he was smiling again.

'Make sure not to get yourself killed and don't let anyone know you bought that from me,' I said.

'Bought what?' Gorge was aiming down the sight of the M1 again. 'They don't make games with these anymore,' he said.

'What do you mean?' I asked.

'Everything is space opera, fantasy, puzzles, everything is big and bold. Nobody remembers the past, the horrors, the humble beginnings.'

I knew what Gorge was talking about, but I was all ready to leave. He was a great guy but could be a little difficult sometimes. I imagined whoever he was behind the avatar was actually someone pretty old, someone that yearned for the past.

'Hey, listen kid, I have one more thing,' Gorge stopped me as Nel and I were beginning to leave. He hurried towards me. He had slung the rifle over his back and was carrying something in his hand. A small data cube.

'Someone knew you were coming by and asked me to give this to you,' he said placing the small cube in my hand. I looked it over. I wasn't quite sure what he wanted me to do with it but I had no doubt the cube and the woman from the funeral were somehow linked together.

'You can use my office, just be quick about it,' he said.

I walked towards the back of the shop and sat down beside Gorge's home-brew computer network. It looked like he had taken ten monitors and wired them together with one holo-projector in the centre. Some of the monitor computers were cracked while others just played static. There was a slight humming in the room and it felt like the temperature was about five maybe ten degrees hotter than the air outside. Some of the wires didn't seem to go anywhere while others were endless, wrapped around small pieces of metal that didn't seem to serve any purpose. I searched for a place to put the cube and found one hidden underneath a plate of food that must have been a few days old. While the rest of the Upsilon was nice and clean Gorge's office looked like it had seen better days.

```
┌─────────────────────────────────────┐
│              Play Data?             │
│              Yes / No               │
└─────────────────────────────────────┘
```

I clicked 'yes' with my finger and watched. Two figures appeared, both clad in black heavy armour. The figures were armed with energy rifles which they were firing at creatures that looked like mutated Wraiths. Some data appeared: **Dargons, Level: 55, Hostile.** I couldn't make out the rest. It was all happening fast but I soon recognized one of the players. It was Damien. Damien was twenty and had been playing *Bane* for four years. He had managed to level his character up to 52 and had been exploring some of the quadrants blocked to players like me for about a year. The data cube I was watching now was recording from the perspective of another player. A third player in what I assumed must have been a four person squad.

I couldn't tell exactly where they were, it could have been one of a large number of regions but I knew it was someplace neither I nor any of my teammates would be able to go without breaking a few rules. I didn't recognize any of the players he was with either, but Damien knew a lot of people. His funeral alone had over forty guests. The figures in front of me continued to fire. The player beside Damien got knocked out as another alien creature - this time with humanoid features - appeared holding a firearm I had never seen before. I could see a skull mask across the lower part of the humanoid figure's face. Was it another player? Damien's teammate fired from the ground as Damien ran out of view and the camera fell backwards. The feed cut to black.

'You're late. Four paladins. Your friend and my brother among them passed through the world gate *At Eternity* and went into the Cold Zone, level 77, inside a dungeon. They believed it was a way to progress the main story of the game...' the voice was that of a young woman, 'four players, three dead in the real world that day, one survivor who died the following day. Real death.'

A woman clad in purple armour with a Ki rifle slung over her back stood in front of me. I wasn't sure if she had come inside while I was watching the data cube or if she had been in the room the whole time. She had dark, dirty blonde hair that seemed to flow down just an inch past the bottom of her neck. It was almost completely shaved on the sides and along her right eye was a tribalistic tattoo almost too small to notice. It was the woman from the funeral. Her avatar only slightly different to how she appeared in real life. Most players either made themselves look like they did in the real world like myself or they went polar opposite like Gorge so her appearance wasn't too surprising.

'They died in the game and died in real life? How is that possible?' I said not wanting to believe it.

'I'm not sure but I need to find out,' the woman said.

'Just who are you?'

'My name is Kira, I am the co-owner of Moonrain Media.'

Moonrain Media were famous for collecting in-game footage. Some of their most famous recordings were *Battle of the Eternal Day*, *Assault on Cthonia*, and *Operation Siege Engine*. They had hundreds of thousands of people that followed them both in and outside the game and were treated as one of the top guilds. Kira was basically their queen.

'That video was my brother's feed, the last thing he saw before he died, it is not fake, I already checked…each and every one of them died either in battle with the man in the skull mask or just after logging out. My brother died of cardiac arrest while still playing the game.' She paused and took a deep breath sending me a quick file to look over.

NAME: SCRAWL

Age: 22	Status: Deceased
Level: 75	Class: Scout

Health: 100   Stamina: 100
Mana: 100

Load out: M7-7 Artefact Rifle, Short grip energy pistol, Pulse
Shotgun, Sharpened Combat, Dagger, Grenades

'What does this have to do with me?' I asked interrupting.

'They were chasing an echo, a very rare one, something in the Cold Zone had called out to them, a whisper in the void, that was what they called it,' she paused, 'Damien spoke highly of you. He talked about you like the two of you were brothers. I lost my family and if anyone understands it has to be you,' she paused again. Even in the virtual world you could cry. The game was capable of total immersion. Every small detail from an eye twitch to the way your chest moved up and down. The tears running down Kira's eyes were just as real as they would be anywhere else.

'You are a Corpse Diver and I'm here to hire you.'

— Quest —
A Whisper in the Void
Created by: Moonrain Media / Kira
Expected Difficulty: Veteran
Rewards: Unknown

Accept / Decline.

3.
The Chase

As I accepted the quest I felt something strange. A chill ran down the side of my arm. It was like the air in the room had changed. I felt a rush I hadn't felt since the first time I logged in. This was going to be the adventure of a lifetime. Damien, I knew would want this. If I could find his echo I wouldn't just be making a name for myself or buying my way out, I would be honouring my best friend. A moment later the rush was gone replaced by fear and Gorge bursting into the back of the room holding the artefact M1 Garand in his hands ready to fire.

'I don't know what the hell you just did but a guardian is coming our way!' he shouted.

'What do you mean a guardian?' I was angry he had interrupted my meeting with Kira.

'You know the overlords that tank players who commit crimes inside the Spire, the ones that are pretty much immortal objects with big guns,' he answered. I knew exactly what the guardians were but why were they coming towards us?

'I told you not to fire that rifle,' I was shouting now. Nervous. If a guardian really was after us there was little we could do.

'NOT MY FAULT,' Gorge yelled, 'I fire weapons all the time in my own shop, got a small dampening field around it so

31

it's a little arena; can't be too careful some of the customers I deal with.'

'Was it the quest you gave me?' I said, staring towards Kira who was watching us in silence.

'Yes, I'm sorry, I should have warned you,' she answered.

'Damnit, now what are we going to do?' before I got all my words out Kira was already arming herself. She held her Ki rifle high into her arms.

'We need an open area,' she said.

I looked at Kira again and scanned both her and Gorge, pulling up as much information as I could about their player characters as the three of us joined together as a party.

NAME: KIRA

Age: 16   Class: Tech-Mage
Level: 60   Health: 100
Status: Alive   Stamina: 100
Mana: 100

Load out: Ki Rifle, Energy Pistol

NAME: GORGE

Age: Unknown   Class: Tank
Level: 60   Health: 100
Status: Alive   Stamina: 100
Mana: 100

Load out: Artefact Rifle, White Lilly, Tree Root

I couldn't see any of their other stats just as they couldn't see my own. That was one advantage players had over each other. It would have been nice to know everything there was to know about both Kira and Gorge, since the three of us were about to work together in battle.

Skills and Abilities were secret unless shared as a part of a guild. Attack power, Affinity, Sharpness, Elemental powers, and Modifiers were all hidden.

Quick Lore

Attack power = raw damage done without elemental powers or modifiers. Attack power is universal and can be multiplied only by additional strength.

Affinity = A player's chance to deal either more or less damage with a melee attack. High affinity can lead to critical hits. High affinity is usually used by tanks and paladins who will use swords and staffs in melee combat.

Sharpness = A player's chance to deal either more or less damage with an energy or projectile based attack. High sharpness is absolutely necessary for snipers, scouts, and other player characters that use firearms.

Elemental Powers = Powers based on Fire, Water, Air, Earth, and Soul. Enchantments that give player characters 'superpowers'.

Modifiers = anything that can be used to take advantage or increase skills such as strength, stamina, intelligence, and elemental abilities. Modifiers can also be used on different weapon types to increase the affinity or sharpness of weapon.

'Nel how fast can you get to the frigate?' I asked, staring at the floating robot that was our only hope of escape.

'Ten minutes,' Nel said patiently. Of course I didn't expect the AI to be freaking out like the rest of us.

'Go,' I commanded and watched as Nel took off through the doorway just as quickly as I gave the order.

Gorge was suited up. Unlike my armour, which could be broken down and put into a case, his was bulky. It made him look more like a tank though he wasn't happy about having to wear his gear. Since opening his shop in the Spire after the *Battle of Vlel* he had been retired.

'It's not coming for you, what are you doing?' I asked, trying to clear my thoughts.

'Rumour gets out I let a guardian take down a customer I might get a bad reputation. Anyway, I've been playing this game a long time...' He paused. 'Guardians show no mercy, they are mindless giants that stomp out everything and everyone they go after. If the guardian really is coming for you I'm expecting half the block to look like it was hit by an orbital strike.'

'That's not a bad idea? Have you anything in here that can do that?' Kira asked.

'Sorry hun, nothing that powerful on this planet,' Gorge replied.

I looked at him. 'On *this* planet?'

'Think this is my only shop?' Gorge was laughing. I was surprised. I guess it was true, he didn't really care too much for the Spire or the people here but it was the best place to make money.

Gorge's face grew wary and when he spoke again his voice was low and serious, 'we have about thirty seconds before the guardian lands.' He moved towards the doorway.

A moment later, we were stepping outside the entrance of the Upsilon. Several other players and NPCs were standing in the street looking up at the sky above. There was a purple light shining down from the heavens like a line of sight. Three seconds later, a giant mech landed with its fist braking apart the ground.

I shot first into the smoke that rose to the sky above us. The mech looked more like a shadow in the mist as it turned towards us. Through the haze I saw it take a giant rifle off its back, a rifle the size of my own hover cycle, and fire a blast of energy in our direction. Players on the street began running in every direction as the wave of red hit the Upsilon and tore it apart. Gorge looked back for a moment and fired armour piercing rounds towards the guardian. Not even a scratch.

'That first shot was a warning!' shouted Gorge.

'A warning to who?' I shouted back as the smoke faded and the guardian stood about twenty feet high looking down on us.

'Anyone not us!' shouted Kira firing from her energy pistol. Her other weapon was dangerous. A Ki rifle would draw its power from mana and health: use it enough you could die.

Guardian Aegialeus
Level: Unknown
Hostile

Nothing we did depleted the mech's HP at all. The guardian was a weapon of mass destruction. I guess it had to be. It was designed to keep the peace and protect the Spire and, most important of all, it was designed to protect the Chels, regardless of the cost.

Gorge took out a smaller rifle as he swung the artefact behind his back. I was surprised he was still holding onto it. The second rifle was named White Lilly and it looked like a cross between an M60 and some kind of railgun. White Lilly was actually a gauss rifle. Holding the rifle with both hands as it pushed him backwards, Gorge fired at the guardian. A hit from a gauss rifle would normally be critical against a player but the guardian stood its ground.

-10 HP

'It did some damage!' I shouted with delight. For a moment I felt like we had a chance.

'Too bad that was only good for one shot charged like that, cool down is five minutes,' Gorge shouted back switching rifles again. The three of us started to run and dodge as the guardian powered up another blast from its rifle and fired, this time taking out the merchant next door to Gorge that had been selling cupcakes.

'That was my favourite snack place!' Gorge cried out firing back at the mad titan with his artefact. There was no effect. The guardian's health might have been dropping but the change was so negligible it didn't even register. All we could do for the moment was continue to fire. The only thing we had going for us was that the guardian itself was a bad shot with poor accuracy. A small weakness we could exploit.

Kira moved her hands in the air, letting her rifle fall to rest down by her side next to her Ki rifle, which hung on a wolf-sling. She was summoning a decoy. A mirror image of her appeared and began running towards the guardian holding a ghostly broadsword. The guardian turned and followed the image as the three of us recharged our weapons and shot at it again. Nothing. The guardian's armour was made from the same metal as a starship's hull. It was no wonder we weren't able to break through. The gauss rifle was good for one shot but we didn't have the time. The guardian fired for the third time and decimated the street and the decoy along with several bystanders who were caught in the blast. I felt bad. This would be all over the net. 'Guardian Attacks City: Player Lives Lost: Corpse Diver to Blame'. I could see it now.

Gorge had a special ability of his own. Several drones appeared from the wreckage of the Upsilon and began flying towards the guardian. Each drone quickly split apart and the pieces attached themselves across the mechanical monster. A moment later, Kira cast a shield around the entire guardian and the drones exploded sending shrapnel flying through the air. A few small pieces managed to break the shield and escape. One, the size of a dime, hit me and I felt my HP drop to 85.

The guardian on the other hand was also harmed.

- 5

- 5

- 5

Over and over, about a dozen times.

'Can you do that again?'

'That was the last of my stock,' shouted Gorge almost cringing. The drones must have been worth a small fortune. Easily 100,000 credits each. If the guardian didn't kill me Gorge was going to fine me a fortune.

'Can we call for help?'

'I've already contacted Moonrain Media and they are thirty minutes out, probably watching us from a safe distance,' said Kira.

That was true and I knew it. She had come alone. I was sure her media company would help her if they could, and it was obvious they had kept in constant contact, but facing down a guardian was a suicide mission. Yet somehow Kira had known there was a possibility of this happening. I would have to ask her about it later...if we survived this.

'I reached out to the Silvermanes but no answer,' said Gorge.

The Silvermanes were a guild Gorge did regular business with and they had enough members they could afford lose a few in battle, especially if it meant not losing their arms dealer.

'What about an admin?' I shouted, wondering if maybe this attack was a result of something being wrong with the game. Maybe we could talk our way out.

'Not going to happen,' said Kira. She motioned with her finger and a hologram appeared in front of her. She flipped it towards me and I saw we were already banned from the Spire. Player bans were rare and didn't always mean a player would be banned from the actual game…that was near impossible with how the game itself worked. Banning players from certain areas was easy though…like uploading a wanted poster that made every NPC a hostile. This was bad. Being banned from the Spire meant no contact with the Chels and no way to progress the game. It also meant I would never be able to trade with any of the merchants in the Spire again, including the black market, unless I found a way to disguise my character. That was possible. I used a hack before to break my way into the Alpha Centauri system. Unfortunately, there wasn't anything I could do about the ban for now. We couldn't face down the guardian, we had no choice but to run.

I took a deep breath, 'we have to split up.' I saw Kira and Gorge nod their heads around the same time as the three of us split off in different directions. Kira ran to the right and Gorge back into an alley parallel to her. I ran to the left. I had a one in three chance I would survive. A one in three chance that the guardian wouldn't choose me.

It chose me.

Luck -10

I was close to a hover cycle so I jumped on. Firing backwards at the guardian, despite knowing it wouldn't make much of a difference. I started the cycle and felt its anti-gravity drive begin to spin. The guardian was locking onto me as I powered the thrusters and surged forward. I was a block away from it when the guardian began skating towards me as if the streets were ice. It rammed buildings like they were made of toy bricks, destroying residences and offices alike. It didn't care for any of the players in its way either. I flew by several who were screaming at me to slow down, only to turn around and see the foot of the iron giant crash down upon them.

A small sphere floated beside me as I raced towards the Pier. It was just like Kira had said, Moonrain Media were watching, along with a dozen others. Several more drones appeared and I crashed into them knocking several to the ground while several more tried to follow behind me. Everyone would be watching. I would lose my job for sure after this…no more playing, no more game. I might as well give up, I thought, feeling more hopeless than ever. But that wasn't my style. I never gave up. I became a Corpse Diver because I wanted to explore the deepest dungeons in the game no matter what the cost and that was exactly what Kira had offered me. This was a once in a lifetime.

This moment…this chase would define everything.

I could feel all the world's eyes on me as I crossed the border from the merchant's district to the financial district and turned the corner again, trying to find my way to the Pier by crossing under a bridge. Behind me, I could feel the ground shake when the guardian ripped it apart. When I hit a straightaway, two airships appeared like daggers from the darkness coming towards me. The guardian was maybe thirty yards behind me and catching up quickly. As it skated, however, it couldn't fire or charge its rifle…another weakness. For a moment I thought the airships were going to fire upon me. Maybe they were friends of his…but as they fired several ballistic missiles, slowing the guardian to a near stop, I recognized the emblem on the side. A sword and a rifle crossed over a shield that looked like an eighteen-string guitar with teeth. It was the badge of the *Ibanez*.

A chat request appeared.

Incoming message

I swiped my finger right and listened.

'Breq, you idiot, what kind of trouble did you get into now?' the voice was that of Cass, who was shouting at me.

'Someone requested a dive,' I responded turning down another street. I could finally see the Pier. There was a wall between the street and the entrance. The guardian had control over the city, a small but crucial detail I had forgotten. The Pier was on lockdown.

'A job huh, really, must be one hell of a job if you have a guardian chasing you,' she responded. The airships were flying back around again.

'Take out the gate,' I shouted.

The guardian was gaining ground. This time I could see its health had gone down about a quarter of the way. They weren't immortal and now everyone watching would know it.

The two airships fired at the gate, blowing it into fragments.

Cass wasn't playing around. The missiles they launched could tear apart a starship's hull, which was the only reason they were working on the guardian. I wanted to scream at her to stop. To tell her that the entire team would get banned.

I couldn't slow down. If I stopped the guardian would fire.

The hover cycle and I moved through the darkness.

'Nel, fire up the frigate,' I shouted into my comm.

A voice, Nel's voice, 'negative Sir,' she said.

'Nel, please,' I shouted.

'Negative Sir, the frigate is impounded; I have acquired other means of transportation,' a bright light flashed blinding me for a moment. As my vision adjusted I could see the Crimson King's destroyer hovering about fifty yards ahead with an open hatch. Ten seconds later I was swallowed up inside. The thrusters on my hover cycle were blown out and the Crimson King's destroyer was flying upwards away from the Spire as the guardian fired one last shot into the air barely missing us. One small camera sphere had made its way inside. I fired at it and watched the small pieces spark and fall apart. At long last I took a deep breath and fell onto the cold steel floor.

'Breq,' Cass's voice came through on my comm, 'boss wants to see you.'

4.
Meet the Boss

I felt the quantum drive kick in as time distorted around the star-ship and we entered one of the pathways. We were on our way to another star system. Probably a good idea to get away from the Spire after everything that had happened. The guardians could hypothetically chase us anywhere in the system and it wouldn't have been long before they came after us in that way. After fifteen minutes, I felt the drive ease off. I was already being greeted like a prisoner by the guards. Among them, several players I had joined the ranks with. Cass was leading them. She looked at me with a sly smirk on her face lecturing me at first...asking what the hell I thought I was doing and how she was scared to death they were going to lose me too. At the same time she was impressed. I had done something no one had attempted before.

Cass had always seen me as a younger brother. I couldn't imagine how torn up she was now that Damien was gone. The two of them always had a connection but it was a relationship they were building slowly. I could remember Damien telling me once about his crush on her...how he met her in the real world for some coffee and donuts, even brought her a rose. Turns out she was allergic and the date didn't quite go as planned but Cass liked Damien too and the two started to see one another more and more during their days off. Both of them were like the older siblings I never had and when the three of us went out together I never felt like the third wheel...it always felt like we were a team.

Cass wasn't happy with me now and after they stripped me of my gear, told me in a cold voice to wait for the boss. As her smirk faded and she turned to face away from me, I could see she was holding back tears.

I didn't defend my actions. I felt like all of it would be too hard to explain. Too hard too understand. But I wanted to. I wanted her to know that Damien was the reason I had gone off on my own. I wanted to tell her about the woman at the funeral, Kira. I still had the data cube on me when they found me, if she watched it maybe it would give her some comfort. No. I watched it and I only felt worse. I wanted vengeance. The skull-faced man and whatever it was they were chasing in the Cold Zone. Damien had always told me he admired my resolution, my determination to level up, to survive, to be independent.

Two S-class soldiers, elite, from the boss's personal guard, stood at the front door of the suite. They had asked me to wait inside. Dressed in red and black armour, they each wore a small cape with a symbol of a wolf. A sect of the Corpse Diver core I had never seen before. Elite players, handpicked from applications submitted to the boss herself. Each elite was at least level 50 or higher.

I was told not to log out or to leave the Crimson King's destroyer.

When you logged out of *Bane* your avatar would still be wherever it was you were last. Logging out in the middle of a mission was a sure way to get killed, same as logging out inside a dungeon or deep space. Usually players had to pay for a room at an inn or board up on a vessel somewhere. Most of the time I put my avatar inside stasis before logging out, even if it meant taking a few extra minutes to break away from any action around me. I knew if I logged out the two guards would execute me. I would lose my job, my reputation, everything.

The suite was nice. Before Nel had taken control of the destroyer the suite must have belonged to one of the Crimson King's generals. The room was filled with dozens of key artefacts some of which were easily recognizable while others were rare and probably worth millions of credits. One in particular caught my eye. Buried behind several artefact rifles that looked like they were historical antiquities there was a broadsword. The sword itself didn't look too different from other broadswords in game, however on the side of it there were several runes scratched into the metal blade.

Since I had nothing else to do, my eyes kept coming back to those runes. Should I? After what felt like an hour of waiting, I lifted the glass plate protecting the sword. Expecting some kind of alarm to trigger and knowing that touching it was the same as stealing, I still couldn't help but want to hold such an incredible object of power in my hand. For all I knew the boss was coming to kill me anyway, so what did I have to lose? I wouldn't let that happen. Already, I was planning an escape: analyzing the room around me and devising scenarios in my head. At best I was going to be demoted and penalized, at worst I would be back on the streets in real life. If the situation looked like it was going south I would at least be holding a weapon.

I reached out and grabbed the sword with both hands.

For a moment I feel like I am stepping outside my body. Transported to some kind of void, I can hear a moan in the darkness that surrounded me. The heat that surrounds me is nearly unbearable, almost as bad as it was when I was trapped inside the *Lockhead* falling into a star. As my eyes adjust I can see a ghostly figure. An elemental with chains wrapped around its wrists. Its body broad and robust, it almost looks like the sword itself has taken the form of some kind of creature. Four long fingers reach out towards me as the creature stares at me like I am some kind of prey...but it almost seems bored. Two wings extend themselves fully, revealing blackened bone with tiny tears. They stretch upwards. The monster moves through the air towards me as the void fades away and I'm still standing inside the suite with the sword in both hands. The creature disappears, swallowed up by the sword which begins to burn against the skin of my hand.

Sword of the Depraved
Cut down by the forces of Lintirmai, the depraved creature known only as *The Beast's Soul* was imprisoned inside a great metal sword made from the hull of an ancient alien starship.
That which may never die must be contained.

Damage: 30 (with 25% chance of 120 damage critical)
Class: None required
Level Required: None
Weight: 10 lbs
Affinity: 50%
Sharpness: None
Elemental: Soul - Steals players' Mana for better attacks
Modifiers: None

As the sword became a part of my own inventory, a screen appeared before my eyes asking me if I would like to rename the item. 'Yes,' I said aloud, wondering if the guards would come in and attack me. Maybe this whole thing was some kind of trap or set up.

An augmented holographic keyboard appeared before my eyes, allowing me to type any name I want. Most of the time I was against naming weapons, since I was always moving from one to the next. Guns and melee weapons could be upgraded, but even after two years there were a ton of weapon types I had yet to try. *Bane* was full of them. There were thousands of iterations of guns and melee weapons some of which could even be combined. Most common were M44 and Ki rifles which could be advanced and levelled up alongside players. There were several hundred variants of pistols as well. With no shortage of weapons I had never bothered to change the name of one. Of course being a Corpse Diver we had an armoury the size of three baseball fields inside the *Ibanez* and I had only been able to use a third of them. Most of my team felt the same; there was no point in naming something and becoming attached to it when we could all die on the next mission. As far as I knew, the boss was the only one who had named a weapon.

I must have stared at the letters in front of me for ten minutes as I tried to think of the coolest name. I settled on *Aegis*.

```
Aegis - Broadsword

Cut down by the forces of Lintirmai, the depraved
creature known only as The Beast's Soul was
imprisoned inside a great metal sword made from the
hull of an ancient alien starship. Passed from one
cursed soul to another Aegis is a living weapon that
not only protects its masters but eventually devours
their very being.

That which may never die must be contained.

Damage: 30 (with 25% chance of 120 damage critical)
Class: None required
Level Required: None
Weight: 10 lbs
Affinity: 50%
Sharpness: None
Elemental: Soul - Steals players' Mana for better
attacks
Modifiers: None
```

'Strange,' I thought, reading how the biographical information had slightly updated since I renamed the item in hand.
Reading it now and knowing I was the sword's new master did
not fill me with confidence.

The boss kept me waiting for six hours.

Plenty of time to familiarize myself with the rest of the room
and practice my kendo kata with my new weapon. My father was
a firm believer in extracurricular activities and I had been studying
martial arts and kendo since I was around five years old. All of

those skills made living on the streets easier after they died, though I doubt he knew or would support the way I used them to defend myself. Those same skills also translated to the game world. Kendo kata would usually be practiced with a bamboo katana or blunt sword but in the game it was all practice. With the skills I learned in real life I could easily adapt any melee weapon and had become an expert in hand-to-hand combat. There were several martial arts created inside the game world too that I had started to learn.

The boss was a woman who went by the name Lady Gray. She had short dark hair with grey streaks and a scar ran down across her right eye and another scar down across her lip. She was tall. Taller than most male players and slim with an athletic build. She looked like she was in her mid-twenties and if her real life body was anything like her avatar she easily could be mistaken for a pop-star or glamour model. When she entered, I was still holding the sword down by my side and starting to sweat. My stamina was low since I had just swung the weapon several dozen times. She smiled as she looked me up and down.

'So, you're Breq; I think this is the first time we've ever officially met.' This wasn't true. She was the leader of the Corpse Divers and I had seen her aboard the *Ibanez* several times. We also met when Damien led me into an interview for the team. In fact she had to sign off on my joining. She probably signed most of my paychecks too. Still, I didn't feel like it was the time or place to correct her.

'That's me, Breq,' I said wondering if I should be saluting or readying my weapon for attack.

Name: Lady Gray

Age: Unknown	Status: Alive
Level: 92	Mana: 300

49

Class: Tech-Mage   Stamina: 250
        Health: 250

Load out: None

I didn't stand a chance. I placed the sword behind my back and felt a sling digitize across my chest to support it. If Lady Gray was going to kill me I was sure she could do it even unarmed. The boss was the first player I had ever even seen with such a high level. She was also a tech-mage with a high mana and could probably summon a weapon with a critical hit strong enough to destroy me in an instant. Most players I came across when not in the Spire or inside settlements were in their 30s or 40s like myself. Lower level players were usually out grinding, while higher players were dungeon diving in quadrants I couldn't legitimately enter. At level 90, the boss was capable of going anywhere she wanted in the entire galaxy.

'Sorry, I didn't mean to keep you waiting,' she said, smiling at me again.

Two chairs materialized inside the room.

'Let's have a seat, I see you've been training, I'm glad you found something to do in this room. We have much to discuss,' she sat down, motioning for me to do the same.

I unclipped my sling and sat down across from her without saying a word.

'I had to do a little negotiating with the Crimson Kings since you had Nel steal one of their destroyers. I'm surprised our mutual friend was able to control such a vessel without any crew. Amazing how far she made it before Cass and the others were able to get aboard.' She paused, 'don't worry, the Crimson Kings won't be causing us any trouble, we've released the prisoners we captured and I've taken care of the rest,' she was smirking now.

She had a twisted look in her eyes.

I sat there and said nothing.

'What we do need to talk about is your situation.'

I continued to wait, not wanting to say anything. I still had the data cube and that new quest I had to complete no matter the cost.

'Whisper in the Void: are those words familiar to you?' she asked.

'No,' I lied.

She stared down at her lap. Her shoulders tensed slightly. 'A Whisper in the Void,' she repeated.

'No,' I lied again.

'Breq, you should know I already spoke to Kira. I know she hired you for a quest,' she said calmly. She was still smiling at me as I lied to her again.

'I have no idea what you are talking about.'

'Oh well, I guess I'll have to rethink my decision to reassign you and the rest of your squad. I do know a few fetch quests that need taking care of though, a Wraith hive or two that need clearing,' she was nearly laughing as she spoke, trying to break the silence that filled the room.

The last thing I wanted was to continue low level quests. I would never get the chance to enter the Cold Zone.

'I'm sorry,' I said looking down, 'I lied.'

'That's better, please be honest with me, you've cost our little group a fortune and become a wanted man, I am your friend, I am here to help you.'

There was a slight pause as an eerie silence filled the room.

'If you spoke to Kira you know it's a quest, a job assigned to me.'

'Yes, have you reviewed it yet?'

The truth was I had only glanced at it earlier.

51

'I was a little busy running for my life,' I replied.

'Take a moment to review it further,' she smiled.

— Quest —
A Whisper in the Void
Created by: Moonrain Media / Kira
Expected Difficulty: Veteran
Rewards: Unknown

Details:
1. Find a way inside the Cold Zone
2. Recover the echoes of the lost (0/3)
3. Kill the man with the skull mask.

Level Requirement: 50 (locked)

I wanted to scream. How had I not seen that earlier? I could view the quest but it was currently unavailable for me to activate. The boss could see it in my eyes. Everything I had done to this point had been for nothing. It would take me another year at the least to level up enough to activate the quest and access the levels needed to make my way inside the Cold Zone.

'I see you've found it,' she said.

'It's not fair,' I was making a fist, pulling at my trousers just above my knee. This time, my shoulders were tense. I felt like I must have looked either completely terrifying or pathetic. It was always either one way or another.

'This is why I wanted you to trust me.'

'So I could see I'm a failure, that I still have a long way to go?'

'No, because I can help you level up,' she smiled standing up.

'Follow me,' she said. The two chairs began de-materializing just as quickly as they came into being. I stood up and followed

52

her away from the room slinging *Aegis* around my back again. As I stepped forward through the doorway, the two of us were teleported and I found myself standing on a glass floor inside an observation room looking outwards towards a planet that covered much of the horizon. 'This world is full of many secrets, some good, some dark; even the game-creators don't fully understand everything they have made here.'

```
Quick Lore
Though many artefacts possess the ability to teleport
one or more players across small distances,
teleportation devices are illegal unless registered and
cannot be activated while inside dungeons.
Teleportation is very dangerous and can result in loss
of inventory, forced death, or change in stats.

Teleportation is only obtainable by the tech-mage
class and has a cool down time of 24 hours.
```

I stood staring out at the luminous sphere on the horizon.

The planet was **Orithyia.** The second planet in the Alpha-1 system. It was beautiful. Though mostly nothing but toxic atmosphere there was a small area in which humanity had built a settlement. The planet had a strange rotation but just enough of a magnetic field to hold an atmosphere similar to that of Earth. The habitable part of the planet had only one season and was near what was the planet's equator, surrounded by massive mountains that made Everest look like an anthill. This kept the toxicity that surrounded the central part of the planet in check. Orithyia, unlike Apus which traded with everyone, was exclusively home to the Crimson Kings.

'We stole their destroyer yes, but we also released their prisoners in return. We even promised to give the starship back. Yet one hour ago, there was a bounty placed on your head. Not the first, mind you, it seems the Chels themselves want you dead and there is a thirty-million-dollar credit reward. Enough to live a good life both in game and home,' she paused and lifted her hand into the air and shaped it like a gun. Then, Lady Gray pointed downward towards the planet and I watched as an orbital strike commenced. Hundreds of warheads fell from the sky, raining fire upon the players and settlements on the planet's surface. I could see the *Ibanez* from the observation deck along with several more battle cruisers and at least one Titan doing the same. The Titan was of course Lady Gray's own personal starship, named *Wave Maker*.

'You're killing them,' I said my voice trembling.

'I'm protecting you,' she said as the two of us watched the world burn.

I understood. Lady Gray was showing me her true strength. She had probably made them promise not to attack or go after any of us for what had happened. If it was true and there was a thirty million credit bounty on my head I would be hunted by everyone in the game. The Crimson Kings had betrayed her even after she released their prisoners in good will and when they placed the bounty on my head she had to show them that her words were words of power. She had to set an example. I was not to be harmed.

'The battle with the guardian has made you famous,' she said turning away from the planet and towards me.

'Famous?' I said wondering how all of this had happened so fast.

'Millions watched you fight the guardian and saw what happened and now with a bounty out for your death millions more are going to be watching your every move,' Lady Gray had been looking around the room as if it was possible someone else might have been listening. Her eyes gave away her actual paranoia but maybe there was something she knew I didn't. It was obvious she had been playing *Bane* far longer than I had and already knew many of the game's secrets. She smiled at me again. That same twisted smile that made me feel like I was actually talking to the devil. I didn't say anything. I couldn't think of anything to say. I had a pretty good life before my parents died but after a year of running away from everything and trying to live on my own I never imagined for a moment I would become some kind of celebrity. Even when I became emancipated and a ward of the company, it hadn't occurred to me that it was possible others would want to watch me play.

'I want to talk to you in the real world,' she said breaking the long silence. I wasn't sure how to respond. There were only a few times players actually met in the real world when they weren't friends or part of a team. I had never met anyone else from the game in the real world and had only met my team because we all worked closely together at Keen Industries. Each of us had to see one another since our immersion pods were so close together.

What more could Lady Gray want to tell me?

What more could she be after?

What could I possibly do for her?

5.
Breach

The boss, Lady Gray, had invited me out for 'coffee and donuts' in the real world and I couldn't refuse. In game, she walked with me to a shuttle and stood at the door as I went inside and she watched as I placed my avatar into stasis. I logged out en route back to the *Ibanez*, where she promised Cass and the others would be waiting for me when I re-entered.

I remembered a story: Erim, the journeyman. A part of *Bane's* lore. Erim had been the one of the first cadets to journey out into the stars in search of artefacts. It was a journey that was - according to lore - set to take twenty-two years, as it was made without the use of world gates and STL. Erim was hellbent on racing across the cosmos in an exot ship, traveling just under lightspeed. Lore stated that he had discovered alien artefacts, weapons of unequal value. I stared down at *Aegis*. Was this one of the artefacts? Why had Lady Gray let me hold onto it? The story of Erim was one that began with hope and adventure and ended in sadness. Erim never finished his journey. Hunted by a rogue cult, his valuables stolen from him, his ship was said to have jumped away into the Cold Zone. No matter what weapon I held I was weak, it felt like I was a prisoner. Our meeting was set to take place mid-afternoon the next day. Lady Gray told me she would send a driver for me and that all I had to do was wait and rest at my place.

When I came out of my pod, I was greeted by Keen Industries security personal. Two of them, both wearing black-collared shirts with a gold patch that shined brightly on the front and black dress trousers. They were armed with a small baton carried on their side sitting beside a walkie talkie. They both also had a smart watch. One was saying something into it but I was disoriented and couldn't understand what it was they were mumbling. The guard closest to me caught my shirt as I began to fall out of my pod. I was nauseous, near vomiting. My vision was also blurred but most of all I felt like I was starving at the same time.

It was common if someone spent more than twelve to fourteen hours inside virtual reality that their physical body would feel some after-effects. I had been playing for sixteen hours. Mostly, because waiting for my meeting with the boss had taken so long. One of the guards had been trained for exactly this type of situation and I felt a needle slide into my arm; it was attached to an IV. Minutes later I was laying in a hospital bed in a fresh scented gown with the Keen Industries logo on it.

'You've made us millions.' The voice came from a suit walking into the room. It was a man in all business attire. He had a small five o'clock shadow, which was weird because it must have been pretty early in the morning at this point given my meeting with the boss had most likely taken place around the middle of the night.

'What?' I asked.

'Breq, your fight with the guardian at the Spire led to more views than the Battle of Broken Dreams,' the suit said, smiling. 'We've already made license deals with several mainstream media companies including Moonrain Media who we know you've been in contact with,' the figure said, 'from now on you get the best: a private room with your own VR set up and a team to watch your back.'

I was overwhelmed.

Things like this didn't happen to people like me.

'What are you talking about? All I did was run,' I said.

'Modest too, you truly are spectacular,' the man replied.

'Really, none of this is necessary,' I started to sit up, to try and get myself out of the bed. This immediately pulled the needle from my arm. I had become used to running out of hospitals. The year I lived on my own, I had gone to several different emergency rooms and every time had to run before they called the state and put me into a foster. I didn't want to live with another family. There would never be anyone else for me.

'Really now, come on, my name is...'

'I don't care what your name is, get me the hell out of here,' I said interrupting him.

He started to laugh. 'My name is Wesley, you can call me Wez, I'm your agent,' he reached out his hand for me to shake.

'I don't exactly understand what is going on but I have some-where I need to be,' I exclaimed.

'Right, your meeting with the lady, we'll take care of that,' he said. Another figure walked in, this time an older man with a long, black beard who looked like he would be more at home in the woods than the city. He was wearing a black suit and a match-ing chauffeur's cap on top of his head. He smelled like cedar and a barrel of beard oil.

'This is Reynolds, you can call him Rey, he will be your driver.'

'Driver?'

'As you can see Breq, we have everything under control,' Wez finished, still smiling. Somehow, I felt like nothing was un-der control, or at least that I had no control over anything.

A few minutes later, the doctor came in and released me to Reynolds who gave me back my clothes and drove me back towards the facility and home.

'My home is that way,' I said, pointing towards the housing area I had been staying in while employed. It was only since Damien had managed to get me a job at Keen Industries that I had been able to emancipate myself. For the first year I was their ward and I was still staying at one of their emergency shelters, which had become a slum for players like me.

'We've already taken the liberty of moving your belongings to your new room,' he said straight-faced. Somehow I didn't remember asking to have everything I owned uprooted and moved.

Overall, Reynolds was far nicer than Wesley and apologized for the agent's behaviour. My battle with the guardian had helped put Keen Industries back on the map. Mostly, the company was in the market of selling and trading in-game assets, recently, however, they had made some deals with a number of media companies to showcase the unique players under their control. My battle with the guardian was broadcast all across the net. During the six hours I had been waiting for the boss I had gone viral. Top that off with our group glassing the planet Orithyia, all eyes were on us.

My new room looked like a penthouse suite. It was entirely open, with a queen-sized bed, kitchen, sitting area, and gym equipment. The walls were covered in abstract artwork that looked like they may have been game related but it was too hard too tell. My first impression was that there was no way I could afford this with what little the company was paying me. It was the real world equivalent to the room I had been held prisoner while onboard the Crimson King destroyer.

'I can't accept this,' I said.

Reynolds looked at me, 'Sir, there is no issue, everything is bought and paid for.'

'How is that possible?'

'Thank the lady when you see her, she insisted that you have this.'

Lady Gray was investing a lot of money in me. Now I was more nervous than ever about meeting her.

Mid-Afternoon

I had a closet full of graphic tees, shorts, jeans, cargo pants, and one all-black suit. I grabbed a set of black cargo pants and a white T-shirt with the red silhouette of a soldier artistically drawn across it, like a samurai pointing his rifle upward into the air. There was a seven-string guitar hanging in the room, nearby it, a turntable and a record collection. Everything I had loved since I was a child. A few of the records looked familiar. I recognized them as being from my father's collection. Real artefacts that I thought were lost when I refused to return to the empty home. All of it had been claimed and bought by the company. Along the wall were several swords. Different types from different eras. There were several kendo sticks and an area open enough to practice my swordsmanship in. The ceilings in the penthouse were tall as well, about twenty feet high. I could see the steel beams and brick alongside one of the walls. The bathroom was just as nice as the rest of the rooms, with a full bath, shower, and a toilet that automatically flushed. Even the cabinets were stocked with deodorants, vitamins, towels, toilet paper, shampoo, and conditioner. Everything I could need or want had been here waiting for me. The fridge was stocked with fruits and veggies as well as water and coffee. Lady Gray wasn't lying. I felt famous.

When I stepped outside my new home into the long hallway I could see there were four more doors to rooms I assumed were around the same size as my own. At the end of the hallway there was an elevator and beside it Reynolds stood waiting.

'Glad to see you found your way alright, hope you managed to get some rest,' he said. The old man was smiling, his hand running down across his beard. I had managed to grab a few hours here and there but I was running on fumes. The only things keeping me going at this point were adrenaline and caffeine.

'Shouldn't I have to sign a contract or something?' I asked, still not able to believe any of this was happening.

'The day you joined you signed up for the possibility of this,' Reynolds replied. I forgot that for a moment. I was still indentured to the company. If they found out about the artefacts I had sold to Gorge, I would lose everything. I felt scared again, that fear of losing it all. Not that I wanted all of this, but how could I turn this away? Damien, Cass, Brand, the others and I had always dreamt of living like this, the only difference was that we wanted to do it on our own terms.

I felt fake.

Reynolds drove me to the donut shop. It was a small place just a few blocks away from the penthouse. I probably could have just walked but he insisted and continued to wait outside as went in. The entire shop was empty with the exception of one cashier and a young girl sitting drinking tea in the back of the room.

I walked towards the cashier and she pointed towards the girl.

'I'm here to meet someone, you don't happen to know Lady Gray do you?' I asked. She continued to point so I walked over to the young girl and looked down at her.

'Here,' her eyes sparkled with amusement.

It was impossible. Lady Gray's avatar was mid-twenties, short dark hair, scars, scary brown eyes and TALL. This woman sitting in front of me couldn't have been any older than thirteen (not even old enough to play *Bane*) and had long blonde hair with big blue eyes AND she was short. The two couldn't have been more opposite.

'Sit,' she demanded, motioning with her finger the same way she had in game.

'It is you,' I said trying to hide the shock and terror in my voice.

She smiled that same mischievous smile.

'Lady Gray at your service but you can call me Alexis,' she smiled again. I couldn't help but cower at that smile as my muscles tensed. I felt fatigued again; still, I hadn't had anything to eat.

'Have a donut,' she pointed towards a tray of different types.

'Thank you, Al…ex…is' I stuttered, while grabbing one of the chocolate-covered donuts from the tray. Probably not the best thing to eat under the circumstances but at least it was something. I had a fridge of healthy food at my new home and had no idea the next time I'd be able to indulge in something sweet and unhealthy. Slowly, I took a large, satisfying bite.

'I love sweets; nothing beats the kind with sprinkles,' she said.

I finished chewing and swallowed. 'You know the sprinkles are actually, like, really bad for you.' I put the shock and awe behind me and put on my serious face. When I did Alexis giggled slightly. 'Why did you want to meet in the real world?' I said, with real concern.

'Because everything you do in game is now going to be live. This is the only privacy we can get.'

'What do you mean?'

'For the past two years you've been nothing special, just a weak level thirty who occasionally sold guns on the black market,' her words caught me off-guard, 'yeah, Keen Industries know about that; before now it didn't really matter, they didn't care what you did so long as you met certain quotas,' she finished taking another bite. She had frosting on the side of her lip.

'Isn't that a breach of contract?' I asked, wondering how much trouble I was in.

'Like I said, they don't care,' she said chewing a full mouthful.

'Okay, so I'm still lost. You said I'm famous now and I now have a new place to live, new clothes, and a state-of-the-art VR system.'

'No one has ever taken on a guardian and survived, no one has ever had a bounty placed on them by the Chels and no one has ever been given a quest to venture into the Cold Zone,' she paused taking a sip of tea, looking at me over the rim as is appraising me. 'If we don't protect you no one will.'

'Why protect me?'

'Apart from the Chels and the Crimson Kings? There's also a potential threat from the man with the skull mask recorded in the data cube.'

'How do you know about that?'

'It wasn't the only copy Kira had.'

'You know Kira!' I exclaimed.

'I helped put together the team that went into the Cold Zone. Damien came to me with the request and I gave them the go ahead. They were all level fifty and had every right to explore the galaxy as much as a level ninety,' she paused, 'I was afraid; I was afraid of going with them, afraid of venturing myself,' her eyes were beginning to water, 'I sent them to their death.'

I wanted to comfort her. There was no way anyone could have foreseen what would happen. That somehow all four of the soldiers that went into the Cold Zone would be killed by whatever the skull-faced man was or that there was some kind of weapon that could kill players.

'It wasn't your fault, it was the game.'

'I had no idea there was a weapon; a weapon that could cause real damage.'

'Of course not, no one could know that, we're still not sure what really happened, IF there is such a weapon, we have to make it public, we have to warn players,' I said.

'We can't, the only way to prove it's real is to show it to the world, but even the footage we have looks like it could have been altered. In order to prove it's real someone would have to be killed live,' she was no longer eating.

'Is that what you are asking me to do?'

'No, I WANT you to complete your quest, I WANT you to kill the skull-masked man and collect the echoes left behind, recover the weapon if you can too, so we can lock it away.'

For a moment I had been afraid she had called me out here to ask me to die but I was wrong, wrong about everything to do with her. The boss wasn't terrifying. She was probably more caring than anyone - besides my own team - I had met in a long time. She wanted the truth just as much as I did.

'What do you know about the Cold Zone?' I asked.

'Level seventy-seven, nearly impossible to access unless you are level fifty or higher and even after that it's nearly impossible to find since there is no direct pathway,' she paused, 'there is also at least one habitable world, code named Nero.'

'Why were you afraid of going yourself?'

'I'm a prodigy and have been playing and beating games since I was four years old but if I lose my character and have to start over I lose everything.'

In that way Alexis was just like me. The game was life.

'Even if you lost your character, we'd all help you get back to being boss of Corpse Divers again,' I argued.

'Thanks, but I doubt Keen Industries will be so patient. And you haven't experienced Prestige mode. Everything is harder after level fifty and if you had built an empire like I have you would understand that it would take me years to reacquire half of what

64

I own.' I had heard about that Prestige mode and could see that high level players were a lot more cautious than those around my level. Even Damien, with the exception of his mission into the Cold Zone, had acted differently after levelling up past forty-nine.

'Quadrants are locked between levels one to ten; ten to thirty; thirty to fifty and fifty plus. Yes, there are some loopholes around the quadrants but once you reach level fifty you are playing an entirely different game, the universe becomes a battlefield and if you don't surround yourself with power you will lose everything.' And now I knew why Alexis had become the boss Lady Gray and why she had destroyed the Crimson Kings in such a spectacle. I'm sure she was wrong about most things but she was right about several. Most players in *Bane* were casual or worked for a company like I did and sat somewhere between one and forty. Players over fifty were guild masters, leaders, titans, and, like Lady Gray, legends.

Alexis looked like she was going to cry.

I felt angry. She was so powerful...she could just take her army and invade the Cold Zone. Everyone like me would follow her in a heartbeat. No. It wouldn't work. The Cold Zone was like the Bermuda Triangle...if an army tried to invade the game would just come up with a way to wipe them out and if it was proven there was a weapon that could kill in real life...everyone invested would be in a frenzy.

'Why do you want this? Why care?' I wondered aloud.

'Damien was the only person that stood up to me in the game, he, and now you, are the only two people in the world that know my secret, that know who I really am,' she answered.

Alexis had taken a bite of her donut again and began to talk with her mouth half full; after realizing she was doing this she stopped and smiled. 'I was at level forty-nine, teamed with three random players in a raid. Three of them were using Ki rifles and let me tell you. I loved them. No one died. We were up against an Aberrant Vrax and no one died. We broke its attacks one after another and finally, when it was limping away in retreat, we all transformed. Swinging from ledges like we were superheroes, we arrived at the top of a mountain pass with time to spare before the Vrax even arrived back to its lair. We were out of our minds. We placed a trap in its path, ran back a bit, waited until it jumped towards us and listened as the sound of four bombs went off. Each hit their mark. It was glorious. The Vrax fell. But in our triumph we failed to notice the mountain crumbling around us. Damien jumped forward and saved my life. The two other players weren't so lucky. Plus ten trapping, plus twenty breaking parts of a Vrax, plus fifty for killing a monster. I levelled up and I knew without people like Damien watching my back I could lose everything. When I established the Corpse Divers, Damien was one of the first I invited to my guild.'

Listening to Alexis, I knew in that moment that I wasn't the only one that had lost my best friend.

EVENING

Alexis promised to give my team and I everything we needed to accomplish our mission and gave me several tips on how I could level my character up quickly without grinding. When I left, I hugged her and she reminded me that she wouldn't be so nice in-game and that I better not forgot she was still the boss and that she wouldn't hesitate to kill me if I made her look bad. I told Rey I wanted to walk home alone. Lying, I told him that I had eaten too many donuts and could use the exercise. He agreed to this, but before he drove off he reminded me that I was a considerable asset to the company and that if I tried to run away they would send a team after me. At the moment I was worth millions.

On the way home I stopped at a small diner and went inside. I ordered some greasy food and condiments and chowed down for half an hour, eating as much of the junk as I could. I figured that after tonight it would be my last unhealthy treat for awhile. As I sat there alone, I thought about Damien's funeral. I thought about the two of us coming here and grabbing a bite to eat after beating our first raid. How after I hit level 10 he bought me a burger made of real meat and nothing artificial. He was always proud when I came and told him of my accomplishments. He was the older brother I never had.

Damien had a lot of friends and yet he had spent so much time with just Cass and me. On first discovering that he knew the boss, I had felt like he had been living a double life, but that wasn't the case at all. He was just kind. He was patient. He never gave in to his fears. Damien lived his life the way he wanted, pushing himself to exceed, to excel at everything no matter what it was. From the moment he had kicked my ass on the street he had made me one of his missions. And that is what got him killed. Survival always has a price.

6.
Class

Damien had become my friend for a few weeks and had been talking non-stop about me joining him as a Corpse Diver in *Bane*. He was excited to have found me, admiring my talent for survival and how I had managed to hold my own for so long since my parents passed. I had just emancipated, leaving my school with high marks and even recommendations from teachers who had been sad to see me break away. It was the usual course but it was the path I was forging for myself. I could only run from the past so long. Damien showed up right when I wasn't sure what to do.

I don't know why I let him in. I had met dozens of people while acting on my own. Many tried to recruit me for this or that but I always said 'No'. Damien just seemed different. He had an energy that drew me to him like a magnet. He bought me a meal at *The Sparrow*, one of his favourite diners, and spoke about being a Corpse Diver with a passion I had never seen before.

'Of course I know about the game, my father was working with Keen Industries on developing software for the pods,' I said, not quite sure if I was trying to get Damien to shut up or not. My father did more than that though. He began working there as an engineer shortly before I was born, while *Bane* was barely in alpha. He moved up, creating non-player-characters and developing software.

'So you've played it?' Damien asked, ordering two shakes from a waitress. The waitress was Cass, though I didn't know it at the time, and she was the reason Damien frequented *The Sparrow* so much.

'I don't want a shake. And to answer your question, no, I never played it. Dad said it was too mature, too real and that I'd have to wait until I was older.'

'Too bad, you'd probably be a pro by now if you managed to get in on the ground floor,' he said, ignoring my shake comment.

'I don't want to play it,' I answered back, still unsure what I was doing there. Maybe I had just been alone so long I needed the company.

'I can see it in your eyes,' Damien began, 'you've lost so much in so little time maybe playing *Bane* is something that will help bring you closer to your father, closer to figuring out who you are.'

My comeback: 'My eyes are brown and you can't see anything in them.'

'You're wrong; you are a warrior like me.'

The rest of the conversation was more about my family and the game. Damien told me about *Bane* and Keen Industries, the dozens of other companies and studios that were working both inside and behind the scenes. An entire sub-culture built around something my father had been a part of. I listened. It was the first time I heard anyone give anything so familiar to me so much praise. By the end of the night, Damien had convinced me and the next day he moved along some paperwork that got me a job as a player. While I would be working for Keen Industries, technically my contract was as a freelancer so they wouldn't be held responsible for anything idiotic I said or did in the game. Damien had to call in about a dozen favours so that I could join the Corpse

Divers though. Taking responsibility for me when I was hardly taking responsibility for myself.

I signed in. Created my character. My original user name was 'Wild_Dog47' but since I had the option to show my real name and because of a point made in my contract, I changed it to 'Breq.'

Displaying your real name had become common practice in *Bane*. Most players, at least those without scripted names, choose to show their real names. Settings could easily be adjusted for safety and privacy but since the game was such a massive part of real life this was unnecessary.

Slightly disappointing was my discovery that I wasn't allowed to customize my appearance at all. Signing in as a solo player I could have made a character with alien characteristics, various body shapes, or even changed the colour of my skin to something strange like blue or purple. As a Corpse Diver, however, there were specific rules to follow set down by Lady Gray.

I could still remember my first day in *Bane*. Waking up in a small cruiser called *Adept,* looking up at the logo of Lady Gray's guild, and equipping my starting set of weapons before dropping into Terminus. The first thing a player sees is a cut-scene. A starship comes out of a rip made in reality hovering above an unknown planet. The type of starship varies depending on how the player came in. The starship moves across the player's vision like a silhouette in front of the planet. The camera zooms in towards the engines and showcases the outside of the ship.

For many players, this was a monumental moment. After a few minutes of spectacle, the camera cuts to black and players wake up as if from a deep sleep to be greeted by an interface that allows them to choose their backstory.

Most everyone had the same origin. We were remnants. All that was left of humanity after a massive exodus through the world gate *At Eternity* which had since gone offline.

The current timeline is three hundred years since the exodus and we have several pieces of backstory to choose from. The first option was that having just graduated from Starlight Academy, now setting off on our own. The second backstory was of waking up from stasis to serve some kind of greater purpose ranging from elite guardsman, paladins, tech-mages, mech-pilots, etc. This made it easy for players to integrate into various guilds and jobs set up by external forces programmed as part of the game. Some were wardens, admin, others part of specific guilds. Some others were playing the game as part of therapy and were bound by certain laws and restrictions programed via external software into their pods before playing.

After figuring out what your backstory was you next had to choose a class:

Soldiers (Five sub-classes Warrior / Paladin / Boomer / Sniper / Tank)

Scout (Three sub-classes Hunter / Rogue / Ranger)

Medic

Merchant / Trader

Engineer / Tech-Mage (being the advanced class)

Specialist

Psion

I chose Scout. If I wanted to at some point I could change it to Hunter or Rogue, enhancing my skills in either combat or stealth. I preferred to play as a balanced character. Besides the basic classes there were dozens of titles someone could earn in the game such as 'mercenary' or 'bounty-hunter' even titles such as 'slayer' or 'captain' and 'commander' depending on how you played and how your guild operated. Also, the more proficient you were in skills had a direct relation to your class and identity. An example would be that a specialist with a high pilot level could unlock the class 'Pilot' or an engineer unlocking the 'Tech-Mage' class.

After getting your avatar and distributing your first set of skill points you were ready to play. The first seven hours covered basic movement and control, plus weapons and practice at a firing range with an energy pistol. A few tweaks here and there by Damien helped give me better control of my new avatar body, but for the most part I grew into it. Just as he had told me I would. I still feel my character growing. Every day, every battle, saw me gain experience and grow stronger: even in the face of non-stop conflict. Damien wasn't a tough teacher, not like Aiden or Brand, Corpse Divers who had been forced to take me onto their team. Damien was always patient. That was a part of what made him a good leader, a good friend.

Weapons training was difficult at first. The two of us walked onto a range: a large arena that looked like the outside world with floating islands and waterfalls that ran upward from the ground. The environment was surreal and yet all of the plant-life looked natural. The targets were holograms placed across an open field at different ranges. I tried various different weapons, including a few heavy weapons that Damien had brought with him for fun.

Pro Tip

Bane is full of different types of weapons. Assault Rifles, Energy Rifles, Mana draining rifles, SMGs, pistols, shotguns, grenade launchers, rocket launchers, melee weapons. In all there are around 15,000 different variations of ballistic and energy weapons alone. All weapons can be levelled up for higher affinity and sharpness as well as increased damage and critical chance. Find a weapon that matches your play style and stick with it. Players that use the same weapon have a stronger advantage over other players who change their weapons frequently.

Weapon Types:

All weapons come in two forms. They are either material weapons that shoot bullets or items made of various substances, or they are kinetic rifles that fire powerful bursts of energy.

Assault Rifles - great short round bursts; provide excellent cover fire and are effective for taking on hordes of enemies in game.

Scout Rifles - Precision rifles that reward a skilled player. Usually semi-automatic but can be found in automatic or modified forms. High accuracy.

Shotguns - Great for close quarters but like their real-life counterparts can be used for range. Pump action and automatic types. Usually limited ammo.

> Sniper Rifles - Kill an enemy from a mile away. Used only by those who have mastered scout rifles and have high sharpness. Known to do immense damage in small spaces. Sniper rifles take the most skill to master.
>
> Pistols - Stealth weapons can be modified into semi-auto or automatic variants that are on par with assault rifles as far as damage.
>
> Explosive Weapons - Grenade launchers, rocket launchers, anti-matter rifles and nuclear detonation canons. All things RED.

I was awful. Seriously, I felt like the worst player in history. For three hours I didn't hit a single target. The game gave some assistance but unlike most games with auto-aim it was still more about skill than mechanics. Damien taught me to aim, to breathe, to look down my sight and how to hold my weapon just right. I became attached to rifles - specifically energy or Ki-rifles - because of their light weight. We spent far too long with the guns: the motion sickness that came after I first logged out was bad enough that I slept fourteen hours the next day and ended up late for my first mission.

My assignment was a beginner's quest in a training zone called 'Point Zero', a zone that might as well have been its own game. Set on a moon in the Terminus binary star system in Quadrant 3, it was world where anything felt possible. I can still remember that magic feeling of floating in zero gravity and the opposite intensity of feeling as we hit 2G, thrusters firing in reverse as we entered the planet's atmosphere. It was so real. If I hadn't known I was in a game I would have thought I was dreaming.

NAME: DAMIEN

Age: 17   Class: Paladin
Level: 30   Health: 100 (+10 Armour)
Status: Alive   Stamina: 100
Mana: 100

Load out: Ki Rifle, Energy Pistol, Combat Dagger

```
Location Discovered: Training Ground Landing Point A /
                        Terminus
            Quest: Quick Salvage
            Expected Difficulty: Low
            Rewards: 500 EXP
```

'That hurt,' I said falling out of my stasis chamber. The *Adept* had just had a rather rough landing on the planet's surface.

'Sorry about that, Nel is new, just starting to learn the ship,' Damien answered. He was wearing his usual gear, equipped with a M7-7 rifle and an energy pistol along with a combat dagger.

'Our imperfect landing was a result of the intervention of Damien,' I heard an automated voice say into my ear. I couldn't tell where it was coming from and it startled me: I jumped back holding my rifle up just as Damien had shown me.

He, however, was looking at me curiously. 'What's the matter Breq?'

'The ship says it was your intervention made for the bumps.'

'Tell Nel if she ever wants those brand new ion canons attached at the front, she will stop blaming me for its faults,' Damien was laughing now. I felt like I missed some kind of joke.

'Ship says you are too poor to buy new ion canons and expects you would most likely buy used,' Nel spoke both in my ear and through the ship's PA. I didn't jump this time. In fact, knowing I had a robotic companion to help me made me feel safer in a way.

'Nel, if you help me level up I'll make sure the ship gets new ion canons from a top dealer in the Spire and you get as many upgrades as you want,' I said, trying to show my determination as a new player.

'Chances of your success are thirteen percent, I will, however, be cheering you on.'

'Stop flirting with the robot,' Damien chuckled. I thought about making a comeback but I had nothing.

Probably, anything I said would have sounded stupid and by the time I had finally thought of something, Nel had already answered back with, 'organics are not my type.'

Damien was moving down the ramp and out of the ship. The planetscape was barren except for a few scattered trees and what looked like Mayan ruins.

> Location Discovered: Training Ground Site B
> /Terminus

'Chel ruins; a city that was once prosperous now long forgotten,' Damien said. It was easy to forget all of this was made up. The world around us felt lived in, dirty, real. 'Did you check your weapons and ammo?'

I had, but just in case I checked the power battery on my rifle again to make sure it was fully charged. Fifty-five percent! If it dropped below that figure, it would drain my HP points every time I fired. I wasn't sure how the charge had gone down so quickly, but we had gone to the range to practice one last time before picking up the game-quest.

I lied, told him it was full, and he threw me an extra battery. I guess he already knew.

```
M7 - 7 Ki Rifle
Description: Standard issue

Level: 1
Damage: 10
Weight: 8 lbs
Weapon Type: Assault Rifle
Rarity: Common
Impact: 5
Range: 6
Stability: 3
Reload Speed: 4
RPM (rounds per minute): 250 bursts
Affinity: 3
Sharpness: 5
Elemental: None
Critical Chance: 20%
Modifiers: None
```

'Follow me, keep low, remember you are a scout. You want to try to use stealth as much as possible when entering into a battle zone. The more you use it the more advanced your detection skill will become,' Damien crouched down and followed a path that descended into the ruins. The path led to a small tunnel. The tunnel was filled with small lizards and red moss. The lizards seemed to blend in with the moss until we began to cross paths with them.

'Don't waste any ammo,' Damien said. He wasn't talking about the lizards. In front of us inside the tunnel was an opening with a giant waterway. A large animal that looked like a multi-coloured hippo with massive tusks was drinking from the small river that flowed north in the direction we were heading. The two of us crept forward and I had to admire the abundance of alien life that surrounded us. Each new animal felt like a new discovery. My senses were overloading with imagery. The various colours and the abstract essence of Terminus.

Half a mile underground we found the wreckage we were looking for. Buried deep below the ruins of Terminus was an alien starship called *Decrepit*. The loot inside the ship was constantly being re-spawned and it was a perfect starting point for a new player like myself to collect some credits and experience points.

Location Discovered: Training Ground Site B - *Decrepit*
/ Terminus

'A light mech and three raiders are guarding the entrance, what should we do?' Damien asked. At *The Sparrow* Damien would frequently tell me things about the game, decisions I would have to make that would define who I was as a player. Here, he was letting me lead.

'Analyze the situation and move in as quietly as possible,' I said.

Nel spoke up, 'it seems your enemy has a hostage. Based on your current skill level and affinity for weapons she has a two percent chance of survival.' I was starting to get used to hearing the voice in my head.

'Damn, wasn't expecting that,' Damien was pointing towards a character tied up next to the entrance. Raiders were common NPC combatants: easy low-level enemies who scavenged ruined worlds; for them to take a hostage was strange behaviour.

'It's been awhile since I've played; this is new,' Damien said.

'Does the hostage matter?'

'Player or NPC, if they are good, they matter, that hostage might be a trader or someone with a high reward, they could also be a bounty of some kind but either way it's our job to get involved,' Damien answered. It was the first time I had heard him speak so sternly and the first time I realized just how seriously I had to take the game.

'Can you take on the mech by yourself?' I asked.

'It's only a level 10. It shouldn't be a problem.'

'You draw out the mech, I'll take down the three guards and rescue the hostage, if she can help I'll give her my energy pistol and if she can't I'll run her back to the entrance and meet back up with you here.'

'That actually sounds like a good plan.'

A minute later we moved ourselves into position. Damien fired first, aiming at the mech, drawing its attention and running further into the caves as we planned. The mech and one of the guards followed while the other two moved closer to the hostage. I crept behind them and from a crouched position blind fired at one: a hit! I felt powerful as my hands shook. It was amazing, my heart raced. I felt like I had gained something. Like having superpowers. Determined more than ever now to win, I fired again just as the second guard turned, aiming down the barrel of my gun as Damien had taught me.

+10 EXP

+10 EXP

+5 Stealth

+5 Luck

As the two guards vanished from the game, I approached the hostage and untied her hands. She was an NPC around my age, athletic, with short blonde hair that was dreaded around the tips. Wearing a tank top and cargo pants, she had a scar across her eye and it was obvious her life had been rough, rougher even than mine. Her only armour was a single shoulder piece, which was covered in alien runes; I could only assume it had been salvaged from the *Decrepit* a long time ago.

Having ripped off the tape that had been placed over her mouth by the raiders she spoke in a language that was hard to understand. Quickly, the game translated it for me. She told me her name was Riley and she had been a scavenger by trade. Both her and her sister lived in a colony, a small settlement based on the planet where players could travel and trade for low level items and implants.

As looked at her, Nel instructed me how to scan other players and NPCs for valuable information. While it was possible the information could be false in the case of players it was less likely an NPC would be able to hide their stats.

Riley
Level 6 (Health: 90 Stamina: 80)
Friendly
No Weapons Equipped

She was five levels stronger than me. Not that it mattered. Without Damien by my side it was nice to have company.

'Chances of survival have increased: you have a very good chance,' Nel announced.

I thanked the robotic voice in my head as Riley turned and looked at me like I was talking to myself. I tried to explain but it was useless. She didn't quite understand what I was or what I was doing. She was focused solely on saving her sister.

'My sister! They took her inside, five of them, they said if we didn't lead them to the ruins they would slay our colony.' **Translation quality: approximate**.

'I am here to help, can you understand me?' I asked.

'Yes,' she answered in common.

'Your sister will be safe, first we have to wait for my friend. Can you fire a weapon?' I held out the energy pistol removing it from my inventory as she took it. A simple yes would have done but she began to move forward towards the side entrance of *Decrepit*.

'We have to wait!' I shouted.

'I can't. My sister is in danger,' she answered back.

I had another decision to make. Damien was right, choices were going to be a huge part of *Bane*. As she moved ahead, I was forced to decide. Follow the woman into *Decrepit* or wait for Damien to deal with the raider mech and guard?

It wasn't hard. I followed Riley inside a small airlock where she pressed several keys and the door opened. Right off the back, we were ambushed by two guards.

```
Raider x 2
Level 3
Hostile
```

Two shots each from each of us and they were down. Another +20 EXP gained. Both raiders were wearing weak body armour that looked like it had been scrapped together from a junkyard. They had focused their attack on Riley giving me the advantage. Since the woman was an NPC she seemed to have a decent amount of health. I wondered if she could be killed at all. Probably, Definitely. The two of us continued to sneak our way through the *Decrepit*, with Riley leading the way.

The other three raiders went down just as easily. I really started to feel a sense of accomplishment playing *Bane*. The rush of living in this world, the gunfights, helping strangers in need. I felt an overwhelming sense of discovery in turning every corner and exploring what came next. Damien was right, this was what had been missing in my life. My chance at something more. I was starting to feel like less of a corporate tool and more like a player.

Riley's sister was named Kess. She was younger than Riley by almost five years. As I followed the two of them out the quest became more of an escort mission. Gun turrets dropped from above as the defence system activated against us. By the time we made it through the ship, I had lost almost half my health. Yet when I was in the airlock and able to look outside, there were half a dozen raiders waiting for me and no sign of Damien any-where.

'I'm going to fail this mission,' I said.

'It seems I will not be receiving future upgrades,' Nel re-sponded.

'Thanks for the vote of confidence.'

I told Kess and Riley to stay behind me near the back of the airlock as the hull door opened. The raiders turned their attention on us as I fired, knocking one down. I hid in the small space between the airlock door and the wall as Damien began firing from somewhere above us. Three, then four of the raiders fell and I turned my attention towards the last one, laying down cover fire. I couldn't get a read on him but the last raider was strong. Most likely a level 10 equipped with heavy armour. Damien took him out by first injuring him in the knee and finishing him with a shot to the spine.

I smiled looking over at Damien. I felt like a new person. Brand new and both of us knew it. He smirked and gave me a thumbs up. We won.

'Who are your friends?' Damien asked as the smoke cleared.

'Riley and Kess, from the settlement,' I answered.

As the two of them walked out of the *Decrepit* they thanked both of us for saving them. Riley gave me back my energy pistol and as they moved away, she encouraged me to find her again in the future, promising she would have a reward for us. A prompt appeared in my field of vision.

Quest Complete!
+500 EXP

I almost immediately levelled up and began distributing points into my focus and attacks. I wasn't going to be a weak player. If I was going to hunt artefacts and save NPCs from raiders I was going to have to be strong. Stronger than them, as strong, no, stronger than Damien.

Three days later I returned to the *Decrepit* with Damien. The raiders had returned and we completed the mission again earning me +100 EXP. After that run through the ship, Damien and I visited the settlement and found Riley and Kess who rewarded both of us with upgraded armour. It was there in the settlements I saw Damien sneak away and talk to someone, another player by the name of Scrawl. Little did I know at the time Scrawl was Kira's brother and the two were planning the biggest dive in history.

7.
Ambush

'Access'

Checking for necessary update files...

Update 1.11.7 found.

Initializing...

Player environment meets necessary requirements.

Retina scan / Identity confirmed.

Dive 100%

Loading player data...

'Loneliness is an infection that will attack you at your core. It will twist your veins and distort your heart until you don't know up from down. It will lie to you and blur what is right and wrong and at that moment it will try all it can to strangle you. Please remember if you can only take one thing from this. No matter how lost, how alone you can still be found. All you have to do is look around you and know we are here.'

    - Damien, days before his death.

The inside of the stasis pod was just like it had always been before but I felt different. I could hear the sound of the dark grey metal hatch grind as it opened and I began to access my arms and legs. Usually there was a small lag joining the game but this time there was almost nothing. My new pod must have been state of the art, maybe I was even the first person to use it. I felt my chest move up and down as my senses sharpened. The game enhanced your senses three times greater than in reality. In the real world I would need to wear glasses or contacts but in the game I had perfect twenty/twenty vision. Even more so with the right implants. I could, if I wanted, have vision like a hawk or cat eyes that could see in the dark. Every implant had their own share of problems though. Trade your human vision for cat eyes and you see less colour. Moving back and forth from one to another could also cause severe nausea and headaches for those that accessed the game too long. It would be like staring at a coloured light bulb all day and all night. Your eyes wouldn't always be permanently damaged but there would be side effects. Everyone that played knew that. The first virtual reality sets were nothing more than headgear. After that came finger sensors and foot pads. Treadmills for running. Over the years VR evolved until finally someone developed the pods. Originally they were created as medical care units. Able to treat patients with severe trauma or bodily injuries. The military used them to train soldiers in real life combat situations. A week in a pod with the right software could be just as real as three weeks in the field.

The pods use light and sound to trick the mind into a kind of transcendent static state that allow several sensors worn on the body to provide reflex movement while a visor stimulates brain activity, essentially upending you inside the game. The pods were designed so that too much pain caused a decrease in health while dampening the actual pain response to the body. The pods were also set up to mediate potentially disturbing experiences, such as torture or death, so that they felt like dreams. If a user died during their time in the game, that moment would be adjusted. Rather than experience events that might cause someone to become unhinged in the real world, players were left with a feeling of having lived but not felt certain events. Examples include traumatic death, torture, etc. this feature could of course be modified based on how the user played the game.

Another built in feature for pods is the ability to speak to an admin. This allows players who became stranded to get help or rescue. Most of the time this feature involves a player-controlled organization, who send help for a small fee. As a Corpse Diver I was required to have my settings adjusted to being as realistic as possible since the game would automatically read over my character and generate loot and EXP based on my personal stats.

Bane was a living system. The game engine was designed from the ground up for military use. Rumour has it that the code was originally designed to run and test an experiment combining time dilation and virtual reality, however none of the time dilation effects worked as intended and so the project was scrapped. Time dilation of course is a difference in time between two observers. Example: if the project had worked as intended someone that played *Bane* would feel like years of their life had gone by only to log out and find that those years were the equivalent to hours in the real world.

The engine itself was seamless. Unlike other VR worlds it was able to support millions of players in true to real life environments and utilize all five senses. Players could live out their fantasies without worry. *Bane* became popular after an overload of fantasy worlds began to drown out the market. Everyone began looking for something new and with a procedurally generated resource system and various degrees of built-in artificial intelligence *Bane* was born. If you wanted to fly you could journey to sector 17 and live on a planet with vast red forests and low gravity. If you wanted to hunt wild animals you could venture into the wilds of Decima-12 and trade with others that settled in your sector. *Bane* allowed players to slightly mod and dress their characters how they saw fit. It was science fiction in genre only. With so many worlds to explore and discover everything was left to the players' imagination and determination.

After *Bane* became popular, credits in game meant real world dollars and that was when companies like Keen Industries and Moonrain Media became involved. Now, there are four million players in a hundred and seventy-seven servers, give or take. That means twenty-two thousand, five hundred and ninety-eight people spread out in seventy-six quadrants: two nine seven players per quadrant equally. Not everyone played at the same time or daily however, so take away maybe a thousand here and there. Dungeons and settlements also shared several of the same servers allowing players the ability to interact. The Spire alone had four thousand five hundred people in it when I arrived. There were probably a hundred bystanders who lost their game when I went face to face with the guardian and out of the five k people in Alpha-1 three thousand two hundred were taken out by my boss. The servers themselves were spread out all across the world.

In real life I had pain that shot through my arms and legs several times throughout the day. Nerve damage that would cause me to feel like I was being stuck with pins and needles. It made lifting anything heavy nearly unbearable and without the money for surgery I would have to live with the attacks for the rest of my life. In the real it was a reminder of the wreck that took away my parents' lives. In the game there was no pain. Replaced by a healthy body, one that could take damage and dish it out.

Bane was limited when it came to character creation. When you first played, it would scan your own body and allow you to build features on top of that. Sure, you could like Lady Gray and change your appearance and height but your avatar had to be 'proportionate' to your body in the real world for your mind to accept the environment around you. The game, like most virtual worlds, allowed you to feel one hundred percent healthy. This was a great feature that made living in a virtual world a reality for many. Some people would spend more time in VR than real life. Leaving only to eat, drink, sleep. Most pods had a system in place that allowed the body to well…you get it.

While most players were between levels 1 and 40, that was because many players found themselves holding down positions around level 35. Some were guards, bounty hunters, raiders, smugglers, merchants. Dungeon divers like myself usually died around level 45 as they explored harder levels in the game, so getting as high as Lady Gray or Damien made you look like a badass. There were also lost colonies. These were player groups that lived on the fringe worlds and explored new areas of space, looking to advance their bank account far more than their EXP. And they had a tendency to get lost. Some would set up on new worlds and invited players to come trade and explore, while others would have no choice but to restart their accounts.

The level of difficulty in *Bane* was a part of what made it so interesting to play. It made the loot worth more and EXP a necessity for reaching worlds that were farther out from the Spire. Other guilds similar to the Corpse Divers existed, we were only #1200 as far as leaderboards were concerned, however we were the only group with a Lady Gray and a Titan.

'Took your time meeting with the boss,' Cass and several others were standing over me as I woke up into the game.

'Mighty hero, Breq, the city-runner,' said Brand, he was another Corpse Diver, one of my squad. Together we had gone on several raids and missions together. It was nice to see his bald head and gnarly face smiling down at me. Brand always looked like he was angry, but he was probably one of the nicest among our ranks.

'Ensign idiot,' the voice was that of Aiden. Aiden was more or less the leader of our group. He was a level 37 and had already made a name for himself with sponsorships from Anomaly Games and Media, Sunblossom Studios, and Hungry Sidekick. Aiden was clearly upset. The deal made with Moonrain Media gave them and only them a hundred percent access to my feed. They had paid a ton of money for exclusivity rights and that meant that players like Aiden had to put their sponsors on hold. I felt bad. I knew Aiden needed those sponsors to make ends meet. He was eighteen and had managed to move out of the housing into a small apartment because of the progress he made. Now, because of me it was possible he could lose it all.

The *Ibanez* is a cruiser that holds roughly ten squads aboard. Each squad consisted of seven players.

Seven was the minimum requirement for some of the more advanced dungeons and raids.

Echo - 1, my squad, consisted of:

NAME: AIDEN

Level: 37   Class: Gunner / Tank

Loadout: M7-7 Ki Rifle (lvl. 7), mini-gun (lvl.2), combat knife, explosive grenades

NAME: BRAND

Level: 32   Class: Medic

Loadout: Automatic Shotgun (lvl. 4), Pistol (lvl. 10), combat knife, med-kit x 4

Name: Shiru

Level: 30   Class: Sniper / weapons
specialist

Loadout: M44 Long Range Sniper Rifle (lvl. 20) w/ modifiers,
short barrel pump action shotgun (lvl. 13), throwing knives,
and extra food supplies.

Name: Pierce

Level: 25   Class: Tech Specialist

Loadout: M7-7 Ki Rifle (lvl. 15) x 2 with duel modifiers, short
grip energy takedown glove, smoke grenades

Name: Eli

Level: 34 Class: Tech Specialist

Loadout: M7-7 Ki Rifle (lvl. 15), EMP Blaster, Microwave Emit-
ter (lvl. 5), EMP Grenades

And of course Cass...

Name: Cass

Level: 34   Class: Scout

Loadout: M7-7 Ki Rifle, M44 SMG variant x 2 with duel modifiers, explosive grenades, and a long sword called *Eta Tau*.

As for my ship.

Along with weapons and tech the *Ibanez* was equipped with several mechs which could be controlled by Nel, Tel, and of course any crew personnel so long as they were level 20 or higher and had a pilot skill 5. Pierce and Eli were our mech techs though Cass was learning. Gorge had told me a few things about them here and there from our trades but for the most part they were a newer addition to the game. Rated on a scale of 1 to 10 in speed and agility, mechs could be loaded with one weapons on each arm. Mechs came in three categories: light, medium, heavy. The three categories consisting of various forms. Most mechs took the shape of bi-pedal machines resembling humans in function while others could resemble robotic animals such as gorillas, there were even four-legged mechs that functioned more as tanks. The mechs were controlled via cockpits much like fighters however once a user interfaced with the controls the mech acted as an extension of the user's body, mimicking their body movements.

The three mechs in our hangar:

Light

A compact frame with repulsors that allow it to skid across any terrain, with an open centre torso, our light mech was code-named *Pilgrim*. The light mech can fly 20 feet above the ground for 20 seconds at a time with a recharge rate starting at 120 seconds (skilled mechanics and techs could upgrade flight time to last minutes and even mod light mechs with wings so they could glide for short distances at various heights).

Weight: 2 Tons (Carbon Fiber alloy / thin ballistic shell)
Health: 500
Speed: 8
Agility: 9
Weapons: Primary - Heavy Laser Rifle (100 Damage at 300 RPM)
Secondary - Shotgun (single shell) (300 Damage 10 RPM)
Melee - Extendable Combat Blade (150 Damage)

Medium

Medium mechs were, unfortunately, not the best of both worlds. Made similar to a heavy mech with few of the advantages of the light. The one in our hangar was named *Radagast*. Medium mechs have a robust frame with a closed cockpit and can function in zero gravity with four repulsors: two on the back of the legs and two on the shoulders. While the medium mech was too heavy to fly without heavy modification, it could hover for three to five seconds with the help of two fusion jets attached to the back of the torso.

```
Weight: 10 Tons (with a thick ballistic shell)
                  Health: 2000
                    Speed: 6
                   Agility: 5
Weapons: Primary - Gatling Laser Rifle (100 Damage
                  at 600 RPM)
     Secondary - Railgun (700 Damage 2 RPM)
Melee - None (however a long enough blade can be
                    modded)
                     Heavy
```

Although unable to fly or hover for any given amount of time, there is no doubt that a heavy mech is a mobile fortress, equipped with sufficient firepower to destroy buildings, slug starships, and fight large enemies or hordes. Their dense armour plating made heavy mechs a force of nature. Unending. Unforgiving. The name of the heavy we had on board was *Vex*. It was also very expensive costing nearly a years worth of an average player's salary.

```
Weight: 20 Tons
Health: 5000
Speed: 3
Agility: 3
Weapons: Primary - Enhanced Mutli-Grenade Launcher
with tracking
(5000 Damage at 10 RPM) for short range.
Secondary - Long-range Laser Railgun
(1000 Damage at 5 RPM)
Melee - None
```

The *Ibanez* had been abandoned by everyone except my squad and a small, four-person crew to run the ship alongside Tel, Nel's big 'sister'. It was our ship now. Another present from Lady Gray. In a way, the others saw it as a reward for rescuing me from the guardian. We actually had our own starship! Something I had been striving for since I started playing and yet somehow it all seemed forced. Unearned.

Since Aiden was the highest level among us he was put in charge. He was also a tank. He was the only one among us with special abilities that included super strength without the use of power armour. Before joining us, Aiden used to fight in an arena in the Spire. Second in command was Eli followed by Cass. Pierce was Eli's sidekick for the most part. Eli had been training him since he started playing and, slowly, Pierce had been catching up with her. Cass was, I supposed, my mentor too now that Damien had passed. I was the second scout in our group and would be following her lead during missions. Our job for the most part was stealth. Scouts were sent in first towards the front line to investigate and if possible, come up with a strategy to fulfill our mission.

Our other scout, Shiru, was a lone wolf before he joined the squad. Having lost his original level 40 avatar aboard the battle cruiser *King Solomon*, he joined us after hardening his skills as a sniper in the wastelands on the moon of Awarath Prime called Luminae - 4. When he joined, he asked us a personal favour. The retrieval of his own echo. We agreed and it was the first quest he went on with us. It was there we watched as he avenged his own death against a group of raiders known as 'Devoted Domination'. I can still remember his battle cry as his eyes turned red and he began sniping them from afar. Shiru started at the top, killing the leader, followed by the rest of the Devoted's crew. His first avatar had been a trader, a merchant that moved goods from one system to the next. Taking out the raiders made Shiru happy; it was clear how personal was the loss of his first avatar. He had spent the better part of the last year levelling up his weapon for that moment. After that, he was one of us. He believed in corpse diving as a kind of tribute to the dead, even if some of us were only doing it because it was all we could do to survive.

I didn't know the others on the outside, like I knew Damien and Cass. When Damien joined another squad, I joined Echo-1 in his stead. For a while this meant having to prove myself to the other squad members, time and time again. Mostly we did smaller dungeon dives, around levels 5-20, with the occasional corpse dive around level 30. Damien had introduced me to Cass outside the game when the three of us went out to an arcade and art show together. It was the first time I had been to the city since my parents passed. It was also the first time I remember really smiling. I could still feel the pain on the side of my face from where she had hit me the other day. I moved my hand along my cheek as we were joined by Nel on our way to see the others. Shiru, Pierce, and Eli were all waiting for us in the bridge.

Giving my AI friend a smile, I walked behind Aiden and Cass. Brand was alongside me and he insisted on placing his arm over my shoulder and acting like we were best friends. I was still in shock. The last few days had been insane and at the moment all I wanted was to get back to playing the game.

When I walked in to the bridge, I could see several of the others sitting and waiting.

Tel was near a coms station communicating with another group, a squad that had just departed from the *Ibanez* a few hours earlier. I couldn't make out the squad leader's voice, but I could overhear some of their conversation.

'Tel, we've got something. Quadrant five sector six. Planet Rem. Just outside the city. Looks like an old transport ship from before the pathways were established. She came down at the base of one of those fungal growths, I'm guessing that's why they didn't spot her from the sky.'

'Copy that Recon. Please advise as to the condition of the craft.'

'Recon. She looks pretty intact. I wouldn't say one piece, exactly, but they sure built these things to last. Two of ours are about to make a sweep of the interior.'

'Copy Recon. Can we drop in with a heavy?'

'Negative. Not enough space, even a light would have issues, these old ships weren't made for anything larger than a lift.'

'Copy that, be on your guard and check for hostiles.'

'Say again. Did you say hostiles?'

'Roger Recon. Make sure your guys take every precaution. There's a chance the core may still be active. That ship is most likely turning into a dungeon now. There is definitely going to be an echo inside. Maybe an artefact or two if you are lucky. Like you said, they built these things to last, I'm sure you aren't the first player to find it.'

'No kidding. But Hollows, after all these years? This looks more scripted than that.'

'Containment packs at the ready, Recon Four. It's not unknown. There should also be an interface in every compartment,
so have your guys monitor their systems periodically. If there's
anything left alive down there it'll be highly corrupted and looking to switch to a new power source. Your atmo-suits would look
like gold platinum to a fading remnant right now.'

'…Err, the guys left those packs in the rover, I'm just going
to run them over to now.'

'Copy Recon. Looks like our team finally showed up so we'll
be down to the surface shortly.'

Tel's voice was similar to Nel's although her character was more
passive aggressive. Tel always sounded like she was annoyed in
some way. Of course Tel was an advanced artificial intelligence
that knew exactly what it was. Not that she would ever admit it
or say it aloud but we could hear it as she went over missions. It
was all routine for her, acting as our director of operations handing out missions and bounties.

LOCATION: PLANET REM
REMNANT STARSHIP

The chance to explore an old starship wasn't an opportunity we
wanted to pass up. Twenty minutes later we were in the Quadrant 5 Sector 6 orbiting above the planet Rem. We dropped five
minutes later, after picking our load out and boarding a shuttle. I
grabbed *Aegis* along with an M7-7 rifle. We were followed by
three several floating spheres that would record our actions
aboard the starship.

— Quest —
Remnant
Created by: Echo-1
Expected Difficulty: Moderate
Rewards: Unknown

Details:
1. Search the Remnant Transport ship for supplies
2. Recover Transport ship data (0/1)
3. Rescue the Recon team
4. (Optional) Recover the ship's core.

Level Requirement: 5

'If I remember the map right, we should head down this hallway to left to reach the bridge. From there we should be able to restore some of the ship's power and find the recon team,' With a flickering light, Aiden pointed down a hallway and Cass turned to look.

'Alright, Breq and I will take point. You just tell us where to go, com three' Cass answered as she began to walk down the hallway. A moment later, the lights went dark. I jumped. 'Calm down rookie,' Cass teased.

It was nice to hear her laugh again. I pulled myself together and fumbled with the flashlight on my rifle. Once it was on, Cass and I made a quick sweep to make sure it was still clear. Once satisfied, we continued forward with the rest of Echo-1 a few yards behind, their own light casting our shadows a long way down the floor ahead. 'This ship's probably three hundred years old, maybe older,' Eli said. 'No way anything could be alive in here, not even Hollows, not to mention Nel hasn't picked up any trace of an echo.'

I turned my thoughts to the past, letting training guide me through the halls as I lost myself in the maze in the belly of the metal giant. The Remnants, whose ship we had so eagerly wanted to explore, had left the Spire just before the world gates had been reconnected and STL drives became a stable part of every large ship. The Remnants were a group of fanatics who had desperately wanted to see humanity colonize the stars: they had frozen themselves in cryogenic sleep and launched themselves away in their massive seed ships, ships which utilized ion drives and a prototype STL drive that was deemed unstable. Seven of the behemoths had been built and launched towards different stars that were believed to have planets capable of supporting life. Since STL travel had become the norm, only three of the Remnants' ships had been found, all with missing crews. It was a mystery and one which our team was hoping to find out more about through a search of this ship's remains. There was a main quest that involved the exploration of one of the lost ships, but it had been given several years ago and before I started playing. At the moment none of us could recall what exactly had taken place.

'Hear something?' Cass asked as she swept her rifle down to her left shining her light down another dark hallway.

I swept my own light over the region that Cass had been looking at, but didn't see anything that looked out of place.

'It was just the metal piping and conduits normal for any starship,' I said.

'I could have sworn,' Cass moved forward, rifle at the ready as she approached a turn in the corridor. Together we looked around the piping, just around the corner of the starship's lower deck.

'Anything?' Aiden asked from behind.

'No, just ventilation or maintenance. It was probably just some local fauna that's taken up residence. They said this place could be turning into a dungeon so let's not get caught inside.'

— Quest —
Survive
Expected Difficulty: Veteran
Rewards: 1000 XP Bonus

A moment later, I was racing down the hallway, stumbling over debris I couldn't see in the dark.

'Right behind you!' I shouted, and Cass stopped and turned around with her rifle at the ready. She couldn't pick a target out of the frantically moving shadows, but pulled the trigger anyway. We heard the scramble of legs but didn't stay to see if we got the kill. No EXP showed.

I rounded the corner ahead and passed through a doorway and paused for the others to catch up. As soon as we were through the threshold, the door slammed behind us. Just as it did so, there were several loud bangs against the bulkhead. Something was trying to get in.

'What was that?' yelled Eli.

'Local fauna?' asked Cass.

'There is definitely an echo here,' said Aiden.

'Were those Hollows?' I asked. I had seen Hollows before but normally they were immobile, just objects to avoid. Ghosts of the past but never much of a threat.

We continued onward toward the bridge, hoping the Hollows were behind us.

'They're supposed to be stationary, which means we are dealing with some kind of variant,' said Shiru.

Aiden's voice came through our coms. 'We need a power pack to restore power to the ship, after that I say we get the hell out of here.'

'That could be a problem. Anyone have a power pack?' asked Cass.

'Nah,' answered Aiden, 'but there should be some around here somewhere. Nel can you scan the bridge? We came in through the upper decks: worst case we'll have Tel blast a hole in this rig and climb our way out.'

'If we blast a hole in the ship, that will just draw their attention.' I wasn't trying to argue with Aiden but I could tell he hadn't thought it through. All of us were scared, yet somehow I felt alive again. It was the same rush of adventure I felt going against the guardian.

Our two leaders started in the direction of the Captain's quarters, but as they did the door ahead of them slammed shut on its own. They froze and stared at the blocked pathway before them.

'The ship's AI is on to us,' Aiden said.

'It's probably locked on to our power signatures, anything living and breathing. Right?' I offered.

The environment was hospitable enough that we knew we would be fine for a few hours, maybe there was time enough to call for another squad or two, but what was more concerning was our lack of protection against the ship itself. When starships crashed on planets, they would adapt and become dungeons. The lore of the world said that it had something to do with the quantum drives creating a time pocket that transformed the area around into a living system.

I'd been so worried, I had forgotten to check on how Pierce was doing. The youngest player in our group and newest member, he was also one of the most intelligent and, it seemed, resourceful. Somehow, he had rigged his short grip energy takedown glove into the terminal.

'Looks like we're good to go,' he said with satisfaction in his voice.

Power was back. The Captain's quarters opened.

'Contact!' Aiden shouted, activating his mini-gun which seemed to almost appear out of thin air. Several well-placed shots hit a strange creature that collapsed on the ground. The creature looked like a cross between a regular soldier and some kind of reptile. Aiden moved forward, stepping over the body, and searched the area beyond.

'Clear!' he shouted. The rest of us moved forward keeping our weapons downrange and ready to fire.

'What is it?' Shiru asked.

'No idea; Nel?' asked Aiden. Besides being our pack-mule, Nel also had a database full of known creatures. Basically she was our guide to the universe.

'Analysis shows Human, Dargon and Brosechel DNA present: it is a hybrid of some kind,' Nel answered.

'Take a sample, we'll bring it back with us, maybe this is what the Hollows were guarding,' ordered Aiden. Brand used a syringe from one of his med-kits to take a blood sample. The blood seemed to move as if it was alive.

'Amazing, some kind of symbiotic life-form,' he said.

'Joking right?' Cass said.

Brand looked up earnestly. 'No seriously, it's going crazy. We could probably use this to improve our armour.'

'I don't know, I took it out pretty easy,' said Aiden, smirking.

'With a mini-gun,' added Brand.

'Let me see it. That may be what we need to get out of here. There was an interface back over there. If I can just set it up properly maybe we can use the DNA in that thing to activate the starship's security,' Eli held out her hand and Brand handed over the syringe.

'Make it fast, I can hear them crawling around outside. If they find a way in, we'll be dead,' said Aiden.

With a glance at me, Cass pointed over to a few crates which looked like they might provide some decent cover and when we had arranged them to best effect, everyone took up defensive positions. As I knelt there, rifle resting on a crate top, a camera hovered above me. I had almost forgot that people were watching all of this. It occurred to me to ask Moonrain Media for help. If there was anyone in the area that could have helped surely they would be on their way?

'Any idea on time?' I asked Eli.

'About five or ten minutes? Depends how badly damaged the drive is.'

'We've got incoming.' There were several Hollows breaking in through cracks in the bulkhead door. I reckoned we were about two minutes away from being overrun.

'Interface connection established. Hacking.' Eli grabbed his rifle and spun around to help us the moment his hack hit 100%. It hadn't taken him long. He had poured almost every skill point he gained into maximizing that skill and I had never felt so grateful to him. Hopefully, now that he had identified us as crew under threat, the ship's turrets would automatically search out and fire on the Hollows from both the inside and outside of the ship.

I quickly raised my sights and pulled the trigger. The rounds connected with a Hollow just as it burst through the final layers of the door, its momentum stopped mid-air as it fell to the ground, the glow in its eyes fading away.

+100 EXP

+100 EXP

+100 EXP

+100 EXP

+100 EXP

+200 kill streak M7-7 Lvl 2

'They just keep jumping into our line of fire,' Shiru said.

'They aren't designed with intelligence,' I shouted over the sound of energy searing the air.

'I think we earned our pay for today,' shouted Cass. 'And once we start data mining back at base, we should be able to find out how the ship got here and what happened to the crew. Might not even need to explore the rest of the ship if we can recover enough info.'

'What about the core?' I said. I was thinking about something Alexis had told me.

Pro Tip

Both starships and dungeons have 'cores'. The core in a starship makes up one of the key components in the STL drive, however in dungeons the core is usually an object of power guarded by a boss or a part of a boss.

If you have the chance, always rip the core from a dungeon or salvage it from a starship. If the core is taken from a dungeon it will turn into neutral territory and is almost guaranteed to level you up. If a core is swiped from a starship it can be sold for millions of credits.

'We've barely made it this far and you want to go after this thing's core?' yelled Cass. She was staring me down.

'I don't want be walking through miles of ship if I don't have to, and especially not when low on ammo. Get that door open and let's go,' Aiden ordered.

As if on cue, the ceiling opened up and we saw a ship appear above us.

Another shuttle. I didn't recognize it at first. It looked like it belonged to some kind of raiding company. Maybe one of the smaller guilds? We began climbing to the top of the starship's hull. The ship beneath us was being overrun with emerging Hollows: black humanoid monsters that seemed to swallow the ship's hull as it began transforming into the fungal landscape.

The cameras that had been near me rushed downwards to focus in as a Hollow grabbed hold of Pierce and pulled him down. My squad UI showed his health dropping fast and he began screaming from the pain. Cass and I were nearest and dropped back down as Aiden, Eli, Shiru and Brand boarded the rescue shuttle. While I provided covering fire, Cass went in hand-to-hand, finally forcing the Hollow to let Pierce go. I could see the shimmer in world around us as the Remnant ship's quantum drive broke down reality.

I was still firing when Cass handed Pierce over to Brand who immediately began treating his wounds. When she came back for me it was already too late. From the outside of the shuttle I turned and saw Gorge and Kira were piloting the rescue craft. It looked like they had made an alliance after the guardian had started chasing me in the Spire. It made sense that Gorge would want a cut of whatever was happening and I was sure Kira wouldn't mind using his resources. So, the two of them had teamed up and had been watching everything.

'Damnit,' shouted Gorge, jumping down beside me, just outside the shuttle. 'Get out of here,' he motioned for Kira to take off.

There were three cameras following us as another group of Hollows began to make their way towards us across the hull of the abandoned ship. As the shuttle rose, Kira provided some quick cover so that Cass, Gorge and I could scramble away from the Hollows by going back inside the ruins of the transport ship, dropping into a corridor that currently sitting above the overwhelming horde. This was it. I thought about Lady Gray and Cass, if I survived this, they were going to kill me.

'You're an idiot, you know that,' I said looking down at the black mass below us. One wrong move and it would all be over.

Gorge only smiled, 'I'm retired.'

An icon blinked in the bottom left hand side of my vision. I motioned with my finger, blinking twice to open it. Gorge and I joined a party together. A moment later another message appeared and a third name. I quickly made the circular motion with my hand as the interface disappeared and I saw Cass standing with her rifle at the ready and a rocket launcher strapped across her back: 'I am going to kill you for this.'

+1000 XP

Nel was with us too. Apparently nobody had helped her into the ship.

Pro Tip
Never under any circumstances dive alone.

8.
Ruins

The first time I dived alone I was only level 5. I had stolen the
Adept and crashed it answering a distress call on an alien moon
called Minerva. I still remember the accident like it was yesterday.

'Trust me,' I said, turning the starship *Adept* downward towards the rings of Minerva, using the ice to slow our descent as
we dropped out of STL too close to the planet's orbit. Minerva
was a beautiful sight, shadowed by the gas giant Aquila-1 which
covered the entire line of sight from the ship. I would have been
in awe if I wasn't too busy crashing.

'Famous last words,' Nel replied, calculating our odds of survival as being somewhere between 'pretty awful' and 'painfully
remote'.

Chasing an artefact across the Jellyfish Nebula we intercepted
a distress call originating from a research outpost on the moon.
Neither of us the type to turn down an SOS, we turned from one
quest to another. Stealing the *Adept* and not telling anyone where
I was or what I was doing was probably not the best idea in the
world, but this wouldn't be the first time I'd taken matters into
my own hands. Damien, my best friend and mentor, had been
pushing me to take control of my own life. What better time than

now. Looking back, I'm still not sure if I would chosen any differently.

The rear thrusters burned out and the ice that built up on the wings of the *Adept* melted away when we hit the moon's atmosphere. When we cleared the boundary, our fall came fast. Thirty seconds between the edge of space and the clouds.

After crash-landing near the SOS call, Nel and I made our way to the research outpost and I met an NPC named Niburi. She was a young girl, in her early teens. She had sent the distress call out herself. Her father had gone missing, having left with a small team to combat some kind of creature in a mission called 'Celestial Pursuit'.

I found myself taking the reigns. Niburi was accompanied at the time only by a rusted robotic companion named Cocoa. The two were a sight for sore eyes. It was my first real solo mission out though and I didn't want to let anyone down. Especially since the quest promised an artefact as a reward. After Nel and I journeyed to her father's last waypoint, I found an excavation site being guarded by a giant unmanned mech. The mech, acting on its own was defending the area. Defending Niburi's father's grave. It was heartbreaking at first. That was my first boss battle. The mech had been programmed to protect Niburi. After her father died in battle, it continued on its mission. Apparently, it had killed the real celestial being of the mission's name, however, the only way it could continue to keep Niburi safe was to keep watch at the excavation site, which continued to spawn low level Wraiths.

Defeating the mech wasn't hard. The hard part was going back. I found the artefact, her father's pendant. It was an heirloom I could have kept and sold as a cosmetic at the Spire (players were always interested in unique accessories) but I couldn't. The look on Niburi's face evoked real sorrow as she screamed and cried in my arms. I told her I knew how she felt. I told her how I had lost both of my parents. I contacted a guild called the 'Astra' in the

Spire and within half an hour they came to pick her up. Some players probably would have left her there. She was just an NPC, what did it matter? Maybe it didn't. Maybe I should have kept the pendant and runaway, but I couldn't. Just as Cass and the others had come for me, I saw in them a reflection of myself.

When Damien arrived to pick me up in the *Ibanez* he congratulated me on my mission. Two months later I accompanied him to the Spire where I met Gorge at the Upsilon for the first time. He was fixing up Cocoa: upgrading the little robot with all new parts and weapons. Niburi walked in at the same time, maybe Damien had planned it, maybe it was scripted. She had joined an archaeology guild and had become a research assistant on a starship set to explore the outer worlds.

Despite the cost of repairs to the *Adept*, Damien had congratulated me on my mission success, but others weren't so happy with me and I almost got kicked from the guild. Cass was the one that came to my rescue. She convinced the others to let me stay, arguing that she would never let me go alone again. Her and Damien were always the two that had my back no matter what I rushed into.

That was over a year ago and this is now. Now, I just have Cass.

LOCATION: PLANET REM
INSIDE THE REMNANT STARSHIP

We only spent a few minutes outside standing above the Hollows watching as they swarmed below us like rats. I checked my gear. My shield was charged. My battle armour still in one piece. I unpacked a dark grey and red jacket from one of my pockets and watched it unfold. Cass followed suit and did the same before leading us into the ship through a small tunnel that was still being held together by metal hinges.

A black shape scurried past the feet of Cass, disappearing into the belly of the starship. Gorge was leading us and halted, holding his hand up as we crept through a narrow dark hallway towards what we hoped was the engine bay of the Remnant starship.

'Was that some kind of rat?' Cass said, pointing with her rifle at the ready. She sounded as unsure as I was about what we might be facing next. Rats weren't dangerous and were pretty common for the most part. Every planet had its own species of rat, of course, and they looked different on different ships, but they were all mostly the same in nature. Rats on the Spire were called Spire Rats, rats on Orithyia were Orithian Rats, rats on Rem were called Rem Rats. Maybe someone knew what the creatures were actually called but for the most part rats were always rats. And always a sign of misfortune.

'Not sure, maybe; seemed like it was running towards something,' Gorge picked up one of the rats and scanned it, like it was a clue to a bigger mystery.

'Maybe running away,' Cass said, just as we heard a low growl break the silence that surrounded us. Gorge let the rat go and readied his weapon, holding it just above his chest, attaching a wire from his cybernetic arm to the stock.

'It's a kinetic mod,' he whispered, as I wondered what he was doing.

'What does that mean?'

'My cyber-leg collects energy and stores it in power cells throughout my body. All my weapons are modded so that I can run power straight through from my body to them.'

It was a brilliant idea. So long as Gorge kept moving he gathered more and more energy that could be used to fight off enemies, without having to worry about the power levels of his weapons or carrying extra supplies like batteries or ballistics. He also never had to worry about a Ki-rifle draining down his own HP, since he always had energy stored up.

'This is totally not a trap, right?' I said.

'No, it's probably a trap, this whole thing doesn't feel right,' Cass was two steps in front of me. I doubt any of us liked feeling so exposed. Enemy snipers could wreak havoc on us from all the places we couldn't see into and monsters could come from any direction we weren't constantly watching.

'We will do everything we can to protect you, but enemies outnumber us, maybe the safest thing for us to do is turn back,' Cass said.

Gorge came to a halt. 'It's too late.'

Everyone was quiet. A wall of mist was blanketing the rooms around us. Kira had managed to give us cover support and divert the Hollows away from our position after we dropped in, but they had probably figured out by now that we were here.

There was another risk: the possibility of running into other players who wanted the bounty on me. The presence of a drone was a constant reminder that everyone was watching us. At any given moment we had a hundred thousand people wondering what we were going to do next. Probably screaming at us what to do and where to go. Based on what I knew about Moonrain Media and streaming feeds, I assumed that the number was rising. I wanted to shoot the camera that had managed to follow us but I knew if I did I would probably be dragged out of my pod immediately for costing the company and sponsors hundreds of thousands of dollars.

As we descended through the darkness, everything I did now was being tracked. No doubt a bidding war was taking place in the real world for ads and relevancies. Not that I really cared about celebrity. What I did, I was doing for myself, for Damien. I wasn't going to let them tell me I couldn't risk my life. I was still grateful though that I wasn't alone. Gorge had come out of nowhere and was surprising me again and again. The more I followed him the more I began to trust him.

'Can we use more light down here?' Cass asked.

'You're the scout, you tell me,' Gorge replied sarcastically.

It was dark. The only light we had came from our rifles but Nel, who followed behind us, could have lit up the hallway in an instant if we asked. That could easily attract unwanted attention though. At least with the light from our rifles we could quickly flicker it and cover our tracks. A creature hiding in the darkness was less likely to attack a suspicious floating light if it didn't know what was on the other side.

'Sorry, Cass, I don't think it's a good idea,' I said, knowing she knew the answer well enough.

'I'm just worried there might be traps or ordinance: something we might run into or trip on that will end all this sooner rather than later,' she replied making a fair point, 'if we see something or attract something, Nel can lay down cover fire while we make an escape, but if we fall into some kind of acid or blow ourselves up we're screwed.'

'Fair enough, Nel, shine some light for us,' I said.

'You didn't say the magic word,' Nel replied as the hallway lit up in front of us and I mumbled, 'please,' under my breath.

Cass was right.

The skeletons of a dozen soldiers stood at the end of the long hallway, next to a barrel of open waste. We saw several dozen small creatures dart away from the bodies and fumes that were leaking into the air. The waste wasn't a threat, nor were the dead. The fumes, however, would have killed us if we had come any closer.

'Air quality check!' I shouted towards Nel.

'Toxic, recommend breathers,' Nel paused, 'immediately.'

We each placed a respirator mask over our mouths and began to move closer to investigate the fallen soldiers.

'NPCs?' asked Gorge nudging one with his rifle.

He studied the dog tags for a moment as Cass and I covered the area. We had reached the end of the hallway and found ourselves at a fork. Two paths. One left, one right.

'Sergeant Bach,' Gorge said, 'definitely an NPC, been dead quite awhile too it seems, decay makes it look like a hundred years or more, body structure and bone is preserved pretty damn good too, though, looks like something might have eaten the skin off it.'

A soft growl came from the left. Both Cass and I dropped and prepared to fire. Nothing. We continued in that direction. Whatever was making the growl didn't sound large. It was the atmosphere around us and the firefight we had been in nearly an hour earlier that still had us on edge. If we ordered Nel to go ahead of us we could probably use her to map out the entire area and we would be less at risk. Any smart diver would probably have done that but over the many missions we've had together both Cass and I had grown attached to our robotic ally. We pushed forward as a team.

'Nel turn the lights off,' I whispered, 'please.'

Nel did what I asked without question, perhaps having noted my heart rate had risen quickly. I could feel something watching us. Something that wasn't quite right with the ship. The three of us turned off our lights and we stood our backs against the wall in complete darkness. There was a beam of light that flashed ahead of us. Someone or something was heading down the path towards us. Cass stepped towards me and grabbed my shoulder, pushing me down lower to the ground.

'Hide,' Cass whispered.

The light was coming towards us quicker now but what was it?

Gorge led us down the hallway, tossing a small piece of twine into my hands. We followed along the wall patting our way across so we wouldn't run into one another until finally we found a small hatch.

'Get in,' Gorge whispered to the two of us.

We followed his command.

Nel couldn't fit, so instead hid above us, flattening out across the ceiling. The beam of light approached closer, angled down towards the ground like it was looking for us, like it had known what our next move would have been. Cass and I squeezed tightly together with our faces down, not wanting our eyes to reflect the light that could might across us.

More noise came from the wreckage that surrounded us echoing through the hallway. The three of whispered into our coms: as soon as the light came close enough we were going to have Nel blind whoever it was and fire on them.

The light suddenly went out.

'Plan B. On three we light up the hallway and fire,' I said.

'One…Two…,' I paused. Nel's lights flashed on and, as we fired, a shield surrounded us like a bubble. The floating head of Kira stood in front of us laughing.

'You three look like you wet your pants,' she said.

'Not funny,' answered Gorge.

'Why are you a floating head?' I asked.

'Stealth tech, artefact clothing,' Kira was still laughing as she hit a button on the upper left-hand side of her outfit, revealing her slim body in the black mesh-and-honeycomb spandex she was wearing.

The bubble was a shield she had thrown down at the last minute, when she realized we might attack.

'Smart,' said Gorge, 'got anymore?'

'Sorry only a few exist,' she answered.

'Too bad,' Gorge grunted.

I had questions, 'how did you find us? Where are the others?'

'Back in the colony on Rem, probably playing scraps in a hangar.'

I looked down for a moment in disappointment.

'Kidding, they're all pretty worried about you guys but none of them had the balls to come back, this area is off-limits now. They are waiting just outside the border. A Crimson King cruiser was spotted descending towards the planet's surface and we think they might be after you.'

'You'd think they would learn their lesson.'

'A cycle of vengeance; all is fair in love and war, for many of them that is what *Bane* is,' Kira replied.

I quickly asked my next question, 'what do you mean off-limits?'

'I mean this transport isn't just some pile of junk etched into the landscape anymore, its turning into a full-fledged dungeon as we speak, there is a guardian outside guarding it and that makes it off limits to anyone that isn't completely invisible,' Kira smiled. Hearing about the guardian made me feel fear. I was beginning to regret our dungeon dive.

'What kind of dungeon gets a guardian?' asked Cass.

'The kind none of us are prepared for; it looks like it's going to be a raid dungeon, possibly level forty-two or higher, I'm not sure, it is still generating itself, seems the Chel take a special interest in Remnant STL technology.'

'What do you mean?' I wondered aloud.

'OK, so we know starships have cores in their STL drives, but so far no one knows where exactly where the dungeon cores come from. The creatures just seem drawn to certain points on the map, usually ruins or crashed ships, some underground caves, but all dungeons are built around a core. '

I cut in, 'and if you take the core it turns into neutral territory, just another piece of the landscape.'

'Yes, but I have a theory that the core is actually what remains of an STL drive after its used up. A material fragment of time and space.'

'Guess that's why they are worth millions on the market,' added Gorge.

Kira continued with enthusiasm, 'a time-light drive gone crazy attracts creatures and mutates them with quantum radiation, they feel territorial and defend the dungeon, protecting the core and other loot the ship might hold.'

I couldn't stop thinking about what Lady Gray had told me. One of her tips to levelling up was to loot the core of a dungeon in doing so you capture that dungeon and gain something close to 50,000 XP. That was enough to level me up to 31 and get me halfway to 32. If Kira was right this wasn't about getting credits anymore. The ship was turning into a dungeon and the core was my chance to level up.

'Okay, what about the robots? Are those with you?' asked Gorge pointing behind Kira.

'Robots?' Kira gasped and turning around, threw down a shield. 'That was my last one,' she yelled as the rest of us began running back the way we came followed by Nel. 'The shield should hold them back for about thirty seconds.'

'What are they?' Cass shouted. I turned back to get a read on them.

Autons
Level 20
Hostile

'Autons, robot workers that are designed to maintain and defend the ship, right now with the quantum drive exploding they must think everything is an enemy, their sensors are probably all over the place,' I called out.

'Did you guys activate the ship's security measures?' Kira asked.

'Maybe,' I shrugged. I could imagine Kira cursing. 'It was a good idea at the time, you know, when we were surrounded by the horde of Hollows.'

The four of us (counting Nel as a team member) had ventured into the heart of a dungeon in the process of being born, completely unprepared for what was happening around us. I noticed several things that didn't seem right as we walked through what felt like an endless hallway: the creaks and growls as the ship moved and sank and transformed around us. Kira had come in through a hatch on the side of the transporter. She had found us by tracking the camera, which I was thankful I hadn't shot.

We hid inside one of the east wings of one of the research stations on the second level, in a room filled with computer terminals that looked like they were part analogue. The room also had several containers that were filled with different coloured liquids. Some kind of genetic testing facility. The hallway was different to how it had looked when we had first come through. The ship was changing all around us, rearranging itself into a maze. In a way it was defending itself: stopping intruders and summoning creatures from the outside world, changing them to defend it to their death. That was why the rats were moving towards the engine room instead of away.

I took a breath and sat with my back against the wall. We had run far enough to have lost the attention of the Autons who had decided to pursue something else. But we weren't alone.

'The Autons will probably be wiped out by the creatures before this place settles,' Kira said, taking a drink of water and handing the bottle over to Cass. Even in game your body still required elements such as food and water to stay healthy. Of course you could also inject yourself with a stimulant or pick up some kind of implant of the market.

I stared at the camera floating above the room around us. It was taking a wide-angle shot. I wondered how many people were watching us fail. Watching waiting to see our next move or shouting at us to do something interesting.

'How many views do you think we have?' I asked, staring towards Kira.

'I can't check statistics from inside the game, maybe a few hundred thousand or so currently, maybe less, I don't know,' she answered. Being followed by a camera was nothing new to her.

I choked for a moment. That was a lot of people watching us sit around. For a second, I felt bad for not being entertaining enough, but pure entertainment wasn't why they were watching. They were watching to see what came next; our reaction; the game's reaction to us; they were watching because this was something new, something real. 'I feel like we're letting our audience down.'

'We're already making history; if my theory is right and we prove that the STL drive turns into a dungeon and we can grab the core before the entire place warps around us, we'll be worth watching,' Kira smiled at the camera.

'Okay, anyone have a plan?' Gorge cut in, sharpening his knife on a small silver whetstones, one of the few items he carried on him at all times.

'Both of you are past level sixty why don't you go first?' I suggested.

'Level thirty or level sixty doesn't make much of a difference if we don't know what we are up against. The two of us may be able to take a lot more damage than the two of you but we will still go down against a horde,' Gorge replied.

'Speaking of levels,' I turned to Kira, 'that quest you assigned me, *Whisper in the Void*, is locked. I can't even begin it and I'm honestly not so sure what I should do, I may not be able to continue,' I said, lying, knowing very well that I was hell-bent on finding a way to solve it.

'There might be a way around that,' Kira began.

'Don't even think it; don't say it,' Gorge cut her off.

'What is it?' I demanded, sharpening my tone for a moment, making it obvious to the others I had been lying before about not being able to continue. The sudden shift in my emotions caught Kira off guard and she broke into a smile. I looked up and saw the camera facing down almost right above me. I quickly calmed myself, 'never mind, it's okay, I'll find a way, I'll pick apart twenty more dungeons if I have to.'

'Quiet,' said Cass. She had been keeping lookout at the door while the rest of us were resting. An Auton moved across the doorway, unaware of our presence. As it walked past in its bi-pedal form, the Auton looked worse for wear. Autons appeared to be like regular people, only their skin was coated in metal and when damaged their bodies took on the appearance of a walking skeleton. They also had yellow eyes. Most Autons would usually move tethered to a power source while others had a battery life and could move freely on their own. This was one of the latter. Most likely rogue or lost. Was it possible for a robot to get lost? Nel had answered that question for me dozens of times on simpler missions. Kira closed her eyes and held out her hand. I saw the palm of her hand begin to glow with a light blue haze as she whispered into the air, gesturing with her hand and summoned a shotgun.

```
Whisper Canon - Silenced Shotgun


Description: 'Pew Pew Pew'


Level: 30
Damage: 60
Weight: 7.5 lbs
Weapon Type: Silenced Plasma Shotgun
Rarity: Rare
Impact: 10
Range: 7
Stability: 6
Reload Speed: 9
RPM (rounds per minute): 100 bursts
Affinity: 9
Sharpness: 8
Elemental: None
Critical Chance: 60%
Modifiers: None
```

As a tech-mage Kira had an ability to store weapons inside a pocket universe called the ether (also known as the immer) and summon them at need. She could only carry three weapons at a time this way but it was pretty damn cool to see it in person. The hand gesture itself was something she had to have mastery of. One wrong move and she easily could have severed a limb, finger, or summoned something else from the white space beyond. It only took several seconds, with the shotgun forming piece by piece in the air as blue energy lit up around her hand. I could feel the heat from the plasma cartridge from several feet away as she turned and lowered herself down towards the ground and fired upwards destroying the Auton's head with a quick burst.

'Silent and deadly,' Kira smiled.

'Nice work, now the others are going to be alerted,' said Cass.

'What? No one heard that shot.'

'Autons are linked, tethered or not, they share a hive-like intelligence,' answered Cass.

Gorge grabbed his rocket launcher off the ground, where it had rested alongside the rest of his gear, 'OK, you heard the girl, time to move out.' Gorge too could store weapons in the immer however his skill at summoning them wasn't on par with that of Kira.

'No map and no idea how to get to the core, what do you plan to do?' asked Kira.

I answered, 'we should hack one of the Autons, we face them head on and capture one before its destroyed. Have Nel download its data.'

'That actually sounds like a good plan,' said Cass.

Several minutes passed as Gorge set up a tripwire and some mines down both ends of the hallway and we waited for the rest of the Autons to show. Several came, just like Cass predicted. Driven by their shared intelligence they looked down towards their fallen and prepped for battle. They were holding M7-3 energy rifles.

```
┌─────────────────────────────────────────────┐
│                    M7-3                       │
│                                               │
│ Description: This weapon is terrifying and    │
│ praised by many for being a low cost, highly  │
│ effective energy weapon. The power cells of   │
│ the M7-3, however, don't hold a strong charge │
│ leading to low stability and impact.          │
│                                               │
│                  Level: 0                     │
│                 Damage: 60                    │
│               Weight: 12.5 lbs                │
│         Weapon Type: Energy Assault Rifle     │
│               Rarity: Common                  │
│                 Impact: 6                     │
│                  Range: 7                     │
│                Stability: 4                   │
│              Reload Speed: 8                  │
│       RPM (rounds per minute): 300            │
│                Affinity: 4                    │
│               Sharpness: 5                    │
│               Elemental: None                 │
│            Critical Chance: None              │
│             Modifiers: Optic Sight            │
└─────────────────────────────────────────────┘
```

Their weapons weren't very strong. I knew dozens of players with M7-3s in their inventory. It was an easy weapon for a player to level up with in the early stages. The robots must have raided the ship's ammo supply before coming after us. They really were adapting to defend the ship. In most cases Autons were unoffensive, keepers of the peace who worked maintenance for ships that didn't have the minimum crew needed. I knew of several dozen hotshots that flew cruisers completely automated with Autons. They could be programmed for just about anything and were even fodder used in tutorial missions. The training ground had dozens to spare for target practice. Now these ones seemed to be growing stronger, more advanced. Their tactics were changing too. The Autons coming for us were tethered by some kind of chord at the hip. A single leader stood at the back in plated armour. Most likely the same kind of hull plating Gorge was wearing but not nearly as strong. +10 defence at the most.

As the first Auton approached the tripwire it stepped right over it. The second was not so lucky.

Luck + 5

I fired through the smoke, holding down the trigger as I faced the oncoming storm, listening to my M7 - 7 tear through their metal plating until their leader untethered from the others to leap forward towards us. My HP dropped to 98 as my power cell spooled and began to charge back up. I could feel the needle sensation in my wrist as the rifle drained my energy. The leader had an M7 - 3 like the others but refused to fire. Instead the robot opted to come at us with a metal spear that looked like it had been made from parts of the ship. The Autons were developing faster than any of us had thought possible.

Kira met it head on using her Whisper Canon as a shield. She kicked the Auton backwards and as it fell Cass yelled out, 'we need it alive.' Kira grunted and lunged forward, blasting the Auton apart at the knees. The battlefield was her home. Her agility was off the charts as she danced around the Auton, cloaking her movements, appearing and disappearing into the smoke. The Auton's sensors couldn't track her and after another three seconds she had its head in hand.

'Nel, can you hack this?' she was nearly laughing as she threw the head on the ground towards us. I picked up the head as Nel lowered a small cable down towards me. The cable had a magnet that attached to the skull of the Auton and before I knew it she was in.

'Dirty, Dirty, mind, a mess, prime directive, defend, systems down, hull breach in sectors 3, 5, 7, and 9. Stasis chambers offline. Hollows creatures pouring inside. Sadness...

'Three doors down take a right, down the maintenance shaft one hundred yards and through the doorway on the left, three miles down...disconnecting,' the plug removed itself from the head and the Auton's yellow, glowing eyes faded away. The hack was successful. More than that though, Nel now knew the whereabouts of all the Autons and could lead us past them.

'Three miles down? Does that mean the transport ship is digging itself into the planet?' asked Gorge.

'Yes, the ship itself is expanding into a dungeon, organic metal, nanites seeping into the crust below the surface as the STL drive decays,' said Kira.

I had a thought. 'How is the STL decay not hurting us?'

'Honestly I'm not sure. We're not actually supposed to be here during this kind of event,' she answered with a shrug, I could tell the question had crossed her mind just as much as it had crossed my own.

I examined the Auton leader one more time, as well as the others that surrounded us. Dozens of rifles lay across the ground but there was nothing worth taking, even the leader's spear had no real value. Gorge picked it up and examined it as well.

'They started making tools,' he said.

'Weapons,' Kira corrected him.

Three doors down we took a right and found the maintenance shaft, or rather, an enormous hole in the floor below us about thirty yards wide. The floor looked like it contained a giant sink hole in the middle of the ship. Surrounding us on several sides were open rooms with terminals from which wires were hanging out. Some of the equipment looked like it had been rusting for years, while other machines looked brand new. The STL was warping the world around us, countering itself as it tried to stabilize. Yet nothing in the known world could stabilize it now. The ship had sunk. The core I was searching for was currently an erupting volcano and I would have to wait for it to cool and turn to 'stone' even if we managed to make it down there.

'How long does this process take?' I asked.

Kira looked over at me. 'Should be a few hours, that's my guess.'

I knew it was all speculation, that she really had no idea, but the world around us looked solid and it felt more fact than fiction to hear her say this.

'Once the dungeon is settled, do you think the Crimson Kings are going to raid it?' Cass asked.

'Yes, I do, I believe that is their second objective,' Kira answered.

I turned away from the hole. 'So the guardian is just keeping them from entering it while it transforms from starship to dungeon, why?'

'I'm not sure,' Kira answered as Gorge and Cass shrugged. Gorge was already putting together the gear for us to go spelunking. The camera was focusing on him as he attached an anchor to the ground and fitted it with a 'cow's tail' and carabiner. He used the twine he carried with a special descender, weaving it into a rope for us.

'Sorry I couldn't pack a harness, this is the best I got so short notice,' he said smiling, 'the twine I carry is actually web from an Arachnid queen I killed back a few years ago. Never throw away anything that seems like it might be useful someday,' he finished tying off another notch for us to hold onto, throwing the rest of the web down the large hole. I could feel it now.

The starship around me shifted as it began to warp and twist. There came the sound of the hull creaking and cracking, like it was under water; the pressure in the air was changing. I began to fear we might get booted from the game for being here.

125

Gorge jumped first, followed by Cass and myself, with Kira and Nel coming down behind her.

'Took your time getting down here,' Gorge said as I landed on the ground.

'I jumped right after Cass, what are you talking about?' I said. But I was already aware that Kira should have landed right behind me yet she hadn't.

'Shit,' said Gorge, 'just sit and wait,' he pointed towards Cass who was eating a piece of jerky next to a fire that looked like it was ready to burn out.

Another twenty minutes passed until Kira appeared. I understood now why Gorge had cursed. The worst was happening. The dungeon had a strange effect on us. Kira stared at us and shook her head biting her bottom lip. To her only a few seconds had passed but she picked up on the strange occurrence. She knew just like the rest of us that time was moving different from one part of the dungeon / ship to another. The deeper we dived the worst it would get.

Again, we had a long wait for Nel to arrive so we could set off. We could still see torn apart fragments of the starship's hull layered along the cave walls. None of us said it aloud. Maybe we were all too scared. Worried what might happen to us. We continued through the doorway on the left and down a three-mile slope. The STL drive had sunk into the ruins of the planet's crust and the core was starting to solidify. The Remnant starship was no more…only a blight on the planet surface. A dungeon was born and that meant there would be monsters and of course the worst would be yet to come.

9.
Stasis

Quick Lore

Bane is full of NPC characters. From merchants and raiders to entire starships full of crew. Some NPC characters align themselves with factions and players while others act as hostiles. Others can be merchants and traders as well as quest givers.

A low growl. More noise from the darkness that unfolded before us. There was a chewing sound in the distance, something that probably each of us found unnerving. A few more steps and we heard the sound of a heavy object being dragged through the dirt, scrapping against the spare pieces of wreckage and metal junk that littered what was once an underground cavern. Dust drifted upward as the five of us marched forward. I could feel the damp air hit my face: even with a respirator covering my nose and mouth I could still taste the copper that was collecting in the atmosphere. Gorge was the only one of us that didn't have a breather on. I guess being mostly machine he didn't quite need it but that didn't stop him from pinching his nostrils time and again.

'Are you sure about this?' said Cass.

'We've gone too far now,' I said. The two of us were nestled between Gorge, who had taken the lead, and Kira who was shadowing us alongside the camera and Nel.

'Lights off,' said Cass, pointing towards a creature approaching us from the right. It looked like some kind of giant bear, only that parts of it were in different states of decomposition. We ducked behind what used to be some kind of metal cargo container. A small creature landed on my hand. It looked like a moth but its back end lit up, turning it into a lightning bug with a dim blue light. Fortunately, the glow did not seem to catch the bear's attention but for some reason I felt hypnotized by it.

```
Voth
Level: 5
Hostile
```

The Voth bit me. I felt it attach itself to me and the moment I grunted in pain, the bear turned towards us. It felt like I stepped into a mound of fire ants. The burning, stinging sensation made me want to scream. Cass looked at me with her finger raised up over her lip. She saw the small creature attached to my hand and quickly struck it down. The Voth was gone but the pain lingered on. The bear was on the other side of the container moving closer to towards us.

```
Thorn
Level: 55
Nuetral
```

Quietly, we attempted to sneak by the creature as it turned away again and continued upward through the cargo container.

+5 Stealth

As we began to clear away from the area we heard a loud roar and saw the Thorn was being attacked by a horde of the vampire moths.

+10 Luck

It fled in the opposite direction to us.

We made our way to the next area and turned on our lights. Just as the pain in my hand was starting to subside, a large explosion erupted from nearby. The dark dungeon lit up around us and I saw a giant Arachnid come running in our direction. Gorge opened fire. The screeching the creature made my eardrums want to bleed. There was a small pile of rubble we ducked behind for cover. Kira landed a better shot than Gorge from behind as the Arachnid, level 30, spit acid towards us. The acid caught Gorge off guard. It was a toxic variant. Not just a normal Arachnid. Blood streamed down from his fingers and he opened his mouth as if he wanted to scream. There was nothing. Like he had put his vocal chords on mute. Despite the pain he must have felt, Gorge never let go of his weapons and fired again. This time a direct hit: right between the Arachnid's eight eyes. Kira ducked back and fired again. So this is what it was like to watch two high level players battle. Her bullet slammed into the spider's torso and it fell striking the ground, throwing up a cloud of dust as its HP reached zero.

Gorge ripped off a part of his shirt and covered his bleeding wound. 'More than acid, I think that thing had poison.'

'Are you going to be alright?' asked Kira.

'Nothing more than a scratch, I can't get poison damaged so I'm just glad none of you got hit, guess that's a part of the reason you let me volunteer to go first,' Gorge was laughing now.

The game had taught us how to kill but that didn't change the fact that any of it felt less horrifying. There was a rush, of course, when you felt your life on the line, but the feeling that you could lose someone you'd become close to never made it any easier. Each of us knew what was at stake now. Even Gorge had been filled in on the *Whisper in the Void* quest and the player deaths that had occurred. He had shrugged it off, as he'd always thought it was only a matter of time before real world deaths took place.

The Arachnid disappeared slowly, leaving nothing but a smudge across the ground and a small pile of loot in its wake. Having picked it up, Gorge insisted we moved on. Unfortunately, since I had missed when I had fired at the Arachnid, I gained 0 EXP from the encounter.

'Hang tight,' said Gorge. There was something moving ahead of us.

Gorge grabbed a small grenade from one of his side pockets. The grenade was only a few inches across and yet he threw it with force, screaming at us to get down. There was a flash of light as several dozen smaller, charging Arachnids disappeared into the mist.

'What was that?' I asked.

'Dark matter grenade!' Kira answered for Gorge.

'Yeah,' Gorge rubbed his hands together happily, 'kind of a home-brew, made it myself. Used to do all kinds of experiments back in the Spire, you know, before my shop blew up.'

Dark matter grenades were dangerous. Unstable energy that could corrode state-of-the-art combat armour and even melt the hull of a Titan. Against organic matter they basically evaporated whatever they came in contact with.

'Did you kill all of them?' asked Cass.

'Think so, looks like we stumbled across a nest,' Gorge answered studying the web around us as Nel shone a light through the darkness. There was no sense in hiding our presence anymore. Any chance we had at sneaking around was lost.

'Anymore useful tricks?'

'I got lots of those,' Gorge shook his head and pulled out a piece of jerky from his satchel, taking a bite and offering another to the rest of us. Like Cass and Kira, I declined.

'I got a chocolate bar too if anyone is interested,' he said.

Kira narrowed her eyes, 'you should have brought more grenades.'

With a laugh, Gorge threw her the chocolate bar. Kira managed a brief smile before taking a bite. Like the rest of us, she was probably wondering how many more surprises he had hidden away.

Lights flashed above us.

Several small plants had begun to glow with a pale amber hue.

'Save your batteries Nel,' I commanded.

'I don't run on batteries, I run on nuclear fusion thank you,' Nel responded. I turned towards the others and we began moving forward. I didn't waste time arguing with Nel, she knew I was joking.

The bioluminescent plants shined like fluorescent lights through the tunnels. We could see several paths ahead of us just past what remained of the Arachnids nest. We took the path to the left and found ourselves traveling through what looked like more of the starship.

'This part must have hit the ground first, the fore side of the transport,' said Kira as we wandered into another large dark room.

'Nel shine your light again,' I said.

'So bossy,' Nel replied, lighting up the environment. It was a stasis chamber.

Cass lowered her rifle. 'A room with a thousand lost thrones.'

'Yeah, think any of the NPCs are still alive? Maybe they could help us?' said Gorge.

'Most likely they'll turn into aberrants or raiders and try to chew our heads off,' said Kira.

Gorge looked over at her and shook his ahead. 'That's comforting.'

We stepped forward and investigated what looked like a terminal in the centre of the room. After touching the analogue screen the terminal flickered to life with a username and passcode required.

```
┌─────────────────────────────────────────┐
│                  HACK                     │
│           30% Chance Success              │
└─────────────────────────────────────────┘
```

I stepped back and let Kira take a crack at it. Her chance for a successful hack was 80% and after about thirty seconds we were in.

```
┌─────────────────────────────────────────┐
│              Terminal - 4                 │
│         Statis Pods Active - 104          │
│        Stasis Pods Inactive - 896         │
│       Open Stasis Pods - Yes / No         │
└─────────────────────────────────────────┘
```

'Can you tell us anything more about the transport ship?' I asked.

Kira tied up her dirty blonde hair in two pigtails. Her eyes glistened and her diamond-shaped face formed a veil over the screen as she studied it. 'Give me just a second I should be able to bring up a log, maybe we can get a quick history lesson before going any further.'

'Well the world is watching,' I replied pointing towards the camera following Kira's every move. Suddenly, she seemed just as annoyed by it as I had been earlier. The drone stayed out of the way for the most part, but it was still weird to think that people were watching our every move. It made making decisions like this seem fatal in a way…like watching a horror movie and yelling at the screen when someone hears a noise and must investigate.

Fortunately, we could at least say that investigating mysteries was a part of our job. Exploring the unknown and all that.

Meer is dead. After his parley with the Chel on neutral ground he was betrayed and ambushed. The bastards murdered him in cold blood. All we ever wanted was our freedom. The chance to set out on our own without their guidance and intervention. We've been destined for something more since we came through the world gate, but they insist that we learn from this. That Meer's death was inevitable and that they themselves had nothing to do with it. They sit safe in their tower on their thrones...the last of their kind and yet no one questions why. Why did their empire fall? We deserve answers. How could they justify the genocide of millions of worlds and yet welcome us to their most spiritual place in the Spire. None of it matters now. The Leviathan is on the move and we launch at dawn. We are fleeing their tyrannical empire and going our own way along with six others. They won't know who to chase first and to make sure they don't come at us with everything they've got we've taken one of their own. I'd never even seen a real Chel before last night but having now seen one in person I'm not surprised by how they have been treating us. We've locked the prisoner in a stasis pod on the fore most part of the ship. Should they come after us we'll execute her.

It won't be long now. We'll take back the stars.

Adam Asher, Captain

Several of the pods started to open.

'I hit NO, dammit, I HIT NO,' shouted Kira, banging her fist against the terminal. Gorge pulled her back and blasted it.

'Hard luck.' Gorge grimaced.

'Probably a safety built into the system in case someone hacked it, if nothing was wrong they could all just go back to bed,' said Cass.

'OK, what now?' I asked.

The four of us stood back to back, looking around at the open stasis pods around us. We could hear the metal pods grind as several of the chambers were stuck. Above us, we could also hear what sounded like an animal screaming. The humans in the pods weren't human anymore.

'The quantum radiation mutated them,' said Cass. As one of the creatures approached us, I got a quick scan of it.

```
Aberration
Level: 45
Hostile
```

'I thought you said this dungeon was going to be level forty-two?' I yelled, firing at the abomination. The creature looked humanoid, only it had multiple elongated limbs similar to an Arachnid, along with a tail that looked similar to the rats we saw running down towards the core earlier. The Aberration was still wearing an old Remnant officer uniform. I could only imagine how difficult it would be to defend against any that were wearing combat gear. Luckily, thanks to Gorge and Kira these ex-crew members would never get the chance to put on armour. Cass and I got about 100 EXP in assists as the two high level players lit up the battlefield around us, firing at the Aberrations on the ground and also at in the pods opening above us. For a moment it felt like we were drowning in the bodies of the awakened dead but we were running. Running forward through the halls of the stasis chamber as the doors around us continued to open, until finally we found a room with a hatch and we closed ourselves in.

'I said I think this is going to be a level forty-two dungeon,' Kira was panting, her rapid breaths visible in the ins and outs of her spandex torso. I felt my own heart beating inside my chest. I wanted to log out. I was surprised the game had continued to let me play this long. If I had to guess, I would bet Lady Gray had overridden several of my safety protocols for the sake of the viewing figures. This unique adventure must be attracting thousands.

'I can deal with Hollows, Wraiths and rats but what the hell was that?' shouted Cass.

'Aberrations, mutated human corpses. Hybrids of man and whatever else lives down here,' answered Gorge. He was eating yet another piece of beef jerky when Kira gave him a sideways glance.

'Rare creatures, usually they are fully formed monsters by the time most players dive into dungeons. Right now they still look human,' Kira added.

We could hear them banging against the metal door.

'Can they break through?' I asked.

'No, that door should hold, they aren't as driven as the Hollows and will probably give up pretty easily. Most likely, they will start wandering the ship or killing one another until only a few of the stronger ones remain.'

'Another terminal up ahead, want to take a look inside?' said Cass.

```
HACK
70% Chance Success
```

It took me twenty-nine seconds to override the terminal. I knew Kira could have done it faster, but I appreciated the +10 XP she let me earn.

```
┌─────────────────────────────────────────┐
│            Terminal - 7                  │
│                                          │
│        Statis Pods Active - 1            │
│        Stasis Pods Deactive - 0          │
│      Open Stasis Pods - Unavailable      │
└─────────────────────────────────────────┘
```

'Do you think that is the Chel they were talking about having taken?'

'What else could it be?' Kira stepped in and began decoding the log.

There is a god among us, living in silence aboard the Leviathan. They told me what happened to Meer but I just can't believe it. He never would have agreed to this...Asher is an insane idealist. He really believes we can find Earth again. It's been years and the world gate above the Spire only goes one way. Even with the new STL drives it will take centuries to map all of the known quadrants. What does it matter anyway? Earth was dying, by the time find what is left, it will be nothing but a wasteland. What Asher doesn't know can't hurt him...I know she can still hear them. They whisper in her ear, in her dreams. Upon her return to the material world she will have her vengeance upon us. Forgive me, for I must forsake my oath. I must make it so that can never happen. If we can't find Earth in a hundred years I'll have no choice. I'll make sure we land on a habitable planet and that the god never wakes again.

- Adrian Parker, First Class Medical Officer.

'That was brutal,' I said staring at Kira.

'What do you say we go have a look, I've never actually seen a Chel. Those rare times when they meet with players, they do so as glowing avatars,' Kira motioned towards a door with a blood splatter on it.

The door looked like it had been welded shut but that didn't stop Nel from finding a quick way in. Once Nel finished cutting open the door, we stepped inside and found another terminal beside a massive stasis pod that must have been twenty meters across and ten feet high. The stasis pod looked like a shark tank the way it was designed: it was slightly curved out from the wall and there was some kind of vibration filling the inside the room. The inside of the pod was covered by some kind of pitch black metal plating.

'Backup power generator,' said Gorge putting his hand against the covered glass before pointing towards another terminal.

```
HACK
80% Chance Success
```

I stepped up and again had a successful hack but nothing appeared on screen. Only a line of code I couldn't decipher. I let Kira try to make sense of it.

Terminal - 8

Before the collapse, my people were hungry and defiant and quickly we turned on one another, Meer promised us food and drink, he promised us a future and for many that was enough. When he asked we follow him I was one of the few to raise my hand and take up arms against the ones who had promised us their empire. As we prepared for war with the eternals we found ourselves trapped. Humanity had divided. The gods had abandoned us and cast us aside. We showed them. We rose from the ashes of a lost rebellion and took one of their own. Turns out I was wrong. The Chel were no different than us. Biologically they were more like us than we wanted to believe. They could mimic the human form, our emotions. The young woman we kept prisoner. Frozen in sadness. She was just like us now, far from home. Far from all she ever knew and wanted. Her elders had taken us in and promised us the stars but when we learned the truth, that we had to earn it, that we had to build the gates ourselves and complete tasks for power we could just take, we turned on them. They were few and we numbered in the hundreds. What chance did they have? They had the immortal giants. The guardians slew hundreds before we finally ran and the rest of humanity bowed. They probably won't even remember us. Doesn't matter. I can see her crying sometimes. I know they are calling out to her even now, they want their child back...And that is never going to happen.

  - *Michel, Director of Operations.*

After the log ended, Kira managed to decipher more of the terminal's hidden code. There was a backdoor built into the computer system and it looked like Terminal 8 was the only way to access it. With a look over her shoulder, Kira questioned whether or not we should open it. Curiosity had the better of us. Even knowing it could be a trap or that there could be some kind of boss beyond the veil we nodded our heads. We had come this far as a team, we weren't going to stop now. The Chel were hiding something. Humanity itself had a secret past that no one had spoken of before. Maybe whatever was behind the black iron covering wouldn't give us answers, but it would give a form, a shape to at least one of the mysteries of *Bane*.

The metal plating began to slowly slide open. The floating camera turned away from Kira and I as we gazed upon the tank. We were about to show the world what a Chel really looked like. Only...

There was nothing there.

10.
Crucible

Nine hours in. My physical body can only stay inside my pod a few more hours before I will get sick. We'd managed to make it halfway through the new dungeon. We opened the sealed door to a stasis chamber we believed would reveal a Chel and found nothing. Not even a dead husk. The chamber was filled with the same liquid protein that was prevalent in regular stasis chambers. The Chel's pod was large but the liquid only ran half way to the top. We speculated that maybe Michel or Adrian had destroyed the creature in order to ensure it couldn't ever wake up, but small cracks in the top of the structure made us believe there was something more going on.

'You remember that hybrid we killed earlier?' said Cass.

'The reptile thing that had Chel, Dargon, and human DNA?' I said.

'Yes, I think it's possible the Chel woke up when the ship crashed and it started banging against the glass, drowning,' she paused, pointing out that the glass looked like it had been smashed from the inside out.

'As the ship sank and began turning into a dungeon the Chel got caught in the transformation and its DNA was spread to various degrees over the entire ship. The creature we encountered had very little Chel DNA, it was mostly a hybrid of Dargon and human, most likely some kind of lab experiment gone wrong,' Cass paused and pointed towards Nel, 'robot! I order you to analyze the materials used in the walls of the dungeon,' she put down her finger and smiled...

'I am an artificial companion, not a robot, you do not command me,' Nel sounded very disapproving of Cass's tone. Cass, however, was a Corpse Diver and in fact Nel had to take orders from her, just as if they had come from me or Lady Gray. The only people who couldn't command Nel were Gorge and Kira.

'Scanning now,' Nel turned towards the wall. I watched as a blue laser shot out from one of Nel's round eyes and moved up and down across the wall. The results were sent to my heads-up display.

Carbon nanotubes

Lithium

Titanium Alloy

Ceramic composites

Steel

Bio-organic compounds (including two unknown samples)

'Nel can you identify the bio-organic compounds?' I asked.

'Can you say please?' Nel responded, before answering: 'Chel, human, Dargon, various insects, rats, moths, and mole DNA signatures found as well as several dozen plant species,' Nel sent me the list. It was half a dozen pages long but proved Cass's theory right.

Many starships were made of the non-organic materials in this list. Carbon nanotubes were stronger than most metals and could be spun together to create the outside of the ship's hull, with titanium alloy and ceramic composites making up the inner shell, reinforced with steel hallways and rooms. Cover all that with an artificial biomass that acted like skin for a ship and you could sail through space against radiation and asteroids all day long. When this ship turned into a dungeon and the core broke down, the biomass fused with the humans aboard as well as the plants and animals that were living in the gardens. The Dargon was probably a prisoner of some kind or lab experiment. The Chel, the other prisoner, had tried to break free only to find its body evaporating before it could escape.

'Can you tell how much of the ship is made of Chel DNA? Is there a concentration of it anywhere?' I asked.

'No; request unable to be completed. The Chel DNA is scattered everywhere, no concentration detected.' Nel paused, 'I would, however, like to inform you that I have detected an echo in the area,'

'An echo? How is that possible?' It almost seemed like Cass's elven ears perked up with excitement. I knew what she was thinking, that there was no way any other players could be alive down here. But there was. Recon. The first team sent inside the starship had never left. It was plausible that they had made it farther down than us…maybe even to the core itself. If Nel was only now detecting an echo that meant that something had killed at least one of them and a new artefact had appeared.

'It must be the recon team,' said Gorge, echoing my thoughts.

'How did you know about that?' asked Cass.

'I have ears everywhere. But in this case, everything is being broadcast over the net,' Gorge answered with a chuckle. Of course. We still had a camera hovering around us, recording and

141

broadcasting everything we did. Right now there were probably hundreds of players searching for a way to dive into this dungeon, hoping they could follow our path to the core should we fail.

'So the dungeon is part Chel?' I asked.

Nel gave a human-like nod, 'yes, that would be the simple answer.'

'Can you lead us to the echo?' I asked, instead of ordering.

'It would be my pleasure Breq; thank you for treating me like the companion I am.' Nel set off to towards a wall in the Chel chamber, which she scanned: a door materialized in front of us.

'Hidden by a hologram, neat trick,' said Kira.

Again, Gorge led the way, followed by Cass, myself, Kira, Nel and the camera drone. The next room was larger than the one we had sealed ourselves shut inside, larger than the Chel's stasis chamber and probably the largest part of the ship we had seen so far. It looked like it had been some kind of garden at some point, but the plants were gone and nothing but soil and broken stems remained. I could still smell the dirt in the humid air as we walked further into the garden. I could see small creatures hiding in the corners of the room but there was no indication that any of them were dangerous. There were Voths flying around as well but not in swarms like earlier. I couldn't help but wonder what had happened to the Thorn we encountered earlier.

Gorge walked through the garden to the next door. Behind me, Nel lit up the area, casting our huge shadows on the far walls. When the rest of us followed, we saw two figures standing nearby. Gorge was standing with his arms up in the air with a rifle pointed towards his head. The echo was coming from a dead soldier in the room. Three Hollows stood in the shadows with their eyes facing the walls. They weren't the predatory kind we encountered earlier. These were more typical Hollows. Ghosts that guarded the echoes of the deceased. They were neutralized at the moment.

'Name and association,' one of the figures, a man, said. The second figure was a tall, beautiful woman with brunette hair. She looked like she was around my age, maybe a year older. She was dual wielding a set of rifles aimed at the rest of us.

'Gorge, space trader, tank, level sixty. Now put down the toy gun before someone gets hurt,' he said smirking.

The man didn't do as our veteran said and instead demanded, 'who sent you?'

In one fluid movement Gorge turned to his right and wrapped his wrist around the rifle and quickly disarmed the soldier. 'Put your toys down girl,' Gorge demanded.

The girl was shaking. She looked nervous. I doubt she had ever met anyone level sixty before. After about ten seconds of staring down Gorge who was now holding a knife to her friend's chest she lowered her rifles.

'Now that's settled, how about we talk. You guys are the recon team right?' Gorge let go of the soldier and handing him back his rifle.

'Yes sir; what is left of the recon team,' the soldier stood up.

'How many of you were there?' Cass asked.

'Five total: two were killed by Hollows and Riley, our third died just recently after the ship started to sink and we found ourselves stuck down here.'

'Names?' Kira asked.

'Chaz, Scout class, Level fifteen,' he responded.

'Naomi, Scout class, Level twenty,' the girl said.

'So Naomi, are you the one in charge?' Cass asked.

Naomi looked at the rest of us. The recon team were scavengers hired out by Lady Gray to investigate the ship just after it crashed. They were supposed to keep an eye on things until we were able to arrive and salvage. The scouts were also prospects of hers for joining our little guild. At this point I wasn't sure whether they would pass with flying colours for having survived this long, or would fail miserably for having failed in preventing the ship from sinking and transforming into a dungeon.

'I was in charge,' Naomi replied.

Cass ran a hand through her red spikes, looking sombre. 'I'm sorry for your losses; why didn't you call for aid?'

'No signal, we haven't been able to get a connection to the outside since the ship started sinking into the sands,' she replied.

'Tell us exactly what happened,' Kira demanded in a soft tone.

'We had been running in darkness for a what felt like forever, maybe not forever but it was a long time. Something or someone was chasing us but we couldn't get a read on it, occasionally the lights flickered on and we could see the shadow of something that looked like it had no real shape or form. It was like a tentacle, decaying everything it touched. I remember turning back and aiming my rifle at it. Nothing, no damage at all. It was like the ship had come to life and was trying to catch us with its tongue.'

'Naomi, do you know what happened to the ship?' I asked.

'It sunk into the sands of Rem?' she said, hesitating.

'It's turned into a dungeon, a Chel dungeon to be exact, got a guardian on the outside protecting it while it transitions and everything,' Gorge explained patiently.

Naomi looked confused, 'a dungeon? Is that even possible?'

Cass was the one who responded first. 'Doesn't matter. It has happened; they were holding a Chel prisoner and after the ship started transforming, Chel DNA got scattered, becoming a part of the dungeon itself. We're trying to track down the core now, maybe we can neutralize this place and get some nice loot out of this whole thing,' Cass said.

144

'More than loot, I'm here to level up,' I said.

'We'll have to raid a lot more dungeons for that, but yeah, that's another reason we are here,' said Kira. Naomi looked at Kira and I could see the realization hit the recon scout that here too was a seriously high level player.

'I had no idea,' she said.

'How did you escape? How did you neutralize the Hollows?' I asked.

'We kept running until the three of us made it past the garden. Eventually, whatever it was stopped coming after us. I had some home-made cryo-bombs and used them on the Hollows, that put them out for a few hours at a time. I'm also using a Biotek rifle, I can load it with special ammo that will boost my party's defence. If I'm able to upgrade it I can boost their attack as well.'

'Wow, that's impressive, must have a pretty good crafting skill to make bombs like that. Why didn't you kill them?' Gorge asked.

'There is something else down here, it escaped into the vents, thought maybe if we kept the Hollows around we would be safe for a little while,' she answered.

'Any idea what it was?' I asked.

'No idea, just that it was level thirty and hostile,' she answered.

'Maybe a Wraith?' said Kira.

Gorge shook his head. 'Doubtful, not this low, probably some kind of Rem fauna that got mixed up in the environmental shift.'

'You guys can theorize all day but right now those Hollows are going to wake up. Since two of you are high level players, we should be able to make our way back to the surface,' Chaz said.

'Can't do that, gotta complete this quest,' I answered at once.

'What, are you their leader?' Chaz asked.

The others looked at me, all of them, Gorge, Kira, Cass, all smiling and nodding their heads in approval.

'Yes I am and we're going deeper.'

'You're all insane,' Chaz said.

'I'm in,' said Naomi.

'Thank you, welcome to the Corpse Divers,' I said shaking her hand and adding her to our party.

NAME: NAOMI

Age: 17	Class: Tech-Mage
Level: 20	Health: 100
Status: Alive	Stamina: 100
Mana: 100	

Load out: Biotek Rifle, Energy Pistol, Charge Blade

'I thought you said you were a scout?' I said reading her class: 'Tech-mage'.

'I lied, at that moment, I thought it was better that you didn't know. A lot of pressure comes with being a tech-mage and I'm still developing my skills,' she answered.

'That's AWESOME!' shouted Kira, 'I'm a tech-mage too!'

Naomi stood staring at Kira for a moment. 'Please, I'm sorry, I'm really not very good, I don't know why I even chose the class, I can't properly use any of the skills; I just have always liked the idea of magic and using elemental powers, but I can't even cast a shield,' Naomi was about to go on but Kira silenced her and created a ball of blue energy in the air. She slung it at the three Hollows who were turning towards us. The ball of energy dissolved them to ashes. The room was silent. Kira's eyes looked like they were glowing from within a halo of golden hair.

'You weren't kidding about the high level enemy, I can feel its presence. And it's not level thirty anymore…it's growing stronger.' Kira looked around the room.

Naomi stared at Kira in disbelief. I could tell she had never seen anything like that. 'Please make me your apprentice!' she sounded excited.

'Wait? What?' Kira turned around staring at Naomi.

'You have to train me, if I could be half as good as you…'

'I'm not really looking to take on an apprentice right now.'

'Hey Kira, remember everything you do is being broadcast live right now, to the world,' I reminded her.

'Maybe,' Kira said, 'first, tell me, we detected an echo in this room, was it your fallen comrade?'

'Yes, we haven't picked up the artefact yet. It didn't seem right.'

'You know echoes attract monsters right? More Hollows and whatever that thing is that has been watching you. They will all come back,' Kira replied.

'I didn't know that, I'm sorry.'

'It's OK, don't worry about it; if not for the echo we probably wouldn't have found you guys anyway,' Kira smiled and gave a thumbs up towards the rest of us and then the camera. She was trying not to appear too arrogant to help a lower level player. Unlike the rest of us, she had a reputation. That was the price of being the head of Moonrain Media.

A moment later Chaz joined our party as well.

NAME: CHAZ

Age: 16   Mana: 100

Level: 15   Class: Scout

Status: Alive   Health: 100

Stamina: 100

Load out: M7-7 Standard Scout Rifle, Energy Pistol

We now had five members in our makeshift squad.

Gorge and I moved towards the artefact unsure of what we would find. Inside the dead soldier's corpse we found a small tome hidden in the coat of his jacket pocket.

The tome was inscribed in a code.

'Think you can decipher it?' I asked.

'No, unfortunately this isn't my area of expertise, tomes can unlock all kinds of different things, even level players up automatically,' he said, handing it over to me. The tome looked like a square piece of rock. For some reason it made me think of a key but that was probably reaching. I set it aside and stuffed it into my satchel with the other gear I had.

'We need to keep moving ahead,' I said.

Kira shook her head, blonde hair swinging to emphasize the movement. 'No Breq, we need to stop, your body can't take anymore of this.'

'How do you know?' I was being stubborn. I didn't care that I was going to get sick, I couldn't just logout in the middle of a dungeon.

'We can double back to the Chel stasis room and Nel can weld the doors shut, from there you can logout and get some rest, the rest of us will follow, I'll have people watching us with the camera to make sure nothing happens and we can log back in quickly if something comes up.'

'Fine, you win, I'll logout,' I was reluctant but I knew arguing with Kira was not going to get me anywhere.

I followed the others back to the Chel stasis room back through the garden. We weren't alone this time. I could feel the presence of something.

'I am detecting a large life form underneath the floor,' said Nel.

As one, we raised our rifles. Chaz was the only one shaking. He was new to all of this. A casual player who never expected to get caught up in something like this.

'See something, say something,' I called out. The floor began to rumble but after a few seconds it stopped. Gorge rested his gun down by his side and placed his ear to the ground.

```
              Vrax
             Level 30
             Hostile
```

I saw the enemy display on my heads up, but I couldn't see the enemy until it was right beneath us. The Vrax was a type of Aberration. An underground animal that lived in the sands of Rem. Usually, they were docile creatures but we were deep inside this one's territory and I could only imagine how the quantum radiation had mutated it.

Gorge fired at the ground and soon the Vrax emerged. It was seven feet tall and fifteen feet long. It looked like a mole, only its tail was longer and its body was covered in sharp black spikes that were poisonous. It also had tusks and teeth like a boar, with a jaw that unhinged and opened outward towards us as we dodged its first attack.

'Fire!' I shouted.

The Vrax had a 1000 HP. We did some damage in our first attack but the creature dove back under ground.

'Nice going, a few more rounds and we'll have it,' I said.

The creature emerged again and again we fired. This time it didn't try to come towards us, instead, swinging its tail and smashing Gorge and Naomi into the wall.

'You guys ok?' I shouted.

Both Kira and Nel were already rushing over. Kira with some kind of injection in hand.

It was a stimulant. As soon as Naomi was injected, her eyes turned green. I could see a yellow energy surround her like an aura. For a moment she seemed invincible.

'No thanks,' said Gorge, holding up his hand as Kira prepped another injection. 'I don't need it,' he cracked his neck and stood back up.

With a shrug, Kira injected herself, boosting her own health as the Vrax swung at us again. I kept firing, standing just far enough away to avoid any damage. Unfortunately, most of my shots were being deflected by the Vrax's thick back hide. Turns out we were lucky the first time, as it charged us head on.

The neck was a weak spot. So were the creature's eyes, which were solid white. Since it lived underground it was blind. The rest of its body was hardened. I guess this made some sense.

It was a creature that had evolved to dig through desert sand. It had four claws on each foot, each measuring about three feet long. It could probably kill any of us in one or two blows.

Quick Lore

The Vrax is a rare alien creature that lives on Rem. In most cases the Vrax is only available to fight during seasonal events such as Winter festivals and Spring Blossom events, having come out of hibernation from deep below the planet's surface. In order to fight the Vrax, a player must reach Level 10, it won't give the light of day to anyone weaker. The Vrax quest is usually given by NPC villagers living on Rem as a special hunting quest, since the Vrax in the area are known for being hostile and destroying many smaller settlements. It can also be encountered randomly.

Chaz stood by my side. I could see he was trying to mimic the things I did. For once, I was the leading scout. I guess maybe I should have told them Cass was in charge, but really it wouldn't have done any good. Cass was covering Kira and the others. Her health had dropped to 75. Had she been hit by one of the Vrax claws? I wasn't sure and didn't have time to think about it. I had to defend, as the Vrax turned away from the three of them and set its sights on us. Somehow, it had figured out we were weaker than the rest. Maybe it was our poor attack damage or maybe something more. It turned its head towards us and for a moment I felt like I was staring into its eyes. Then it span again and I felt the whiplash of its tail as the air turned to a sonic boom and Chaz and I were thrown back against the wall.

My health dropped to 90 points. My stamina 50.

I got up as quick as I could, but the Vrax was charging towards me.

Naomi shot me with her Biotek rifle. I felt my HP rise. 95.

Somewhere between being blown against the wall and standing up, I had dropped my rifle. I pulled my sword, *Aegis*, from my back and held it like a shield. The creature's tail hit the blade full force. Like a razor, *Aegis* cut the Vrax's tail clean off. The creature cried out and made a number of unholy sounds before turning towards me again. It opened its jaws and inside I could see the face of a man screaming out with red in his eyes.

Vrax Aberration

Level 35

Hostile

The creature was transforming. Health regenerating.

Something about cutting off its tail had sent it into overdrive. As the face inside its mouth stared at me, I watched as he monster unhinged its jaw ready to charge. And the creature had also regenerated its tail. This wasn't a normal Vrax. This was something unique to the dungeon. I stood ready for the beast to come at me. If I timed it right, I could swing *Aegis* and knock the creature back. If I missed I would die. Game over.

The Vrax charged and I waited for what felt like the longest second of my life. It was faster than I thought but not fast enough. I swung and clipped the creature with just enough force to deflect it past me. In doing so, I fell to the ground but I had given my team the chance to attack.

From all sides Cass, Kira, Gorge, Naomi and even Chaz fired on the Abberation until its health had dropped half a bar. It began to dive back underground but Kira had cast a shield across the floor. As she held her hand against the ground I could see the shield glowing red around us. The Vrax was in a frenzy as it turned towards me again. This time I was ready. I dived with my sword in hand and cut across the face of the man I had seen inside its throat. A line of text appeared, 'killed Adrian Parker, First Class Medical Officer Vrax Abberation.' +5000 XP. I was now less than 500 points from levelling up to 31.

Aegis also levelled up.

```
Level: 3
Damage: 60
Weight: 5 lbs
Weapon Type: Melee
Rarity: Rare
Impact: 10
Range: 0
Stability: 10
Sharpness: 8
Elemental: None
Critical Chance: 60%
Modifiers: None
```

Nel lit up the room. My feeling of delight collapsed. Naomi was laying on the ground. One of the Vrax spines had pierced her stomach.

'Get me a med patch quickly!' Kira screamed.

'I'm out,' I said.

'Same here,' said Chaz.

Gorge looked sorrowful. 'I don't use patches.'

Kira was in tears.

Scanner in hand, Nel was standing over Naomi's avatar. 'Poison. Chance of survival seventeen percent and falling.'

Naomi was smiling, despite the blood pouring out of her mouth. 'I have my pain dampened, I'm not going to logout until the very end.'

'You'll survive this; you have to, I've decided to take you on as my apprentice,' Kira cried.

'That's great...let me...let me show you what I learned watching you,' Naomi's voice was trembling. Her health began dropping again, as did her mana. A small blue orb of energy floated above the palm of her right hand as her eyes turned yellow.

15% chance survival
10% chance survival
5% chance survival
0% chance survival

Naomi was gone. I brushed my bangs back trying to wipe away the trace of tears from my eyes.

A few minutes later an artefact appeared beside her echo. It was a blue gem. A permanent reminder of the blue orb she had conjured just before her death. Kira claimed it and attached it like an ornament to her Ki rifle.

After that, we made our way back to the Chel stasis chamber and I logged out of the game. My pod opened and I felt disoriented. I vomited down my chest as my throat burned and my hands began to shake.

Reynolds was waiting for me, dressed in black as ever. 'Good show today kid,' he handed me a small wet wash cloth. As he checked my heart rate and blood pressure, I didn't say a word. I heard him mention they lost the feed for a few minutes in the dungeon, some kind of weird feedback. I wanted to hit him in the face but I stopped myself. Clenching my fist, I was angry at the mission, angry at the company, angry at myself, even mad at Damien for dying. It wouldn't do either of us any good. I relaxed and let him hand me a handful of vitamins and pills and told me to get something to eat along with some rest.

Half an hour later, Reynolds left and I was laying in my new bed. I couldn't stop thinking about Naomi. I logged onto the net and brought up the live dungeon feed. On the screen was my body, laying alongside Cass, Kira, and Gorge with Nel standing guard beside us. Our avatars were sleeping inside the Chel's stasis chamber but that didn't mean we were really safe. Chaz was still there in the game. He was keeping watch too. I couldn't believe he hadn't logged out yet. Hopefully, we wouldn't have to carry him the next day. If we had logged off any earlier, I was sure now that the Vrax would have swallowed us all whole.

A small sub-group dedicated to following our feed was holding a virtual vigil for Naomi in the city of Alet on the water world known as Loomis which had been her starting area. Like the rest of us she had become famous. The first casualty in our quest to clear the Chel dungeon.

Another sub-group had managed to translate the inscription on the tome I had found.

'No Level Required.'

11.
Debris

I woke up at 9 a.m. the next morning after just four hours of sleep. Reynolds was there again. Turns out he had a key to my suite. Not that I was surprised to see him, but it was quite uncomfortable given how ugly I felt. My head was pounding. Still, he had medicine and breakfast waiting. Breakfast was scrambled eggs alongside some kind of fake bacon and toast. Although Reynolds had seasoned the eggs in a way they tasted great, honestly that didn't stop me from adding half a bottle of ketchup to my meal. That was a habit my mom had always picked on me for. Ever since I was little, ketchup had been one of my favourite condiments and I could eat it on anything.

Cup of black coffee in hand, Reynolds sat beside me while I ate. I asked him if I could have some and he told me I was too young and handed me a bottle of water instead. I wasn't too young and it wasn't like he was drinking real coffee anyway. Real coffee had become rare, like many other things people had taken for granted.

'Seattle's best faux coffee,' he smiled through his long beard. 'You should know that views skyrocketed last night when you confronted the mole creature. Crimson Kings are making a move towards that area though so better watch your back. They've started a petition to have you banned from the game. Calling you a cheater. Even blaming you for that young girl's death.'

'Blaming me for her death,' I slammed my fist against the table. I wanted to cry. Naomi's death wasn't my fault. It was an accident. She was a hero who had done everything she could to save her team in the worst scenario possible.

'Calm down. Didn't you see the vigil they held for her? That girl is a star. More famous now than she could have ever dreamed. People are already printing T-shirts with her face on it.

'Meanwhile, I've news about that dungeon your avatar is sleeping in now. Currently it's locked and it looks like it's going to remain locked unless players are level forty-five or higher and a part of a raiding party. You and your band of misfits were lucky you were already inside, otherwise you would have gotten crushed by the guardian. Not to mention the Crimson Kings are amassing a small army on the outskirts of Rem. Everything you are discovering is wild, everyone is watching to see what happens next. Even the developers had no idea the AI was going to do what it did.'

I finished eating and pulled up the net. Reynolds was right. In the hours after her death in the game Naomi's social accounts had to be temporarily disabled as she become a public figure. Fan pages were popping up and agents from all over were already trying to discover her real name. I had about a dozen messages asking for interviews and demanding I make some kind of statement but there was one particular message that stood out.

Breq,

This is Naomi. My real name is Hannah. Please don't feel bad for what happened. I wish you and Kira all the best. It's going to be awhile before I am able to start a new character. Starting at level 1 is going to suck but I'll catch up. Thank you for making me a part of your team even if it was only for a little while.

I will be watching you. :)

- Hannah

The message included ways to contact her in the real world alongside a picture of what she really looked like. I was flattered. Even Reynolds saw I was turning red.

'Got a fan message?' he laughed.

'No, a message from a friend,' I replied.

'Looks like more than that,' he finished, wandering over towards me. He tried to look over my shoulder but I closed out of the net before he could spy on me. He was probably reading all my messages anyway, it wasn't like my life was private anymore.

'A thirty-minute workout, then you can log back in,' he pointed towards some of the exercise equipment that came with the suite.

'Isn't it a bad idea to work out right after eating?' I asked.

'Ideally, you would eat three to four hours before you exercise but your time is valuable and were not going to do anything that requires that much sweat. Mostly making sure you're breathing okay along with some stretches before you cram yourself back in that pod all day.' With a chuckle, Reynolds tossed me a pair of spandex pants and a tank top. 'Put these on, they will help.'

A part of me still felt like I was running on fumes. Four hours wasn't enough sleep, but once I was back in the game I could grab a stimulant from Kira and that would keep me going for awhile. Reynold's workout consisted mostly of repetitive exercises that worked on straightening my back and stretching my muscles. Turns out he was also licensed chiropractor and he gave my posture a quick adjustment before I changed into a set of clothes to wear inside the pod.

Chaz had spent thirty minutes watching over us before logging out. I guess like the rest of us he couldn't quite come to terms with Naomi's death. It was Kira who logged back in and told him to get some rest. As I had guessed, Chaz was a casual player but he was trying to make his way into playing professionally. The Corpse Divers recon mission was his way of trying to see if he had what it took to make it into a real guild. Before logging out he had spent a total of fifteen hours in game. I could only imagine how sick he had felt. Kira had logged out after another half an hour, once Gorge had logged back in to take over the watch. For some players it was possible to sleep in-game. Gorge crossed his legs and stood against the wall in a meditative state. He was letting his mind rest while the rest of him in the real world lay still in his pod. At a moment's notice he could spring to life, but until then he was just like the rest of us.

'Access'

Checking for necessary update files...

Update 1.11.8 found.

Initializing...

Player environment meets necessary requirements.

Retina scan / Identity confirmed.

Dive 100%

Loading player data...

Chaz was waiting for me when I logged in.

I woke up on the metal floor. My avatar coming to life. As I started to move, my head was pounding and my ears were ringing. The world was a blur until I blinked a few times and found myself staring at a crack in the ceiling. I leaned forward and pulled up my display. Everything was still there, just as I and left it. I wiggled my toes and moved my legs, repeating some of the exercises I had done in the real world. After warming up for a few minutes, I crawled towards my rifle and picked it up. I looked it up and down, making sure there were no flaws present and checked the weapon's level, comparing it to my own affinity and sharpness. I did the same for *Aegis* and breathed a sigh of relief.

'I'm sorry I couldn't do more to save Naomi; did she manage to find you?' Chaz said, extending his hand. I grabbed it and let him help pull me up. I stood there a moment just taking everything in. My eyes and ears continued to adjust. His voice sounded muffled at first but after a moment everything was clear.

'Yes. Did you have something to do with that?'

'I got your contact information from Kira and I sent it along to Naomi; I'm sorry if that was out of line…she thought you were really cool and I felt like I owed it to her, she saved my life more times than I could count and now I just want to survive, I want to beat this dungeon and take the core in her name,' Chaz said making a fist.

'She'll be back, you know she will,' I reassured Chaz. That was true but it wouldn't be the same. Naomi would probably have to start on a separate server and realistically it would take her months to get close to our level (and even then, there would probably always be something of a gap in level). *Bane* was no easy game, even if you were just grinding low level dungeons. Still, I had no doubt I would see more of Naomi / Hannah and thinking about her made me feel happy. The last time I had liked a girl had been in middle school: between my parents dying and living on the streets relationships had been the farthest thing from my mind.

Some twenty minutes after I'd returned to *Bane*, Kira and Cass logged in. Gorge, Chaz, Nel and I had already been discussing where to go next. It seemed that during our time away the starship's transformation had settled. The core had solidified itself in the engine room. Based on the knowledge we'd gained yesterday; Gorge had drawn a small map of what he believed was the shortest route to get to there. It was also likely the most dangerous.

Nel used her laser to open the welds that had sealed the door inside the stasis chamber, and we moved back through the garden. The remains of the Vrax Aberration hadn't yet disappeared and it looked like something had been feeding on it.

'Voth,' said Kira, looking closely, her black spandex uniform stretching tight as she bent over. 'they've eaten a lot of the body's specialized organs; probably that will mutate them even more.'

Each of us had to plug our nose as we passed by the monster's corpse. The smell reminded me of rotten banana peels and only eased up when we found ourselves back in the room that Naomi and Chaz had been hiding out in. It was here that we passed through another sealed door into the R & D stations.

'Figures they would have everything so close together,' said Cass.

The R & D stations were smaller rooms filled with terminals and various types of research equipment and tubes. Some contained small creatures: alien fauna from different quadrants. There were a few Dargon embryos and even a large liquid container with a dead Dargon-human hybrid, like the one we had killed near the surface.

Sitting in the second research station, Cass put her rifle down, setting it to lean against the wall. There were several cells. Each one was rigged with glowing green bars whose energy hummed through the air. Only two cells were occupied. The creatures inside were neither creature nor man. They looked like shells. Husks that had turned to cocoons and broken apart.

'Why go to all this trouble? What were they doing here?' I asked.

'Trying to find a way to survive,' answered Gorge.

I still didn't get what the Remnants had been trying to achieve. 'They saw the Chel as an enemy, they saw them as a threat, and they were trying to find a way to become stronger, but why?'

'Maybe the Chel really are the enemy. After all, what do we know about them, other than they built the first world gate and they like to remain hidden deep inside the Spire?' Cass lifted her red head away from the screen she was studying.

'That's blasphemy, you know that?' Gorge's voice was amused, 'they might send a guardian after you just for talking like that.'

'The Remnants fought the Chel and when they were neutralized they ran into the stars like heretics,' offered Chaz.

I studied my teammates. Both Cass and Kira's eyes had hardened since we began our adventure below the surface. I felt like I had become closer to all of them. For the first time I noticed how callus my own hands were becoming. I hadn't levelled up yet but I could feel my avatar growing in strength.

Turning away from the others, I looked carefully around the lab. Even if the Chel were the enemies of our species, it didn't change anything. It would take an army to go against a single guardian, so if war with the Chel was what the game had in mind, we as players were nowhere near powerful enough to win. Not to mention how it would break the economy built around the Spire. If we had somehow stumbled upon a main quest line, we could be doing more damage than good.

'This isn't normal,' said Cass.

'No shit,' I replied.

'Watch your language,' it was Nel who pulled me up.

'Sorry, but this whole dungeon, this whole thing, has been set up since we arrived. Maybe we stumbled upon it but maybe we didn't. It's just too much pure coincidence,' I stopped. The camera was hovering closer to me now. I didn't want to say another word. I felt like I was preaching. 'It was a mistake for us to come here,' I finished.

'A blessing and a curse sometimes take the same form,' said Gorge.

We continued towards the core with little resistance. A swarm of Voth attacked us, but we cleared it away without too much trouble. There were a few Autons in the lower level as well but many had been ripped apart by some other creature and those that remained were barely functioning. Then there was a moment when Chaz had tried to open a sealed chest he had found, only for it to come to life. If Gorge hadn't pulled him back at the last minute he would have been swallowed whole by the mimic.

As well as these encounters, we had an anxious few minutes passing through a tunnel filled with floating Hollows. Everyone managed to sneak by them. I gained +10 stealth for that. We passed from tunnels that looked like they were a part of the ship to caverns that smelled like the inside of an empty fish tank. Inside one of the labs we found a video recording. One of the experiments run on the ship involved creating homunculi. When the crew had spliced human and alien DNA in their labs, they had yielded deformed creatures that fed on blood. Some of the specimens were still living inside jars. They could sense our presence as they followed us across the room reaching towards us to press their hands against the containers.

After three hours in game, I finally gained enough XP and levelled up to 31. It felt great but I still had a long way to go. If I was going to succeed I would have to do more.

While the others took a break, I was able to access my skills. At level 1 you automatically have 5 points in every category. There are an initial 60 skill sets in *Bane*, though some players manage to find extra sub-categories or pick up brand new skills as they play, making for a total of over a hundred skills available for top tier players. Every time you level up you are given a total of 15 skill points to allocate. A few of these can boost your affinity, sharpness, elemental powers, critical chance, etc., but for the most part skills simply allow players to function properly inside of *Bane* and they also dictate how NPCs (whether they are human, enemy, or animal) react to your presence. The botany skill for example: plant science allows players the advantage of learning new lore about the plant life found on certain worlds, including knowledge of what can be crafted from certain vegetation. A player with high botany and handicraft skills can actually extract poison from plants to use on their weapons, while a player without these could end up suffering badly if they tried to do the same.

As a scout, I had poured most of my points into evasion and stealth (otherwise known as detection) and as well, to resisting attacks such as fire, ice and poison. Skills points can also be picked up in-game while playing. Such as when I earn a +10 Stealth bonus: this temporarily boosts my stealth stats for a limited time. The time duration varies, however, and can wear off at any time. Bonuses like that feel like adrenaline in real life. Besides the sixty skills listed there are also hidden skills players can't access or manipulate, often related to intelligence or memory. Also, if you are incapable of a skill such as a particular type of crafting in real life, then adding it as a skill is useless. Your avatar is an extension of who you are. At level 30 I had spent 450 points. I now had 15 more points to use.

Level 31 Breq
15 Points Available

Adrenaline 45	Artillery (Heavy Weapons) 15
Affinity (weapons) 15	Attack Boost (DMG) 5 (+5 Bonus)
Agitation 15	
Animal / Aquatic Expert 35	Blast Attack Boost 5

Blast Resistance 35

Bleeding Resistance 45

Botany (Biology) 5

Bow Expert 5

Capacity Boost (Carrying) 5

Capture / Tame 15

Carving 10

Charisma 25 (+10 Bonus)

Constitution 5

Critical Boost 50

Critical Affinity 50 (+10 Bonus)

Defence 5

Detection (stealth) 15 (+10 Bonus)

Divinity / Fame 5

Evasion 5

Fire Attack 5

Fire Resistance 5

Focus 35

Fortification 5

Gambler 5

Fortifying 5

Guard 5

Hacking 25 (+10 Bonus)

Handicraft (crafting) 5

Heat Resistance 15 (Armour Bonus +10)

Health Boost 15

Hunting (survival) 5

Hunger (cooking) 5

Ice Attack 5

Ice Resistance 15

Intimidation 5

Iron Body 5 (Armour Bonus +10)

Latent Power 5

Luck 25

Medical Specialist 15

Mind's Eye 5

Navigator 5

Nullification 5

Paralysis Attack 5

Paralysis Resistance 5

Peak Performance 5

Piercing (Damage Boost) 5

Pilot 5 (+10 Bonus Active)

Poison Attack 5

Poison Resistance 5

Poison Duration 5

Psionic 5

Recovery 5

Stamina 25

Sheath Speed (reflexes) 5

Strength 5

Stun Attack 5

Stun Duration 5

Stun Resistance 5

Survival (general) 15

Having already thought about my build, it only took me about thirty seconds to decide. I put all 15 points into Detection (stealth) bringing that skill to 30, with a +10 bonus currently active. Most of my skills were based on dives I had run, hence my bleeding resistance and ice resistance. In this dive, I didn't want anything getting the drop on me.

Pro Tip
Decide early on what kind of player you want to be.

NAME: BREQ

Age: 17	Class: Scout
Level: 31	Health: 100
Status: Alive	Stamina: 100
Mana: 100	

Load out: M7-7 kinetic Rifle, *Aegis* (melee),

We set out again. Back into the metallic ruins of what was once a ship. I could feel it. All around us was a presence unlike anything I had felt before. I moved ahead, in front of the others. Kira followed close behind. We had one more door left to open. Drawing up to me, Kira hacked it in about three and a half seconds.

It was the engine room and it was in the same shape as the rest of the vessel. Ruined, there was debris thrown around. Some of it looked like it had aged a millennia. Crucially, we could see the core sitting only just ahead of us. The core itself looked like a metallic sphere hovering just above a rectangular podium. Several metal columns around us were etched with images showing what looked to be human soldiers fighting against hordes of alien monsters. But there were no actual monsters, no alien creatures, no Hollows around.

The room was silent and still. The air untouched and stale. Not even dust remained. For a moment it was hard to believe that this dungeon had once been a ship. As we approached the core, we saw behind it, hidden in the shadows of the floor something else. A black box, the kind for audio records. Kira picked it up and let it play.

All I can do now is rest...May God forgive our souls.

- Adam Asher, Captain

There may have once been a body but it was gone. No bones, no remnants, nothing but the audio recorder, the artefact that had been left at the end of the dungeon for only those brave enough to dive this deep to find. I turned away from Kira as Captain Asher stopped speaking. There was a low growl at the end of the message. Something unsettling.

'How much time do you think passed?' Kira asked.

'Since he made that recording?' asked Gorge, coming into the room. 'It's not absolute time, of course, it's relative. In here it looks like more than a thousand years. The core sat here at the eye of the storm.'

'Have you ever seen anything like this?' I asked.

'Not in *Bane*,' Gorge answered after a pause.

'Another game?'

Gorge was not meeting my eye. 'Not a game, it was an experiment, it was virtual reality, yes, but it failed.'

I didn't press him. Whatever Gorge was thinking, he wasn't willing to share out right and I wasn't going to push his buttons.

'Take it, it's yours,' Gorge said pointing towards the core.

The sphere was small enough it fit into the palm of my hand and as I pulled it down from the air I felt my muscles tense. The core was heavy. Not ridiculously heavy, but much heavier than I had anticipated, ten pounds at least. As soon as I touched it, the metallic core stopped glowing. Cold to the touch. I could feel the heat from my body move over it as I wrapped my fingers around the sphere.

'So that's it? We've won?' I said, holding the core in my hand.

'Only the beginning,' answered Kira.

The metallic sphere began to peel apart, as if centuries of waiting had finally caught up to it. As the metal shell fell to dust I felt something strange against my skin.

'Nel, what is this?'

'That, Sir, is an egg.'

'What the hell do we do with this?' I looked the egg up and down. It looked like a dinosaur egg, at least the kind I had seen in holos.

'Keep it safe, could be one of a kind,' said Gorge.

'Once we get back to the surface we can have it analyzed,' added Kira.

'OK, should be a short trip back to the surface right? Destroying the core turns a dungeon mute.' I placed the egg in a safe-box and inside my bag.

Gorge was walking slowly around the room, studying the images on the columns. 'Maybe, I'm not sure that was really the core,' he answered.

'What do you mean?'

'Look here,' Gorge moved around the base of the pedestal we had taken the metal sphere from and pushed down against the surface. The chamber around us moved, my stomach telling me it was descending.

'We're inside an elevator shaft?'

'Is that a question?' Nel responded, scanning the walls around us as the sensation of motion continued.

If this were an elevator, we were going deep. 'This starship was nowhere near this big when we entered.'

Nel turned her life-like eyes to mine. 'It is fused with the planet's crust; it can do what it wants.' Then she swivelled back to the wall.

'Finding anything interesting?'

'The crust is speckled with a metallic coating, nanites,' Nel answered.

'What does that mean?' Chaz asked.

'It means we aren't alone!' Kira shouted, readying her rifle as the elevator stopped. The walls began to move close in upon us as though alive.

'What the hell is it?' Chaz was the first to fire, aiming low into the wall.

'What was left of the Autons. Evolved,' Gorge threw a grenade and the nanites scattered across the floor. Hundreds of tiny hands appeared, as if they were drowning. The hands soon began to take other forms as they gathered together in a puddle. We could see a door leading to another hallway behind them: the nanites were blocking our only escape…the way to the dungeon's true core. As the nanites melded back together, they began to look like a mechanical Tyrannosaurus Rex made of fused bio-organic hands. The head and body of the assembled creature moved like a current of water across ropes of wire that resembled veins.

Even as it took form, all of us had opened fire on the robotic monster; I was hoping that if we could do enough damage it would fall apart at the seams before attacking. With hope, I saw the skull fracture and the faux Tyrannosaurus face turned into a giant hand as it tried to reform.

'Run past it!' I shouted. We barely had seconds to make our way around. Some enemies are too strong to face head on. Sometimes fighting doesn't even feel like an option. Once we were all in the far room, Gorge slammed his fist down on the ground and a shield appeared up around the door keeping the Auton monster out but also giving it time to fully transform.

```
Auton Guardian
Level 75
Hostile
```

'Nel can you scan any weaknesses?'

'None identified,' Nel replied almost at once.

'Scan it again!' I shouted.

'High pressure; high electrical charge; high energy output; electromagnetic pulses; nuclear fission; dark matter,' Nel stopped.

'Blast it with all we have; Gorge, is there a way for you to trap it inside a shield?'

'No, that was the last one I had,' he answered.

We were running out of time. The Auton Guardian was beginning to break through as our barrier lost energy. It was also getting stronger, regenerating from the metallic dust that lined the elevator shaft.

'The self-replicating cells of the Autons, they evolved, multiplied,' Kira said.

'Percent survival is...' Nel was cut off by Gorge screaming at her to shut up.

'Aren't Autons supposed to protect humans?' Chaz shouted.

'They are made to protect the ship and now that we're threatening the core they have turned on us,' Kira replied.

'Okay so kill the core: stop the monster,' I said running down the hallway. Ahead of me was something that probably was the real core. This time, rather than a metal sphere there was a pedestal holding what looked like a piece of blue blown glass with a red centre.

On the pedestal just below the sphere I saw the face of Skull-Faced Man carved in gold. I wasn't sure if it was my imagination or some trick of the light, maybe even something in the room playing with my mind. Maybe it was the game itself. I raised my rifle.

Gorge had caught up with me. 'You destroy the core we won't be able to sell it.'

I didn't care and pulled the trigger, pouring shots into the core... to no effect. My gun stopped firing and I drew *Aegis* from its sheath. I was seeing red. The image of Skull-Faced Man burned into my mind. I ran as fast as I could towards the core and hit it just as Cass cried out.

'It's through!'

I could feel the electricity run across my blade as my health dropped twenty points and for a moment I thought I was going to be forced out of the game. My hands felt on fire.

+ 5000 EXP

+ 10 Adrenaline

+ 10 Critical

+10 Intimidation

+10 Peak Performance

Turning, I saw the nanite creature dissolve, just as it was about to take a bite out of Cass's left arm. The others looked at me with relief. I placed my sword back into its sheath and picked my rifle back up from the ground. My sword, *Aegis*, had levelled

172

up. I hadn't. Destroying the core gave me no bonus. I was supposed to loot it. To reach level 32 I still had to collect close to
20,000 EXP. I could do this. I had to do this. I still had a long
journey ahead. For every dungeon there is always a boss. A beast,
a being that lives to protect its home, its sanctuary, whether it be
good or evil it just is as it always has. The lights in the room
turned off as all power died and the dungeon which had just come
to life passed away, just another ruin on Rem.

Aegis - Broadsword

Cut down by the forces of Lintirmai, the depraved creature known only as the beast's soul was imprisoned inside a great metal sword made from the hull of an ancient alien starship. Passed from one cursed soul to another *Aegis* is a living weapon that not only protects its master but eventually devours their very being.

That which may never die must be contained.

Level: 4
Damage: 65
Weight: 5 lbs
Weapon Type: Melee
Rarity: Rare
Impact: 10
Range: 0
Stability: 10
Sharpness: 8
Elemental: Soul – Steal a player's mana for better attack.
Critical Chance: 60%
Modifiers: None

As we made our exit my rifle became unique and I decided it was the right time to give it a name.

AKA *Naomi.*
M7-7 Ki / Energy Rifle

Description: Robot killer.

Level: 3
Damage: 60
Weight: 5.5 lbs
Weapon Type: Scout Rifle / Ki Rifle hybrid
Rarity: Rare
Impact: 8
Range: 8
Stability: 9
Reload Speed: 8
RPM (rounds per minute): 300 bursts
Affinity: 9
Sharpness: 8
Elemental: Unknown
Critical Chance: 80%
Modifiers: Bonus EXP gained against Robots

And, of course, the last item added to my inventory was still a mystery.

Egg
Unknown
Unknown

12.
Dominance

It took three hours to reach the bridge.

'So what are you going to do with the egg?' Gorge asked. I was holding it in the palm of my hand as we were resting now back at the bridge. The egg looked like that of an Ostrich, with a rune in it. If *Bane* had been a fantasy game I would have guessed it was a dragon's egg of some kind but *Bane* was not a fantasy. The egg was definitely alien. The rune felt familiar. I couldn't quite remember where I had seen it before or if I had. Maybe this sense of familiarity was just something I had created myself to make the situation feel more under my own control. With everything that was happening both in the real and the game world. I felt powerless. Defeated. Trying to survive. Trying to uncover the mysteries of my friend's death while millions watched, without my really knowing why. I wanted to speak about this powerlessness aloud, but it wouldn't matter. Everything was changing. Since Damien's death it was obvious now that *Bane*, like the starship that turned into a dungeon, was evolving into something more than a game.

In case it was possible we had missed something and could discover what the egg was or some kind of clue as to why the ship appeared so powerful in the first place, Nel was downloading more information from the ship's computer. The entire ship had gone quiet since we destroyed the core, minus a few Voths here and there. We even passed by the Thorn and saw that its corpse had been picked clean by several of the smaller creatures that were scurrying away from us inside the darkness. The Hollows had disappeared as well. Perhaps they weren't drawn to the energy anymore.

'Sir, it's possible the egg may be an ingredient of some kind, perhaps for the perfect omelette,' said Nel. I couldn't tell if the robot was being sarcastic or serious, but it had been so long now since I ate, I was starving.

'I'm not going to cook it,' I said.

'What do you think is in it? If you did decide to cook it I hope you share with the rest of us,' Gorge smiled, taking the egg from my hand and looking it over. He licked it.

Hurriedly, I stretched out a hand to take our discovery back from him. 'We'll analyze it back on the *Ibanez*, Nel's sister Tel can figure it out.'

'There is a forty-nine percent chance that she won't,' Nel said.

'Sorry, no offense,' I added.

'None taken, anything my sister can do, I can do as well, I do not believe that either of us is capable of discovering information that does not exist,' Nel sounded affronted, 'perhaps we should dispose of the egg before it hatches and kills all of us; there is a ninety-seven percent chance the egg is a hostile entity.'

'We can't just kill it,' I said placing the egg back into a protective casing inside my satchel, 'no matter what we aren't going to do that.'

'OK, so no killing it, no eating it, what's the plan? Put it in a zoo?' asked Gorge.

'Study it, use it if we can,' I answered.

'Neat; so what are you going to call it?' Gorge was smirking now. I could tell he was still thinking about eating the egg.

'I'm not sure,' I answered.

'If it's a new species you can name it after yourself or after someone you care about,' said Chaz, as if he was hinting I should name it after him.

'Maybe Spot, Spot is a good name,' Gorge said.

'You could name it Nel, or Mel, or Nel two-point-o,' Nel offered.

'Think it's a girl or boy? Both?' Chaz said.

'I don't know; I don't know what I would name it; I DON'T KNOW ANYTHING ABOUT IT,' I was getting frustrated.

The only two not obsessively talking about the egg were Cass and Kira.

'I still think we should eat it,' said Gorge after a moment of silence.

Somehow, Nel seemed to have formed a comedic rapport with Gorge. 'There is a ninety-eight percent possibility Breq will attempt to kill you if you eat the egg,' she said, with a clear note of amusement in her voice.

Kira, who had been ignoring all of us, drew a rune in the air with her fingers. She had been quiet most of the walk back, concentrating on rebuilding her mana and stamina. Something told me that she had seen an artefact similar to the egg before but I didn't ask. She wasn't a Corpse Diver and it was not my place to investigate her past or try and interrogate her for information. A grappling hook appeared in her hand. She fired it just north of the wall where earlier the dropship had come and rescued us. She shot the other end into the ground and the rope began to transform into a ladder.

'We need to get out of here and find somewhere safe to regroup,' she said.

Cass was reading a holographic map and spoke without looking up. 'Already contacted the *Ibanez*, they should be sending a ship to pick us up, waypoint is northeast after we reach the surface, maybe a ten-minute hike, five minutes if we aren't slow from where we are now.'

'Something is wrong, do you hear that?' Kira said.

'Yeah it sounds like gun fire,' I answered.

'Sounds like a battle coming our way,' Gorge unshouldered his rifle.

'OK, don't panic, Corpse Divers won't let anything happen to us, not to mention there is a guardian protecting this place, no one can come close to penetrating those defences,' Cass said.

Slowly, we began climbing the ladder, even as the sound of gun fire grew louder.

Transports and fighters flew overhead while others descended towards the surface of Rem from orbit above. Some were falling while on fire, others were retreating away from enemies overhead. Another set of fighters were flying towards us: strafing the area as Crimson King soldiers moved towards us. We had reached the surface.

'We have a siege,' said Gorge.

'What the hell is going on here? I thought a guardian was supposed to be protecting this place?' said Chaz.

'Looks like they sacrificed a Titan to take it down,' said Cass pointing towards the wreckage of a Crimson King Titan in the distance.

'We are worth millions,' said Kira.

I couldn't believe what I was seeing. 'Not that much, really?'

'They also want vengeance, Lady Gray killed thousands of players in your name,' Kira added.

Barricades and fences held back a swarm of Crimson King soldiers while refugees ran down our left flank looking for any cover they could. There too were the remains of the giant guardian that had come to protect the dungeon. On the surface of the ship, all sounds were loud. When we crawled outside the ship, we crawled through a small dampening field that had blocked most of the noise of the siege around us. We were lucky the battle hadn't grown to the point that we had our heads blown off as soon as we came above ground. We slid behind the ruins of the starship that was still sticking out from below the desert sands.

The dead guardian differed from the one in the Spire. It was four times as large, with a body that looked more like a gorilla than the other had. Still, somehow the Crimson Kings had slain the mecha giant. Its twisted body lay across the landscape like a sinking ship, as fighters descended from the sky above.

180

'Okay, we have to move if we are going to survive,' Gorge had jumped up on a projecting girder and was studying the situation, 'it looks like there are three or four guilds at work here: the Crimson Kings are gunning for us, but they are being held back by Lady Gray in alliance with the Astra Exploration team. She's probably promised them study rights to the planet and dungeon.'

'How are you getting this information?' asked Kira.

'Remember, I'm tapped into everything. Lady Gray's Titan is in the atmosphere and I can hear them talking to one another, bits and pieces mostly, I can't concentrate on everything but I got just enough to know we ain't alone down here.' Tapped into Lady Gray's Titan? I couldn't believe it. If anything she was probably letting him listen while keeping tabs on us at the same time.

I was relieved. Gorge had played a part in a large share of famous battles and if we were going to survive out here, following his lead was our best bet.

'Three Titans and several cruisers are firing at one another above us, looks like the Kings are playing their biggest hand yet, forces from six different quadrants have pulled together and dropped out of the world gate,' Gorge paused, 'nearly every resource they have is being put to use.'

'New waypoint,' Cass looked up at me from her map, 'we have to rendezvous with Kilo-squad and regroup, they are going to escort us to a safe rally point so we can get off world.'

'Kilo are south of us,' Kira said.

'Get ready!' Gorge shouted as we stood behind the cover of a substantial protrusion. A blast of energy flew overhead, destroying the hole through which we had climbed. The Crimson Kings were making their move. If we had made it to the surface any later we would all be dead.

Battle screams from the Crimson Kings troops mixed together with those of the refugees trying to flee. The refugees were heading towards an aid ship called the *Dauntless*. The aid ship was run by players that helped other players that found themselves in a tough situation. There was a cost, of course, and no doubt the *Dauntless* was making a fortune. As a Corpse Diver we were forbidden to use such contacts and would have our contracts terminated if we did, however, this situation might make for an exception.

'We need to follow the refugees, we can escape with the *Dauntless* and have them take us back to the *Ibanez*,' I said.

'That will break our contract!' shouted Cass at once.

'Not necessarily, since I am paying you for the mission I can pay for your passage: any means necessary to escape,' Kira said.

'We can work it all out when all of our lives are out of danger,' I pointed towards a Crimson mech walking our way. The Astra Exploration group were retreating and the Crimson Kings were coming our way. A private yacht flew across the sky above us. The *Youthful Indiscretion*. It had a polished hull covered in scorch marks and was equipped with a single luxury suite and ion defence canon. On the side was the logo of Sun-blossom Studios. They had been filming the action, only now it looked like they had gotten caught in the middle of the battle.

'Kilo squad is going to cover us,' Cass said in an encouraging manner. I didn't believe her. I trusted her, but I knew she was wrong in this case. The Crimson Kings were out for blood and nothing would stop them. Not to mention Kilo squad weren't exactly special forces, while *Dauntless* had players with abilities that would and could protect us.

'I'm going to the *Dauntless*; you can follow me or not.'

Cass shook her head. 'Fine.'

And looking around, I could see that everyone else agreed it was our best option as well. We waited another minute before moving. Then, cloaked from the Crimson King's radar by Kira, we slipped past the mechs that were converging at our last known location. This was our chance to join the refugees: now or never.

Luck was on our side and we didn't have to fight our way through. Having turned herself invisible, Nel followed close behind us. She could attach herself to the outer hull and follow us from afar until we were able to meet back up with the *Ibanez*.

The *Dauntless*'s soldiers were scanning the profiles of all whom they let aboard. Most were NPC characters, while some were actually players caught up in the fight. I noticed several of these players were aligned with the Crimson Kings but I couldn't make out whether they were traitors or spies. Either would call cause for concern. While not everyone would know our faces, thanks to the camera, those aligned with the Crimson Kings would.

We sent Chaz in first. He behaved as if unaware that we were using him as a guinea pig, though I was sure he knew it. He was the only one of us that didn't have a target pinned to their back. With a thumbs up, Chaz made it through their security check and turned to enter inside.

Time slowed as fire erupted from the interior of the *Dauntless*. An explosion. A bomb set off by one of the passengers. *Dauntless*'s soldiers ducked for cover. I saw Chaz's body fly backwards towards us. He was alive. Just barely. His health was in the low twenties. Kira rushed towards him and gave him an injection. As my ears rang, I looked around and saw crew from the *Dauntless* fall to the ground, their health zeroed out. We should have seen this coming. I tried to scream but my mouth wouldn't move. My body was telling me to log out of the game and forget all of this but I couldn't. I couldn't abandon everyone after all that we had just gone through…from out of the frying pan into the oven. That old-world expression echoed in my mind. Damien use to say things like that a lot. He wasn't the only one though. Lady Gray had said it to me once, a long time ago, when I first joined the Corpse Divers and watched an orientation video. She had said joining her clan was both the best and worst mistake I would ever make in my life…that being a Corpse Diver meant more than just playing a game…that I, as a new recruit had jumped head first from the frying pan into the oven.

Bullets were flying across the field. More soldiers were falling. I could see the shadows of mechs behind me. Hand to her mouth, Cass was calling for an airstrike, screaming at some holographic person. Nel was visible again. Gorge's mechanical arm was missing and the Youthful Indiscretion that had been flying away from the battle before was crashing.

The Crimson Kings had come for us.

> ### Pro Tip
> Know your enemy.
> Strategize and plan accordingly. Sacrifice if necessary.
> Push them in the direction you want them to go by making them believe that it was their decision.

13.
Lure

The sky had turned red. As my hearing came back, I could hear refugees screaming and guns firing (at us?) from the haze of smoke that surrounded what was left of the *Dauntless* and the *Youthful Indiscretion*. Only one of the three cameras that had been along for the ride was actually looking at me now. The other two were focused on the chaos around me.

A figure emerged from the smoke. He was wearing solid black body armour with a golden skull mask underneath a hood; there was a rifle in his hand. This wasn't the same masked figure I had seen kill Damien in the Cold Zone but there was something familiar about him. It was the leader of the Crimson King's honour guard. As Gorge stood in front of me, holding me back with his mechanical arm, I could feel the rage building inside of me.

185

How many players had just died because we had walked into their trap? The CKHG was named Set. His profile was public and I was easily able to scan most of it.

NAME: SET

Age: 21	Class: Tech-Mage
Level: 60	Health: 150
Status: Alive	Stamina: 105
Mana: 100	

Load out: M7-7 kinetic Rifle, Star-killer (melee) Smoke grenades.

'Well, well, well…look what we have here, looks like a couple rats that got caught in a trap,' Set said, laughing, 'not the one I had planned mind you but I guess it will do; nice job Ra.'

A second soldier walked out of the smoke and threw the head of one of Kilo squad's members down into the dust, 'our vengeance waits.' This second figure, Ra, looked similar to Gorge: he had an Orc-like appearance with red skin and cybernetics across the whole of his body. He looked more machine than man and his limbs were auto-cannons. Like something out of a comic book. He too was wearing a golden face mask over his usual helmet, along with a hooded black coat. Unlike Set's mask, which was a skull, Ra's was more human in appearance. I couldn't read his profile and when I did try I felt my vision blur.

Just trying to get a scan on him was a dangerous thing.

'You have us, let the refugees and other players go, end this siege,' said Gorge.

'As if. You think we're going to let the Lady get away with what she did to us!' Set was shouting. The second figure, Ra, put his hand up and at once the smoke seemed to begin to clear away and several soldiers that were firing on the refugees from behind the smoke stopped. The fighters above seemed to stop as well. Angrily, Set turned to Ra and snapped, 'what the hell? We aren't actually going to listen to them are we?'

The second figure didn't say a word that we could hear. Instead, he communicated with Set and the others by some other means, a private channel or even text. *Bane* had built in several workarounds for access to allow players with disabilities to immerse themselves inside the game, including a link that allowed players that were deaf or mute to communicate via text.

With Ra's hands being replaced by canons, we weren't able to see if he was actually moving his fingers or not.

'Ra asks that you, the one named Breq join us, become a member of the Crimson Kings and all your sins will be forgiven and together we will share with you the secrets that will allow you to cross into the cold,' Set said as though reading, then, in his more natural voice added, 'cross into the cold? What does that mean?'

I knew exactly what Ra meant but I wasn't going to take his deal. The last thing I was willing to do was abandon my family. 'No.'

'Fine, not the game I wanted to play but we'll do things your way,' smiled Set, 'looks like the boss wants to take both of you alive back to the Spire, collect the bounties on your head. Your lady up there in the sky: looks like she's in for one hell of a nasty surprise,' Set might well have been laughing as he pointed upwards towards the sky.

'No, that can't be possible,' said Gorge.

I was shaking. 'What? What's not possible?'

'The *Wave Maker* is falling,' said Gorge.

'That can't happen? They can't take out a Titan?'

'Three against one; the Crimson Kings have brought everything to this siege, sacrificed an entire Titan against the guardian and now have two more colliding into your boss's ship,' Gorge shook his head in disbelief. Cass was standing behind us now, while Kira, holding Chaz, who was still recovering, was holding him up against he limped towards us.

'Disarm yourselves now or logout,' Set ordered.

'Perhaps we can compromise; maybe take a few pictures; make amends,' I heard Nel's voice from behind us. Although Nel was an AI and a part of our team, this intervention and attempt to speak for us all was unprecedented. Something strange was going on. 'I believe that if we all become friends we can do wondrous things,' Nel continued floating towards the front of the line. Set and Ra were standing on higher ground than us.

'Stand down robot,' said Set.

'I don't actually stand, think of the adventures we could have: the Corpse Divers and the Crimson Kings...we could be King Divers, all of the quadrants could be ours,' Nel stopped just in front of us.

'I said, stop talking,' Set was getting angry. He lifted his finger, poised to order one of the mechs to fire on Nel.

I wanted to scream. The Crimson Kings were no better than Lady Gray: carelessly decimating another planet along with innocent players and NPCs.

Nel's somewhat mocking voice continued, 'it could be so easy.'

None of us logged out or disarmed.

'Doesn't look like they are taking this seriously,' Set said, looking across at Ra, 'should I show them how serious we are?' Set was smiling again as he took out a small knife from behind his back and began to cut his arm. With his arm bleeding, he scattered drops of his blood on the ground in front of us. Hands, just like the nanites from the dungeon, began to emerge from the ground. We stood back and readied our weapons. Kira, still holding Chaz, moved away, taking cover near some of the soldering wreckage from the *Dauntless*.

'I tried doing this the easy way,' Set said.

A creature that looked like a sabre-tooth tiger, made of metal and black bio-organic fluid began to take shape. Set was a tech-mage and his blood must have been infused with nano-machines…nano-machines he was using to create the mechanical golem that now stood in front of us.

'Nice kitty,' said Nel unperturbed, 'remember it is not too late.'

The creature roared but waited for Set's command.

'Interesting, why don't they shoot us?' muttered Gorge, looking towards me.

'Capture,' Set said to the creature.

'Never mind,' Gorge's question had been answered, as Set marked Gorge, Kira and myself with his finger.

'Kill the rest,' Set was pointing towards Cass and the other players, including Chaz, that surrounded us.

'Can we take it?' I asked.

King Golem
Level: 30
Hostile

'Sure; it's not all his strength. He's probably just baiting us again,' said Gorge.

'Very well,' I replied. Set could only conjure creatures half his level. He had shown us a weakness. Plus I knew we weren't alone. Kilo squad might have all been killed but for sure there was a second team in play. Like the Crimson Kings, the Corpse

Divers weren't so hasty as to come unprepared. By rambling on about making peace, Nel had been buying us time.

'Now would be a good time to get down,' Nel said turning towards us.

From several hundred yards behind us, Shiru fired a shot at the tiger, just as we ducked our heads down out of the way.

The golem's health fell about a quarter of the way down. Shiru was firing with bullets strong enough to tear through a small fighter. These might have cost a fortune to buy or craft, but there was no better time to use them than now. Echo-1 were behind us, watching the whole thing, waiting for the right moment to strike. As the smoke continued to clear, it became evident the Kings were surrounded.

'Damnit,' said Set ruefully.

Gorge almost broke out laughing. 'Didn't you know?'

Set looked at Ra. 'Can we kill them all now?' he asked.

Now it was Ra's turn to looked at Set and back over to us. The three mechs that Ra had earlier ordered to stop firing turned their guns towards us.

'Give up now and we won't kill your characters,' Aiden's voice echoed around us.

'More blood for our brothers,' Set said, motioning for the mechs to fire. At that moment three shots ripped through the smoke and air around us. All three mechs dropped. Pierce, Shiru, and Brand were with us too.

'We aren't alone and we don't have to run,' I said with relief.

Set looked over at Ra again, 'please, I have this; we don't have to go that far. This was supposed to be easy, we had them.' He sounded like he was begging. 'There is honour in dying like this,' Ra answered, as one of his auto cannons turned into a hand reaching out and grabbing Set's mask. He began squeezing it in his fist, killing Set and breaking the mask to pieces. The golem began to react as if it had been set on fire.

Name: Ra

Age: Unknown	Class: Tech-Mage
Level: 90	Health: 250
Status: Alive	Stamina: 300
Mana: 200	

Load out: Unknown

I could see it. He had been hiding behind some kind of artefact. Both masks were artefacts. A master and an apprentice. Ra had killed Set and absorbed him into his own being. It was brutal. I bet even Gorge had never seen anything quite like it. We were up to three cameras again now and all of them turned towards Ra and the sabre-tooth tiger that was evolving to take a new form.

```
King Golem Type-II
Level: 60
Hostile
```

Shiru fired several more shots before jumping away as a Crimson attack ship flew down from the sky bombing his location. Shiru wasn't dead but it would be awhile before he could reload and fire again. For now, he had to avoid the attack ship. The rest of Echo-1 moved forward towards us, joining our fight against the King Golem Type-II. Even Nel had joined the fight alongside us, firing at the creature with a stun baton. As I fired at the creature alongside Gorge, Cass, and everyone else, I could feel the electricity through the air and the hair on the side of my arms stood up. Beside us stood dozens of refugees, those who had survived and had heard everything that was happening. Both players and NPCs joined the fight, as dozens of us fought to take down the creature in a battle that felt like it had turned into some kind of in-game event.

With hand gestures that commanded the golem like a puppet, Ra stood back. He had revealed himself completely now. His face was young with black hair. It seemed like he was blind in one eye and had been in an accident. A scar ran down across his neck, where it looked as if his throat had been slit. He moved his fingers quickly, giving commands to the Crimson King army that surrounded us. We had just barely survived their trap long enough to take back the advantage.

A Jocia Trader flew overhead. It was a courier starship. Attached to it was a cargo container that dropped about fifty yards away from us. We began to run towards it, hoping that it was some kind of gift from our allies. Our assumption was correct. The Jocian starship had been hired by none other than Naomi. On the side of the container was a note. 'Thanks for naming your rifle after me, I hope this helps.' Inside the container was a blue mech. The kind made for a peace-loving, electricity-wielding robot.

'Nel can you interface with this?' I called out.

'No problem,' Nel answered, flying towards the mech and integrating with it the same way that she would integrate with a starship. The mech's head looked like a larger version of Nel, with a small thin torso and long arms and legs. Each hand had four fingers and attached to the back of the blue mech was a rifle. There was an auto-rifle alongside it as well. The mech stood about thirty feet high, with an eight foot rifle. There was a small battery pack attached to its back along with several other plugs and wires wrapped in cloth. Taking control of the mech, Nel immediately ran up to the golem, slamming it into the ground head first and firing into its torso, ripping it apart.

Naomi's Grace
Medium Mech - Hybrid

A robust frame with a closed cockpit with four repulsors, two on the back of the legs and two on the shoulders along with two fusion jets attached to the back of the torso. This blue mech was custom designed in only a few hours. Commissioned and paid for by Moonrain Media.

Weight: 7 Tons (with a thick ballistic shell)
Health: 2000
Speed: 8
Agility: 5
Weapons: Primary - Large TX - 7 Auto Rifle (100 Damage 200 RPM)
Secondary - Large M7 - 3 Auto Canon (50 Damage 300 RPM)
Melee - Great Sword of Alet (300 Damage)

14.
Mercy

Quick Lore

When humans came through the first world gate and found themselves stranded at the Spire, the Chel didn't approach them. Instead they waited for humanity to come to them. The first humans found they couldn't interface with any of the Chel technology which was operated via a genetic code and so an expedition was led inside the lost chamber. The first dungeon. Inside the chamber the entire expedition team disappeared, however, soon after Chel technology was compatible with human genetics.

Even at level 60, the golem stood no chance against Nel and the rest of us. After five minutes of fighting, Ra stopped moving his fingers. Ra's life force was being drawn into the machine, but that still wasn't enough. The golem type-II stopped moving and began to dissolve as it tried to crawl away from Nel. After it dissipated completely there was silence and Nel turned her rifle towards Ra. Ra took off running.

I ran after him as quick as I could, rounding a large piece of debris to find him standing at the edge of the ruins of the *Youthful Indiscretion.*

'It's my turn now,' he said, before running inside. I slung my rifle down at my side and took out my sword. I thought about firing but it seemed like a waste of ammo. This was over and all of us knew it. Ra was running for his life now. I soon caught up to him near the bridge. He vanished before my eyes as the blast of light appeared straight behind me. I was blinded for a moment. A stun grenade? No. It was a flare.

'Awww, did that hurt?' he mocked me, disappearing again. Despite the fact I couldn't see him, his footsteps were echoing around me.

This wasn't a chase. Not like I imagined. Ra was using implants. Some kind of stealth. Ghosting. Spectral armour? I picked up my rifle and tucked my sword away. I should have shot first. I turned back towards the hallways that led outside. Some intuition told me it would be better to go back then blast the wreckage from orbit.

I soon found myself drowning. Mud began pouring in from outside as the walls began caving in. The longest I had ever held my breath under water had been two minutes. My parents use to take me swimming at a local park. 'It is good to get out,' my father would say. I thought once I had set a world record. As the mud poured in now I held my breath for two and a half minutes before finding a pocket of air that led to another level above. Ra thought he could get rid of me. Something about the chase brought fury into my mind. I was filled with rage. I moved faster, knowing my life was in danger, that I could lose everything because of one simple mistake.

Finally, I reached a door. An armoury. My luck was failing me now. There was nowhere else he could have run. I opened the door and dropped down to my knee, firing several shots. If he was invisible, I would have to hope I hit him before he realised I had caught up.

'I FOUND YOU,' I shouted. Ra was standing in the corner of the room. He moved towards me. His mouth gasping. Everything went red. All around me I saw images of Damien. Ra's body was wet and I could sense the cold coming off of him.

Behind him several more creatures appeared from pools of black goo. He was summoning wolves from the pools. Then Ra looked like he was coming at me from every direction, that he was filling the room. Damien; wolves; darkness. I felt like I was losing my mind. I screamed again and everything disappeared. Suddenly, I am face-to-face with a bizarre soul of decay and heat. Six crazed eyes stare at me with a terrifying grimace and another moan surges from its thin mouth, expressing unfathomable agony. Four thin horns adorn its head, which itself is almost bark-like. Chains wrap around it, as if to keep the creature contained; the creature seems to take pride in this, before taking a step forward, its two legs carrying firmly its infernal body with a sedated energy. The creature looks at me for what feels like hours, but as the seconds disappear it seems bored with my presence.

'Mercy,' Ra called out. We were standing back outside the wreckage of the starship. I had dragged him out, breaking his arm in the process. The only reason he hadn't logged out yet was he was begging for his life. He must have set his pain receptors to their lowest point. Looking around I could see why *Bane* was a mature game. Why those too young to understand couldn't play it.

'Was there mercy for the refugees you killed? the NPCs? The players whose games you ended? What about the crew of the *Youthful Indiscretion* or Lady Gray and all of the crew aboard the *Wave Maker*? Was there mercy?' I was screaming, but I managed to check myself and wait for Ra to give a response.

'There was no honour in what you did to Orithyia: my home, my family has fallen apart, I offered you a chance to escape fate, to level up, the secrets of the game,' Ra was pleading for his life. There were no secrets I couldn't discover on my own but something he had said earlier had stayed with me. That he would help me 'enter the cold'. Did he know what I was truly after? Did Kira talk to him? Or someone else at Moonrain Media? I wanted to take Ra prisoner, to interrogate him. There had to be a way to find out what he knew.

I threw him down on the ground and stepped away. By the time Nel fired upon him, it was already too late to take him prisoner. Ra had logged out just seconds before abandoning his body and his years of investment in this character. Mercy had been lost. Ra was dead. He would have to start over at level 1 just like thousands of others.

'You are one wicked little bot,' said Gorge, 'that was brutal. Even for me as a spectator.'

The remaining Crimson Kings on the surface surrendered to the Ad Astra Exploration society. In space, the two Titans that were working against Lady Gray jumped away, retreating to the far off reaches of space. We were victorious again. The Crimson Kings who had come after us were gone. The Battle of Rem had been won in our favour.

Aiden approached me. I was so glad to see him, I was ready to give him a hug but instead he punched me in the face.

'Idiot, we ARE a team, all of us, YOU had no reason to run off like that; you are lucky you didn't get more people killed,' he breathed a sigh of relief, 'but I am glad you're OK.'

'Don't let him get to you, that was the most fun I've had playing in a long time,' said Brand, who gave Chaz a curious look.

'That was insane, I can't believe we survived,' said Shiru standing beside Pierce.

'You know, you probably just made that bounty go up another million,' laughed Eli who was admiring Nel's new mech, 'we need to get you back to the *Ibanez*, this new suit is a marvel.'

Several dozen ships appeared as time and space folded in the skies above. First was the *Gowaur Clipper*: passenger carrier The *Gowaur Clipper* had an elegant, white polished hull and long-range fusion engines with automatic repair systems. It was equipped to hold 320 passenger seats and a landing shuttle. At the moment it was empty and ready to escort refugees off planet. Next came *Robert Goddard*: research spaceship. The *Robert Goddard* had a rebuilt hull with large observation windows. It was equipped with an astronomical sensor system and was scanning the area around us as it would continue to do for days to come. Several drones flew around it as a defence mechanism. Another passenger carrier arrived soon after, called the *Solar Queen*. Empty, with enough room for 100 passengers, it landed on the ground and acted as a medical bay for refugees and players who were injured.

Another starship, dropped into view, *Light of Teva*: private yacht. The *Light of Teva* had a ring-like primary hull connected to several smaller ellipsoid structures. It was equipped with a single luxury suite and defensive ion cannon. It landed near the *Solar Queen* and provided a second option for refugees as well as protection from alien fauna and rogue raiders that still roamed the wastes.

All of the starships that came were paid for by Lady Gray. Maybe she felt responsible for the chaos in a way, but the truth was that each and every starship that landed had requested a visit from the five of us: myself, Cass, Kira, Gorge and even Chaz. Together we had become legends. Views had gone up exponentially. Our entire dive including the battle above had been live for the world to see and now we were the heroes of *Bane*.

In the aftermath, we found several piles of loot dropped by the golem that Ra and Set had created. The more interesting items that we procured:

The Punisher - Silenced Shotgun

Description: The weapon has its receiver located behind the pistol grip to save on weight. The pistol grip is made out of plastic. The stock is made out of red oak, but other stock materials are widely available. There is a spray-painted skull on the side of the stock, which has mostly faded away.

Level: 3
Damage: 40
Weight: 5.5 lbs
Weapon Type: Silenced Shotgun
Rarity: Rare
Impact: 10
Range: 3
Stability: 5
Reload Speed: 5
RPM (rounds per minute): 8-16
Affinity: 4
Sharpness: 7
Elemental: None
Critical Chance: 80%
Modifiers: None

Flaming Choppa - Auto Rifle

Description: A body made from melted chains, the Flaming Chopper is a custom designed auto rifle for those looking to melt their enemies with flames.

Level: 5
Damage: 80

Weight: 5.5 lbs
Weapon Type: Auto Rifle
Rarity: Rare
Impact: 10
Range: 8
Stability: 1
Reload Speed: 5
RPM (rounds per minute): 300
Affinity: 6
Sharpness: 6
Elemental: Fire
Critical Chance: 60%
Modifiers: Flamethrower attachment under sling.

Aiden, of course, stored the weapons but I wasn't too upset. We had made a small fortune for ourselves and the other divers and I didn't need to keep swapping out my weapons anymore.

All of us celebrated the fact that *Naomi* had levelled up again.

```
AKA Naomi.
M7-7 Ki / Energy Rifle

Description: Robot killer.

Level: 4
Damage: 65
Weight: 5.5 lbs
Weapon Type: Scout Rifle / Ki Rifle hybrid
Rarity: Rare
Impact: 8
Range: 8
Stability: 9
Reload Speed: 8
RPM (rounds per minute): 300 bursts
Affinity: 9
Sharpness: 8
Elemental: Unknown
Critical Chance: 80%
Modifiers: Bonus EXP gained against Robots, Bonus
EXP against Hollows
```

And I was less than a thousand EXP from levelling up again myself.

Before logging out, one last ship came. *The Lady of Lani* passenger carrier. *The Lady of Lani* had a narrow hull and an upgraded STL drive that required frequent maintenance. It was a luxury ship. Expensive. Made like a billion-dollar yacht. It was equipped with 100 passenger seats and a landing shuttle along with a pool, game room, and private suites. The entire ship had been cleared out and made available for us and the rest of Echo-1.

Inside *The Lady of Lani*, Kira found me and took me aside. Kira was an expert at slicing and data mining and while we were taking a quick break she had been busy extracting information from the data in Ra's equipment.

'Breq, there is something I found that may be of some interest. I dug this data cube from Ra's mech, if I hadn't put so many points into hacking it would have been impossible to crack.'

Inside the Spire, inside the chambers below the Chel there is a dungeon. Inside the dungeon is an artefact. An artefact that alters time and hides player levels from the game structure, allowing them and others connected to them to pass through quadrants without restrictions.

Ra wasn't lying. There were secrets.

15.
I-U

Quick Lore

A young monk ventures fourth into a portal made of fire. When he emerges he finds himself met by a wonderful world. Snowflakes fall from the air as he stands in a thick layer of snow. The light plays tricks on his eyes as shadows cover the landscape. His imagination goes wild as he fears he has crossed into a world of treachery and lies. After a minute, he can hear the songs of strange creatures. Some look at him as he moves forward, pushing his way through the cold. He prays that they have no ill will towards him for he knows he is nothing more than a trespasser, a stranger in a strange land that might or might not be a threat to all they hold dear. He keeps his distance. He sets his eyes on the horizon and begins his life as an adventurer, a wanderer, an explorer in a new world. With some courage, some resourcefulness, and a bit of luck, he might actually survive. Even if this place becomes his deathbed he knows...he's known...from the moment that he walked through the fire this place became his new home.

I should have stayed logged out when I had the chance. I managed to get a bite to eat and a small nap but just as I started dreaming I was called back to action. Woken up by one of the security guards that now stood outside my penthouse. I had two guards in total at my door now. Two guards that would accompany me anywhere I went in the real at all times. I wasn't a prisoner per se, but every move I made had to be recorded. I couldn't just wander off on my own. Apparently, I had started getting death threats and my mail was now being monitored. The guards were protection but a part of me wondered if they were trying to hide something. I lost access to all of my personal social sites: I was told it was too dangerous, Keen Industries had hired a public relations officer to post for me. This news didn't make me too mad, I barely used any of it. Still, it felt strange not being able to look up other players or friends. I couldn't look at Damien's profile anymore either or bring up any of our video files, gameplay or not. I couldn't even contact Hannah anymore.

Update 1.11.8 found.

Access granted.

I went through it all again and came to back inside *The Lady of Lani*. A message had been sent to me by Aiden asking that I meet him on the bridge. Kira, Gorge, and Chaz had been asked to attend as well.

The inside of the *Lani* was sleek and clean, unlike on most ships, small robots maintained both the inner and outer walls of the vessel, continually polishing it twenty-four seven. The entire ship was automated. The rich didn't have to worry about leaving a mess or tending to their own discomforts. There was even food waiting for me as I gathered my newly minted gear and set out walking through the pristine hallways. There was something off about the whole thing. The ship felt too nice, too spacious. Even the bed was more comfortable than the bed I had been given in the real world. If I could have, I would have laid there for another fifteen minutes.

It was possible to 'sleep' inside virtual reality but most experts advised against it. Waking up in a virtual environment was dangerous and could cause cognitive dissonance. I couldn't blame those that had rested here though. In many ways this world was better than the world back home. It certainly beat the cot I had been sleeping on before becoming Keen Industries MVP.

Most of the ships I had been aboard, even Titans, were always dirty, lived in. Here, the scent of vanilla filled the air as I walked towards the bridge. I found the others gathered around. Not just Kira, Gorge, Chaz, and Aiden, the rest of Echo were in attendance as well. Kira was sipping some kind of tea while Gorge sat in the corner, Indian style, cleaning one of his rifles. Chaz was having some kind of beer. *The Lady of Lani* was exquisite, a paradise, and for a moment I couldn't imagine ever wanting to play the game outside this ship. In a way that was the beauty of *Bane*, the beauty of virtual reality. Worlds within worlds. In this space you could be whoever you desired and so long as you worked hard enough you could acquire power, skill and - if you were lucky enough - fame.

There were no cameras following me. None in the room. I thought maybe Kira might have had some hidden but that wasn't the case. For the first time in days my actions weren't being broadcast to the world. I gave a sigh of relief as I looked around at the others. The room was oval and had a giant table in the centre, surrounded by eleven seats. Egyptian artwork hung on the walls. Not actual Egyptian artwork but something made to imitate - with a slightly more modern take - the *Book of the Heavenly Cow*. I wondered was there a hidden meaning. The Ancient Egyptian text told the story of humans rebelling against the sun god Ra and losing. The loss brought death to the world as humanity was 'separated' from Ra who resided in the sky on the back of Nut, the heavenly cow. The loss also put different gods in different positions of power as they had been during the Middle Kingdom.

'Want anything to drink? This ship can make anything,' Chaz raised his beer enthusiastically.

'I'm good, thank you,' I answered. I only ever drank anything when necessary. Food, drinks, it all cost in-game currency and I could never afford to pay out unless I was using something to help with my health or stamina. I once thought about getting an implant to bypass all material needs but it would have cost six months of what I earned. Right now, it was all free and I still couldn't bring myself to avail of it.

'What about food? These robots can cook up anything from anywhere in the world, you can try whatever you like and the taste is supposed to be ninety-seven percent accurate of the real thing,' Chaz added.

'Not interested, thanks again.'

Aiden studied the room as I studied him. He seemed more highly strung than ever holding his shoulders back and his head high. His eyes and mouth looked almost completely motionless. After standing around a few minutes he asked everyone to have a seat. There were eleven seats total and ten of us.

'Who are we waiting for?' I asked before sitting down.

Aiden smirked, 'nice observation.'

'Not going to answer the question?'

'I can't say, I was called here just before you. Things have changed. Become somewhat complicated.'

'What's changed?'

'People are scared, scared of what all of you are doing out there in the wild. Other corporations are requesting that Keen Industries reel you in.'

'What do you think?'

'I don't think. I'm only here to follow orders.'

The room became silent. A door opened and standing before us was Lady Gray.

'Now that everyone is here let us get started,' she said. I couldn't help but think about the little girl I had met at the doughnut shop. How was it possible the two of them were one-and-the-same? In the donut shop she wore a light dress and was dressed like a kid but here she was older looking, full grown almost, ripped tank top made of ballistic thread hanging just above her waist with small plates of armour around her shoulders, her legs wrapped with leather armour over the top of baggy cargo pants tied with tribal bands. She had a necklace of Vrax teeth hanging down around her neck. Knowing her, she probably ripped them out herself. Along her back was a giant sword and across her hip a small energy pistol. Her hair was short and dreaded, braided with bands in some areas while the rest of her hair was being held back by a black bandana. Everyone was sitting now. Including myself. I hadn't even realized I had sat down. A holographic contract appeared before Kira, Gorge, and Chaz.

'The three of you already read it before coming to the meeting I assume,' said Lady Gray, 'by agreeing to being here, you three are honourary members of the Corpse Divers, crew of the *Lani*, *Ibanez*, and *Wave Maker*, and agree to the terms and conditions that apply, blah, blah, blah, etc., etc., I really hope the three of you read it and aren't wasting any of our time,' she finished.

Kira, Gorge, and Chaz (who was smiling like a kid in a candy shop) pressed down with their thumbs on the holo and it disappeared.

'Great, welcome to the Corpse Divers, let's get down to business,' Lady Gray pronounced, 'first thing first,' and she looked over at Aiden who in turn looked towards me. A moment later I was staring at my own reflection.

Aiden's face, body, it all morphed until he looked just like me. 'What do you think?' he asked, sounding just like me.

I wasn't sure what to say as he looked at me. Slowly, he moved away from his chair and moved towards me. The only difference between us was our clothes. I felt sick. Was this some evil ploy to replace me? I felt like I was about to be kicked from the game.

'A perfect copy in almost every way,' Lady Gray said.

'What is this for?' asked Gorge.

'Patience, we're getting to that,' the Lady said.

Aiden morphed back again. Changing his appearance so that he returned to normal. 'It's an artefact. Picked it up off the wreckage of the *Malevolent Crescent* from a quest I picked up called *Desolation, Secret of Trials*. A rare artefact that allows a player to copy the avatar of one other person. There is no time limit and I can change between my own appearance and the selected avatar at any time,' Aiden explained.

I found my voice. 'I've never heard of that quest.'

'It was an old one, I ran it almost three years ago and have been holding onto the artefact since, Lady Gray instructed me to never use it unless absolutely necessary,' he continued, 'the artefact is a once-in-a-lifetime drop, not the kind of thing you would hear about in message boards but rather something rumoured to exist but never found.'

Lady Gray began to speak, 'That said, the artefact was discovered shortly after a main quest had been completed. I have no question in my mind now that as we advance the main quest more and more strange and unusual artefacts will be appearing: the rules of *Bane* are shifting and we have more at stake now than ever before,' she paused, 'as of this moment Aiden will be taking Breq's place in front of the cameras.'

I wanted to scream. It wasn't fair. After everything I had done, they were going to toss me aside. I was angry. Angry at everything. Damien wouldn't have let this happen. I didn't say a word. I felt like my lips had been sewn shut. I wanted to beg. Beg for my life back. For forgiveness, but there was nothing I could do or say. Everything was being done for me and I was lost. Why Kira, Gorge, and Chaz had been brought into this was a mystery to me but it wouldn't matter soon. I stared up at Lady Gray who was standing and smiling now. I imagined her taunting me, waving her hands up in the air and pointing down at me. Casting me aside. Casting me out.

'With that said, I have a new mission for the rest of you.'

I felt like Lady Gray was looking right at me, through me. I could hear the significance of her words in her voice, the way she almost trembled when she spoke, 'Breq, Cass, Kira, Gorge, Chaz: the five of you are going to infiltrate the Spire and dive down into the tower's lower levels. You are to investigate rumours of a dungeon, a dungeon that holds the key to breaking into the Cold Zone.' My heart began beating faster than ever. A second ago I thought I was going to be begging for my life but now I knew the real plan… I was going to be fighting for it.

Lady Gray was one of the few people that knew the truth of Damien's death, of the players killed in the Cold Zone and what it meant for the game as a whole. She wasn't turning a blind eye to the truth even if she was too scared to risk everything she had acquired and venture there herself. The rest of us were pawns. Players in a game she could move from one place to another on a whim. She was smart. If I was in her position I would do exactly the same thing.

With the aid of holographic images, Lady Gray explained the plan to us. We were going to separate into two teams. The five of us would take the *Lani* and venture back towards the Spire while Aiden, disguised, would re-join the *Ibanez* along with the others and lead the Crimson Kings on a wild goose chase across the galaxy, venturing after an artefact called the Soulcursed Silver Edge, a rumoured sword of power that once belonged to an ancient alien civilization. The cameras would be following him, while we found a way into the deepest, darkest parts of the Spire and from there hopefully to the Cold Zone to confront Skull-Faced Man and avenge Damien's death.

```
Quick Lore
```

An unexpected encounter with a Wraith, a howl in the void, a planet in ruins. What once must have been a beautiful, thriving world is now nothing but dust and dying forests. There is a rustling of leaves and suddenly you're face to face with a young figure that looks like that of a man made of heat and embers. Two black eyes stare at you with a hollow dread and again a howl rages from its abysmal mouth in a show of force. This is not a man. Not a beast either. Nor like any creature on any other world. Two lights on dangling stalks adorn its withered head, which itself is covered in glowing tattoos. It looks more like a reptile now as your eyes adjust to the dark light. From gnarled nostrils set within a shriveled nose escapes the smell of death. Chains are stuck within its flesh; the creature seems to take pride in this. The creature bolts toward you and you can see four legs carry its glowing body smoothly with a chaotic energy. Two draconic wings extend themselves fully. Blackened bones and ripped membranes stretch upward before gently lowering again. The creature comes closer and closer, its eyes never leaving yours. The last thing you see are the teeth which glow white in the night as it opens its jaws and you can't help that you aren't running. You know you are going to die...you just wish you could catch one more glimpse of it, one more glimpse of the face of death.

I continued to read up on the many creatures that had been discovered across the worlds. Each quadrant had its own rich collection, each was filled with both the most beautiful and deadly life-forms. All of them surrounding the Spire, the core world, the first quadrant. The heart of it all. And at the centre, the Chel. The tower from which they bestowed powers to their most valuable players and from which all the energy in the galaxy flowed. A city protected by guardians.

Our meeting came to an end soon after Lady Gray explained the plan. The *Lani* was ours. Nel was also going to accompany us, her mech suit packed away in the hangar alongside several fighters. Once the others departed for the *Ibanez* we would be on our own.

16.
Far below

LOCATION: *THE LADY OF THE LANI*
DEEP SPACE
THE WORLD GATE *LUX AETERNA*

The engines kicked in as we crossed from the gate closest to Rem and passed through the world gate *Lux Aeterna*. We were weightless for a moment as reality seemed to shift around us. Passing through the world gates was a fast travel option that allowed us to bypass the need to use our quantum drives. This saved money, fuel and other expenses we would need to make our way into the Spire. Lady Gray had deposited a nice sum of cash, passed down to us from the company (who knew little of her plan). She was the driving force behind our cause. Unfortunately, this also meant her keeping track of Aiden and the others so that we could synch up our game time.

We had three days to prepare our dive into the Spire's underground, but first we had to find a way back to the planet. Aiden and the others already set out on their quest for the Soul-cursed Silver Edge. They were moving on the far side of the Spire, away from us, and had already run into trouble with a bounty-hunting guild called the Pristine Gunslingers, who were working alongside Avenging Claw. The two groups weren't really a threat to them and watching the live feed it looked like Aiden, playing me, was having a blast taunting them.

'So this is how everyone else sees us,' I said, watching the feed beside Kira and Gorge. I couldn't help but admire the way Aiden and the rest of the team handled the bounty hunters. We had one camera with us now, Kira's camera that recorded without streaming anywhere. Should anything happen to us the stream would upload to the net and everyone would know what we were planning. We were en route to the planet Maitreya, a jungle world with beaches, Icopods, giant reptiles, bio-tech mutants and several small settlements, home to the infamous MonsterStrong, Steelstars, Trembleriders, Lost Hooligans and a group of raiders Gorge use to be good friends with called the Silvermanes. Gorge was a considered a captain among them as well as an elite member of their own honour guard. He had fought beside them at the Battle of Vel, an enormous battle event that took place both on the ground and in space, in which five guilds battled for control of the planet Vel and the surrounding system.

Vel was an Earth-sized world but mostly mountains and rock. It had two small oceans on the surface and three more below the surface. Turns out almost all of the rock was salvageable. Mountains made of diamonds. Mountains that could be turned into starships, guns, swords, armour. I wasn't sure if the Silvermanes were all players or both players and NPCs but that didn't matter. The Battle of Vel was one of the largest events in the history of *Bane* with a total of twenty-seven Titans destroyed. Three of them destroyed from the inside by none other than Gorge himself. The entire battle had cost millions of dollars in real world revenue but once the Silvermanes gained control of Vel they were able to quickly re-coop their losses, selling resources and artefacts via the black market and the Spire. Gorge retired shortly after and started the Upsilon shop in the Spire. A part of his reward was a twenty percent discount on Vel materials for his service.

'It's like a game show, only they don't realize we're fighting for our lives,' Kira said.

'Fighting for their lives as well: if we do discover a weapon that can kill players in real life than there is going to be chaos,' Gorge added.

I looked over at him, 'if there is a weapon do you think we can destroy it?'

'We'll have to run tests, a full scan of it, find out how the man masked with a skull was able to do what he did and than find a way to patch it, fix the game. If that doesn't work we'll tell the truth and shut down *Bane*'s servers. Millions of players will lose their line of work, their escape from reality, and, like us their livelihood…but death is not a doorway, we can't allow innocent people to play the game if there is a weapon that can kill them,' Kira was earnest, studying the video she had shown me days earlier. She zoomed in on Skull-Faced Man. Before our quest even began, she had hired another mercenary group to investigate this strange character but they came up with nothing. Not even the best slicers could figure out Skull-Faced Man's true identity. With no other choice, Kira brought me into the fold, knowing my connection to Damien and the Corpse Divers. Gorge and Cass joining us was a happy accident. Chaz joining us…just an accident. Not that we didn't enjoy having him on the team, but when we let him know just how high the stakes were we all thought he would run, back out, never to log in to *Bane* again. We were lucky to be proven wrong. Chaz had already demonstrated that for a casual player he could hold his own and now that he was a part of our team he wasn't just playing for fame and glory, he was one of us.

'So why Maitreya?' I asked Gorge.

'Besides what I told you, we'll need the help of one of their techs, an old friend, to scramble your, our, player identities to enter the Spire. Without it we'll be disintegrated the moment we enter the system. Guardians, bounty hunters, raiders, NPCs: all of them want us dead, the rewards have even gone up. Five million each. Enough to live the good life both in-game and the real world,' he answered with a slight smirk. There was a part of me that wondered if he was having fun with all of this. This cat-and-mouse game against the universe. I felt like we were leading some kind of rag tag group of rebels in a resistance against the tyranny. Like all the epic stories of heroes rising from nothing that I had read as a kid. Now I was one of them. That was the point of *Bane* to begin with. To forge your own path and be a part of a greater universe. A galaxy of terror that only the strongest and most determined players could traverse.

LOCATION: *THE LADY OF THE LANI*
MAITREYA – UPPER
LOWER ATMOSPHERE

'Coming in hot, might want to buckle up,' Nel said through a loudspeaker. Nel, of course, was flying the ship at top speed down through the atmosphere of Maitreya.

'Are we crashing?' asked Chaz worried.

'No, of course not, Nel is an advanced AI whose primary concern is preserving the lives of our avatars. I don't think Nel would crash the ship,' I almost stopped mid-sentence as we hit turbulence and the gravity fluttered. I felt like I had three-Gs pressing against me as my insides turned on their side. Chaz was lucky, he had his pain receptors turned down for the moment. Something I knew he was going to change once we reached the surface of the planet...which in this case was about thirty seconds away. We weren't crashing but we were in for a rough landing as *The Lady Luni* scared the tops of trees and landed hard against the ground in a clearing just northwest of the coordinates Gorge had given us.

'It seems new information is available. The planet of Maitreya has less than one G of gravity,' Nel said, apologizing. I guess not even an advanced AI like Nel could have expected that.

Luckily, we were all alright. We grabbed our weapons, gear and Nel, along with several hover cycles. I decided to take along the grey and red jacket I had been using. It had become a lucky charm since I opened it up. Kira changed from her battle armour into a more casual stealth outfit that consisted of a ballistic shirt and skirt. She kept her combat boots from before, only I could see she had loaded a small dagger into the side. Chaz and Cass continued to wear their battle armour over their standard environmental suits except Cass had added a brown scarf to her outfit. Chaz also had a double-handed sword that had a secondary function allowing it to activate an energy shield. Gorge had shaved a part of his beard; he looked more orcish than human. Having taken off the arms, his armour covered only his chest.

The trees of Maitreya were massive. Three times the height of anything on Earth and ten times as dangerous. We were fortunate that Nel had been able to find such an open area to land. In fact, the open area looked like it had been cleared out for that very purpose.

Gorge pumped one of his shotguns, 'several different groups roam the jungles, a few of them friendly to the Silvermanes, but since we are aliens here they are likely to try to pick us off. This landing area is probably a hunting ground, a trap.' He had three times his usual gear. Partly because less gravity meant he could carry more, but also because he was planning to trade some weapons for information. Truth was, he had no idea where to find his 'friend' or even if his 'friend' was on the planet at this time.

Having discussed this, we made the gamble to come here anyway. Worst case scenario, it was nice to have a change of scenery compared to the deserts of Rem.

Three hours later, having dodged pit traps, laser mines, stun gates and wild boar we found ourselves in a 'tree' spying on one of the Steelstar camps.

'They have hostages,' said Chaz pointing towards a cage.

'Looks like a Silvermane soldier; why didn't he logout?' I wondered.

'And lose everything? Probably hoping for a rescue party, which means if we wait long enough we should be able to meet up with them as well,' said Kira.

'Not going to work, Silvermanes are trained so that even if they are captured they will continue to wait days, weeks, even months. Only under the worst circumstances do they sacrifice a character. Sometimes, other gangs will ask for ransom but its more likely they are holding the player hostage in order to take control of this piece of land,' Gorge told us sombrely, 'we have no choice, if we want to meet up with the rest of the Silvermanes we have to rescue the caged one and have him call for support.'

'Enemies are surrounding the starship,' Nel reported.

'We're three hours away, what can we do?'

'I could call the ship towards us and control it via sky-signal so that it will remain in orbit until we are ready to abandon the planet,' Nel answered.

I thought about this. 'Not a bad idea, but that leaves us one mech down and missing supplies and shelter should everything fall apart.'

'Not a problem. Controlling the ship remotely will be more beneficial to our quest.'

'Why didn't you suggest that earlier?'

'It was an unnecessary action; controlling the ships system remotely requires half my processing power and means I am unable to use certain abilities such as stealth, remote hack, and augmented weapons.'

'Okay, we'll watch your back Nel. Take the ship up and we'll call for it when we need it, maybe we'll get lucky and they will think we left the planet.' I was a little frustrated, but it was the best decision. Maybe I should have let Cass or one of the others make the call, but it seemed that alongside Gorge I was leading our little squad.

'Flying the ship, remotely, gives me an idea!' I exclaimed.

Everyone looked at me with surprise.

'Nel can you fly the ship over the enemy's camp, really low?'

'With seventy-five percent chance of success.'

'Great, that's good enough: bring the ship in as low as possible, focus all shields on the lower decks. When we attack, drop a cargo container from the bottom hull on top of their network antenna so they can't communicate with any other groups that might be in the area. Chaz, Kira, Cass flank them on the left while Gorge and I hit them from the right side.'

It took three minutes for the starship to traverse the three hours of terrain we had journeyed on foot. Taking off and frying the scouts, Nel directed the ship to hover right above the prison.

'Cass, take point, stay here and provide sniper cover to both sides,' I ordered, still wondering how the hell I had started to take charge. Cass, Kira, and Gorge were all still ranked higher than I was but they were letting me run this operation. I guess I was lucky, without having realized it earlier. Since we had been chased by the guardian in the Spire, the three of us had grown to trust and rely on one another. Cass and I had always been a part of the same squad but now things were different. It felt for the first time since starting my character with Damien by my side that I truly was a member of a team.

The shields of our ship covered the lower hull and our plan went off without a hitch. It was the first real success we had as a team with no losses and no repercussions. Even Nel was impressed. The lighter gravity made our attacks that much more deadly as we jumped across from one tree to another, taking cover on the high branches and picking the raiders off one by one. We gained a little experience from the player kills but not much. Most were low levels. The highest was a level 20 Paladin.

The prisoner himself a level 15 scout. Too young to have fought in the Battle of Vel, but still he recognized Gorge from footage he had been shown by his superiors.

'It's an honour to meet you,' he said.

'Thanks, we have a problem. I need you to contact Trace. I'm calling in a favour,' Gorge said.

'You can't be serious? Trace? That's impossible,' the scout replied.

Gorge looked at the soldier, frustrated, and grabbed him by the neck, picking him up and tilting his head sideways said, 'we just saved your life, your career; now contact Trace or, unlike the Steelstars, we'll show no mercy,' there was a slight pause as Gorge put more pressure against the scout's neck. For the first time since trading with him I remembered just how intimidating Gorge actually was, 'how is it that impossible?'

The scout mumbled the words, 'Trace is dead.'

Gorge threw the scout to the ground before reaching his hand down and lifting him back to his feet. When he crossed his arms I could see again how strong Gorge actually was. Cybernetic limbs, enhanced strength. He closed his eyes and asked, 'how did it happen?'

Trace was a tech-mage. Level 60. One of the best. He could slice into anything. During the Battle of Vel, Trace had been the reason Gorge had managed to sneak inside three Titans and destroy them from the inside without getting caught. Trace was a ghost. No one but the Silvermanes spoke of his legend. And now a Silvermane scout spoke of a man who came down from the heavens in a starship that looked like a rotting hand and had destroyed one of the Silvermane settlements...'capturing' all the players inside. The man had a skull for a face.

After the scout, named Yueng, told the story to us, we all knew what had happened. Skull-Faced Man wasn't just working inside the Cold Zone anymore. He had attacked a settlement here in our territory...the Silvermanes weren't captives: they were dead. Gorge uncrossed his arms and smashed his fist against a wall. The wall quivered and cracked, a loud echo of cybernetic steel beating on metal that swallowed us whole. Yueng looked terrified that Gorge was going to kill him but as Gorge turned towards the young player he managed a smile, 'where is the settlement?'

'Trace was working on developing some new tech just north of here, modding some old starships we found. We were stripping them down for the track but he had other plans for them. It was a pet project of his I guess, I don't actually know much about it..'

'Can you take us to it?' Gorge interrupted.

'Yes I can, but you won't find anything there...Trace's stuff has already been salvaged. Spare parts for the races; rumour has it if you win you get a key to his vault, recovered by the main sponsors of the race, a group called ShadowMask. The key opens a secret underground bio-lab where the settlement was. Least that's what I heard,' Yueng responded.

'When are the races?'

'Tomorrow: one race, a sprint from the beaches to grey gardens, an abandoned ship factory.'

'So are we going to steal the vault key?' I asked.

'No, we are going to win the race,' Gorge smiled back at me.

THE REAL WORLD

I managed to get a hold of Hannah via a DOS messaging system, practically analog, on one of the old net servers. A private network set up by Alexis, aka Lady Gray, so that I could interact with her and any other members of my team without the company knowing. I told Hannah bits and pieces of what we were planning and that she should ignore the video feed of Aiden and watch the races instead. She had already figured that out in her response to me, saying how Aiden stood a little taller than I did so the camera was always hovering higher above the ground.

Hannah sent me a real life picture. She looked much like her avatar only her skin seemed to glimmer and she had shorter hair with curls. I sent her a photo of myself in return. I looked identical to my avatar minus some muscle, and in the real world my hair wasn't quite as nice or shaved on the sides but that was how I chose to play the game. There was no point in being anyone else even if I had the chance to change the things I didn't like about myself. She admired that and promised that after I made my way back outside the Spire we would meet in the real. That she wasn't far and that she would be in touch. I was excited about the idea, nervous honestly, I couldn't wait. Every second I was logged out I was waiting for her messages. Despite everything that had happened, it was starting to feel like there was a silver lining.

> **Quick Lore**
>
> Besides tactical combat, *Bane* is full of other mini-games such as racing, gambling, endurance tests, 'box' games, and games of intelligence. Many of these games are organized by players or player organizations and have unofficial rules inspired by games of old. That is to say that many of these rules can be easily broken.

LOCATION: *THE LADY OF THE LANI*
MAITREYA - THE SOUTHERN REACH

The *Lani* landed in a hangar just south of the start of where the Silvermanes, Steelstars, and Hooligans were readying their vehicles to race. There were several dozen other factions running about too, including the media associations Fluke Arts, Superdoor Studios and Green Camel Games. Gorge, Kira, and myself were each adorned with black masks and hooded outfits to mask our appearance. We were entering the race under a subsidiary of Moonrain Media called *Terminal Velocity*. We were sponsored in part by Moonrain Media, Upsilon, and the Silvermanes, from whom Gorge had acquired a third generation fighter for us to use in the race. Grateful for our having saved his character, Yueng was a huge help in leading negotiations with the Silvermanes, convincing them not to turn Kira and I over to the Spire (though Gorge was free to do as he wished), as well as providing us fake identities to use while we were in public. The Silvermanes agreed to help us under the condition that if we won, we were allowed only one thing from Trace's secret vault and everything else belonged to them. We were also told we could keep the fighter, assuming we weren't killed during the race.

Gorge was a great mechanic and with the help of Cass and Chaz stripped the Gen-3 of unnecessary parts. Kira and I flipped a coin to decide who would be putting their life on the line and I lucked out again. Gorge even disassembled Nel's AI core and installed it into the racer. At least knowing that I wouldn't be alone made me slightly less nervous. We installed a cage, a small shield from the mech and refurbished the wings with carbon from the hull of the *Lani* so she would be lighter. Unfortunately, we couldn't install any weapons but I was able to take my rifle along with me. Since we weren't going to be breaching into space we uninstalled the ship's cockpit shielding. I would be flying in open air but the mask I was wearing would make sure I wouldn't pass out. I'd also have a small life support system in the ship. Each ship was equipped with a tracker that also acted as a detonator that would explode should the ship exceed a thousand feet in altitude, meaning we couldn't fly up and over. Bringing weapons and killing other opponents was acceptable, but to cheat by flying into space and back down to the surface of the planet below was not.

From the beaches of the Southern Reach to the Grey Gardens in the North. First place earned the vault key being auctioned off by the Silvermanes along with a hundred thousand credits. Second place would earn fifty thousand credits and third place ten thousand. Any racers to cross the finish line after that were given an achievement point that allowed them to enter another race for free. First time entrants like us had to pay ten thousand credits to compete and complete a practice lap. The practice lap was simple enough. Three laps around in and out of the jungle. All you had to do was survive.

```
Laps complete 3/3
Place: 5 / 12
Time: 3:47
Kills: 0
EXP: 200 XP gained!
```

With that done we had only a few hours to prepare.

The rules of the race were simple.

A hundred players move from point A to point B.

No rules.

TO: Hannah

FROM: Breq

SUBJECT: Gen-3

You wouldn't believe what I got myself into. I've attached some video feed. Never thought I would be a part of a racing team but it actually feels really cool. Terminal Velocity, our Gen-3, isn't much to look at but it's fast for what it is, plus it isn't like we are going to be flying across the sky.

I'm nervous, I feel like everyone is counting on me to win this but I'm just not sure if I can. I know Damien would tell me to try my best but he's truly gone now isn't he? I'm doing all of this for what? Vengeance? To save strangers who I don't know, half of whom want to turn me into the Spire for a reward. Aiden's been leading them on one hell of a chase. They've already jumped ship twice and trekked across three different worlds. He looks like he's having the time of his life.

I just don't know what to do. It's not like Damien is going to come back and neither is Kira's brother. How are we even supposed to know if Skull-Faced Man can kill without one of us dying? Maybe it was some kind of weird mistake and we are chasing a ghost.

I feel guilty but at the same time I think this is the most fun I've had playing Bane since I first began. And outside I still feel like a prisoner. I can't wait for this to be over. To be able to walk down the street again as myself. To go out without a bodyguard.

I'm glad we were able to find a backdoor to message one another. I can't wait to hear what you've been up to.

- Breq

TO: Breq
FROM: Hannah
SUBJECT: RE: Race

This backdoor is incredible. Thank Kira for me. I love the video.

You ARE a REAL racer. I can't stay on here for long. I've actually just started a new character. Naomi_2.0. Hard to believe it wasn't taken.

Believe in yourself. You've got this. You'll win.

I'll be watching.

- Hannah

17.
Terminal Velocity

A hundred players. Fighters, shuttles, escorts…most all of them stripped of weight, weaponized, painted in various colours and markings. Sponsorships sprayed on the sides. The smell of burning ion engines and thrusters in the air as we all line up in five rows, twenty players each. I was in the middle. We paid a little extra for the bump up but it wasn't much. Even if I had been at the front I would be shaking. Sweaty palms. I had brought my rifle along with a small bag of supplies in case I should crash. I even brought the egg with me hoping it was maybe my lucky charm. I wanted to piss myself. I could hear the roar of the crowd and I was sweating hard underneath my hood and mask. I was identified as Gen-3, the *Vigilante*. I was about to fall under a microscope, it wouldn't be millions of viewers but thousands watching me race. Half were probably watching in the hope of seeing some cool crash.

We had to wait for a loud crack. A carrier floated in the sky was going to jump with their quantum drive the moment we started. The jump would cause a small burst around us as the air pressure changed. Those with cockpits probably wouldn't feel a thing while those without protection, like myself, risked falling unconscious.

227

Once again I was high on luck. When it happened, I felt my ears burst, while beside me another pilot's eardrums were bleeding. I was safe for now as the crack ruptured the sky above, turning the daylight to darkness like an eclipse of the sun. There was silence and a moment later I was off, flying at over two hundred miles per hour in six seconds across an open landscape.

Maitreya, a jungle planet, was covered in dense trees and alien life both large and small. Dozens of red lizards ran across the ground in a stampede below us in the clearing as we approached the opening of the actual jungle. Several of the starships fluttered and slammed on their breaks, unable to make the first opening that led to a small path cut out specifically for the races. Many more racers slammed into the trunks of trees, igniting fires and foliage in waves of orange and green. The opening led way to a path for those brave enough to enter.

Nel helped guide me as best she could given the circumstances, but when we came to several cutaways in the path, we choose to go left every time. There was no telling when we would hit a dead end and that was exactly the point. Only a few ships flying above, slower than the rest, had the advantage, hovering just above the maze of green.

One path along led inside a small cave and we were flying straight into a waterfall. I took the risk. Gambling with my life and luck again. The water led back out into the dense jungle where Icopods waited to snatch unsuspecting players who had either slowed down or stopped at the exit. Several more players went down. A few activated their ejection seats, another item Gorge had stripped for weight. All in all, our Gen-3 was one of the lightest in the race. Gorge had done this before, it was probably one of the Silvermane's favourite past times. They had enough money and material to race in whatever way they wanted. There were twenty-two Silvermanes in this race and they sponsored them along with another ten including myself. It was easy to imagine that they had cut the same deal with them as they had for us. They wanted that key and whatever Trace had in his bunker. The real question was, how did ShadowMask manage to get their hands on it first?

I didn't have time to contemplate. The question came and went. I was relying on my instinct. The game. Damien had always said I was a natural fit for the world of *Bane* and now I was living proof. A living weapon…my first race and I was already in the top ten as we screamed around a rocky curve and passed into another clearing. I could see the others in front of me. There were maybe thirty racers still alive at this point but I wasn't about to look back and count. That would mean defeat. All of my flight training, honing my skills as a pilot, as a player had led to this moment. I was alone and yet I stood together with my team. The *Vigilante* was a symbol of what we could do if we put our heads together. I guess the only thing we didn't think about was a toxic rain storm.

'Poison gas dead ahead, the rain is toxic to organics, you,' Nel said, along with some other things I couldn't quite make out. The wind was so loud even with the mask and hood I had on. As we crossed from clear blue sky into black clouds I could see the smoke rise from burning cloth as my hood began to unravel.

'This mask is made from the hull of a broken Titan, wear it with pride,' Gorge had said, handing the mask to me only that very morning. It had been made from the remains of one of the Titans he had destroyed. A trophy that belonged to the Silvermanes and now it was the only thing between acid rain and my own skin.

Nel took control of the fighter as we slowed down and I covered the visible parts of my body. I was still wearing my diver gear, so luckily my arms and chest weren't in any kind of danger. Nel took us higher into the air and flipped the ship upside down. I was thankful Gorge had decided it would at least be a good idea to keep the five point harness plugged inside. The rest of my gear was strapped below one of the console controls, but a part of me still worried I would lose my lucky egg.

'Three minutes and we'll clear the clouds,' Nel said.

I counted the seconds till I had control again. With the blood rushing to my head I began to feel like I was going to faint. Then the life support system kicked on and a needle slipped into the back of my spine. Nel had been a good pilot but could only keep the fighter steady for so long. After all, Nel had been programmed to protect me at all costs and flying into a toxic thunderstorm was the opposite of that programming.

Three minutes passed and we turned right side up. Nel gave me back the controls and I saw my health had dropped to 55. Why didn't I feel any pain? Internal injuries. Nel's maneuver had managed to injure me but far less than landing...or crashing.

'I suggest we give up, we are now twenty positions behind,' Nel said.

'No way, we have to push through.'

And we did...right into another cave. This time the cave went down into the planet. I couldn't decipher whether the tunnels had been made for the course or if they were old mines that had been stripped for resources but it all looked the same. We had no visible light besides the ships in front of us and I copied their movements like a shadow in the night. Occasionally, a bright light would tell me I was heading in the wrong direction or that I needed to turn right instead of left. Again, another light, another race in front of us would appear and lead our way. We followed this course until we were back in fourteenth place and back outside in another clearing.

Laser fire came up from behind us. A player who had loaded their fighter - a new one - to the max with weapons. They had sacrificed speed for artillery. Not a bad plan but I was still too fast for them. Nel guided me, telling me when to zig and zag, turning a sharp left at one point to escape a missile that had locked onto us. The fighter continued their assault only to crash and burn as they focused too much on their target and not enough on the landscape.

Giant geysers erupted form the ground hundreds of feet high. I was in twelfth place now. Apparently, the fighter behind me wasn't the only one not watching the landscape change around us.

'Focus,' I said it over to myself again and again . As I looked down towards the ground, I saw a small shuttle crashing in front of me. It had been high enough to skip the trees and caves and strong enough to withstand the rain but the pressure built up from the planet itself erupted against their hull, melting it, causing a fracture that took them to the ground.

'Eleventh place,' I grinned.

I could see the other ships ahead of me and knew I wasn't far behind. I continued to push the limits of my Gen-3, shutting down power to my life support system and to some of the minor operating systems to increase thrust. We were overheating as we entered another jungle, slowing down from three hundred to one hundred and fifty miles per hour. Knowing these ships could go far faster than that didn't help me feel any better as a racer passed me: a shuttle that had been stripped bare besides a thin, almost translucent shielding that had protected it from the rain. I could see the pilot inside, a young woman about my age, wearing pirate gear with a sniper rifle across her back. I realized now I had no choice. I asked Nel to take over the controls and I unlocked *Naomi* from the sling I had attached on my waist and aimed. I fired at the shuttle, watching as the pilot fell backwards and the ship ran into a tree. The fire ignited behind us as we flew past. I aimed at the next ship in front of us. It was still far away but I had learned to become a damn good shot. I fired and felt my health drop as my rifle stole my own energy from me.

My rifle levelled up.

Naomi.

M7-7 Ki / Energy Rifle

Description: Robot killer.

Level: 5
Damage: 75
Weight: 5.5 lbs
Weapon Type: Scout Rifle / Ki Rifle hybrid
Rarity: Rare
Impact: 8
Range: 9
Stability: 9
Reload Speed: 8
RPM (rounds per minute): 300 bursts
Affinity: 9
Sharpness: 8
Elemental: Unknown
Critical Chance: 81%
Modifiers: Bonus EXP gained against Robots,
Bonus EXP against Hollows

Nel handed control back to me and began repairing the ship using a self-repair mode Gorge had installed in case of emergencies. Nanites broke loose from the wings of my Gen-3, leaving only crossbars to hold the two thrusters in place, but they repaired one engine and I was back to two hundred miles per hour. The same couldn't be said for my second thruster. I could feel the fighter pulling to the right as I relaxed and prepared to crash.

Out of the jungle and over a lake. I sank the right thruster into the water and watched as parts of it tore away but the spray was enough. More than enough to cool it. Three hundred miles an hour.

A giant sea creature emerges from the depths, tentacles grabbing two of the ships in front of me. I fly through dodging the creature's tendrils. I can see a large beak appear from the depths of the lake, like some kind of Kraken.

Three more of these creatures emerge and I find myself rolling through the sky like a leaf on the wind. Fifth place. No sign of the others. I begin to fear I'm lost or maybe I missed a turn but Nel assures me I'm on the right path. We're more than a third of the way. I look down at the egg and realize its gone. Cracked open. I feel something touching my leg. A small blue creature that looks like a baby fox with small horns across its head is rubbing itself against my leg. I loose focus for a moment before pulling it up into my lap where it tucks itself down below my arm.

By the time I was about to cross the finish line I was in third place.

It wasn't enough.

I lost.

```
Laps complete 1/1
Place: 3 / 100
Time: 3:47
Kills: 2
EXP: 500 XP gained!
```

18.
Sliver

Bane, sure it is immersive. A player can easily sink five thousand hours into it even if parts of it might feel mundane, like clocking in and going to work. Wait times, drinking, eating, taking elevators, flying from one place to another without fast travel, walking from A to B, buying, selling. All the immersive features that feel novel at first…people used to believe it would get old quick while others thought it would be taken for granted. Dozens of games provided similar worlds built on themes of racing, fighting, trading, exploration but none of them combined it the same way.

The more players immersed themselves, the more they found *Bane* a second life, an escape, a place to free their mind and for some even develop ideas. People made a business out of playing the game, crypto currencies, economy, a population of players that love and live it even the boring parts. So many worlds, so many ways to escape. Some set up pleasure palaces, some weapons shops, others joined guilds and chased adventure. Some even built manufacturing plants on planets creating an endless stream of goods, so long as they could collect the materials.

Grey Gardens had once been a pristine shipyard run by players and NPCs but now it was in ruins, a mass of mechanical pieces covered in green vines that rose from the ground. Every so often a tree would be growing where there was once an assembly line.

Pieces of leftover materials still lay scattered about in small ponds of toxic water. The entire area was coated in a small metal dust called the grey, from which it earned its name. Someone had built this place up only for it to be torn down and taken back by the fractal pieces that make up the world itself...

...And for that too to be torn down.

Losing was the beginning. 'This can't be happening,' I yelled out. Nel displayed an image in front of me of the winner. The ship that won belonged to a pilot that went by the name Lappa. His avatar was tall and skinny, decked out with cybernetic arms and spiky purple hair. He had been racing for a group known as the Alpha Centauri Corporation but his avatar's tattoos etched across silver metal and tan skin displayed red sigils and the bottom of a skull across his chin. They were a dead giveaway as to what organization he really belonged to. Crimson Kings.

But still not the worst thing happening at the moment.

The egg, the egg I had been holding onto since discovering it inside the wreckage of the dungeon *Lockhead*, the egg I had been harboring from the deserts of Rem and all across the jungles and caverns of Maitreya had hatched.

No Name

Owner: Breq	Neutral
Level 1	Health: 100
Skills: Unknown	Stamina: 100
Mana: 100	

The creature, whatever it was, had become mine as a new alert in my user interface appeared for just a moment showing the creature's health, stats, and history. I quickly moved it out of the way, since I had too many other things to concentrate on at the moment but it was there and I could feel it.

Quick Lore
Familiars are creatures assigned to players like pets. Unlike pets however Familiars are connected to a player's life-force and cannot be traded, sold, or killed by players. Familiars are one of the most rare creatures in all of *Bane*.

I didn't mind that the egg had hatched, but it could have happened at a better time. Still, the creature's big round eyes glimmered with a purple hue that made it hard to stay upset. I'm not going to lie. It was cute. Like a puppy or a kitten with small horns and a long reptilian tail covered in small metallic scales. The creature was some kind of hybrid. Of what I wasn't sure. I was already waiting to hear Kira say that we had to to run a scan on it immediately, that we had uncovered some kind of new and exotic alien life.

At the moment though I was in over my head. The race was finished but something had gone wrong. Nel told me that the winner was already turning and flying back.

Three Titans came out of the air. Hundreds of ships detaching themselves and flying out from the sides like wasps around a broken hive. The race was over but we were still running for our lives.

I commanded the creature to stay still as I turned our fighter around and began heading back towards the forest. I still had a detonator aboard so I couldn't fly up and over the trees but I could easily go back the way I came. An explosion behind me. I could only hold out hope that the others weren't waiting for me there. That they had gotten out before any of the chaos. The three Titans had taken out the shipyard and now I was dodging debris falling from the air. Not that it was an issue. Since the beginning of the race I had started to feel like a A+ pilot.

Once again running for my life, I drifted into the tree line and back down the broken path and into the caves just as Nel began to receive a communication from *The Lady of Lani.*

'Have….Key…fast…can,' it was broken chatter and static. I couldn't understand but at least I knew they were safe. Kira was safe and that meant I had to have hope. The cave made certain I wouldn't receive any more of the message. What I heard was impossible to understand besides a few words. Words that would be essential to my getting out of this alive. I asked Nel to find a way to unscramble the message but we were already too deep and in the darkness. I had to give up control of the fighter to Nel, who had mapped a course based on our first run. The Crimson King, first place winner of the race was already coming up behind me. I could see a look of terror on his face. What was it that had him so afraid? My question was answered when Nel told me we were being followed by several FTC fighters, soldiers sent by the Spire itself, special forces division. Nel fed me intel but I could only concentrate on half of it. The three Titans were under command by someone named Nightswan, who was onboard the *Galactic Pegasus*, which, from what I saw, was almost twice as large as Lady Gray's own Titan. The two smaller Titans were named *Strength of a Devoted Dominion* and *Yell of the Collapsed* respectively.

All I could think was that they had found me. Somehow, someway, they figured out that it wasn't me on the camera, tracked us down to this backwater world and now they were here to finish the job. No. That didn't make sense.

The small creature stood up on my lap, looking back at the fighters coming after us with a snarl and display of sharp teeth. For a moment I was afraid if I commanded it to sit back down I would be attacked, or worse, the thing would jump out of the ship and make for one of them. I commanded the creature to back down and told it I had control.

Our survival was all that mattered. The Crimson King began flashing a light behind me, using it to guide me through the tunnels. He was only several yards behind now as I led us back into the jungle.

A message relayed to me through Nel: it was the winner telling me we had to work together to survive. Before I could respond the *Strength of a Devoted Dominion* appeared above our heads and he was gone. His fighter destroyed by a railgun. They were aiming down at us now from above. We'd be lucky if they didn't glass the whole planet.

My thruster began to overheat again and this time I had no lake to dip it in. I wasn't going to venture back that way either. I would rather be struck down by a Titan than face the Krakens again. I was the only one left. Several dozen other racers had already turn tail and had started to go back, I could see the *Yell of the Collapsed* had moved ahead and was picking them off one by one. It wasn't me they were after. Of course not. The key. The message; the static that covered Kira's voice. She was trying to tell me something and I just had to figure it out.

I drifted right this time: instead of flying into the jungle I flew beside it, using the tall trees to shelter myself from the Titan's line of sight. I thought about stopping but they would be tracking my heat signature and abandoning the ship would mean abandoning Nel, and after all we had been through I couldn't do that.

FTC (For the City): a group of soldiers that dedicate their lives to protecting the interests of the Spire and, most importantly, the Chel. Never seen in streams and rarely seen in any day-to-day activities. Many of the FTC lived off world in space colonies and on hellish worlds that were used for their training. I had heard rumours that half of the FTC were actually prisoners or people that had been kidnapped and forced to play the game a certain way. They had no identity. Their armour and masks were all colour-coded based on the terrain. Dozens of FTC divisions existed, including Torture, Crossbow, Paladin, Garrison, Covert, and Chaos. Those were the few I had heard of anyway.

Damien told me once about how he ran into an FTC officer on a dive not long after he had hit level 50 and it was the first time in the game he had feared another player (besides Lady Gray I'm sure). The FTC officer and Damien were chasing the same echo through the wreckage of a freighter. The freighter had become overrun with Hollows and while Damien was barely holding his own the FTC officer moved at ten times Damien's speed. Some kind of implant? Mechanical enhancement? No. It was a power given to the soldier by the Chel, some kind of sufficiently advanced tech that looked like magic. Damien gave up the chase and fled.

Given the attack and hunt that was on, the FTC weren't going to leave any witnesses this time around. They were known for being scary but this was beyond. Player killers. That was all they were in the end. In the sky above I could see what looked like a silver ship flying around the *Strength of a Devoted Dominion* and a moment later the entire Titan was descending towards the ground towards me. Nel gave me manual control and I pushed my fighter to the max, ordering the newly hatched creature to stay tucked down as we hit three-G. I could barely move to turn us away from a rock that seemed to appear from the ground.

The Titan was crashing. Behind me I could hear it tearing the jungle apart as it turned the ground to cinder. By the time I cleared it, there was ash raining down from the sky above and the silver ship that had taken down the Titan was flying in front of me with its hangar open.

The silver ship was *The Lady of Lani* and, said Nel, it had been newly refitted by Lady Gray. Tracking Nel they had pinpointed my location and come as quick as they could, taking out the Titan so that we wouldn't be destroyed mid-rescue. My friends had saved me again. I smiled and began to slow down, crashing to the ground inside the hangar before several Silvermanes appeared, putting out the fire on my thruster and surrounding me with raised TX-7 assault rifles.

'GUNS DOWN!' Gorge yelled, 'he's a friendly.'

Slowly, I lowered my hands which had been above my head and the Silvermanes lowered their weapons and began helping me out of the ship. The creature I had been keeping safe jumped up on my shoulder before landing on all four feet on the ground in front of me. The Silvermanes looked at it with curiosity, one of them pointing his rifle at it, 'he's with me,' I smiled removing my mask.

LOCATION: HANGAR
THE LADY OF LANI

Everyone else soon appeared and we were back in the air, flying away from the wrecked Titan and the fighters that were swarming around it like maggots. Moments after we came to a landing at the finish line in Grey Gardens, my entire team ran towards Nel and I. The familiar immediately took to Kira, jumping into her arms and licking her. I prayed its saliva wasn't poisonous. Given where and how we found the egg anything was possible. We were dealing with something unexplained, unexplored, and as far as I knew totally new to the game.

'It's a familiar! I never thought I would see one,' Kira said studying it with some kind of multi-tool device I assume she had been carrying with her for just such an occasion. 'There is evidence that it shares DNA with Chel!' she exclaimed.

240

'Are you serious?' I exclaimed, 'how is that possible?'

'Remember the dungeon? They were holding a Chel prisoner; now if I had to guess this is some kind of pre-cursor, a *proto-chel*. Some of the data we uncovered revealed that they were reverse engineering the Chel's genetic makeup in an attempt to duplicate their powers,' she showed me a holo filled with research data. I guess I knew where her free time had been going.

'I still don't understand? Why does it look like a fox?'

'Looks like a reptile to me,' said Gorge.

'It's possible that we all see it somewhat differently, some kind of active camouflage, advanced evolutionary trait, or that it somehow creates an image of something slightly different than what it is in our mind.'

'Like a glitch in the game?'

'That's one way to put it but it's not really a glitch, it's intentional.'

'I think it looks like a fish creature!' said Chaz chiming in.

'That's…weird,' said Cass, 'it's obviously some kind of wolf.'

'It looks like an animal with horns and a long tail to me. Its ears are sticking up and curving back like fox or wolf but now that I look at its face it kind of looks like a Komodo dragon,' I said.

Kira smiled, 'looks like a kitten to me. As it developed it must have been adapting to the world outside and since it travelled from one world to another and so quickly it developed this strange defence mechanism, hatching during the race and attaching itself to you,' Kira caught my eye, 'congratulations Dad!'

I shrugged. Sure. Why not. The creature seemed to understand commands pretty well and since I had no choice in the matter it wasn't like I was going to argue. It could be nice to have a side kick.

'That's great and all but what are we going to do now? This entire planet is under siege and we don't have the key,' I placed the creature on top of my shoulder.

'Give it a name,' Kira interjected.

'Not what we are going to do about the creature, about the vault key.'

'Yeah, Gorge and Cass already stole it,' Kira had an impish smile.

I wanted to scream.

'We used the race as a distraction. Now, give it a name!'

'I can't think of anything right now.'

'Boop! Bop; Spot,' Kira was ignoring me, focusing on the creature.

'MEL,' I heard Nel's voice coming from the wrecked fighter.

'No,' I said, turning about. The little creature turned alongside me following my movements.

'Something more masculine; how about Brutus,' said Gorge.

Both Cass and Chaz were silent but I could tell from their expressions they were trying to think of something to add to the discussion.

'How about Hatch or Hatchet since it y'know, hatched from an egg?' Chaz drew the shape of an egg with his finger in the air.

'I have a K-Dog named Hatch at one of my lairs,' said Gorge.

'You have a lair?' Kira said looking at him.

'Yes, I have a lair,' he said moving on. It would figure Gorge had a secret lair that none of us knew about.

'I'll think of a name later. Tell me how you got the vault key,' I said, trying to turn the conversation around. I felt left out. This was the first operation that the others had run without me since we started our journey on the Spire. I felt betrayed. Alone. Used.

'We'll do better than that, watch this holo,' Kira patted my arm.

I sat down and watched.

LOCATION: UNKNOWN
UNKNOWN

Gorge stared down the sights of his rifle. He was standing outside some kind of interior hallway with Kira and a dozen Silvermanes. The footage was captured using Kira's cube. They were aiming at an airlock door. All the lights were off and I could only make things out because the footage had been doctored. I could see the silencers that had been added to all of their weapons. Gorge, who usually went in loud, was wearing an all black stealth suit that hid his cybernetic features. Kira and the Silvermanes wore similar outfits, hers, however, had a red stripe across the side. Metal gave way and popped from the other side of the door as a ship docked. They weren't inside the *Lani*, it was some kind of Silvermane ship connecting to the shipyard.

'Ready,' Gorge called out. His voice stern. The Silvermanes grunted and whispered around him as a bright light appeared and everyone found cover behind a shield. They all kept their weapons trained on the door as a dozen raiders entered.

It took two seconds and they were gone. Rag dolls scattered across the floor. Three more raiders came from the darkness as the team entered inside the shipyard, fighting their way down several flights of stairs. Gorge, Kira and the Silvermanes dropped one body after another like they had been holding back this entire time.

'Incoming,' Kira yelled, taking point as a missile came from the raiders below. It was answered by automatic fire and the death of three more raiders dead. Gorge and Kira used single shots while the Silvermanes shot in short bursts.

Kira dropped into a crouch next to Gorge and smiled.

'You're crazy,' she said, raising her rifle, sighting out another raider. The stairs provided great cover, shielding their profile as they moved from corner to corner, firing at their targets from thirty feet on high.

Two more raiders waited at the bottom but they weren't firing. They had no idea what was coming for them. Only the dozen at that entered at the top had any idea that there was a threat. Gorge, Kira, the Silvermanes silenced the two and entered another room.

'We're going for the station, split, two teams, one takes comms,' Gorge pointed, motioning for two of the Silvermanes and Kira to follow him.

Kira nodded and let out a burst of suppressive fire as they entered another stretch of hallway.

'Traps?' she asked.

'Probably not expecting anything like this,' Gorge answered.

They used the opportunity to sprint down and dive into a hole behind a small crate. Gorge waited three seconds and fired, taking out the remaining raiders.

'Back on your feet,' he said.

'I'm right behind you, old man,' she called out, reloading her rifle.

'Is there any way you can scan ahead?'

'No problem…Five more raiders and a boss. We can trail them if we need to, by now they know we are coming, they might be planning something.'

'Advance, it isn't going to matter. Circle around me after I go inside.' Gorge ran forward and slid into the room ahead and took down four of the raiders before standing up. By that time Kira already had ShadowMask at gunpoint.

'Key,' she said, holding out her hand.

'You will pay dearly for this,' ShadowMask said in a deep groan.

'You're just another gangster, don't get your hopes up,' she smiled, taking the key and knocking ShadowMask to the ground.

'Not much of a boss,' Gorge said.

'Should we kill him?'

'First, Yueng, scan the key. Is it the real deal?'

One of the masked Silvermanes took off his helmet and revealed Yueng's face. He nodded his head and smiled confirming that Kira was holding the key to Trace's vault.

LOCATION: HANGAR
THE LADY OF LANI

Kira stopped the footage there.

'After that we made our way out and split into two groups to throw off the scent. Half of us came to the *Lani* while the other half made a run towards the other side of the planet; five minutes later the Titans appeared. We're assuming after ShadowMask departed, a message was sent to the FTC command who jumped here from a few systems over. Guess he had more friends than we gave him credit for and now they are searching for the key. It's likely he never had any intention of handing the key over to the winner anyway,' she said.

'So you didn't think I would win?' I asked.

'Not at all,' she exclaimed with a slight stutter, turning red. 'We couldn't take any chances.'

'You could have clued me in on the plan.'

'We were worried if we told you, maybe you wouldn't have given the race your all,' she said her face still blushing. She was probably right. Not to mention I would have wanted to be a part of their raid.

'So are we working with the Silvermanes?' I asked.

'Same deal as if you had won.'

'How long till we reach the vault?'

'Fifteen minutes, give or take, we are plotting a course that takes us out of view of the Titans, hoping they don't put any soldiers on the ground near there either or we'll be in for another firefight we don't have the resources for,' she answered. 'Now how about giving your familiar a name?'

'I still haven't thought of anything.'

'How about Blade!' Gorge said.

'Actually, I'm pretty sure it's a girl,' Kira said.

'How do you know that?' I asked without thinking, Kira knew everything, she had already scanned the familiar three times and looked it up and down in her lap while I was watching the holo.

'Ekke!' said Chaz.

'You know that is slang for a loser right?' Kira.

'Not a loser, just someone that doesn't go into crowds and draws a lot, I use to be a proud Ekke, thank you,' said Gorge. 'Sorry,' he added, taking the hint not to suggest anymore names.

There was a moment of silence.

'Aiko,'[1] I said.

'I like that,' Kira smiled, 'hello Aiko.' The little creature smiled.

I moved my finger in the air motioning for my user interface to appear in my vision. I studied it for a moment and gave my familiar a name.

+50 XP - 'You're #1'

---

[1] From the Japanese 愛 (ai) meaning 'love, affection' and 子 (ko) meaning 'child', as well as other character combinations.

I levelled up.

```
┌─────────────────────────────────────────┐
│              Level 33                    │
│          15 Points to Spend              │
└─────────────────────────────────────────┘
```

Adrenaline 45

Affinity (weapons) 15

Agitation 15

Animal / Aquatic Expert 35

Artillery 15

Attack Boost 5 (+5 Bonus)

Blast Attack Boost 5

Blast Resistance 35

Bleeding Resistance 45

Botany 5

Bow Expert 5

Capacity Boost 5

Capture / Tame 15 (+ 50

Familiar Bonus) = 65

Carving 10

Charisma 25 (+10 Bonus)

Constitution 5

Critical Boost 50

Critical Affinity 50 (+10 Bonus)

Defence 5

Detection (stealth) 30 (+10

Bonus)

Divinity / Fame 5

Evasion 5

Explosives 15

Fire Attack 5

Fire Resistance 5

Focus 35 (I add +5 points) = 40

(+5 Piloting Bonus)

Fortification 5

Gambler 5

Guard 5

Hacking 25

Handicraft (crafting) 5

Heat Resistance 15

Health Boost 15

Hunting (survival) 5

Hunger (cooking) 5

Ice Attack 5

Ice Resistance 15

Intimidation 5

Iron Body 5

Latent Power 5

Luck 25

Medical Specialist 15

Mind's Eye 5 (+10 Piloting

Bonus)

Navigator 5

Nullification 5

Paralysis Attack 5

Paralysis Resistance 5

Peak Performance 5

Piercing (Damage Boost) 5

Pilot 5 (+20 Bonus)

Poison Attack 5

Poison Resistance 5

Poison Duration 5

Psionic 5

Recovery 5

Stamina 25 (I add +5) = 30

Sheath Speed (reflexes) 5

Strength5 (add +5) = 10

Stun Attack 5

Stun Duration 5

Stun Resistance 5

Survival 15

Tool Specialist 5

Training 5

Name: Aiko

Level 1

Friendly

Mana: 100

Health: 100

Stamina: 100

Adrenaline 50

Agitation 15

Attack Boost 5 (+5 Bonus)

Blast Attack Boost 5

Blast Resistance 35

Bleeding Resistance 45

Charisma 75

Constitution 25

Critical Boost 50

Critical Affinity 40

Defence 55

Detection (stealth) 30

Evasion 25

Fire Resistance 15

Focus 35

Guard 5

Heat Resistance 15

Health Boost 15

Ice Resistance 15

Intimidation 20

Luck 25

Nullification 5

Paralysis Resistance 15

Piercing (Damage Boost)   15

Poison Resistance 15

Recovery 35

Reflexes 35

Stamina 55

Strength20

Stun Attack 35

Stun Duration 5

Stun Resistance 15

19.
Trace

TO: *Hannah*

FROM: *Breq*

SUBJECT: *Family*

As much as I try to tell myself it's just a game the truth is it is so much more than that. Life is all about making choices. I made a lot of really bad ones since I lost my parents. I can see that now. I turned my back on the world, turned my back on friends, the family I had left. I turned my back on the values that made me who I was. My father had worked in R & D, worked for Keen Industries. He once told me that what he was working on was going to change the world. That the world was changing, falling apart, that it had been falling apart for a long time. The oceans rose, millions died. Disease. Hunger. War. He told me how after the coast rose him and mom had lived on something called 'the raft'. It was a community brought together around barges and an old oil rig. It was one of many settlements. I envied it now. He told me of the freedom. Fishing from the sea. Catching a shark in the early morning of spring. Staring up at the stars in the middle of the night. In many ways I was like him now. A scout, living with my own community.

When I was young we lay on the roof and he pointed out the constellations and planets. Mars. Jupiter. I could remember watching meteors fall from the sky and looking at the moon through a haze of grey. Maybe that's why I like Bane so much. No matter where I am I can see the stars no matter how artificial they are. Before he died he also told me of the cold. Of the fevers. Of the coughing children and how the water had started making people sick. How humanity had turned their back on nature and so nature turned her back on humanity. When mom became pregnant the two of them left 'the raft' and found work in Recovery Zone. It was here I was born. Here that both of them died. Am I to blame for that?

Before working at Keen Industries my father was a part of a relief effort that gave food and shelter to the homeless. Maybe that was a part of the reason I ran away. Sleeping in the shelter, eating soup from the kitchen, wondering whether I too would catch a fever from the red tide. Living so close to the edge made me feel alive. I was lonely without them but I could look at others, others like me who had lost everything and I could see them. The good that they had done, the good they done for me. At the same time I was so angry. I saw the good that had been taken, stolen from me. For that first year I was filled with nothing but rage. I hated them for dying, for leaving. I hated the company. I hated the world. By the time the second year rolled around it was too late. I had lost my family name. I had lost my place in the world and couldn't go back no matter how badly I wanted to. I was alone…after that I met Damien and I wasn't.

Sorry, I'm ranting a little now. I just thought you should know.

- Breq

LOCATION: SILVERMANE COMPOUND
MAITREYA

We had to fly around three times before landing half a mile from the bunker. I left Aiko in Nel's care. While it was true I was tethered to the creature, I could still put it in stasis if I had some kind of special quest I was working on. The problem with this meant that if anything happened to Aiko while I was away, I would still be responsible even while on my mission. I trusted very few players as much as I trusted Nel and as Aiko and I said our see-you-laters, I promised my familiar that I would return.

Kira assigned us the quest.

Explore Trace's Vault
Created by: Moonrain Media / Kira
Expected Difficulty: Unknown
Rewards: Unknown

As we took a shuttle down to the surface below, Nel had to take the ship off-world so we wouldn't be discovered by any of the dozens of FTC fighters flying overhead every eight to ten minutes. We stuck to the trees as much as we could before finally making our way inside the back of the compound, which was made of spare starship parts that couldn't be salvaged. Parts of reactors made up walls and a massive wing stood straight up from the ground like a giant buried sideways in the ground. The compound itself was unguarded. Nothing but scraps. Yueng planted a charger on one of the walls and we stood back as it blew apart. Dust and debris fell around us as we adhered respirators to our face. It was a safe bet that the vault was booby-trapped, so we were going to be taking extra precautions anyway. Not that it would make a difference. Poison gas was one thing but if the vault was rigged with acid or lasers we wouldn't stand a chance. Assuming it had a failsafe that would lock anyone out that wasn't Trace was also a fair bet.

Detonating the wall, we were swarmed by several Wraiths, bio-engineered in Trace's lab and fitted with collars. Three of them went down without a hitch, but the fourth and final one began to mutate into something else as the others fell. Some kind of aberration. It was harder to kill than the others but nevertheless it still went down. Several of the Silvermane scouts that accompanied us had taken major damage.

The second trap before reaching the vault entrance was just as difficult: a small minefield. Gorge and Chaz took point, disarming all of them one at a time. We wasted nearly forty-five minutes walking ten feet just to reach the access panel to the vault.

'No wonder he didn't get much company,' Yueng said as Gorge handed him the last mine.

'Acid mines; we were right, I think this vault is going to take more than just a key to get inside,' Gorge walked up to the panel. In front of him was the insert for the key, alongside a hand print screen. I wasn't sure what he was thinking. Instead of trying to hack his way through, Gorge simply laid his hand on the screen and inserted the key. In that moment I was sure we were all going to be blown to pieces. Never had I been so happy to be wrong. Gorge looked back at us and smiled, 'that's my ol' buddy.'

The vault opened to a staircase that led to another door. This door looked ancient, alien. Runes were etched all across it, like it had been dug up from ruins somewhere.

'Stronger than ship metal, this is one of the most rare elements in the game,' Kira said, studying the door with her hand.

'I'd be careful,' said Chaz, 'might still be traps.'

'Probably not. We made it past the welcome mat,' she smiled back, motioning for Gorge to lead the way inside.

'Bet you wish you had a camera on us right now,' Cass laughed.

Kira wasn't so cheerful, 'capturing things with cameras is about making memories immortal, I'm not sure I want to remember any of this, if those Wraiths and mines are anything to go by, I'm afraid of what we are going to see inside.'

As Gorge opened the door I felt the hair on my arms stand.

It was cold. Freezing inside. The vault, of course, was bigger on the inside. We weren't surprised by that. Trace was more than a slicer, he was a master of deception. The simple staircase that we followed down to the alien door had actually taken us several levels below the surface of the planet. The moment Gorge opened the alien door the one behind us closed and we were sealed inside. This also wasn't a surprise. The inside of the door had a place for identification and the key as well. That was Trace's failsafe. No one could enter or leave without his permission and somehow Gorge had earned that. Fighting side by side with Trace must have brought Gorge close to him. Maybe as close as the five of us now. No. Closer. I had the feeling Gorge knew Trace in real life. Something about the way he spoke about him. The way it reminded me of my love for Damien and Kira's love for her lost brother. These thoughts put me in mind of why we were fighting. There was no bargaining with Skull-Faced Man but if he was outside the Cold Zone did we really have to go through all this trouble anymore? Shouldn't we be searching for clues on the surface, putting out bounties...no, that would end with others getting killed. We had to move forward with what we knew.

Moving forward was all we could do. Gorge led us through the vault, which looked like a high tech but abandoned zoo.

'Why are all the animals gone?' Chaz asked.

'Moved to a separate location? Maybe they disappeared with Trace's death,' Gorge answered.

'You mean his capture, Trace wouldn't go down,' said Yueng.

'He's gone and you know it, the only reason we were allowed in is because this is mine now,' Gorge replied.

'Yours?'

'A couple days ago I noticed the appearance of a new item in my inventory. It was a red key card, sent by Trace. The two of us use to joke about key cards and how they were used in some of the first games to open doors. Once, when the two of us were on tour, all we had for entertainment was an old system and we would take turns playing for hours.'

'How old are you again?' Chaz cut in.

'Old enough,' Gorge grinned.

'The two of you served in real life together?'

'It was after the fall, resources were scarce and the tides rose. I was young and found honour in defending what we had left.'

'What happened?' Chaz asked.

Gorge turned away and pointed, 'what we are looking for should be just ahead, I think in one of the locked boxes over there, I've added all of you to the vault's personnel so you shouldn't have any problems opening anything without permission but be careful. Trace never liked strangers messing with his things.'

As the others walked towards the chests to search them, Gorge grabbed me by the hood of my jacket and called out to Kira. He pulled us aside, 'follow me.' Kira's ear twitched. Together the three of us went deeper into the vault and passed through another alien door.

'The two of you remind me of Trace and I,' he said.

'Thanks, I guess,' Kira replied.

'Right, you should be thanking me, what we are after is going to take us straight to the last level of hell,' he replied.

'What exactly are we looking for?' I asked.

'It will look like a metal brace, small, should be a few of them actually, a prototype, a type-one and a type-two. Somehow I can't help but think Trace had made them for us. I've been thinking about this since the three of us were attacked in the Spire. Trace had a way of reasoning, seeing things no one else could. Patterns. He developed the braces as a mod originally to hide his own identity. Maybe he was paranoid,' Gorge stopped, holding his hand up and the three of us ducked down readying our rifles.

'Something is wrong,' he said closing his hand in a fist.

There in the darkness, thirty yards ahead of us, stood an old man with grey hair and a white beard wearing a pair of brown rags. Chains were wrapped around his wrists and a collar around his neck.

'Is that Trace?' Kira asked.

'No, maybe what he looked like in the real world but not in the game,' Gorge answered.

'What is that?'

'A mimic: guess not all of his experiments disappeared.'

'Do we kill it?'

Gorge paused for a moment, then smiled. 'I kill it.' And with that he stood up and the mimic turned towards him and jumped. Gorge pulled out a knife from the ether and slashed its neck. The mimic screamed and the alien door behind us closed shut, separating us from the others. Grabbing the mimic's wrist, Gorge pulled its arm back behind its back standing up and forcing the mimic version of his best friend to its knees. Taking his knife, he dug it again into the creature's neck. I turned away and closed my eyes. I couldn't believe Gorge could kill the creature without so much as a single hesitation. When I opened my eyes he tossed me a bloody metal bracer.

'Trace always said I should be the one to kill him. It was cruel joke,' Gorge grinned cleaning the mimic's blood from his knife wiping it off on his dark sleeve. Kira and I both looked at him, I was sure he could see the fear and confusion in our eyes. A cruel joke? What kind of relationship did the two of them have?

'That's one. Two more to find.'

'Do you think the others are going to be guarded by Trace clones?'

'Nah, that joke is only funny once. Test out the bracer.'

I handed the bracer over to Kira and at Gorge's urging she left our party.

'Now scan her,' he said.

Surprisingly, Kira's identity read as that of someone totally different.

Name: Rama

Age: 17	Class: Paladin
Level: 16	Health: 100
Status: Alive	Stamina: 100
Mana: 100	

Load out: Empty

Even her inventory read empty. It was the perfect disguise to use against a machine. Not that it would work against a player very well.

'That must be the type-one,' said Gorge, 'the prototype couldn't hide load out and the type-two will let you create a hologram over your own avatar to disguise against other players…kind of like how Aiden is pretending to be you right now,' Gorge laughed, perhaps enjoying the thought that Trace had got to that idea before anyone else. When Kira rejoined our party her real stats became clear to us again. I wondered aloud why the bracer wouldn't work in parties.

'Trace wouldn't hide from his friends; he was selective as to who could see him, but if you were in his company you were a part of his family,' Gorge smiled.

There was a banging on the door we had come through, then it opened (Gorge wasn't lying about our access) to reveal Chaz, who was battered looking, as though he had just survived some kind of arena. 'Found one of the gauntlets!' he shouted.

'Bracer,' Gorge corrected him under his breath.

Chaz continued without noticing, 'funny thing, one of the chests turned into a monster and we had to fight it. After we killed it, we found the gauntlet in the guts. It was epic.'

Kira held up the second one and without speaking of Gorge's battle with the mimic, we pressed on towards the inner sanctum.

> Location Discovered: Hall of Great Fortunes
> /Maitreya

Once inside the hall, we had to solve several puzzles to unlock a chained door. The puzzles were simple. There were several rooms inside the hall, each holding a switch. All the switches had to be pressed at the same time. For one person this would have involved creating some kind of golem (something only an advanced tech-mage like Trace could have done) but since Gorge had brought a team, we each took room and counting backwards from three activated the switches. It took us three tries to manage this in unison.

The chains opened and inside was a massive computer terminal alongside a 3-D printer, one of the largest I had seen inside *Bane*. Alongside it were dozens of mechs in all shapes and colours. It looked like Trace had been building some kind of mechanical army. Some of the mechs looked like they had been re-skinned from other, older games while others had gears and stickers attached to the sides as though they were built to run on steam or water. Different mechs made from different materials and different technologies.

'What is this?' Chaz asked.

'The Hall of Great Fortunes, otherwise known as the armoury.'

'Any of these ever used?' I asked.

'A few of them during the Battle of Vel,' Gorge pointed at one in particular that had a large dent in the side.

'This is an incredible find, no wonder the Silvermanes want it,' said Cass, 'imagine what Lady Gray would say if we returned with even one of these.'

'Don't even think about it; we made a deal,' I said.

'I know, but just imagine how fun driving one of these would be, I bet they are as tough as guardians.'

'Not quite, most don't even work. Trace scrapped parts from one to build another, adding and modding a few here and there but at this point they are probably no more than husks,' said Gorge.

'Guess he didn't want them to fall into the wrong hands,' Chaz said.

'To many, his hands were the wrong hands,' Gorge smiled.

My concern was that one of the mechs would react to our presence. Another trap or some kind of trial for us to pass. Didn't matter what Gorge had said, I imagined at least one would be living. It would swing a mighty sword down and strike us with fire for intruding on their underground kingdom.

No blows came to pass. The terminal in the back reminded me of a throne. Some of the larger mechs seemed to be bowing.

The terminal had a large screen and another input for the key.

'Going to use it?' Kira asked.

'No, we are here for one thing,' Gorge responded.

'Seems a waste not to check and see if Trace might have left you a message or something,' she said.

'Speech doesn't work on players.'

Kira moved closer, her fingers tapping across the terminal's keyboard.

Gorge shook his head, grey beard wagging. 'Neither does charisma.'

Kira almost broke a smile.

'Remember, I assigned us this quest, it was to explore Trace's vault, not just retrieve the gauntlets,' she was smiling now as Gorge too began to grin.

'Fine, you probably won't be able to understand anything on there anyway, Trace had a way with words, making his own languages, probably take anyone unfamiliar years to decipher.' Gorge placed the key inside and gave the terminal his hand print. A flash of red light quickly scanned the entire room.

The words, 'OD UST HLE' appeared in red letters across a black screen and Gorge looked afraid. For a moment I thought maybe he had logged out or that his avatar had frozen. The rest of us read the letters, unable to figure it out. Chaz and Kira both attempted to say them aloud.

'What does it say?' I asked.

'Don't trust the Chel,' Gorge replied.

'That's not all.'

'The last three words are a code for "do not trust". HLE is code for Chel. The UST mean "they see us", and OD means that death is upon us.'

'That's never scared you before why does it now?'

'Because Trace never used the word death when talking about a game, he always used the word frag, or the phrase player-death.'

'He knew the end was coming, I'm sorry, I shouldn't have...'

Gorge held up his hand, 'it's alright, you were right, I needed to see this. He knew it was coming and he knew we would come looking for a way to stop it; maybe he didn't plan to die this early in the game but he understood well his part in this.' Gorge held out his hand and transformed in front of our eyes into a new person. A human version of his own avatar without scars or cybernetics that was mid-twenties with a five-o'clock shadow and short hair wearing a white tank top and black cargo pants. The avatar was skinnier than Gorge's actual avatar but he was still able to control it just as easily. He was almost in tears as he looked down at his hands and the bracer that had appeared wrapped around his wrist. He looked at his fingers like he hadn't seen them in a long time, the same with his wrists and again towards his right leg before moving his hand back up against his arm.

'That you? Not bad,' Kira said.

'This was me.'

And like that, the image of his earlier self was gone.

Quest complete!
+ 5000 EXP
+ 20 Detection (stealth)
Temporary Bonus
+ 10 Forager
+ 10 Constitution
+ 10 Divinity / Fame
+ 10 Charisma

20.
Vault

While we were inside the vault the Silvermanes had been planting small shield generators around the compound both hiding it and protecting it from the FTC who were still patrolling the planet. We were lucky. If they wanted to, they could glass all of us. Most likely, they too were searching for the vault. Most likely too, at some point they would tire of their quest and make this world inhospitable.

'Nel, you have the tow in place? Can you bring the ship around?' I asked through a long-range comm.

'Sir, this channel is not secure, yes,' Nel responded.

'Thanks for the warning, don't let them track you,' I replied, turning towards the others, 'they know we're on the planet, they are going to be tracking the skies, Nel is bringing the ship around but it might be awhile. I don't think we should log out until we get to safe space.'

'That's great, two Titans in the sky; they probably have radar over the whole planet. How exactly is the *Lani* going to pick us up?' Chaz asked anxiously.

'Don't worry about that,' I smiled, 'as for the others, any Silvermanes that want to come with us are welcome, we are taking the fight to the FTC, to the Spire, we're not running anymore.'

The Silvermanes that were nearby turned to me for a moment, but quickly went back to their own business.

'They aren't coming any further, our deal is done, they want us gone by tomorrow. If we aren't they are going to turn us in for the bounty,' said Gorge.

'That's the kind of thanks we get,' Kira shrugged.

'That's the game, I would be hard pressed to find any other guild who honoured such a bargain,' Gorge responded.

'We won't have to wait long,' I said tracking Nel and the *Lani*.

Three minutes later I was right. Meteors began to rain down from the sky. Thousands of them.

'What the hell is that?' said Chaz.

'Nel is creating a diversion, get ready,' I smiled. It was tactic I had read about a player using once. I couldn't remember the players name but the idea was simple. They needed to land on a planet that was heavily guarded so they towed an asteroid towards the planet and broke it apart at the last second, just enough that it would rain across the sky and disrupt any radar in the area.

The *Lani* landed a moment later, opening the back hatch. While Nel waited for us in her mech, Aiko came rushing out of the ship. Already distinctly larger, Aiko jumped on top of me and licked me with her long tongue. It felt like sandpaper but I was happy to feel like I was coming home.

'I know if not for Trace you wouldn't be the man you are today and that you did this for him, but it was nice working with you again. Take care of your new friends,' Yüeng said to Gorge shaking his hand.

'Thank you, don't let the FTC get a hold of this place, I've unlocked all the doors, no keys required anymore.'

'You're kidding! Thank you old friend,' Yueng smiled.

As we boarded the ship I asked Gorge why he had unlocked the vault.

'Nothing there but relics, I deleted the terminal, the logs. They might find a few items worth a few thousand credits. Let us go before trouble,' Gorge hit the hatch button and the light of Maitreya faded away.

I sat down in a room I had all to myself. A guitar sat next to my bed. I thought about playing it for a moment. I wasn't that great in real life but *Bane* had a way of improving anyone who was musically inclined. Had this been a fantasy game I think I would have played a bard. In some ways I wish life could have been that simple. I envied my old life as a diver. Exploring the unknown for artefacts and echoes. Discovering the secrets of the dead. It was easier. Now I felt like I was leading the galaxy into a war that was impossible to win.

LOCATION: *THE LADY OF THE LANI*
DEEP SPACE

From the observation window I could see the three planets in the Maitreya system. We were nearing the world gate but this time we were going to bypass it and drift in deep space until the STL drives could jump us straight into orbit above the Spire. Simple plan. We would jump, dive, land at the Pier, walk right in and steal our way into the Chel's temple. From there we would sneak or fight our way underground. Fingers crossed. I felt the hair on my arm stand up. Another ship was following us.

I picked up my comm, 'we have someone on our tail.'

Nel responded, 'Sir, it looks to be a freighter of some kind.'

'Armed?'

'Negative.'

'Can we shoot it down?'

'Not from this distance.'

'Is it going to hit us?' The freighter was traveling faster than we were. Something about it seemed wrong. It came from nowhere.

'Negative. Should I fire?'

It was obvious. They were going to board us. But the question was whether or not they were friendly. Maybe even traders of some kind.

'Have they hailed us?'

'Communications are being blocked through the system by the FTC. If they have tried, we are unable to know.'

'Contact the others, have them meet me in the ready-room.'

'Negative.'

'What do you mean negative?'

'Detecting radio silence and stasis.'

I cursed under my breath. This was a terrible time to log out. The others should have been more cautious. Not that it would matter. We were all running on fumes. The battle ahead of us was weighing heavy on our minds and no one would have expected this.

'What about Kira? Cass? Can you reach them?'

'Negative. As I said before...'

'I know what you said before Nel. What are our options? Can we contact the Silvermanes?'

'Negative. The freighter is already prepping to board us.'

'Any idea who they are?'

'Scans detect a vast variety of weapons. Most likely raiders.'

'What guild?'

'No affiliations exist.'

'Any idea how they tracked us?'

'Most likely they saw the *Lani* leaving the planet and are investigating.'

'Options?'

'Let them board and see what they want or fire upon them.'

'Can we disable their ship?'

'Negative. Anything at this range will permanently destroy their vessel.'

I didn't want this decision.

It was possible they meant no harm.

'Fire!' I shouted. From the observation deck I watched their ship disappear. Whether they were friend or foe remained a mystery.

'How many players were on board their ship?'

'One hundred and twenty-two.'

'Raiders?'

'Unknown.'

I knew the truth. The freighter could have been about to board us or it also could have been fleeing the FTC. They could have been asking for assistance. They could have been offering assistance for all I knew.

'I had no choice.'

'I know,' Nel's voice was calmer than usual. I tried to remind myself that this was a game. That I had just saved my crew.

'Send everyone a message about what just happened. I am going to retire to my quarters.'

'I shall write it in one of those pretty fonts,' Nel answered.

Aiko climbed up on the bed with me, laying her head down in my lap. I brushed my hand down her head and the metallic scales turned to blue fur. I continued to run my hand down Aiko's back and legs. As I did, she adapted. The metallic scales were an armour that seemed to disappear into the ether. The animal before me now looked more like a wolf than a dragon. Even Aiko's eyes blinked with a different intensity than they had before. Suddenly, there was a knock on my door. Aiko's armour returned as she growled. It was Kira.

'There is something I feel I should share with you,' she said.

'Aiko calm down,' I said running my hand back down her head. The scales turned back to fur before I touched her. She knew Kira wasn't a threat and had already begun to transform back to her softer side.

'Interesting; that's new,' Kira said sitting down beside me.

'Yeah, my cute little monster,' I smiled, turning towards Aiko who made a funny squeak.

'Do you think it can talk too?'

'Doubtful,' I replied scratching behind Aiko's long ears, 'what is it you had to tell me? Is it about the freighter?'

'No. And to be honest, I believe that you did the right thing.'

'I'm not sure.' I felt full of guilt.

'You did.' She moved closer to me, then backed away as if she wanted to comfort me but couldn't.

'Would you have made the same call?'

'A lot quicker than you,' she answered. It didn't make me feel any less bad about what had happened. I reminded myself again that this was all a game.

'I'm sorry, I'm not sure if I can talk right now, I kind of want to be alone.'

'I know. Don't beat yourself up about it. We have to stay focused.'

'Where were you?' I wanted to scream it, to yell, to fight over what I had done but that wasn't going to happen. I knew the others would have made the same call. We had no choice.

Even if they were fleeing the planet they had the numbers and three of us had a giant reward plastered across our foreheads.

'I was doing some research.'

'Into what? Why so important you couldn't wait?'

'Gorge hasn't been completely honest with us.'

'What makes you say that?'

'It's complicated, let's say I did a little digging.'

'What do you mean it's complicated? Were you spying on him?'

'Yes, I guess you can call it that.'

'That's low.'

'I'm a journalist, I search for truth.'

'Any means necessary.'

I was bothered by the fact that Kira had spied on Gorge, but it wasn't a surprise. Alexis, aka Lady Gray, had spied on me and it wasn't like anything in my world outside the game or my own quarters was private, in fact the only privacy I had was between myself and Aiko. I was bothered but I wasn't upset. Gorge, on the other hand, probably would have been furious.

'I don't actually think he's a player.'

'You mean you think he's an NPC?'

'Right, I couldn't track him down in the real.'

'So you couldn't spy on him and that's your problem?'

'Don't put it like that. I just think maybe we should watch our backs.'

'If he is an NPC does it matter? The artificial intelligences in *Bane* operate independent of one another and can basically think for themselves. Honestly, there isn't much to distinguish them from humans as far as free-will. The only real difference is we have bodies we can return to whenever we want. If he is an NPC he knows his limits.'

'That is a part of what is bothering me. He knows about the game, the mechanics of the game, the man with the skull mask. What if Gorge managed to get hold of a weapon that could kill players.' Kira was terrified of the idea, of what could happen.

'Do you think Skull-Faced Man is an NPC gone mad?'

'I don't know.'

'So that's your fear, an uprising. NPCs killing players. If that happens they will just scrap *Bane* and lock the servers. Probably physically destroy the servers. They might do that anyway if we expose the truth. A weapon capable of causing such neurological harm that it kills the player. They might ban VR just for that.'

'I know,' Kira was nearly in tears.

'I'm sorry. I know what this world means to you. The memories you have here with your brother.' It was more than that. I felt just as badly that I didn't want to lose *Bane*. My memories of Damien; my new family; my new life. It was all here. All in this virtual environment made of numbers and probabilities. There was nothing in the real for me. Nothing I truly wanted to go back to except Hannah. If I had to choose, I don't know which I would pick.

'There actually isn't a way to shut down *Bane*,' she said.

'What?'

'Its code is a part of the net, everything. All technology since its inception. If it gives rise to some kind of rebellion against humanity, against its creators and we try to shut it down, it will simply move its core programming from one host to another. Even if it moves like a ghost in the machine it will survive in the cloud until someone copies it into another VR game or it adapts.'

'What are you talking about?'

'I'm talking about an artificial intelligence that was built to live forever.'

'So *Bane* is immortal and you're scared that it's planning an uprising in the real world.'

'I'm terrified.'

A few minutes later Kira left. It was a lot to take in. Not the kind of thing I wanted to worry about. Kira was wrong about one thing though. *Bane* wasn't just one intelligence. It was a living system, a living world, but it was populated by humans and many different artificial intelligences, each with their own personality. If Skull-Faced Man was one side of the coin and Gorge another, than it was at war with itself. In that way it was more human than we had ever given it credit.

I continued to pet Aiko for another hour. I could feel the bond between the two of us grow and it wasn't just some kind of game mechanic. Aiko might have been my familiar but it was by choice. It was something real. Something that defined not just our relationship but the game itself. Like the real world *Bane* was full of choice. Aiko was more than code just as I was more than flesh and blood.

21.
Escape

We had time to spare. Lady Gray contacted us via holo and let us know how Aiden and the others were doing. We could watch them at anytime but it was more personal this way. It kept our group closer. In a way it made it easier for us and for me personally, hearing first hand that they were alive and well. I enjoyed hearing about Aiden's love for the spotlight. He led a group of bounty hunters into the event horizon of a black hole, navigated the depths of the **Ophiuchi cloud**, and led a salvage down the **Grain Star System** in Quadrant 18. It was fantastic. He had done all of that without breaking character. He wasn't just impersonating me, he was making me more famous. Leading adventures worthy of being caught on camera. I have to admit that I was jealous in many ways. He had discovered several artefacts on his salvage, which would make him a fortune. Even the smallest item he acquired now was worth three times the rifle I had discovered in Alpha Centauri A.

To the outside world Lady Gray was corrupt and evil, an elite player who ruled like the Queen of Hearts. To those who came to know her she was nothing like that. That was a part of her facade, the face she put on to keep her guild, her team, her empire safe. More and more, I was grateful that Damien had invited me to take part in *Bane*, to become a Corpse Diver. I was more determined now than ever to break into the Spire to avenge his death and I was grateful too that I wasn't alone.

My conversation with Kira had left me uneasy. So much so that I didn't want to log out and use my time in the real world. I knew I had things I had to catch up on. Reynolds would be mad if I didn't eat or exercise for one. On the outside I felt like a rat in a cage. A boy behind bars. My time felt better used studying star maps and learning lore than it did running a treadmill. There was still so much to discover inside the game. So much territory left uncharted even within the 76 quadrants. The 77th, the Cold Zone, was just one of many mysteries left unsolved. The most important mystery at the moment was the world gate closest to the Spire. The world gate known as *At Eternity*, where humanity had crossed from Earth to the Spire for the first time. Since that exodus the gate had gone cold, Earth itself still undiscovered. Not that anyone truly cared.

Aiko and I went walking through the ship. It felt empty in the silence. I could feel the air circulating through the vents around me, hear the slight vibration of the void outside as we continued, our ion drives pushing us faster and faster as we slung-shot around planets and asteroids every chance we had. We were pushing the engines to their limit.

Gorge was sitting inside the observation deck. Outside the large windows we were crossing through some kind of nebula. I could see sparks of electricity in the air as clouds of purple and red dust swirled around us in a display of beauty that was too hard to put into words. The clouds looked like funnels surrounded by electric sparks. Any one spark could send us crashing, destroy our ship as we made our way across the void. If not for the hull shielding us from the radiation outside we would be dead. Even here there were so many things surrounding us that could kill us it made our plan seem more and more irrational.

As Aiko and I sat beside him, Gorge looked at peace. His eyes gazed at the gas clouds as they moved, crashing into one another in a display of brilliance. It was hypnotizing, the clash as fractals moved from one space to another. No sound, just the crash of colour. Hundreds of thousands of patterns per second. I wondered if it was possible that Kira was right? Was Gorge just as enamoured with the beauty of *Bane* as I was? Or was this actually his home? Was he looking at the nebula or staring through it at some kind of code? As I sat next to him, I thought about asking him some questions but at the same time it all felt better unsaid. I just wanted to be in that moment. Trust is the most important thing a team can have. If I couldn't trust Gorge, if Kira couldn't trust Gorge or I couldn't trust Kira and Gorge together what would become of us? I could feel the seed growing within me. A seed that meant I was losing my faith.

We sat for twenty minutes without saying a word. Eventually, I managed to relax, laying down on my back with my head on Aiko's fur looking out at the wild space that surrounded us. I watched as we came out of the clouds and put the nebula behind us. We had entered the edge of Quadrant 13 and were making our way to a gate known as Snowflake to jump to Quadrant 5. From there we would use our STL drives and jump straight to the Spire. All according to plan. Maybe this was what the Chel wanted us to do. We were playing right into their hands. No. Lady Gray had assured us that Aiden was doing a convincing job. I guess knowing that nearly everyone wanted to kill me left me a little paranoid. Paranoid that even the stars around me were shining in my direction. Looking to blind me. Paranoid that the moon itself was full only as a spotlight.

'Do you think we'll make it?' I asked, breaking the silence.

'Yes, I believe what we are doing will change this world,' Gorge replied.

His words were completely honest, and he said them without any hesitation but they felt static. I couldn't help but analyse what he had said. 'Change this world', that could mean so many different things. What we were facing was bigger than this world alone. If someone could die in *Bane* that would mean the tech was there so any virtual world became a threat. If it was an NPC that killed Damien and the others, then that meant artificial intelligence was the threat. Everything was falling apart and that was something I had become a part of. I, Breq, the harbinger of the coming apocalypse.

'Are you afraid this will end the world?' I asked.

'Nothing truly ends. Many would risk dying in here than living on the outside,' he replied.

'How can you say that? None of this is real. *Bane* is still just a game.'

'Is it a game when one's own life depends on it?' his words made me feel more uneasy. Maybe Kira was right. I had to think back, replay every conversation we had ever had over again in my mind. The answers had to be there. There had to be something 'real' I knew about Gorge, something about him that I could use to convince myself that he was a human and not some puppet or ghost in the machine.

'If *Bane* is shut down, people will move on, find another game, or make a different game with more restrictions. It might be less fun but it would be less dangerous.'

'The tech in *Bane* can't just be copied, it has evolved as it was created. It would take a lifetime to recreate what this world has conceived.'

I looked over at Gorge, 'in some cases change like that is necessary. Don't you think?'

273

'*Bane* is more than a game, its a lifestyle. A lifestyle isn't something that can be shut down or taken away.' He was still staring, rapt at the view.

'Is *Bane* your life?'

'*Bane* is my freedom,' he said, before we both became silent again. In the distance we could see the world gate, a small speck of shiny metal that sparkled like a diamond. It wasn't a round circle like most gates nor was it a cone like others. The centre of the gate was an octagon-shaped pattern with smaller structures branching off, each of which had large towers attached to them, along with another circular pattern. It did, in fact, look like a snowflake hence its name. The gate was farther away from star systems and planets than most world gates, something else that made it strange, and yet here it was, clear as day, a snowflake drifting in the void.

'Why do you think they put it out here? So far away from other worlds,' I asked.

'Maybe we can ask the Chel when we see them, they are supposed to be the ones responsible for building the gates and seeding them across the galaxy.'

'If all goes according to plan, we won't actually run into any Chel.'

'Plan for the worst; we're attempting something that's never been done; not even sure if we can do it, we might make our way to the dungeon beneath the Spire and find nothing but a void, a broken piece of a larger puzzle, unfinished, unrefined, an empty space that was never meant to be seen…or we might find ourselves in the middle of an invasion, a hive of all our worst nightmares come to life,' he spoke as if he was some kind of wise old man, 'as long as we have faith, trust in one another, I feel that we will be alright. Having trust has saved my life more than a handful of times and it will be our actions that define what happens now, not just in this world but the next.'

I nodded my head and agreed without saying another word. His words seemed less cryptic but still, Gorge had said nothing that made me feel like he had a life in the 'real' and I felt that seed of mistrust feed on the soil of his words. I was about to say something else when an alarm came on overhead and the lights in the *Lani* turned red.

'WARNING, an unknown vessel has just exited the Snowflake,' Nel's voice came on through the intercom, 'please report to the bridge, IMMEDIATELY.'

Anyone not logged in was notified via an emergency SOS that we were in danger and that they were to login as quickly as possible. As I soon learned, for Chaz that meant leaving behind some studies he was working on and for Cass that meant getting out of a bath. Kira, Gorge, and myself were at the bridge ten minutes before the others. Cass logged in from a pod separate from the one she would use at Keen Industries and it was obvious there was some small lag in her actions. Nothing detrimental but if we were caught in a fire fight that could mean the death of her.

'What's wrong with your connection?' Gorge asked, first to notice.

'I'm at home; I've been building my own pod, it's not perfect yet and I am bouncing off my neighbour's signal,' she answered. I was impressed. I had no idea Cass was smart enough to build her own pod: even if it wasn't a hundred percent, it took real engineering to program and place all the right parts.

'That's amazing!' said Chaz studying her.

'It's the pods connection, nothing is different here,' she smiled.

'Sorry, yes, you're right, I know that, I've just never met anyone that's built their own pod before.'

'My pod is custom built,' Gorge interrupted.

'Really?' Chaz turned looking at Gorge in amazement. Kira and I looked at one another. That admission felt like a red flag.

There was more to Gorge than his avatar, more to him than what either of us knew.

'Let's focus,' said Cass.

'What kind of ship came out of the Snowflake?' I asked Nel.

'Long range sensors can't confirm the model or identity of the vessel,' Nel answered.

'What if we get closer?'

'At the moment we are far enough away that we are still hidden by the clouds of the Apus Asteropaio Nebula. They won't detect our energy signature for another five minutes.'

'Can we retreat back into the clouds?'

'At our current position and the position of the vessel it will be impossible to escape their long-range sensors. Given the alien nature of the vessel, it is possible that they may already be aware of us.'

'Can we tell if they are armed?'

'The sensors on this ship are not calibrated to detect arms at this range.'

'How long to calibrate them to detect the vessels armament?'

'Thirteen minutes,' Nel responded, despondent.

'Not enough time,' said Cass.

'Okay, so either we run, fight, or ignore them and hope they ignore us,' Kira said, her voice shaking.

'What are the chances they are bounty hunters?' I asked.

'Unknown,' Nel answered, 'running calibration.'

'The calibration is going to take too long,' Cass's voice was frustrated but I knew Nel was just doing that to protect us. There was a good chance even if we didn't engage the alien vessel we could still calibrate our sensors and get a read on them in the next fifteen minutes. The more information we had the better our chance of survival.

'Can we contact Lady Gray? Call for backup?' I asked.

'Negative, it seems all communication is being blocked,' Gorge was reading from one of the terminals. It looked like he had already tried to send a message to someone.

'So we wait?' I asked.

'We prepare for the worst,' said Gorge.

'What about using our STL drive now?' said Kira.

'If we do that we will have to wait for them to recharge and our plans get pushed back,' said Gorge.

'But we'll survive,' Kira answered back almost shouting. I felt like I was I child watching two parents argue. We had to make a decision before we were all at each other's throat. The seed was growing.

'Nel, set us on a course towards the Snowflake, we'll get as close as we can; if our sensors pick up anything at all jump with the STL drive to quadrant five and immediately contact Lady Gray to let her know what is going on,' I ordered. Everyone looked at me and for a moment I felt like a real leader.

The ion drives kicked as we flew forward towards the Snowflake. I could feel the hair on my arms stand up as my heart beat faster. I was anxious. Nervous. My plan had to work. Our sensors scanned the alien ship a moment after they scanned ours. Nel brought up a hologram in the centre of the bridge. The ship before us was battleship with a skull-faced man painted across the side.

'Pirates?' Nel asked.

'No, not pirates, that's him, Skull-Faced Man,' my mouth dropped open. Kira and I stared up at one another. I heard Aiko growling.

'Heavily armed, shields just as strong as a Titan, we could hit that thing and it would be no different than a car running over a small rock,' said Cass.

'Options?' I asked.

'Jumping in three, two, one...' it was Nel's voice. Skull-Faced Man's vessel had started firing at us. I was screaming, ordering Nel to stop but it was already too late. In the blink of an eye we jumped far away from the Snowflake and our enemy.

LOCATION: *THE LADY OF THE LANI* DEEP SPACE - UNKNOWN

The bridge was shaking, fire erupted from one of the terminals, along with smoke and several of us lost our balance and fell. We were hit by something hard. I screamed for a situation report but Nel had gone quiet. The *Lani* had started drifting as the engines shut down. We were in the middle of deep space with no bearings. Skull-Faced Man had managed to hit us just as we jumped, the impact of which folded space-time inwards as well as creating a hole in the side of the ship and with disabling our engines.

'Damn, bastard, he was right there!' I shouted.

'We couldn't do anything, if we stayed we would have been destroyed,' Kira shouted.

Knowing she had to have been just as angry as I was made me feel slightly better, but it wasn't fair. We were face-to-face with the man that killed her brother, the man who had killed Damien, and we couldn't do a damn thing. I banged my fist against a terminal and screamed for Nel. There was no answer. The ship's lights were on and there was oxygen, so I knew none of the critical systems had gone offline but something was wrong.

22.
Danger Beast

Hack 100%

Nel was gone. I managed to hack into the *Lani* using an override and brought up the ship's systems.

Air: Online
Gravity: Online
Communications: Offline
Hull Integrity: 35%
Weapons: Offline
STL Drive: Disabled
Ion Drive: Offline
Shields: 15%
Agility: 0%
Armour: 55%
Fuel: 10t (currently running down)
Max jump avail: 0 Ly (25 max)

We had made the jump but Skull-Faced Man had crippled our ship. The blast in our hull had de-pressurized our ship and caused the jump to drive our shields down to 15% and degrade our ship's

279

armour down to 55%. The hull integrity was holding at 35% thanks to some closed doors but we were separated from the armoury, our personal rooms, medical, storage, hangar, and the mess hall. Basically we were all trapped on the bridge. The ship's fuel tank was hit as well. Usually we carried thirty to forty tons of fuel but now it was down to ten and dropping. With our STL drive disabled and our shields down we were sitting like a derelict.

'Everyone alive? Anyone injured?' I shouted.

With a small growl, Aiko crawled towards me, uninjured.

'Alive,' Gorge answered first, moving his cybernetic jaw back into place.

'Here,' Kira said next, adjusting her neck.

'Present,' Chaz called out from the ground.

'I'm okay,' said Cass, 'is Nel offline?'

'Nel isn't answering, I think the intercoms went down with communications, I'm trying to get in touch via a terminal,' I answered. I moved through several lines of code. I was unsure of what I was doing, for the most part just feeling my way across the ship's terminal. It was a simple text-based graphic system similar to MS-DOS. After struggling for a few moments I managed to open a channel with Nel.

'Alive?' I typed.

'As living as a robot can be.'

'Condition?'

'Damaged; body in self-repair mode; diagnostic not good.'

'Can you control the ship? Where are we?'

'Arrays disconnected; damage to ship is devastating.'

```
Air: Online
Gravity: Online
Communications: Offline
Hull Integrity: 34%
Weapons: Offline
STL Drive: Disabled
Ion Drive: Offline
Shields: 14%
Agility: 0%
Armour: 55%
Fuel: 8t (currently running down)
Max jump avail: 0 Ly
```

Nel showed me the ship's stats again. They had dropped since I looked at them last, but that wasn't important. I knew that was happening.

'Can you get us out of here?'

'Negative.'

'Can you tell us where we are?'

'Negative.'

There was nothing Nel could do to save us. *The Lady* was falling apart.

'Finish self-repair, disconnect from ship's servers and meet us on the bridge; be careful not to blow out the air,' I typed to Nel.

'Affirmative.'

I filled everyone in on the situation. We had few options but luckily we did have a way to communicate in a way that would have been impossible if we were limited to the game.

'Cass can you logout and contact Lady Gray and send us a rescue?' I asked.

'No problem, but we still don't have any idea where we are.'

'Can we pull up our jump co-ordinates?'

'We were set to make a jump to quadrant five but we missed, most likely we overshot it because of the energy surge, we could be anywhere between the Spire and where we want to be,' answered Gorge.

'Can we figure out where we are via the stars?' Chaz asked.

'You are welcome to look, but without a star map or at least one already identifiable object we are lost,' answered Kira.

'I'm logging out now, I'll have Lady Gray see if they can get a lock on Nel from the Titan. Since Nel is Corpse Diver property, she might be able to locate us via item finder,' Cass said.

'Nice idea, we'll wait,' I smiled as Cass logged out, her avatar going blank in one of the bridge's command chairs.

THREE HOURS LATER

Air: 60%
Gravity: Online
Communications: Offline
Hull Integrity: 25%
Weapons: Offline
STL Drive: Offline
Ion Drive: Offline
Shields: 10%
Agility: 0%
Armour: 45%
Fuel: 5t (currently running down)
Max jump avail: 0 Ly (25 max)

Nel came through an airlock attached to the broadside of the bridge Usually used for ambassadors or VIPs, the air dock was just large enough for a person six-foot tall and three feet wide. Enough for Nel to slip through. If worst came to worst we could use space suits. The ship was becoming nothing more than salvage.

We had started losing air not long after Cass logged out. The hull was also being bombarded by small meteorites, which meant we were inside some star system but I was unsure which one. We even tried Chaz's idea of looking at the stars but nothing did any good. There was nothing we could identify, even with Nel's help.

I sat with my back against the wall, Aiko lay beside me with her head on my lap. I was afraid. Afraid that would be the end of all of us. That our luck had run out. Why was Cass taking so long?

'What if one of us goes outside and re-aligns the array?' asked Kira.

'It could work but whoever risks it could die in the process,' Gorge said.

'Why not you?' she called back.

'I'm not ready to give up my life when help is on the way,' he answered.

'Maybe the lack of oxygen won't kill you; as soon as our avatars start to suffer from an inability to breathe we'll automatically be logged out. We won't have a chance,' said Kira.

'You don't think the same thing will happen to me?' asked Gorge.

'No, I don't. I think you are more machine than man.'

'Stop it, both of you. Why are you arguing? We still have several hours before our air goes bad. Cass has plenty of time to rescue us,' interrupted Chaz.

I was tired of them arguing but knew there was little I could do to stop it. The seed Kira had planted within me had begun to bear fruit and it was obvious she was harbouring some kind of anger towards Gorge.

THREE AND A HALF HOURS...

'You know, going up against Lady Gray, it wouldn't be a fight, it would be an act of murder,' Chaz said. I was wondering why he said it. Nobody stood a chance against the Lady on their own. That was a fact. She was a high-level player that wasn't just a prodigy but she had armour and equipment that cost just as much as her Titan.

'Why would you want to go up against her?' I asked.

'I'm just thinking aloud: what if she cut us off, we'd have no choice,' he answered back. The thought hadn't crossed my mind. Lady Gray had invested so much into us, it seemed pretty lame to think she would let all of us die out here in the void.

'You're worried she abandoned us?' Kira asked,

Chaz was sour. 'I'm pretty sure I just said that.'

'Sorry, yeah. If she did that, she would lose her reputation. And if something happens to us in game our secret goes public,' Kira pointed out.

'You're blackmailing her?' Gorge laughed, questioningly.

'Not blackmailing, I just made sure there was some insurance in place should anything happen to my avatar.'

'Blackmailing; lucky you don't have an accident in the real,' said Chaz.

'She wouldn't do that,' I immediately spoke up.

'How do you know? Do know the Lady personally?' Chaz asked.

I wasn't sure exactly what to say so I said nothing.

'Of course he has met her in the real, don't be stupid,' said Gorge. Chaz went silent after that as was Kira.

Another hour passed while Nel tried and failed to reboot the communications. I thought about logging out to get something to eat. I was feeling uneasy in the tight space. The walls felt like they were starting to close in on me. I could feel the seeds of doubt, or mistrust, my loss of faith growing as I looked at the players around me. Chaz, the noob, Kira, the intimidator, Gorge, the robot, Nel, the mule. My own familiar Aiko felt like my only true friend.

'You have a heavy heart,' Gorge was staring at me.

'How would you know?'

'You lost your friend and since that time haven't stopped. Now here we are, all of us, face forward against a wall we can't climb nor move around. Four of us trapped in a void,' as he spoke of our being trapped in the void, I wasn't sure if he was talking to me or himself. His eyes looked around the room and back towards me, 'I understand what it feels like to lose a part of yourself, to lose family, to lose what makes you whole. To run for so long only to be forced to stop.'

'What do you know?' asked Kira.

'And you; you lost your brother. You lost your family and yet you are still here playing the game, searching for truth, running the business you and your brother built. It's amazing. Neither of you have stopped to breath the air around you, to look forward into the future, to define yourselves. Both of you are so young and yet so full of pain, suffering, guilt. Believing that it should have been you that ventured into the Cold Zone. Believing that it should have been you that died. Afraid of everyone and everything you meet and yet you still move forward.'

'I AM NOT AFRAID!' Kira shouted. Gorge had hit a nerve.

'Afraid of me, of what I am. Don't think I'm unaware you ran a search on me. You are afraid of what you can't find. Afraid of the unknown.'

'And who wouldn't be afraid of the unknown?'

285

'The unknown is why we are here. It is not wrong to be afraid of it, however it is wrong to hide away your true self and live a lie. I know you think I'm not real,' Gorge was smiling through his beard.

Kira looked like she was ready to draw her gun. I could see her hand shaking. Gorge hadn't moved but it was painfully obvious he would be faster if they both drew on one another, not to mention that Gorge was cybernetic and could probably take even Kira's strongest weapon.

'I am not an NPC.'

'Tell me what you are,' Kira demanded.

Gorge looked down. I could see a pain in his eyes. 'I'm sorry, I thought we could all trust one another, knowing who we were in *Bane*, in this world and that our actions would be enough,' he began. He looked over at me and Aiko, 'I can see doubt in your eyes.'

'Who are you?' Kira demanded again. Gorge turned his gaze back to her.

'I'm paralyzed from the waist down, I lost my arm and leg in the war. I eat through a tube in my stomach and have a nurse that works on my body. My pod is special. Linked to the game via a neural interface with wires running straight in through my spine. Experimental. In the real world I can't move on my own, In *Bane* I'm me again, I have my body, my arms, the phantom pain disappears, I can live the life I want. I can eat food through my mouth,' Gorge spoke with such sadness I felt my heart ache. Kira on the other hand looked like she wasn't sure if she believed him.

'I've sent you my file, uploaded through our party. I did a great job of hiding who I am in the real world because of the name I made for myself in-game. I'm sorry you misread that. I bulked a bunch of excess materials and sold them. That was the hardest part, selling it all, losing my merchant license on the Spire and becoming a fugitive, hiding my identity.'

I felt like I had betrayed him. Gorge shouldn't have had to tell us any of that. Not now, not ever. It wasn't our business who he was in the real. Even if he was an NPC it shouldn't have mattered because he was and always had been on our side.

'I'm sorry,' I said.

'No worries, I'm sorry that I wasn't honest sooner. I'm more machine than man. I live in *Bane* more than I live in the real world. Trace was one of my best friends. I hid parts of my story away because I was just as afraid as the two of you. Afraid of being seen as weak. Afraid if you knew who I was in the real you would feel sorry for me, that you might treat me differently. The two of you are not the only ones that have lost someone because of the man in the skull mask.

'At first I joined you because I believed in your cause and what the two of you were facing. I am a part of this whether you want me with you or not. Understand that experience has taught me one thing. We will fail if we don't trust one another.'

And with that Gorge had cleared the air and I was left feeling like an idiot for my actions.

'We will never think of you as weak,' Kira said. It was her apology and in that moment I knew that we were a team again.

FIVE HOURS LATER

```
Air: 30%
Gravity: Online
Communications: Offline
Hull Integrity: 15%
Weapons: Offline
STL Drive: Offline
Ion Drive: Offline
Shields: 5%
Agility: 0%
Armour: 35%
Fuel: 0t
Max jump avail: 0 Ly
```

The Lani had been pulled into orbit around a gas giant.

Comms back online

FTC Comm Intercept.

Field Unit: We have unauthorized vessel in grid 15. Sending a unit to check it out. Have support on stand-by.

FIVE AND A HALF HOURS

'Stand back behind me,' Gorge said turning the bridge into a barricade moments after we intercepted the FTC chatter. We knew they were docking at our airlock. This was a matter of life and death, the three of us currently had the most recognizable faces in the game. For half an hour we waited for them to reach our location and scan our ship. They would read six life signs. The four of us stood with our weapons ready and I ordered Aiko to stand down behind me next to Cass's avatar.

'At best they sent a six-man team, ten at most: if we manage to take them out we can use their ship to get out of here, we got this,' I said encouragingly. Gorge grunted and Kira nodded her head. I was hoping for more than that but it was the best I would get given the circumstances. Nel was behind us as well beside Aiko and Cass. Worst case scenario, we would go out in a blaze of gunfire.

'Attention, this is the *No Guts, No Glory* asking the crew of *The Lady of Lani* to surrender, we are coming aboard. Your vessel is heavily damaged and floating in FTC territory,' the voice said.

'Nice name for a ship,' said Gorge, 'get ready.'

Sparks flew from the airlock as three FTC soldiers stepped through onto the bridge. As we opened fire, we were hit with a pulse that jammed our guns. Another three soldiers appeared with stun batons and swords. They wanted us alive. I unsheathed *Aegis*, preparing to attack, but before I could Aiko jumped out from behind us. Transforming from a wolf-like creature to a larger, almost dragon-like monster Aiko's jaw unhinged and bit down on one of the soldiers. Another two fell backwards as Aiko's tail extended outwards, swiping back and forth. As the first soldier fell to the ground unconscious, most likely dead, Aiko clawed and tackled the other three. About ten seconds later, our guns came back online and Aiko sat there dog-like, blue and white fur soaked in a pool of blood.

'Good boy,' I said, not quite sure what exactly happened.

Chaz was looking with amazement at the dead soldiers. 'Wow.'

'None of them are players,' said Kira.

'That was amazing,' said Gorge excitedly, 'your familiar is one badass.'

I wasn't quite sure what to think. Aiko had levelled up twice. I put 15 points into Attack Boost and another 15 into Defence.

'Having a familiar means always having someone at your side; the moment Aiko sensed you were in danger she reacted,' Kira said reassuringly.

We moved through the airlock and boarded the FTC ship. It was a small shuttle. Nel carried Cass's body and we said goodbye to the *Lani*. As we drifted away we took one last look at our luxury liner, noticing how it looked like it had been run through a trash compactor. The entire hull was like crinkled paper, broken bits were floating in space, even pieces of *Naomi's Grace*, Nel's mech, were splintered where the entire backside of the ship was separated from the rest. Behind all that debris there was a blue ball of fire surrounding what had been the STL drive.

'Do you think it would have turned into a dungeon?' I asked.

'Maybe, once it crashed somewhere, given enough time,' Gorge said.

'Blow it up,' Kira said.

'Why not leave it?'

'If it becomes a dungeon it will have records of what happened, hidden messages, parts of our history will remain in the ruins,' she answered.

Gorge took the controls of the shuttle and destroyed the *Lani*.

'Done,' he smiled.

'Sorry about your mech Nel,' I said softly.

'Apologies. Would you like some cookies before we die?' Nel asked before going into a temporary sleep mode.

'So where are we?' I asked.

'Quadrant Three, FTC space, let me give us a little boost and we'll be just inside the Ilioneius Star System,' answered Gorge.

From the shuttle we could see a gas giant three times the size of Jupiter. Similar in colour to the nebula, the planet was made of red and purple gas clouds with dozens of storms raging across the surface.

New Location Discovered: *No Guts, No Glory*
/ Ilioneius Star System

The message appeared. This was my first time in this system.

'Can we jump to the Spire in this?' Kira asked.

'No, we can't, they will ask us for codes. They probably already have a second unit on their way after us,' Gorge said.

'Good thing I'm back,' Cass said behind us, 'what the hell happened?'

Kira hugged her, 'almost died, pirated an FTC shuttle.'

'The *Ibanez* is on its way here along with Shiru and Pierce, they are going to provide us some support, sorry it took me so long.' Cass smiled.

'What about Aiden and our facade?' I asked.

'Oh, you just bought a brand new state-of-the-art, high end and luxurious destroyer called the *Crimson Killer*,' Cass said laughing. Now not only was I wanted throughout the galaxy by the Spire, the Crimson Kings, and anyone looking for a payday but I was rubbing it in their faces. I shook my head in disbelief; still, I couldn't help but smile.

SEVEN HOURS LATER

LOCATION: THE *IBANEZ*
ILIONEIUS STAR SYSTEM

We boarded the *Ibanez* and it was a relief to feel safe again. Both Shiru and Pierce joined our party and handed control of the ship over to Nel, who came out of sleep mode apologizing that

that unfortunately the cookies had all been eaten and thanking them for not damaging the ship with their amateur flying.

We had one day left before our mission to the Spire.

Logout.

23.
The Core

THE REAL

After logging out, I could feel my hands shaking. It had been almost an entire day since I last ate and slept. Reynolds was waiting for me like usual, with a ball of rice and a protein blend. Although I felt like I couldn't stomach the chalk taste, I downed it as he watched in approval. I was a puppet still and had to do what the company wanted. After dinner and another hour of study, I said goodbye to Reynolds and turned off the lights in my penthouse. It was still all so unreal. The bed was softer than anything I'd ever slept on before and some nights it seemed easier to sleep on the floor with a blanket beneath my head. This night...the night before our next quest I made a decision. I wasn't going to live as a pet rat in a cage. I was young, human, and I wanted out. Maybe I was going stir crazy, maybe it was the pressure of the game. I contacted Hannah through the backdoor Kira had built and in the darkness of the night I planned my escape.

It was almost midnight and the only sounds that could be heard were those of taxis in the streets. I had snuck out by crawling through a small vent in the penthouse. I wasn't sure exactly where it led but I was determined. Hannah had sent me a rough blueprint and I followed it like trying to make my way through some hand-drawn maze. At that moment I really did feel like a rat. King Rat Breq. Maybe if I died I could make that my new player name. No. I wasn't going to die. A few hours outside and I would be back, way before I had to login again. It's not like they could force me to play. Worst case scenario, I oversleep and we postpone our plans again.

The others and myself were starting to get used to distractions. It seemed no matter how many walls we climbed there was another, higher one, right after.

It took half an hour to make my way to the lower levels and find a balcony with a fire escape. After that it was easy to find my way down to street level and contact Hannah who was coming to pick me up.

When she arrived, she was more beautiful than I imagined. This was the first time we had met in person and neither her avatar nor her camera feed could do her justice. Hannah pulled up exactly as she said she would, on an old vintage motorcycle. She had her hair pulled up in a double knot. Underneath the padded red zip up jacket she was wearing was a shirt that said GO ECHO! with a cartoon version of the *Ibanez* and Nel giving a thumbs up. Below that, she was wearing black pants that hugged her hips and a pair of boots that made her stand almost as tall as I was. I was speechless at first. Thinking maybe I should make a joke about her t-shirt but then I already knew she was wearing it to be funny. I smirked as she threw me a red and black helmet and told me to get on.

The streets lit up around us in a blaze of red, yellow, and green. The sound of the motorcycle echoed through my helmet and I felt the cold wind hug my neck and push back against me as I hugged Hannah around her waist. I wanted the moment to last forever. For the night to never end. As she leaned around a turn, I leaned with her and felt our bodies and the machine move in synch with one another. Without saying a word, the two of us were one-and-the-same until we finally arrive at an all ages club.

Playing *Bane* had made the days blend together. Each felt the same. It wasn't like I took off for the weekends or holidays. In fact holidays were busier in the game because of special timed quests and rewards. Tonight was Friday night. The venue was called *Club Kaiju* and the inside was just as one would expect. The walls were covered in posters of famous Kaiju and mythological monsters such as Cyclops, Kraken, and even a giant mural of Yamato no Orochi, the eight-headed, eight-tailed dragon, painted with neon colours across the back wall of the dance floor. At the entrance where we checked in and grabbed our wristbands there was a bust of Frankenstein's monster standing to greet us. *Club Kaiju* was more than an all ages dance club though, there was a small bowling alley with pins that looked like giant monster teeth and of course laser tag and an arcade.

Holding hands, the two of us walked inside. Hannah had reached for mine first. I was still nervous. Unlike in *Bane* I had very little real world experience when it came to socializing or going on dates. Most of my time before my parents died I spent being an introvert, writing and studying. After they were gone, I made a few acquaintances on the streets but couldn't afford to go out or do anything. When Damien and I became friends, I found my social life increased ten-fold, but almost every conversation I had was related to *Bane* or some kind of new game tech that was coming out.

Inside, we made our way to one of the 'bars' which served sandwiches, burgers, chips, coffee, energy drinks, and pop. Back behind the bar was a solid metal statue of Cthulhu and several other Old Ones. Hannah ordered something called 'the Rattler', which was a mix of herbal tea infused with citrus and some generic energy drink and I treated myself to a blend called 'Destroyer of Worlds' and a nice greasy burger. The cups they served our drinks in were shaped like small chalice with claws to grab onto. I must have been starving, the way she laughed as I devoured the whole thing.

I tried my best not to talk with my mouth full as I told her first hand about all the adventures I had been having in *Bane*. I told her about my earlier adventures too. The ones with Damien and before…outside the game. As we sat together for an hour I told her about my parents and she told me about hers.

Hannah's father was a mechanic and she had been an only child after her mother died when she was young. Her father had helped her build her pod. Turns out her mother had once been a pro gamer back in the early stages of virtual reality. Hannah joked that her death in *Bane* wasn't her fault but a curse that had been placed on her family after her mom had kicked some serious ass back in her day.

Once we ran out of our drinks we made our way to the arcade and underneath a poster of Sasquatch fighting Grendel we played an old arcade game with a fantasy setting. I picked a Paladin and Hannah picked a Mage. The game was so old-school it took us several tries before finally getting the hang of the controls. It was the first time in years I could remember playing something besides *Bane*. Two other players joined us and we started ripping through the first few levels before losing all three lives we had. The arcade was full of wonders just like that. Games from the past, from an age forgotten. Most all of them were released before we were even born but it felt important to keep their memory alive. They were a part of our history. Maybe that was romanticizing it a bit, but each and every game we played felt like a work of art. Each created by a group of individuals who had to conceptualize, code, paint, play-test, program. Some were made by small teams while others had been created by hundreds, if not thousands, of people working around the clock.

In one of the fantasy games we played called *Stormcaller* I picked up a weapon that reminded me of *Aegis*. A large, thin, slightly curved blade made of ivory and a grip made of gold, dust-covered leather. Sharp on both ends the blade's twisted cross-guard was smooth and seemed to move as if it was an extension of the character on-screen arm. I imagined that this must be what I looked like when swinging a melee attack with my own sword.

'I bet we could get someone to create a mod for these weapons!' I joked.

I was trying to be classy. Maybe a little suave, but most of the night I felt like I was tripping over my words, only for Hannah to come rescue me. Ever since we started talking everything seemed to click into place. I wasn't the only one that had lost someone, something. I wasn't the only one trying my best to survive this world. Searching for answers that didn't really exist. As I looked around *Club Kaiju* I saw others like me who were walking along the same thin line I was. Some were farther along than others but we were all doing our best to feel alive, to find happiness, to find family. We were living real lives and after Hannah and I both lost all three of our game lives in *Stormcaller*, we were outside the arcade dancing.

Electronic music played and Hannah did the shuffle, moving her right foot forward and walking in place with her knees held high. The next moment her left foot was crossing her right and she was turning around all while her arms and hips moved side to side.

It was almost midnight when the music started to slow down and she placed her arms around my neck. She leaned her head into me and for a moment I heard her whisper something in my ear. I wasn't sure what it was, but it sounded like…'please don't go.'

'Please don't go where?' I wanted to ask, but kept the words to myself. I wanted that moment to last. I wanted to feel the warmth of her breath against me as I held her and we swayed to the sound of a ballad from the past. Oldie music. Slow pop from the early twenty-first century that made me feel like we had time travelled into the past. Maybe she didn't want me to go back home. Maybe she didn't want to stop dancing. Maybe she didn't want me to go back into *Bane* knowing that it was possible I was putting my life on the line. The image of Skull-Faced Man flashed before my eyes and I felt fear. I held Hannah tighter until the music changed again and I watched her shuffle once more with a smile lit across her face. A smile I would never forget for the rest of my life.

Just outside the dance floor I could see several people starting to huddle together. They looked like they were whispering as one of them checked the net and I saw a holo of one of the scenes from *Bane* play. A moment later an entire wall was lit up with highlights from the last few days of my life in *Bane* and people were staring.

'You're Breq!' someone shouted.

Another soon followed and a mob was forming. It had taken them so long to realize who I was, I thought maybe I had nothing to worry about. But I was wrong. I grabbed Hannah's hand and the two of us began to retreat. I felt like we were being chased by a killer mech. That rush I had the first time in the Spire over again. Twenty, maybe thirty people were taking pictures of the two of us now. Even as I blocked my face I knew this incident would be hard if not impossible to hide from the company. We ducked inside the laser tag arena, jumping the gate and flying passed the staff. He shrugged it off and blocked the mob from following behind us.

Hannah and I sat with our back against a wall under a purple black light laughing and it was in that moment I kissed her.

A few minutes later the lights in *Club Kaiju* came on and Reynolds entered, surrounded by dozens of personal bodyguards wearing black suits. He looked at me in a way that was both scolding and proud and told both of us to come along. Escorting us to a limo outside he told us to wave to the crowd surrounding us that had grown to nearly fifty. Both Hannah and I did as he asked, smiling and waving as if we were a part of some kind of parade before Reynolds opened the doors to the limo and the three of us entered inside.

There was no lecture, no remarks such as 'don't do that again', there was nothing but an awkward silence as Hannah rested her head in my lap, falling asleep as we drove her home.

'Access'

Checking for necessary update files...

Initializing...

Player environment meets necessary requirements.

Retina scan / Identity confirmed.

Dive 100%

Loading player data...

NAME: BREQ

Age: 17   Class: Scout

Level: 33   Health: 100

Status: Alive   Stamina: 100

Mana: 100

Load out: *Naomi* - M7-7 Ki Rifle, *Aegis* (melee) Short grip energy pistol, EMP grenades.

LOCATION: THE *IBANEZ*
ORBIT ABOVE THE SPIRE

'Maintenance ship zero-one-nine-zero-one-zero-nine request docking,' Nel was talking back and forth with a dock closest to the Chel tower. We had forged access codes claiming to be a work ship with a hold full of fork lifts that had just come out of production. Once landed, we would have to pass through a scanner that Nel would hack remotely and we would land. After that it was as easy as walking into the Spire with our disguises on and Shiru and Pierce by our sides. Aiko would accompany me while Nel stayed and guarded the ship with one of the mecha/guardian armours we had picked up courtesy of Lady Gray. Then, once we made it inside the tower, we would have to track down some secret passage no one had discovered before and find or fight our way through a dungeon into the depths of the Spire's core. From there we would discover the artefact Ra described, the one that allowed a player to hide his or her level from the game and thus access all zones, including the Cold Zone.

The plan was full of holes but there was no stopping what we had already put into action.

Half an hour after logging back in, we docked with the station and began making our way through it. The Spire was just as glamorous as it always had been. Large buildings towered around us as the futuristic cityscape covered the horizon with neon lights. Grey and black metal bridges connected one location to another. I felt like an ant. It was like standing in the centre of London or New York Times Square. Hundreds of players and NPCs moved around us as drones monitored the actions of everyone from above. Everyone had somewhere to go or someone to meet.

Some of the players were dressed causally while others wore power armour and showed off their heavy weapons. Some players around the tower were wearing formal priest outfits and were screaming about the Chel being the saviours of the human species. They were easy to ignore; the poor, who also lined the streets, were not so easy walk past. Dozens of players who had become down at luck and refused to start a new game for one reason or another were begging for credits, to join parties, or searching for adventurers to help them on quests. It was possible some of them were fake but the truth was most weren't. They were lost and yet desperate to hold on to their characters. Maybe they had a high ticket item that had cost them everything and they were just looking to get a new start without resetting their game.

One of the beggars stared intensely at Shiru and Pierce, seeming to recognize them from the holo feed in the real world. When he scrambled to attack, Gorge had to knock him away. The attack drew the attention of some of the FTC security guards, but they looked the other way the moment the scavenger backed down. When we finally were clear of the street traffic, I listened to the crowds and skimmed for a moment through some of the headlines via my interface. Besides some headlines about my 'adventures' and the usual races and arena events taking place, rumours were spreading of players disappearing and dying in the game.

'It was only a matter of time,' said Kira catching wind of the headline I was reading.

'The skull-faced man isn't just laying low in the cold zone anymore, should we even go through with this?' I asked turning the holo program off.

'We still need to be able to chase after him, if this goes right we won't have to worry about being bound by any of the game's rules.'

'This is a big risk.'

Kira shrugged. 'Sometimes it takes a leap of faith, a big risk to move forward.'

'I would rather take the fight to him.'

'And die in the process, at least we might be able to uncover something here that will give us the advantage.'

'We are going to have to face this head on eventually.'

'And we will, this is about being several steps ahead. We aren't going to win by shear luck or numbers. When the truth gets out that we can die in the real world all hell is going to break lose. Right now there is nothing but rumours and a few deaths here and there that look unrelated. People are still playing. What happens when hundreds or thousands of players start to go missing?'

'Chaos, both in *Bane* and the real world,' I answered holding still for a moment pulling my hood over my head. Kira and I started running forward to catch up to the others. Our conversation had taken a dark turn. I wanted more than ever to attack Skull-Faced Man when we ran into him but we stood no chance. Even if he showed up now it would be no good. We still had two dives left and a lot of work to do before we could face him.

Several smaller guardians stood at twelve and fifteen feet tall, staring down from the gates that led inside the Chel tower, their red eyes regarding and analyzing the citizens of *Bane* that walked around them. I prayed under my breath that our disguises worked as they were supposed to. Landing had gone according to plan and we had tested the technology multiple times onboard the *Ibanez*. Aiko heeled by my side as we crossed the threshold that led into the tower gardens. From there we took an elevator to one of the sanctuaries in the lower levels. Kira and Gorge believed it was here that we would find the key to going deeper. They had come with some expensive scanning gear, but it turned out that wasn't needed. Like the good familiar she was, Aiko found the secret entrance for us as though it had been calling out to her.

A panel on a wall opened to reveal a library full of ancient text: alien text that was discernible on sheets of metal that glowed with a blue light. A part of me wondered if the alien text was just Greek writing, a placeholder set in the game that no one was meant to find, or if there was something more to this place. The Chel had their own real language but it wasn't fully translated in the real world yet. Designed by several human scholars and the game's artificial intelligence itself their language had evolved many times over since the game's launch each time falling farther and farther away from what we could decipher in real life. Not without our trying.

Kira filmed everything we saw with a handheld holo recorder attached to the edge of her rifle while another camera floated above us. We weren't streaming but if anything went wrong the recorders were set to upload everything to the Moonrain Media servers. It was our contingency plan.

Inside the library we found another hidden passage that led us into the catacombs of the Chel tower. The underground passage was full of fossilized, wild alien fauna that must have once been the inhabitants of this world now long extinct or living, endangered, far outside the city. I couldn't help but notice a small resemblance that Aiko had to some of the wild creatures. The entire catacomb felt like we were walking further into the Chel's past. A tower that became a tunnel that ran farther and farther down. As the bones disappeared, more of the wild blue text appeared. This time it was written in the walls glowing with a fungus. Three dead astronauts stood at the end of the tunnel. Hanging by their necks.

It was an Easter egg set to another world. Another time and place. The three dead astronauts were wearing the uniforms worn by the original humans who had came through the world gate. Gorge theorized that they were the ones that entered the first dungeon and made the Spire accessible.

'This feels like endgame content,' said Kira.

'More like something that was cut from the game,' added Gorge.

'It's scary as hell, I don't like this. It doesn't feel like *Bane*,' said Chaz. He was wrong though. Horror was and always had been a huge part of the game, but then again he had only seen a few Hollows and monsters in his time. The rest of us had seen the terrible forms found in the void. The eyes that stare back from the abyss. And just like that, we found ourselves being watched. Hollows. Hundreds. Shadows that stood tall, their eyes staring towards the walls. The entire room opened up as if it was the inside of some kind of hive. The walls were even etched in a honeycomb design as if dozens of giant shields had been welded together. As the scenery changed I began to wonder if we had gone from walking through the bottom level of the Spire to the inside of some kind of ancient starship.

We moved closer to a giant door that looked like it would hold the answers. Maybe it was the key. The artefact we were looking for now felt so close. All that stood between us and the door were a few hundred Hollows. We moved as silently as we could, until we were just ten yards from the door. One of us had tripped an alarm. Aiko began to growl as several dozens of the Hollows turned towards us.

That was the moment I lost it.

I ran forward towards the door as if pulled by a force of gravity. Adrenaline. I heard the sound of rifles going off from behind me as I pushed myself forward. I could hear Aiko growling and biting.

Gorge, Kira, Cass, Chaz, Pierce, Shiru all disappeared from my sight.

LOCATION: THE IMMER
THE FIRST DUNGEON

A creature rushes forward, its two legs gracelessly carrying its wicked body with a sedated energy. A skeletal tail writhes behind it; coarse hairs cover its body in patches. Five cruel eyes stare at me with a burning rage and a loud blare reverberates from the creature's cramped mouth as if a warning or challenge to me. I'm not inside the Chel tower anymore. I'm not sure where I am. There is nothing but my body, my weapons, the creature and time. A vortex of light surrounding us. I feel it move closer towards me. It knows what I am. It is a challenge.

The next moment I feel I am falling. I can see seven worlds. Seven planets aligned in a sigil. Each planet revolving around a single blue-and-yellow star, pulling on one another as they continue to keep their shape. A starship flies past me. I'm in space, in the void. No, I am running inside of the starship. I'm on the back of a mech that is running through walls. Running away from something. Something horrible. My rifle is in my hand. The creature with five eyes is chasing after me.

As I turn to fire, using my life as an energy source, I woke up back in the real world. The game kicked me. My heart was beating out of my chest as I struggled to catch my breath. I was having some kind of panic attack. Disoriented. My nose was bleeding, my clothes were covered in blood, and I felt like I had just been slammed hard on the ground. Did I die? Did I lose everything? I tried to stand but I was too weak to lift myself up. I tried to scream. I tried to search around the room for Reynolds or any of the doctors and nurses who had been monitoring me. I was alone. Bleeding, broken, and sitting paralyzed in my own piss.

I moved my lips again and again until finally words.…'Access'

Initializing...

Player environment meets necessary
requirements.

Retina scan / Identity confirmed.

Dive 100%

Loading player data...

Name: Breq

Age: 17   Class: Scout
Level: 51   Health: 100
Status: Alive   Stamina: 100
Mana: 100

Load out: *Naomi* - M7-7 Ki Rifle, *Aegis* (melee)
Short grip energy pistol, EMP grenades.

Update 1.12.01 found. Access granted...

24.
Focus

HACK
100%

Adrenaline 45

Affinity (weapons) 15

Agitation 15

Animal / Aquatic Expert 35

Artillery 15

Attack Boost (Damage) 5 (+5 Bonus)

Blast Attack Boost 5

Blast Resistance 35

Bleeding Resistance 45

Botany 5

Bow Expert 5

Capacity Boost 5

Capture / Tame 15 (+ 50 Familiar Bonus) = 65

Carving 10

Charisma 25 (+10 Bonus)

Constitution 5

Critical Boost 50

Critical Affinity 50 (+10 Bonus)

Defence 5

Detection (stealth) 30 (+10 Bonus)

Divinity / Fame 5

Evasion 5

Explosives 15

Fire Attack 5

Fire Resistance 5

Focus 40

Fortification 5

Gambler 5

Guard 5

Hacking 25

Handicraft (crafting) 5

Heat Resistance 15

Health Boost 15

Hunting (survival) 5

Hunger (cooking) 5

Ice Attack 5

Ice Resistance 15

Intimidation 5

Iron Body 5

Latent Power 5

Luck 25

Medical Specialist 15

Mind's Eye 5 (+10 Piloting Bonus)

Navigator 5

Nullification 5

Paralysis Attack 5

Paralysis Resistance 5

Peak Performance 5

Piercing (Damage Boost) 5

Pilot 5 (+20)

Poison Attack 5

Poison Resistance 5

Poison Duration 5

Psionic 5

Recovery 5

Stamina 30

Sheath Speed (reflexes) 5

Strength 10

Stun Attack 5

Stun Duration 5

Stun Resistance 5

Survival 15

Tool Specialist 5

Training 5

AKA *Naomi*.
M7-7 Ki / Energy Rifle

Description: Boss Slayer

Level: 33
Damage: 275
Weight: 5.5 lbs
Weapon Type: Scout Rifle / Ki Rifle hybrid
Rarity: Ultra-Rare
Impact: 10
Range: 9
Stability: 9.5
Reload Speed: 10
RPM (rounds per minute): 300 bursts
Affinity: 10
Sharpness: 8.5
Elemental: Shadow
Critical Chance: 91%
Modifiers: Bonus EXP gained against Robots,
Bonus EXP against Hollows, Bonus EXP
against Bosses

— Quest —
A Whisper in the Void
Created by: Moonrain Media / Kira
Expected Difficulty: Veteran
Rewards: Unknown

Details:
1. Find a way inside the Cold Zone (acquired)

2. Recover the echoes of the lost (0/3)
3. Kill the man with the skull mask.

Level Requirement: ~~50~~ (UNLOCKED)

My hand had touched the door for just a moment. After that, I woke up in the real world. I could remember bleeding. I remember being alone there. I remember the smell of my own piss as I tried to move, to lift myself up and pry myself from my pod even if it meant I would land flat on the ground. I remember being paralyzed and finally mouthing the words that logged me back into the game. And for seven hours I have no other memories of where I was or what had happened. I disappeared behind the veil. Gorge and Kira had tried to open the door from the outside but there was nothing they could do. The door was a solid object that reacted only once and to me. When I reappeared I was level 51. Almost all of my new points had been put into defence and re-sistance. I felt like my avatar had gone through hell but at the same time I felt stronger, faster. I felt the affinity I had with my weapon rise and when I looked at Aiko I felt our bond had grown by a factor of ten.

'It worked!' shouted Gorge.

'Worked? What worked?' I shouted back, still disoriented and unclear at what was happening to me.

'You've passed level fifty; the time dilation; the military ap-plication buried in *Bane*,' he said. That was right. *Bane* was based on code engineered to experiment in time dilation for military training. Somehow, I had cracked that code. It was an event much like the one that had happened to us on Rem but on a much, much larger scale. I looked back at the door. It appeared as a normal door now. I didn't feel drawn towards it or anything. Rather, I felt relief as I started to move away from it, like some-thing horrible had happened to me there. I could smell the dust and decay of the tomb around us in the air. The Hollows were the echoes of the dead who had failed. Failed to come back. Several were starting to gather and move towards us. The others had done a great job defending the door in my absence but it was my turn now. I powered on my rifle and fired. The damage *Naomi* did was almost three times what it would have been seven hours earlier. I felt like no time at all had gone by…like the game had only just kicked me out and I had immediately logged back in, but as the smoke cleared Gorge quickly filled me in.

'You were gone for seven hours here but behind the door you must have been trying to survive for months on your own,' Gorge was smiling.

'Most likely around seven months,' Kira interjected.

'When you passed through the door a neural interface in your pod must have activated, blocked your brain from retaining any memories of what was happening inside, but from how you spent your points it's obvious you were doing everything you could do defend yourself. Can you remember anything from the other side?' Gorge was looking me up and down, studying my body and armour. My armour was darker, dustier, and had several dozen scratches across the front and side which came from a giant creature.

'I remember waking up in the real world and being alone, my nose bleeding,' I said.

'It could have been some kind of glitch?' said Kira.

'Maybe a hallucination?' added Chaz.

'Most likely a failsafe measure when you found your way out,' Gorge said.

I believed him. It felt right. The way my body felt. The way I had spent my experience points, all of it. Aiko came up to me and rubbed her head on my leg. 'I missed you,' I said, without realizing just why. On the other side of the door I knew I had been alone: trying to survive. Just as lost and confused as when I woke up. I survived. I lived. Mission complete.

'Let's get out here,' Chaz yelled.

'We still have to find a way into the Cold Zone,' Cass pointed out.

Somehow I knew. I knew the answer. '*At Eternity*, the world gate, that's the answer, we just have to activate it,' I said. How I knew this and why I was certain of this was a mystery to me. Lost in the memories I had erased of my seven-month venture. Memories that couldn't exist in the real world. Only it seemed that I retained small pieces of information from that experience.

'Good enough for me,' said Gorge.

'And now we have our advantage,' Kira smiled. The others agreed and we began to move out. Passing back through the shadows of the tomb that was entrance to the first dungeon and back through the catacombs and into the library. When we reached the panel that had led us to the secret entrance, we found it closed. It didn't take Gorge much effort to punch his way through, albeit at the risk of shattering his cybernetic hand in the process. As the wall tore away he smiled and said that he had always wanted to do that. Outside, in the basement of the tower, we were welcomed back by several FTC troops that were waiting for us.

I felt my focus grow. My latent power +10. Time seemed to slow down for a moment as I looked at the world as though through a blue filter and I aimed my rifle at the first FTC trooper on my left. I fired. I felt my rifle as if it was an extension of who I was. Repeatedly, I imagined pulling the trigger and my targets falling one after another. Time returned to normal and four of them were down. As the fifth dived for cover, Aiko was already behind him.

'What the hell was that?' Kira exclaimed staring at me.

I looked at my rifle. 'I don't know.'

'That was the power of shadow. A psionic power up, your latent power,' said Gorge answering the question all of us were wondering. I double checked *Naomi's* stats. He was right. There it was. Elemental: Shadow.

'My psionic level is only five though?' I said doubtfully.

'Doesn't matter, you gained an exploit with your weapon, that's the kind of power players usually beg the Chel for,' Gorge answered. I could tell he was awestruck by everything that had happened, maybe jealous even. I couldn't blame him. Something new, something strange had happened to me and it wasn't just something in the game. I might have been the first human being to experience the effects of time dilation and not lose my mind. That being the case it only raised more questions...why didn't the time dilation kill me? If it worked, why wasn't the military using it to train soldiers? Why was this not exploited before in *Bane*?

'Why did it work with me?' I asked unsure if Gorge or anyone else for that matter had the answers.

'Because of the neural interface in the pod. You haven't retained any training or skills, only your levels and power ups. Seven months of your life flashed before your eyes. Your nose was probably bleeding in the real world because of the stress on your brain,' Gorge answered without hesitation. I knew he had done his research.

'What would happen if I went back and did it again?'

'You would die. You're lucky you found a way out when you did, if you had stayed any longer your mind would have eventually shut itself down.'

'Do you think we should go back? Do you think you guys should travel through the doorway?'

'No, it's too much of a risk, we've gotta keep moving forward,' Kira answered.

'I have one more thing I have to do,' Gorge said trailing behind us.

Right after he said that, Gorge lit up the secret room with an explosion that caused us to run farther inside the tower. The library, catacombs, all the tunnels and secrets were gone.

'What did you just do?' Chaz yelled.

'I made it impossible for anyone else to exploit *Bane*,' he said.

A part of me questioned whether or not using this kind of exploit was the right or wrong thing to do. *Bane* was a game with rules but I wasn't actually breaking the rules. I was using a program inside the game. I had levelled up on my own, fighting for my life for seven months whether I had the memories or not. I was there, it was real to me.

We crossed paths with another Hollow in the tower. This one was different. It looked like several dozen had gathered in mass together, forming one solid black body, The Hollow mimicked our steps as we moved forward, neither attacking or moving in our direction. It stared at us with dozens of glowing red eyes that looked like orbs of energy.

Hollow Mass
Level 55
Hostile

It was stronger than I was, but weaker than all of us put together. In fact a part of me wondered if maybe our group was too overpowered now. We stood before it and readied our weapons. Gorge fired first and the Hollow absorbed the blow disappearing. Small footprints surrounded us as if the Hollow had split into dozens of invisible forms before it reappeared behind us. It still didn't attack as it hovered over Shiru. The rest of us turned, far too slowly, as Chaz and Pierce brought up their weapons and fired. Shiru was lifted into the air as the Hollow Mass transformed into a snake-like creature with fangs covered in red orbs.

We fired relentlessly at it until Shiru fell to the ground, hitting the red orbs and causing the Hollow Mass to retreat to the front of the tunnels again. For a moment we stood silently, before slowly moving as one, with the Hollow Mass keeping pace alongside us. Once again, it was mimicking our movements, anticipating our choices, looking for the right time to strike. Without saying a word, Kira and Cass moved forward and motioned for Gorge and I to move in the other direction.

Our party split into three groups, as far apart from each other as we could manage inside the entrance to the tunnels. The Hollow Mass moved closer, centring itself between our three groups and the exit. Several more eyes appeared across its body. Each eye was fixed on one of us and followed our movements as we continued to spread out as much as we could. Gorge signalled for us to cover our eyes and threw a flash grenade in the air.

The light blinded the Hollow Mass and made it go into a frenzy. As it thrashed around, Aiko jumped behind it and bit down on its neck, snapping it before any of us could get a shot off. If it had been any other animal besides Aiko it would have had poison damage, but being my familiar Aiko had gained the same resistances that I had. This transformation had gone unnoticed by me until now, but I checked Aiko's stats and saw the change that had quietly taken place over my seven hours lost in time.

NAME: AIKO

Level 10   Friendly

Health: 100   Stamina: 100

Mana: 100

Adrenaline 70   Agitation 15

Attack Boost 15 (+5 Bonus)	Health Boost 15
Blast Attack Boost 15	Ice Resistance 15
Blast Resistance 35	Intimidation 20
Bleeding Resistance 45	Luck 25
Charisma 75	Nullification 15
Constitution 25	Paralysis Resistance 15
Critical Boost 50	Piercing (Damage Boost) 25
Critical Affinity 40	Poison Resistance 55
Defence 75	Recovery 45
Detection (stealth) 40	Reflexes 35
Evasion 55	Stamina 55
Fire Resistance 15	Strength 20
Focus 35	Stun Attack 35
Guard 5	Stun Duration 5
Heat Resistance 15	Stun Resistance 25

In the remains of the Hollow Mass we found an artefact of a player recently killed, someone we had passed on our way from the hangar to the tower. Chaz picked up the artefact. It was a small wooden figure shaped like a mech. Nothing too special to us, but something that must have had special meaning to the character it came from. Chaz placed it in his satchel and we pressed forward. We still had a ways to go before we were completely outside the tower and it was possible we were in danger, especially now that Gorge had set fire to the tower's basement.

Aiko was leading us now, followed by Gorge, Kira, myself, Cass, Chaz, Shiru, and Pierce. We were nearing the surface level and could already hear gunshots from the streets above. Something had gone wrong while we were underground.

'Looks like our luck is up,' said Chaz. He was right. Inside the tower, blocking our way out, was a guardian. It was one of the smaller ones. Four-legged, like a centaur, and eight feet tall. Bulky armour that made it look like it was competing to win some heavyweight championship and a giant mace made of dwarf star alloy. The guardian targeted us as soon as we entered the room, swinging its mace down on the ground and cracking the floor below. No way the Chel were happy about us trespassing.

'Form up, we can take it,' yelled Gorge.

'IT'S A GUARDIAN!' yelled Pierce. Like the rest of us, he was unsure if it was even possible to take out one of these mech-like creatures.

'Circle it and draw its attention, stay apart. The centaur can only go after one of us at a time,' Chaz yelled. He was right. The noob had taken the lead. We separated out in a circle and began firing. I wasn't able to get time to slow down again but I was still satisfied with my new affinity to *Naomi*. In a way, I felt like Hannah was actually fighting alongside me. Our party surrounded the close-quarters guardian while Aiko transformed and began jumping around drawing the guardian's attention away from the others. As the guardian caught on to what we were doing it began to target us one by one. First, it set eyes on Pierce. Pierce jumped back and dodged losing half his health to a glancing blow of the mace, but still remaining in the game. His weapon had taken a nasty hit and he was out of commission until Chaz threw him an energy pistol. The rest of us distracted the guardian with flash grenades. Biding our time. It was a long drawn out bout but the

317

guardian continued to weaken. Eventually, it came after me and I unsheathed *Aegis* from my back.

Aegis - Re-forged Broadsword

Cut down by the forces of Lintirmai, the depraved creature known only as the beast's soul was imprisoned inside a great metal sword made from the hull of an ancient alien starship. Passed from one cursed soul to another the *Aegis* is a living weapon that not only protects its master but eventually devours their very being.

That which may never die must be contained.

Damage: 300 (with 25% chance of 420 damage critical)
Class: None required
Level Required: 50
Weight: 10 lbs
Affinity: 90%
Sharpness: None
Elemental: Shadow - Unknown
Modifiers: None

I could still see tiny blemishes where I must have broken *Aegis* and re-forged parts of the sword. I thought of the Paladin in *Stormcaller*, the game Hannah and I had played. The way the sword had been sharp on both edges. The way it moved like an extension of the character's body. I wanted to move like that. I sank one edge of *Aegis* into the guardian and jumped upward, swinging my body in the air, using my blade to climb up on top of the guardian's shoulders. Once there I held *Aegis* with both hands and sank it into the neck of the guardian.

It fell downward with my body still on top of it. Nothing but a lifeless piece of junk. There weren't even any parts we could scavenge.

'That was awesome!' Chaz shouted towards me. He was giving me a thumbs up. Together, the seven of us and Aiko had killed a guardian.

Outside, we found the streets were no longer filled with the hustle of players and NPCs. They were empty.

'The Hollow Mass...' Cass.

'The reason it was so large...' Chaz.

'Nel, can you bring the ship to us?' I asked through my comm.

'Already on my way, urgent transmission, must hurry,' Nel responded faster than I expected. It wasn't the usual witty response either. Nel actually sounded very worried.

25.
Trespass

LOCATION: OUTSIDE THE TOWER
THE SPIRE

We were trespassers.

I aimed down the sights of my rifle as we took cover behind burning rubble just outside the tower. Between us and the tower gates was a long courtyard that hours earlier had been filled with a beautiful exotic garden of flowers ranging in colours from red and white to purple and grey. Most of the flowers were withered now, while others lay on the ground, burned. The air smelled of gunfire and smoke. Several dozen Hollows were forming around us. I fired and reacted as one appeared almost above me, reaching down to grab me and pull me away. It only took one shot from AKA *Naomi* for the Hollow to turn to ash and cover me in a dust that dissipated only moments after touching me. The dust was poison but I had built enough resistance in the Chel dungeon that it didn't have any lasting effect. Nothing noticeable anyway, as my health only dropped from 100 HP to 98.

In her battle form, Aiko leapt at one Hollow after another. It looked as if she was getting stronger with every kill, however she was starting to lose control. Another came from behind her and I screamed, telling her to turn. She did as I commanded but it was almost too late. Aiko kicked the Hollow, taking a small amount of damage before tearing into it with her teeth. If she had been a player the touch of a Hollow would have hurt her, maybe even killed her, but given her nature my familiar was immune. I also noticed her health was regenerating. Aiko had ten kills and counting before I called out to her at the top of my lungs, urging her back to us but catching the attention of three more Hollows.

Cass threw down a shield, giving Kira enough time to trigger a blast of cascading energy that wiped the area around us clean. My two friends were drained of their mana, while the rest of us looked upward. The tower itself had been attacked from the right side and in the distance we could see the edge of a Titan, rising just enough above several of the smaller buildings that we knew that a large battle was raging around us.

'Do you think that is Lady Gray?' Chaz asked.

'Not hers, different details, doesn't look like it belongs to the Kings either,' said Pierce.

'Maybe someone else wanted to take a crack at becoming famous,' said Kira. She was right. Since the chase there had been dozens of players that had attempted to copy what we had done and this was one of the reasons for the Spire's increased security.

Nel was coming in hot. I could still see clamps hanging down from the *Ibanez* where they had been blasted, broken apart in a desperate attempt to free the ship. As the back hatch opened to let us inside, we noticed another Hollow Mass forming across the street. Hurriedly, we exited the courtyard. Nel was there as the hatch opened, sitting inside a heavily modified version of the mech 'Vex', awaiting our arrival.

```
Hollow Mass 1
Level 41
Hostile


Hollow Mass 2
Level 62
Hostile


Hollow Mass 3
Level 53
Hostile
```

A fourth one was coalescing but Nel destroyed it with a guided grenade before it fully formed. They were weaker in their fluctuating state. Not that it mattered with three already coming towards us. Unlike the one in the tower, these three Hollows were shaped more like golems than snakes. The lowest level monster had a giant face covering its torso, along with massive teeth and one red, glowing eye. The other two were shaped like the silhouettes of giants come to life. As Gorge ordered Cass, Pierce and Shiru to the ship to provide support, Nel opened fire. The rest of us were taking cover behind another piece of debris, to blindfire at the three creatures.

'Fire at the red orbs,' yelled Pierce. He was already inside the ship, holding a scanner in his hands. The scanner was old-school tech. A mod made by one of Gorge's friends and a part of an ever growing collection of his that was filling up the storage on the *Ibanez*. During Aiden's time with the ship Gorge had him gather several supply caches he had planted throughout various systems. The objects from them ranged from low-tech scanners like the one Pierce held in his hand to weapons of mass destruction that could wreck starships. Other items in the collection included rare artefacts that Gorge had given Aiden permission to trade for upgraded weapons and armour. Another reason he had been able to buy the *Crimson Killer* so easily. Gorge, of course, didn't care. He considered it all a gift ever since Lady Gray had made him an official member of the Corpse Divers after we escaped the dungeon on Rem. I admired him for that.

The scanner read enemy weak points and pointed them out. It could also be modified to attach to a mech suit or heavy rail gun but none of us had the time or engineering skill to quickly succeed in doing that.

'Let's roll the dice, see how much damage we can do,' yelled Shiru supporting a rocket launcher. The rocket erupted, hitting the low level Hollow Mass in the lower jaw. Now with broken lower teeth, the creature lurched towards the ship. Nel stepped forward, drawing a large eight-foot sword. Another modification made to Vex. In losing about ten tons of armour and re-fabricating the frame, it was obvious that during our time away from the *Ibanez* everything had gone through a serious upgrade (or downgrade if you wanted a to still use the Vex as a mobile fortress). What was once a heavy, moved somewhere between a light and medium mobile suit of armour. The mech didn't walk, instead it hovered across the pavement towards the Hollow Mass like it was on ice skates, gliding as it danced, blade in hand.

Hollow Mass 1 died almost as quickly as it formed, as Nel swung the eight-foot blade into its broken jaw, breaking its upper row of teeth and next slicing it in half. The Hollow turned to ash. The second Hollow turned its attention away from our blindfire and began making its way towards Nel.

Nel was ready. Lifting the sword into the air and gliding forward, Nel thrust the sword into the Hollow's chest only for the Hollow to grab hold of it with both hands and toss Nel backwards. With a sound of thunder, Nel hit the ground and created a small fissure in the pavement. Steam blew up from underground. Although Nel had been stranded for only a moment, it was enough time for the Hollow Mass to jump on top of the mech suit and begin tearing it apart. The monster slowly changed form, one hand enlarging while the other grew smaller. It was manipulating its own body mass. The Hollow's enlarged right hand turned into a blade and Nel ejected, skidding across the ground towards the ship. The Hollow continued to go rampant against the shell of the mech before picking it up and swinging it into a nearby building. The smoke covered the streets and it became harder to breath.

As the dust from the air filled my virtual lungs, I felt my health drop. Kira moved beside me and handed me a breather from her stash. I was lucky she carried a spare. Somewhere along the way I had lost mine.

Both Hollows were making their way towards the *Ibanez* now. Pierce and Shiru had already picked up a railgun called *Heavy Hitter* and a grenade launcher called *Catapulta*. Both did some serious damage but the Hollows were regenerating faster than we could damage them. Against just one, all of our attacks together could it down, but against two we were struggling. Gorge began planting several explosives on the ground running in the blindspot of the two beasts. Presumably, he was hoping to blow a sink hole in the street. His last three charges were thrown just in front of the two giants and he pressed the killswitch. The world went silent. The blast wasn't enough. The streets caved in but only barely. Re-enforced from below the streets of the Spire were made to take heavy damage. Gorge's attack was useless.

'Plan B: focus fire on one and have Aiko distract the other,' I yelled.

Aiko went after the second and strongest of the Hollows only to be knocked back with a yelp. I ran towards her. Aiko's health hadn't dropped at all but she was stunned. Not enough resistance against an enemy at level 62. Most likely it saw Aiko coming and had poured its mass into that hit. I ordered Aiko to hold back while we formulated another plan.

'Use the *Ibanez*'s defensive weapons!' Cass shouted.

Pierce was already moving through the ship. Great minds. It would still take him a few minutes to warm up the artillery though.

'Three minutes,' Pierce cried out through the comms. He must have sprinted, using all of his stamina to get to the control room that fast. We could already see the turrets on the side of the *Ibanez* targeting the two giant Hollows as we drew them away from the hangar. Shiru grabbed another heavy weapon and Pierce had no choice but to close the door and lock us out. With no escape, we had to finish the fight. Shiru immediately began firing at the Hollows, turning their attention away from us.

He held it for two minutes before running out of ammo and taking cover behind some store wreckage. All he had now was a Ki rifle.

The second Hollow hit Gorge, knocking his HP down to 30. Gorge's cybernetic arm was torn up and he could barely hold his rifle as he used it to stand himself back up.

The third Hollow hit both Cass and Chaz, knocking their HP down to 40. The attack wasn't very strong but both of them had tried blocking, with all of their stamina being used in the process. Kira and I flanked the third Hollow, firing blue energy at it from behind. The smell of burning metal and concrete dust in the air was all around us. I could feel my lungs choke as I pulled *Aegis* from my back and attempted to climb atop the giant the same way I had the guardian but found myself knocked back against the side of a wall, leaving an impression as I fell to the ground. My armour's shield fell to 0, my HP dropped 10 points and I was sitting at 80. Kira wasn't so lucky when she attacked after pulling an extendable staff from her stash. I could see bolts of red and yellow electricity cover the area around her as her shield burst into pieces of digital debris. She managed to deal a heavy amount of damage to the creature but her health dropped down to 20 in the process.

It was enough. The turrets from the *Ibanez* locked onto the Hollows and began firing. Red orbs began to appear all across the Hollow's bodies as they made a noise that sounded like I imagined how the Wilhem scream sounded. The stronger Hollow poured its mass into one swiping attack extending its arm like a whip as its body shrank and a moment later the turrets were gone. The firing stopped and there was silence again. Damaged but not done, the two monsters fused into a massive Hollow with a level of 115. Shiru fired a shot from behind cover. Draining his HP with the Ki rifle he managed to stop the Hollow mid-transformation. It took quick notice of him focusing its raw energy into a single melee attack. Arm bearing down over him, Shiru continued to fire until there was nothing left. His HP dropped to 0 and his avatar rolled over dead.

'No!' I shouted getting the monster's attention. It turned its second attack towards me as I rolled. More angry than afraid I stood up and fired again until Gorge called out to me to get cover.

A hundred thousand HP. The Hollow mass increased as it sucked up pieces of debris from around its body including the corpse of Shiru. Most of it looked almost mechanical as pieces of window, steel bars, blocks of tile and concrete swarmed around red orbs, covering the Hollow in a hardened shell. At its core I could see Shiru's body wrapped like a fly in a spider's web. It absorbed him and whatever echo/artefact he might have left behind. The massive Hollow stood twenty-five-feet high, like the most powerful of guardians.

```
┌─────────────────────────────────────┐
│           Hollow Leviathan          │
│              Hostile                │
│             Level 115               │
└─────────────────────────────────────┘
```

The Leviathan's jaws formed teeth as it began to take the form of a giant alligator. A black alligator with red orbs, covered in metal plating made from ruins. Its teeth bit down hard against the back of the *Ibanez* as Nel announced they were going to take off and that we had to regroup with them several blocks away. Chaz and Cass raced into a nearby building, only to be followed by the Leviathan, which tore through the Spire like it was made of paper mache. I felt the world slow down again as I regained my focus. I moved with the shadows around me, letting the darkness guide me through the void as I shot from my rifle, my life force draining away until my HP was as low as 40. I missed. I shot again. This time my life force drained to 20 and as the world sped back up around me: I felt my adrenaline spike. I had hit one of the red orbs and knocked the Leviathan on its side.

Just as I had hoped, Aiko took advantage. No longer stunned, my familiar grabbed hold of one of the red orbs and bit down hard, tearing away bits and pieces of armour revealing red flesh below the surface. The Hollow was evolving into an organic being made of flesh and bone. Basing its form around a mutated form of Shiru's avatar.

Cass and Chaz were a safe distance away but they were going in the wrong direction. Kira, Gorge and I regrouped with Aiko as the Hollow appeared stunned, sitting silently in the ruins. We knew it was recharging but without all seven of us firing at once our weapons weren't enough to damage it. Not to mention we could hear more Hollow Mass creatures forming in the city blocks around us. Several dozen starships were attempting to flee the planet. Some were being shot down but it wasn't clear who was doing the shooting. Flares of light came from the sky above while bolts of lightning erupted from the ground.

'This is our fault,' I said looking at Gorge and Kira.

'This was inevitable,' Gorge said.

'You blew up the Spire, pissed off the Chel, started a war,' I was angry. This wasn't a part of the plan.

'That doesn't explain what happened, this battle we walked into began before we blew up the basement,' Gorge pointed out. I knew he was right. Something outside our circle of influence had started all of this and it just happened we were caught in the middle. I suppose I wanted to blame someone, anyone, for what was happening.

'It's not Gorge's fault; not yours either,' said Kira.

'Thank you, wasn't sure if you were on my side or not,' Gorge said.

'If you hadn't blown up the Spire dungeon, I would have,' she said back.

Gorge looked at me. I was trying to understand. 'I know,' he said putting his good hand on my shoulder, 'if anyone is to blame it is the Skull-Faced man. We are pawns in a game of chess. Lady Gray, the Crimson Kings, humanity, Chel, and the man in the skull mask. The game is advancing faster and we have to move forward. We need to move ourselves. Adapt. Evolve. Right now we are a block away from the rendezvous point and the Leviathan is going to be back up soon. Shiru sacrificed himself already, let's not waste his effort.' Gorge gave me an encouraging smile and turned towards Kira who nodded back towards the both of us. I smiled.

The Leviathan stood up quicker than any of us expected. It was already upright, looking straight ahead, over us, as we began to move again. Yet the Leviathan looked frozen, as if it was null.

Its eyes were big, empty. From the ground it looked soulless, like a statue that had been carved from black ivory. I focused again, letting the shadows and time overtake me. It was beginning to feel like a drug. I felt all my pain dissipate as time slowed and I fired destroying another red orb. The Leviathan lashed out turning its attention back towards us. I knew I had scored a critical hit and it wouldn't take much more to kill it. We cleared the corner hoping to see the *Ibanez* pointing its forward gun our way, just high enough so that it would take out the creature.

We rounded the corner and the blade of a massive guardian swung overhead, cracking against the Leviathan. The disfigured form of Shiru vanished into a digital cloud of dust. The guardian was an old friend, alive and well, remodelled but still much the same minus a few upgrades. It stood 45 ft off the ground with a sword that looked part battle-axe in one hand and a hammer in the other.

Guardian Aegialeus Level: 300 Very Hostile

26.
Down

'RUN,' I screamed as loud as I could. We were frozen. It would not have mattered if we ran anyway. The guardian ignored us. Instead, the unexpected occurred as it turned and ran towards another Hollow Leviathan that was beginning to form. We ducked down behind more ruins and waited several minutes until we could hear the Hollow Mass Leviathan and guardian fighting one another in the distance. Whether it was the same one that had distracted Aegialeus from us or yet a third Leviathan which had entered the battle, it didn't matter. We knew that for the time being we were out of harm's way.

The *Ibanez* landed, with Cass and Chaz in their mech suits, the *Pilgrim* and *Radagast* waiting for us in the hangar. Pierce was controlling the ship. All guns were active and ready to fire. Although Nel had taken serious damage, she would be all right after a few hours, thanks to the help of self-repairing nanites. Gorge's arm too would be repaired shortly. It had been thirteen hours since we descended into the Spire's atmosphere and began our mission but none of us could logout, not yet. *At Eternity* was waiting for us just at the edge of the system. So close to the finish line we had to see this through, not just for us, but for those we had lost. There were even people like Gorge and Lady Gray who depended on *Bane* wanting our mission to succeed. Damien's death; Kira's brother; their deaths would be meaningless if we didn't succeed. Even if we broke *Bane*.

As we rose up away from the city, I could still see the guardian. This time it was in battle against two Leviathans. Each one looked just as dangerous as the one it had slain saving our lives. It was hard to believe. Without knowing it, the Chel had actually helped us.

Nel gathered us together at once. 'We have a problem,' her voice still sounded worried.

'What is it?' I asked, wondering how could we still have a problem when we were exiting the planet's atmosphere. Away from the guardian, away from the Hollows and the Chel. What more could be going wrong?

There was a slight pause, three words I never thought I would hear: 'you have died.'

'What do you mean, I'm dead?' I asked. I was shaking when I looked over at Kira. She was crying, watching something. At first I couldn't make it out. Maybe my mind didn't want to believe what I was seeing. *Bane* had to be playing tricks. On the holo feed I saw Skull-Faced Man holding a gun. The same one used to kill Damien. Holding it to Aiden's head...to my head. A moment later Aiden was gone.

The feed was thirty minutes old. Playing in a loop.

'When Aiden died your location became publicly available,' Kira began, 'everyone knew we were inside the Spire. The Titans that crashed, the dead in the streets, the war against the Chel that started. Lady Gray was cleaning up. The Titan we shrugged off as belonging to a random player. Lady Gray had bought and paid someone to crash it. Everyone, the whole damn system, was attempting to come after us so she killed as many as she could. She made the Hollows. The Hollow Mass. The Leviathan. The guardian didn't attack us because it still couldn't see passed our disguises. The Crimson Kings, Lady Gray and the man in the skull mask, they can all see us, my feed, my camera, its hacked.' Kira was crying but I could tell she wasn't done speaking, 'they are all waiting for us at *At Eternity.*'

27.
Mek

I watched the video over and over again. Rewinding backwards I watched it all from the beginning to end. It began with Aiden and Eli inside the *Crimson Killer* in Quadrant 12. They had just finished fighting a horde of Wraiths on a planet called Quala. Aiden, wearing my face, looked like he was having the time of his life. It was surreal watching him play me. His body, his eyes, all identical. The only difference was that he was a better player and it was obvious. The way he moved with such agility, endurance. I was surprised so many could be fooled thinking he was me.

After clearing the Wraiths, Aiden was showing off his newest mech suit. A light unit called the *Bright Wind of Eternal Night*. It looked identical to *Naomi's Grace*, including sword and battle rifle. Just like *Naomi's Grace* it was custom modded and blue. On the side were dozens of decals, courtesy of the dozen sponsors. More money for the company. At least they were making the best of it. I couldn't blame them. I didn't want the fame. I hated it. The penthouse suite. Being watched in the real world. The thought of being watched twenty-four/seven made me feel uncomfortable. Taking control of my career and letting me go covert was the kindest thing Lady Gray and Aiden had done for me.

Now…now it was all my fault. I had made Aiden a target. My face led to his death. His blood was on my hands.

Inside the *Crimson Killer* Aiden had received a message from Lady Gray calling for assistance at Quadrant 1 near *At Eternity*. The message was fake. Lady Gray's face and voice were convincing but it wasn't her. Kira had cleared that up almost immediately. Lady Gray hadn't arrived until after Aiden and Eli, when she saw the trouble they were being led into. Aiden, being the hero, had powered up the STL and jumped. He was there before anyone, having jumped into the quadrant just a few hours after us. According to the time stamp on the footage it would have been about the time I was inside the Chel dungeon. Minutes after entering Quadrant 1 and approaching the vicinity of *At Eternity*, Skull-Faced Man's starship appeared. The cameras had managed to good to get a good shot of it. I felt like I was watching an alien invasion film. The way the masked man's ship appeared was like something from a caffeine-fuelled nightmare.

'What do we have here?' Aiden asked. He already knew the answer. He had just as much intel as the rest of us to look at after hours and he had been following our progress since the beginning, keeping up to date on everything. Even promising us his support should we need it. Maybe that was another reason he had jumped so quickly. The message from Lady Gray, the thought that we were in danger. Like Damien, he wasn't one to hesitate. Like Damien he was just as dead and there was nothing I could do.

I was helpless: watching the video made me sick BUT I had to watch. I had to see it all the way through. I wasn't the only one. This was the only source we had for Skull-Faced Man's defences, maybe even his weaknesses, if there were any. Kira and Gorge studied other parts of the video as I watched on. The *Crimson Killer* was fired upon. Skull-Faced Man's ship disabled their engines and then his soldiers boarded. Not just the masked man but several dozen soldiers dressed in solid black armour that made them look like they had all been copied and pasted from the same source. Autons? No, they moved like players. NPCs.

Eli was injured first. Wounded badly, he logged out and his avatar stood helpless as Skull-Faced Man came into view. Brand was the next to fall. He was knocked so hard against a wall he died almost instantly, all the while Eli's avatar stood like a statue. The masked man didn't destroy the avatar with his gun, instead summoning a blade of white light that stretched three feet out from the top of his wrist. It was blinding at first, until the camera adjusted, focusing in on the weapon. With the blade he shattered Eli's avatar and it disappeared like it was never there. It was the first time I had seen an energy weapon used that way. While it was possible, it was not common. The weapon, if not unique to him, had to either be an artefact or ultra-rare.

Skull-Faced Man then grabbed one of the cameras and shot Aiden in the knee as he attempted to logout. There was no injury. Yet it was as if the wound had caused some kind of glitch in the system and Aiden was unable to log out of the game. Skull-Faced Man slowly walked towards him, carrying the camera, filming from his own point of view.

'Careless are those that trespass. Careless are those who believe they are free. Careless are those that seek to escape that which the fates have bound them,' Skull-Faced Man spoke in a deep, smooth voice, 'careless are the pretenders.' And Aiden was gone. A moment later the feed went black before switching to Kira's feed and at the same time revealing my true location to everyone watching. As the feed continued, quick clips of Aiden's death were replayed, cutting in and out with our own exploits as we began to exit the first dungeon. The interruptions stopped when we made it to the courtyard, about the time Nel contacted us telling us about the 'urgent transmission'.

336

Kira managed to data mine several pieces of information from the video, relaying them to us from outside the game, sending us intel via messages from a terminal at Moonrain Media in the real world. Skull-Faced Man had no visible player data and neither did any of the soldiers. That in itself was a form of intel. The second and most valuable piece of information she found was the name of the gun he was using to kill players. It was an artefact. Player made. It had been designed to block a player from being able to logout by fragmenting player in-game commands and overloading the player's neural interface, blocking pathways in the player's real body, causing cardiac arrest by starving the brain of oxygen.

Two shots. The first shot disabled the players' in-game commands and the second shot destroyed their neural pathways like a virus.

```
┌─────────────────────────────────────────────────┐
│                    M.E.K.                        │
│                                                  │
│       Description: Master Encyption Key          │
│                 Level: 100                       │
│                Damage: Fatal                     │
│                Weight: 7 lbs                     │
│  Weapon Type: M7-7 Ki Rifle w/ Battle Rifle support │
│             Rarity: One of a kind                │
│                 Impact: 10                       │
│                 Range: 10                        │
│                Stability: 10                     │
│              Reload Speed: 9                     │
│     RPM (rounds per minute): 20 bursts           │
│                Affinity: 10                      │
│               Sharpness: 10                      │
│              Elemental: Shadow                   │
│            Critical Chance: 98%                  │
│         Modifiers: Sniper Scope 3x Zoom          │
└─────────────────────────────────────────────────┘
```

On our way out from the first dungeon and the Chel tower, a mass of bounty hunters had gathered waiting for us. That was when Lady Gray had taken quick action, paying a new player to crash a Titan and attacking the surface of the Spire with everything she had. The city was decimated and our guild had officially declared war on the Spire, war on the Chel. There was no way we could have known. No way we could have stopped any of it. How many had to die before they just let me be? It was our mission, our job to stop the Skull-Faced Man before something like this happened, but Kira confirmed it. While Eli and Brand were alive in the real, Aiden had passed away.

To everyone else, we were in the middle of the biggest scam in gaming history and the price on my head had doubled. This time, it seemed even Keen Industries were offering a reward.

'I just bought you out!' Kira shouted, as she logged back in.

'What?' I asked.

'The company, Keen Industries, they just turned their back on you. All of you. Even Lady Gray. I just bought out your contract, the penthouse, Reynolds, everything. You, along with the Corpse Divers, are now a part of Moonrain Media.'

I couldn't believe it. Everything was all happening so fast, but it was that easy…the switching of hands. Keen Industries wanted to be as far away from all of this as possible. Knowing what could happen. Knowing it could all go south. This was their contingency plan. A deal made in the dark between Lady Gray, Moonrain Media and Keen Industries.

Waving her arms excitedly, Kira continued, 'you don't have to do this; we can all logout, go home. I can cash it all in and we can all be free of this, this world. We don't have to risk our lives. Keen Industries were happy to let you go. You are absolved of all debt. The penthouse is yours. You aren't going to be under watch anymore,' she was about to continue but I couldn't let her.

'If we stop now it's all in vain, that isn't what my brother, your brother, that isn't what anyone who has died would want. Whatever happens, whatever it takes. No matter how big the crisis. We have to go on.' I couldn't help it. Something had changed in me. Something had grown. To everyone else I was now *Bane*'s number one villain. In the real world I was part of the weirdest conspiracy theory ever but here I was thinking myself some kind of avenging hero.

I wasn't. And truth, every story needs a monster.

28.
Catharsis

TO: *Hannah*

FROM: *Breq*

SUBJECT: *Endgame*

After our attack on the Spire I succeeded in clearing the bottom level of the tower and the first dungeon. I made it. Level 51. Not that it was necessary. It wasn't easy either. I've lost parts of me in this game. Memories. Something isn't quite right and I can feel it. The world both inside and out is changing. Skull-Faced Man isn't in the Cold Zone anymore. He's here...right now raging a battle against Lady Gray and the rest of the Corpse Divers near the world gate At Eternity. That's not all though. The gun, the MEK. It was made by a player. My world has turned upside down. One moment I feel like I'm a hero and the next I'm destroying starships with only a slight hesitation. A few weeks ago I was a nobody and now I'm being followed by more than a million viewers, while Kira once again streams everything we do. In this case we want the world to know. This isn't a game anymore. At least not one in which we are in control.

We're moments away from joining the battle and I'm scared. I'm scared I'm not going to come back, that I may never see you again.

Since I lost my parents I thought I would never find happiness again. I thought the world was broken. I thought I was broken. You made me see the world for the better. You, Damien, Kira, Gorge, Aiden, Eli, Pierce...you made me feel like I was a part of a family again and I'm scared that all of this will be for nothing.

The back guns on the Ibanez are firing. Players are dying. Not at the hands of Skull-Faced Man but by orders I gave. One after another. I can feel the warmth on the walls around me. The shields are taking heavy damage. We're being followed and attacked from behind. Bounty hunters, assassins, players looking to make a name for themselves and others thinking we are easy prey. I can't help but wonder if you are back there with them maybe trying to slow them down or, worse, on the surface of the Spire buried among the ruins.

I've already erased half this message. Trying to write it to you. To put into words all the right things I want you to know. To leave behind a record of what happened. We have so little time left. I hope this is enough. I want you to know that I didn't just do this for you or the rest of my team. I didn't do this for Damien or for the paycheck. Kira gave the others and I an out. All of us refused. I'm here now on my own accord. My own free will. My destiny is mine. Please be safe. Skull-Faced Man has used the MEK twice so far that we know of and there are a dozen more rumours of death circling his appearance. I'm not going to tell you to stop playing. I know even if I did it probably wouldn't stop you. Some have no choice. Others like myself have chosen to stand for those who have adopted this world.

This world we're ready to die for.

The people we are ready to die for.

If something happens to me…you know.

- Breq

I feel like if I was a hero I had been severely wounded. Lost. Out of my mind. The darkness of space driving myself and my team forward. Dozens of players chasing us. I gave Nel the order to destroy them by any means necessary while I tried to record my last will and testament. Not that I didn't have faith in our abilities. Three starships had already fallen. Small, light freighters. My personal inbox was blowing up with threats from people in the real. Even news agencies were asking me what I'm planning and for details as to what exactly was going on. I ignored them. Sending a message to Hannah had already taken up too much of my time but I was not the only one locked in their room writing to people I cared about. We had to leave a record. The truth would come out eventually and when it did the world would shake until the events of this day faded. Some of the messages I received were from casualties of Lady Gray's attack on the Spire. Others, from those blown away in the last few minutes by the *Ibanez*. All of us aboard were collecting small amounts of EXP whenever a starship went down and at the rate we were going I might even level up again. Only a few of the messages were encouraging, a handful of people who still believed in what we were doing.

'Kill anything that comes after us,' I ordered. Kira and Gorge were probably better leaders than I was, so too was Cass, but command had fallen to me. Each of us had played our part. Each of us had strengths and weaknesses.

I was sitting in my room next to Aiko. I held a seven-string guitar in my hand. I had barely picked it up since playing *Bane* and I had an exact duplicate sitting in my penthouse at home. I strummed a few chords. I remembered my father teaching me to play. Coaching me while he played bass or drums. Teamwork was key. He was teaching me, even then. The more I reflected on everything the more I felt responsible. Reports were coming in. News of our merger with Moonrain Media. The entire world would be watching us again. I contacted Cass and together with Aiko began to walk towards the armoury, placing the guitar back against the wall of the room. It was a reminder that *Bane* was more than a game, infused as it was with such fine detail.

Inside the armoury I needed to recharge my rifle and secure ammo. Might as well use this time to talk to the others.

'Cass, you and Chaz shouldn't come with us,' I was looking her in the eye as we stood in the centre of our armoury. I was gathering ammo. At this point there was no way I was letting go of my gear.

AKA *Naomi.*
M7-7 Ki / Energy Rifle

Description: Boss Slayer with Shadow ability to slow time.

Level: 33
Damage: 275
Weight: 5.5 lbs
Weapon Type: Scout Rifle / Ki Rifle hybrid
Rarity: Ultra-Rare
Impact: 10
Range: 9
Stability: 9.5
Reload Speed: 10
RPM (rounds per minute): 300 bursts
Affinity: 10
Sharpness: 8.5
Elemental: Shadow
Critical Chance: 91%
Modifiers: Bonus EXP gained against Robots, Bonus EXP against Hollows, Bonus EXP against Bosses

Aegis - Re-forged Broadsword

Cut down by the forces of Lintirmai, the depraved creature known only as the beast's soul was imprisoned inside a great metal sword made from the hull of an ancient alien starship. Passed from one cursed soul to another the *Aegis* is a living weapon that not only protects its master but eventually devours their very being.

That which may never die must be contained.

Damage: 300 (with 25% chance of 420 damage
critical)
Class: None required
Level Required: 50
Weight: 10 lbs
Affinity: 90%
Sharpness: None
Elemental: Shadow - Unknown
Modifiers: None

'Shove it; like I'm going to let you go alone,' she said, equipping a weapon from one of the adjoining lockers.

'You aren't strong enough.'

'Strength is how you wield yourself as a weapon,' she responded. Cass was right. Maybe I just wanted the affirmation. I was talking to everyone, one-on-one. If we weren't all in this as a team we would lose. This wasn't just another player event or raid.

'Okay, I'll count on you to have my back,' I said extending my hand. I wasn't going to try and talk her down. I knew it wouldn't work. She and Damien had been close. She was just as invested in this battle as I was. If she could have gone head first into the first dungeon I'm sure she would have. Before we left the armoury to make our way back to the bridge Cass showed me her weapon. It was an artefact rifle similar, stat wise, to my own.

```
                        Tyr
            TX-7 Artefact Energy Rifle


                    Description:


    When the moment comes and the moon turns bright
    as blood, there a new brother shall cause the return of
    monsters and end an age of warlords. On this day the
    sky will turn red and together two shall feast on the
                    flesh of the damned.
```

Two Viking runes were carved into the side of the rifle.

```
                     Level: 30
                    Damage: 200
                    Weight: 4.5 lbs
        Weapon Type: Scout Rifle / Ki Rifle hybrid
                    Rarity: Ultra-Rare
                     Impact: 10
                      Range: 9
                    Stability: 9.5
                  Reload Speed: 10
        RPM (rounds per minute): 300 bursts
                    Affinity: 10
                   Sharpness: 8
                 Elemental: Unknown
                 Critical Chance: 91%
    Modifiers: Bonus EXP gained against Robots,
                Bonus EXP against Hollows
```

'I've been saving this for awhile,' she said.
'How did you get that?'

'Earned it when I started playing, it was a level three weapon when I first acquired it; I was only a level ten. Found it inside a giant cauldron, that raiders were cooking Kel in. No matter whether I've used it or not the rifle always seems to keep pace with me. Last time I had it out, I was running to save your scrawny ass in the Spire. Lucky I didn't use it on you,' Cass smiled, polishing the runes on the gun. She was proud of the weapon and rightly so. An artefact rifle that levelled up without being used could have gone for a nice cut of credits on the black market. She could have sold it at any time but she held onto it.

Cass gave me a long look. 'Maybe talk Chaz away from the battle, he has more of a life outside the game than the rest of us. I'm not sure he truly understands what is going on.'

She was right. If any of us had no reason to fight it was Chaz. He had joined us after the dungeon on Rem and had never even met Damien.

'Chaz, I'm going to ready an escape pod for you,' I spoke to him through a comm.

'Negative sir, I've already booted up the *Pilgrim* and *Radagast* for Pierce. Together the three of us have spent a small fortune on some custom cosmetics and upgrades. Had them sent aboard the *Ibanez* while she was still docked in the Spire. A few surprises. Sealed the cockpit, added a few boosters, multipliers, oxygen tanks; I may not be joining you on the frontline but Pierce and I will be your support in space.'

'You don't have to come with us,' I said.

'All due respect, I'm a part of this now: same as you, same as the others.'

'Thank you.'

I couldn't think of anything else to say so took a deep breath and confirmed the arrangement with Pierce. Tel was going to control the *Radagast* and Pierce was going to fly the *Ibanez* after the rest of us boarded Skull-Faced Man's ship. If all went according to plan, they would defend us against any players or NPCs in the area.

As I arrived alongside Gorge and Kira on the bridge, I reminded Chaz to make sure his weapons and armour were maxed out. He was still new after all.

'Everyone say their goodbyes?' Gorge asked.

'Affirmative,' both Kira, Cass and I said, more or less together.

Gorge nodded, his repaired arm smoothing his beard. 'Good; should we go over the plan again?'

'Pretty cut and dry: break in, kill Skully, break out,' said Cass.

'That's oversimplifying it, but yes.'

'How exactly are we breaking in?' I asked, not quite caught up on details.

'Nel is attaching a giant drill to the front of *Eternal Night* and we're going to slam it into the side of their hull, take 'em by surprise,' Gorge gave a cheerful laugh.

'Wouldn't it be better if we teamed up with Lady Gray and took out their ship? Anything to avoid engaging in close combat,' Cass asked.

'Would be, but the Lady and several others are already there and in battle, not to mention Skully's ship is twice as strong as a Titan; we don't have the fire power,' Gorge answered.

'Gorge, I want to apologize again for thinking you were a robot,' Kira said.

'It's okay, I've told you a dozen times I don't blame you,' he answered back.

I was sorry too but the two of us were way past that now. We all had experienced moments of doubt in one another, that was a part of what made us grow as a team. Together we had grown in trust, life, strength and self-confidence. Each one of us levelling up.

The ship shook as one of the vessels behind us broke through the shield.

'Damnit! Nel, give me a quick update on the shields!'

'Shields are at forty-two and holding; how or why is a great question,' Nel responded.

'Pierce is re-routing power from the STL drive, we won't be able to make any jumps for awhile,' Cass said, looking at ship's various energy levels.

'So no jumping out if something goes wrong,' I said.

'No jumping ever again, not without a new drive, Pierce is going to have to eject the core or we won't make it,' Cass looked worried but I knew Pierce must have had a plan. I was right. Cass and the rest of us watched as Pierce ejected the core behind the ship and it ignited, killing another dozen players in what looked like a small supernova.

'Extraordinary,' Nel said, clearly impressed.

'That was our engine,' I said back.

'Only our jump engine, we are on our way to a world gate are we not?' Nel had a good point.

I doubled over in pain as I grasped my stomach. Cramps almost crippled me and for a moment it seemed there was no end to the pain. What if it got worse? These thoughts alone made my heart race faster, never mind the pain itself, all I could think about is what I would lose if the game kicked me out. I felt thirsty and tired but determined. It was clear all of us were feeling the strain of spending so long in virtual reality. For the moment all I could do was remind myself that once it was over I would be able to rest as long as I wanted.

'Are you sure we're ready?' asked Kira.

'As ready as we'll ever be; we have no choice,' I replied still holding my stomach.

'Open your master preferences, turn your pain dampening down and override your pod logout control with this command,' said Gorge handing me a piece of paper with code written on it.

'What is this?'

'This is how I manage to stay logged in almost days at a time,' he answered, 'it's an override, a mod designed for disabled players like myself, so that we can log out at the time of our choosing. You'll still feel some of the fatigue but I've got something for that as well,' he finished, pulling out from a backpack a small packet of herbs, alongside a bag of jerky.

An override, like the MEK, able to modify in-game controls. A part of me wondered if it was designed by the same player. Doubtful. This code, the handwriting, looked like it had been designed by Trace. I entered it just as Gorge suggested. Almost instantly, my stomach cramps began to dissipate. I thanked Gorge as he was crushing the herbs together in a steel bowl using the bottom side of his knife.

> **- 1 handful of Blue Tea Leaf**
> **- 1 teaspoon of Spring Rue**
> **- 3 bits of Black Fenu**
> **- 1 batch of Candy Peppermint**
> **- 3 bits of Winter Grass**

'What is this?' I asked.

'Ingredients, which fused together will help keep you grounded.'

'That's an old shaman recipe isn't it?' said Kira.

Gorge looked across at her with respect. 'Yeah, cool that you noticed.'

'You add the candy peppermint for taste, do you have any-more?'

'I've got enough for all of us.'

He still hadn't opened the meat. I asked about it, 'what is the jerky for?'

'Me,' he replied, taking a bite and offering us some.

We were close. Another few minutes and we'd have to swap the shields to the front of the ship. We could see a projection of Lady Gray's Titan and Skull-Faced Man's ship sitting one on top of the other, surrounded by hundreds of swarming fighters. The exact size of each fleet was unknown. The Skull-Faced Man's ship looked like it could hold thousands of such craft, which just made the idea of attacking them head on feel that much worse.

'Another ship approaching from the rear,' Nel said.

'Take it out,' I ordered one last time.

Luck + 5

Latent Power + 5

Focus + 5

Intimidation + 10

Survival + 5

29.
Scout

Quick Lore

World Gates are massive. Large circular objects that
float near the edge of advanced systems, world gates
such as *At Eternity* are usually the circumference of
dwarf planets. A few World Gates take different forms,
with variations in chambers. They collect and store
power via cells attached all around their interior side,
generating enough power to warp time and space.
Warp Gates are accessed via a transmission code
found in the codex of starships. They can, however, be
hacked and / or activated via an internal interface.

Location Discovered: *At Eternity*
+1200 EXP

The hangar door opened and we flew forward. We were several
hundred yards from the hull of Skull-Faced Man's ship. It was
massive. An orbital carrier, twice the size of Lady Gray's Titan.
While Nel operated *Eternal Night*, we rode inside a string of drop

pods attached the back of the mech like a kite. Aiko was scrunched in beside me, making it hard to see the outside, but I could feel we were covered in flames as several dozen boosters kicked on and off. The drill Gorge had attached to *Eternal Night* was used for mining ore from uninhabitable worlds and stood just as large as the mech itself. One of the reasons we had to use so many boosters was because of the unimaginable weight both the drill and mech produced. It was only in the absence of gravity that both moved together as one piece.

Nel reached out, extending the mech's body through space as small pieces of debris cracked against the outer surface of her mecha. Pressing forward into the hull again and again, like trying to chisel through a tank. After a minute the drill punctured through. I didn't feel the impact or the shock waves of the clash of heavy metals. We all just drifted beside the enemy vessel until a large gap appeared, a white-hot ring calling us inside and a battleground for the nanites of hull's repair systems. Now we had less than a minute to dive into the rabbit hole. The tip of the drill broke off. It was smashed at one end but both Nel and the rest of the mecha were in one piece. Unfortunately, the mecha as too big to move into the confines of the ship and Nel was forced to abandon it for the time being.

Inside, we took a moment of silence. It was the first break we had since leaving the Spire. Everything was moving so fast; I was amazed I still had so much stamina.

Cass and I agreed to scout ahead as much as we could, making sure to stay about a hundred yards clear of the others. Aiko followed us taking point. The three of us were scouts so it made sense. Everyone was using their class and class abilities to their utmost. Ready for this encounter, Kira had even acquired a psi power called *Healing* that would allow her to heal us if we were in close range. The power cost 20 mana a time, with a 90 second cool-down per player, but it was comforting to know that if we found ourselves in a tight bind she could use it to our advantage. For his part, Gorge had acquired a new psi power called *Hull-breaker* that would allow him to use his fully upgraded arm to punch a hole through even the strongest metal. He could optimize the efficiency of the strike depending on how much mana he used.

Location Discovered: Orbital Carrier
+1000 EXP

The inside hallways of the carrier were a bloodbath. Dozens of fallen Corpse Divers were strewn about. Lady Gray must have led them to battle but there was no sight of her anywhere as we crossed from one section to another. Most of Skull-Faced Man's army was made from deformed Autons that looked like they had been slain-hacked and revived from dungeons across the whole of the game. One Auton we ran into looked familiar. Similar in structure and size to the one we defeated on Rem, it was a shadow of what it had once been. Maybe we had just grown that much stronger. Cass and I cleared it out with ease.

Making our way into a smaller corridor, we discovered a holo-map of the area and added it to our inventory. The map appeared in the bottom left hand side of my field of view and would disappear unless I summoned it to me via my interface. The map made moving forward easier than we had anticipated. It was as if Skull-Faced Man was drawing us to him. The basic layout of the orbital carrier was the same as a Titan, only the insides were more spread out. We crossed through a dozen empty hangars and an unused armoury. Following a second run in with an Auton we found ourselves in a giant library, filled with empty book shelves and tables. The orbital carrier was a battle station that could function as a city. Normally, they would come fully armed, automated, and with an artificial intelligence similar to

Nel or Tel, that would attack any players who did not have access. This carrier seemed to be missing both an artificial intelligence and defences.

'Removed for parts?' asked Cass studying an empty wall where a defence turret should have been placed.

'Maybe they moved them to the outside of the ship,' I said.

'That's a good theory, would make sense if they truly believed they were impregnable,' she was quick to point out that we had crossed dozens of these empty turrets and that when the *Ibanez* was coming in close our shields had drained to ten percent power before we hit the hull. Pierce and Chaz were still aboard our home vessel, now separate from our party. I was just grateful that if anything happened to them they would only lose their characters and not their lives.

'I'll give you evens on bones,' Cass said.

'What?'

'I bet half the turrets have been replaced on the outside of the ship but the other half are guarding his chamber.'

'Like a lair?'

'Exactly, imagine this entire ship like a dungeon, we're on the first level, the closer we get the harder it's going to be. The Autons, turrets, all of it is to wear us down until he can finish us off.'

'That sounds like a sound strategy. We aren't dealing with a normal NPC or boss. Skull-Faced Man thinks like a player would and he has the homefield advantage. How many levels down do you think we have to pass?'

'If I had to guess, from where we butchered a hole inside his ship, three, maybe four levels down. That's as long as we are actually moving in the right direction.' Cass seemed unsure of herself.

'I have a feeling we are.' Was I trying to reassure her or my-self? But it was true, I could feel the game pushing me, guiding me. That sixth sense I had become accustomed to every time I logged in. And it was on overdrive at the moment as we pushed further and further into the orbital. I felt like I was awakening.

'Breq! Watch out!' Cass yelled, as some kind of camouflaged creature leapt out from behind the next corner. I couldn't see it but Cass's eyes were more advanced than my own. She fired several dozen rounds at the near-invisible chameleon and it fell in front of me turning red and black before burning to ash and dis-solving around me.

'What was that?'

'I'm not sure, I didn't have enough time to scan it.'

'Another one!' I shouted.

This time I fired. Time slowing. I could feel the shadows move around me. My rifle powering up as I pulled the trigger.

Wraith / Hollow Hybrid
Level 31
Hostile
Poison Attack x 50
Bite x10

'It's a hybrid. Probably why we've seen so many dead bodies but so few Hollows,' I said, sending Cass the information I had gathered.

'How did you scan it so quick?'

'One of my special abilities, ever since I finished the first dun-geon I've been able to slow down time,' I responded focusing on the walls around us.

'That's dangerous!' Cass said scolding.

'How? It's a player ability.'

'No wonder you are experiencing pain, you are pushing yourself past your own limit with that skill. Something like that would take years to master if anyone could master it at all. You aren't slowing time, you are speeding up your own reflexes,' I knew she had more to say but we didn't have time. Another Wraith hybrid was coming towards us. Instead of pulling my rifle I unsheathed *Aegis* and slashed it in half. The Wraith was a lower level than the last one.

'Does this mean we are moving away from Skully?' Cass wondered.

'No, it just means we haven't learned about what is going on yet,' I answered, motioning for Cass and Aiko to follow.

'How are the others holding up? Have they run into anything behind us?' I asked cautiously.

'Report?' Cass ordered through a comm. I could have done the same but delegated the task to Cass so I could concentrate on the room before us.

'No signs of danger; we're right behind you about fifty yards,' replied Kira.

'Over,' said Cass nodding her head towards me.

'At least we haven't missed any,' I smiled, raising my rifle up again and aiming. Another Wraith was moving in the distance. I focused on it.

'Good shot,' Cass said.

'My affinity has gone up too, same with my passive sharpness.'

'Maybe I should go back down and dive into that dungeon,' Cass laughed.

I knew it was a joke but the thought of going back there made me feel sick. Losing seven months of memories and not knowing how I survived was not something I'd recommend to anyone.

'I honestly have no idea what happened to me down there but I know it wasn't good. I poured all my experience into defence and somehow developed a power to slow down time by fusing my affinity for rifles with my latent power, stealth, and focus. Every so often I can feel something inside me, like a nightmare I can't remember trying to dig itself back out from below the surface,' I stopped. A new Wraith ahead of us. This time it was a level 41, fast, faster than the others. Not even Aiko had time to respond.

Both Cass and I missed as the Wraith jumped on Cass knocking her back to the ground. Another grabbed Aiko and the two began sparing like wolves. I raised *Aegis* and attacked the Wraith on top of Cass, only to be knocked back by its tail. A barb had detached itself into my side.

Poison Resistance -10

Stun Resistance - 10

Stealth - 10

Health dropping - .01 /second (poison / bleeding)

Pro Tip

When utilizing *Resistance* in combat upgrade your Guard and Defence skills.

'Kira, we need some help!' I shouted through my comm. Shouting was a bad idea. With Cass down, several dozen more Wraith hybrids were making their way towards us at top speed. Gorge shot the one on top of Aiko, freeing my familiar. Two more attacked as Kira summoned a whip made from electricity. She wrapped it around the Wraith's neck and pulled, breaking it apart.

Cass's health had dropped to 89 while Aiko was still sitting at 95.

Myself, I was losing health rapidly. The longer the barb stayed in me the more damage I was taking.

'Can you heal me?' I asked Kira.

'If we get the barb out,' she yelled back. The two of us retreated behind the others and Kira ripped the sharp barb from my side. I was bleeding out and poisoned. My health had dropped to 75. By the time Kira began healing me I was down to 65, but she managed to bring me back up to 98.

'Good enough!' I said, taking my rifle and helping the others clear the Wraiths attacking us on all sides.

'They are coming through the vents!' shouted Cass.

'Gorge can you make a path?' I shouted.

Gorge nodded, activating his *Hullbreaker* ability and running towards the horde. He slammed into them, Kira right behind, followed by the rest of us. As Gorge took more and more damage, she healed him as quickly as she could, until we finally managed to cross a bulkhead door and seal it from the other side. The Wraiths beat at the door. It would be minutes before they came through. If they were intelligent enough, they might form a mass like the ones in the Spire.

Worse…a Leviathan in an area this small would be unstoppable.

'We need an escape route,' Kira shouted.

We all scanned the room but it was Aiko who began scratching at one of the walls.

'Thin enough you can break through?' I asked Gorge.

'I'll try,' he raised his artificial arm and used his ability again to break a hole wide enough for all of us. The drumming against the bulkhead door stopped. The Wraiths had either gone to find a way around or had lost interest, it was impossible to know.

The next room led us into another open chamber.

'Should I call upon the *Eternal Night*?' Nel asked.

'Not yet, let us scout the area first,' I said.

'Pity,' she responded.

The chamber was eerily silent. We had already taken more damage than I would have liked, meaning a severe drain on Kira's mana from healing us so much. The Wraith hybrids were loathsome creatures. Designer weapons created by Skull-Faced Man or someone else?

The room we found ourselves in us had four switches. Each one of us stood beside one and on my nod, activated it.

And found ourselves face-to-face with a new enemy. Thinking of the Skull-Faced Man's ship as a dungeon we had made our way through the first levels and now we were face to face with what I would call a sub-boss. Maybe not as strong as the Skull-Faced Man himself but we all knew the struggle that was ahead.

```
The Monitor
Level 93
Hostile

Abilities:
Shock Absorption
Resistance
Stun x 10
Strength x 50
Absorption x 10
Damage Booster x 2
Melee x 10

Weapons:
Artefact M7-4 Ki Rifle Prototype
Artefact Necro Sabre
Artfact Iron Armour
```

The Monitor looked like a knight that had walked out of the dark ages only there were small gaps between its iron-scaled armour through which I could see the hatching of wires and the crisscrossing of cybernetic mesh. The Monitor was definitely a cyborg of some kind, with two red, glowing eyes and four claws for hands. It held a heavy long sword in its hand called the *Necro Sabre* that put *Aegis* to shame. On its back was another artefact rifle.

'Three artefacts,' Cass yelled out a warning us.

'I see them, sending you information now,' I responded, updating everyone with what little information I could gather.

The Monitor turned towards Gorge, attacking him first. Our opponent leaned down on his sabre as Gorge caught it in his right hand. There was almost no time for Gorge to respond as the ground cracked below his feet and he held both hands up in the air, holding back the cyber-knight's blade.

Aiko leapt to attack, but was blown back as the Monitor showed us it also had some kind of psionic power that could manipulate the gravity around it. It was pushing harder against Gorge now. The rest of us formed a circle and fired everything we had. Time slowed again as I watched the energy blasts from Cass and Kira's weapons head towards the Monitor, only for its body to break apart. Flying into pieces, one arm came towards me while another stayed attached to the torso holding the sword against Gorge's already busted arm. Another arm and leg were shooting outwards towards Cass and Kira. As one of the Monitor's arms wrapped itself around my neck I yelled, 'Nel, call in the *Night*!'

'I called the *Night* thirty seconds ago,' Nel said proudly. Another two seconds later and the blue mech broke through a wall and Nel quickly slid inside the empty cockpit as it opened up, so she could punch down on the Monitor, forcing the cyber-knight to let go of its sabre and permanently postpone the attack on Gorge. The two went head to head, with Nel quickly gaining the upper hand, having caught the Monitor off guard. The sneak attack alone had caused a massive amount of damage to the monstrosity. Nel continued to beat the Monitor until there was nothing left and the arms and legs that had detached towards us as singular weapons fell to the ground like pieces of salvage. The whole thing was over in a few seconds.

Another figure stood at the end of the room clapping.

Skull-Faced Man.

'Well done,' he said. At that moment, Nel's mecha ran towards him at full speed, slamming a metal fist into his human hand. The masked man blocked the attack and was more than capable of holding his own. Skull-Faced Man clenched his hand into a fist tearing against the giant mecha's metal skin. Almost immediately, Nel ejected as Skull-Faced Man threw the mecha through the air across the chamber, the ruined exoskeleton hitting the wall behind us.

'I have come to rescue you from burden,' the masked man said.

Nel powered back up and I received a message.

```
┌─────────────────────────────────────────────┐
│            Nel has joined your party.        │
└─────────────────────────────────────────────┘
```

NAME: NEL

Age: Unknown   Class: Artificial Intelligence

Level: 100   Health: 210

Status: Alive   Stamina: 1000

Mana: 0

Load out: Ultimate K.O. A01 Dictator Auto Assault Rifle, *Invictus Dagger*

'Way to go little robot!' I shouted watching Nel rise back up.

'Can robots do that?' asked Cass, unsure.

'Does it matter?' Gorge added, pointing, so that our focus returned to Skull-Faced Man. He had taken heavy damage from the Monitor, his health sitting at 55.

'Little robot is with us to the end now,' Kira said.

'Special circumstances,' Nel responded sounding more confident than before. Then her voice rose to a shout. 'ULTIMATE KNOCK OUT!'

I could see the power rising around the floating robot as she practically warped from one area to another, teleporting towards Skull-Faced Man with her hand taking the form of a clawed fist. Nel was quick, but not quick enough. Just as with the Monitor,

Skully could control gravity. Right before impact, Nel's fist hit a wall made of air. With another hand, Nel summoned her rifle from the air and began firing. Each bullet fell flat, torn asunder by gravity wells created by Skull-Faced Man.

The thirty seconds it took Nel to join our party and attack the masked man was all it took to witness her destruction. Nel was gone; she lay on the ground in front of us like burnt-up rubble. I received one last message, 'I'm sorry I lied about the cookies.'

```
A01 Dictator - Auto Assault Rifle added to inventory.

A01 Dictator - Auto Assault Rifle

Description: Designed by robots to kill robots and
painted a pretty, bright blue.

Level: 50
Damage: 600
Weight: 7.5 lbs
Weapon Type: Auto Assault Rifle
Rarity: Ultra-Rare
Impact: 10
Range: 10
Stability: 3
Reload Speed: 9
RPM (rounds per minute): 300 bursts
Affinity: 9
Sharpness: 8
Elemental: Aether (can be stored and summoned by
user on command)
Critical Chance: 60%
Modifiers: Built-in artificial intelligence named Q-el.
```

'What THE HELL!' shouted a voice in my head.

I had summoned Nel's rifle the moment it entered my inventory, taking a quick look at the stats, sheathing *Aegis* across my back and my own rifle down across my side. I was slower with so many weapons but speed wouldn't matter. My enemy was faster than I was…more powerful in every way.

'Nel is gone,' I said. A moment later Q-el was rebooted, moving with its own volition in my hands, forcing me to scan the room like I was holding a camera in my hands.

'Analyzing combat situation,' Q-el said in a voice like that of Nel.

'Anytime now!' I shouted as the skull-faced man looked towards me.

'Chances of survival are less than surviving falling into the sun.'

'Logout!' I heard Cass shout as Skull-Faced Man made a move towards her. She was scared and I couldn't blame her. We might have been here to defeat Skull-Faced Man but it was a battle for life and death. Logging out at the last minute was a part of the plan. A worst-case scenario.

There was nothing. Nothing happened when Cass shouted. Skull-Faced Man moved quicker than I imagined. He held out the MEK rifle and fired a shot into Cass. The first shot cut away her connection with her controls.

She was alive but paralyzed.

He was toying with us.

Gorge tried logging out next. Shouting so we could all see and hear. Nothing happened. Kira tried and nothing happened. I tried and nothing happened. Broadcasting to the world, we were four players trapped off-grid against an enemy that was overpowered. Skull-Faced Man didn't have to shoot us to keep us from logging out. From the moment we entered inside the carrier we couldn't log out. The world was going to watch us die if we didn't think of something fast. Another shot and Cass would be dead. I could hear her screaming from across the room, grabbing the part of her leg Skull-Faced Man had shot. The pain she was feeling had to be intense. Real.

'Let her go!' I shouted while thinking this was no time to play the hero.

Skull-Faced Man appeared in front of me, grabbed my neck, and lifted me into the air.

'Imminent danger!' Q-el said as he was taken from my grasp. Skull-Faced Man stared at it for a moment and smiled. The A01 disappeared from my inventory as he shattered it with his other hand, tossing it to the side.

'I've killed you before: this face, the face of the fallen, the pretender come to die,' the masked man said, studying me. Time had slowed. Shadows surrounded both of us. Everyone else seemed to move in slow motion. Even Aiko who was running towards us. I lifted my hand trying to tell her to stay back, to stay away. To warn all of them it was too late. The shadows were interrupted only by a blinding light.

'Breq...Breq, wake up.'

'Damien?' I open my eyes and I'm in the real. In my bed.

'Yeah, bro' it's me, what are you doing?' the figure standing before me looked and sounded just like Damien but...

'You can't be here; you can't be alive?'

'Living and breathing just like you. Are you okay? You've been asleep for hours I thought we were logging in today? You wanted to do that echo quest in Alpha Centauri right?' his voice so familiar, just as I remember it.

'You're dead.'

'Come on, cut it out, I'm right here, I've been right here.' His voice begins to fade. I feel something pulling me away but I don't want to go.

I sit up in the bed. I'm dressed just as I was the last time I saw him.

'Skull-Faced Man, he killed you?' I said it like it was a question.

'Who?' he responded.

'Skull-Faced Man, he's, we were fighting him. Kira, Gorge, Cass.'

'You went on a mission with Cass?'

'This isn't real,' I declared.

'Are you okay? Should I get a doctor?'

'This isn't real,' I declared again.

A moment later, Damien was gone and I was back in the game. Skull-Faced Man's hand wrapped around my neck. His mask moved, as if he were smiling.

'You are Damien's friend. That must make the rest of you Corpse Divers, artefact hunters,' he said, looking around the room studying us.

'What is it to you?' Cass shouted laying limp, crying on the ground. She was fighting for control, fighting against the effects of the MEK.

'You are the ones that brought me here. I owe you my thanks, your kind, you came into the unknown, rescued me from the void. You answered my call. I am here to free you from yourselves. Save you,' Skull-Faced Man spoke but it felt like he was talking in riddles.

'Speak plainly, what are you?' Gorge demanded.

Skull-Faced Man put me back on the ground gently and let go of my neck. I felt my muscles relax as my body became my own again.

'Kira, you look so beautiful,' the Skull-faced man said looking at Kira, 'and Cass, just as vigilant as ever.' He continued looking around the room.

'You, I don't know,' pointing towards Gorge.

'YOU WILL!' Gorge shouted, activating his *Hullbreaker* ability. A moment later, the masked man teleported away from me and crushed what was left of Gorge's artificial arm in his hand, tearing it away from his shoulder.

368

'Not so fast; I'M NOT done talking.'

Gorge screamed in pain as the Skull-faced man threw him down to the ground. I couldn't tell if Gorge had passed out or was laying low. His health had dropped to 35. No way he could take another hit, even with his ability active, his strength was useless. The skull-faced man drew his MEK rifle and held it out with one hand and fired into his chest. Gorge was paralyzed as Skull-Faced Man sheathed the rifle back around his back.

'Apologies, we'll know one another soon, just give me a moment,' Skull-Face Man continued to speak softly, as if to himself, looking around the room. His eyes moved to his right side as he quickly dodged a bullet from up high. One of the air vents in the room was open and inside was Lady Gray pointing a high-power Ki rifle. She had fired and missed.

'Join us,' said Skull-Faced Man, pulling her from the vent across the room to the floor in front of him. She immediately summoned a blade into her hands and leapt through the air. Her agility was unreal, if my focus wasn't so high, I wouldn't have been able to follow her movements at all. I tried to use my shadow ability but it was useless. Cass brought her rifle up from her hip. She was still in miserable pain, bleeding on the floor. She aimed down the sight balancing it on her knee. Skull-Faced Man caught the bullet and grabbed Lady Gray, pushing her back at the same time.

'What are you?' she mumbled.

'The essence of all that will be,' Skull-Faced Man said, unsheathing the MEK from his back. Lady Gray's health had dropped to 85% but she was still in better shape than the rest of us. Gorge hit the ground, cracking it behind both of them, causing the masked man to stumble. Taking advantage of the moment, Lady Gray once again drew her sword and swung it towards our enemy. Slashing with an attack that should have dealt 300 damage, our guild leader sank her sword into Skull-Faced

Man's shoulder. Even as time slowed, I still couldn't get a read on him.

'Breq, it's me Damien…HELP ME!' a voice rattled inside my head. For a moment I looked at the masked man and instead of seeing a monster I saw my best friend. Damien and Lady Gray were fighting one another with Lady Gray even starting to gain the advantage. I knew it wasn't real but I wanted to help. My allegiance was to Damien, my friend: what if this whole thing was some kind of lie. What if he was alive?

Cass fired again, missing and tearing apart Lady Gray's shoulder.

'Damien?' she said, tears rolling down her eyes.

'ITS NOT HIM!' I shouted.

'That's my brother,' I heard Kira mutter almost like a whisper.

'NO, IT'S SOME KIND OF MIND GAME!' Gorge shouted, lifting himself up from the ground. His health had been regenerating and was already at 45%.

'He can read our minds,' it was Lady Gray who said it. Disarmed by Cass, she now stood at the mercy of Skull-Faced Man. From the ether our opponent summoned a sword. Shorter than my own, it looked like a futuristic katana. A weapon I had seen Damien once use long ago, a favourite of his, kept in his inventory for close-combat situations.

'That doesn't belong to you!' I shouted pulling *Aegis* from its sheath and running as fast as I could across the room. I was dragging *Aegis* across the floor as I sprinted forward, pulling it up only at the last moment to cross blades with the katana. Skull-Faced Man didn't bother to knock me back this time. He was smiling from under his mask, as if he was enjoying the fight.

I was using the shadows. Time had slowed again and I was exhausting my own ability in parrying his blows. My focus grew as I began to gain more and more experience at moving my body through the darkness. The masked man moved quickly, considering he should have been frozen just like the others.

After three seconds I felt my mana hit zero. Time restored itself and Gorge threw himself in front of me, taking the blow from the katana at point blank range. His health had dropped to 15 and I ordered Aiko to pull him back. My health stood at 85, mostly damage I had caused to my own body. Lady Gray was bleeding out. Her health had dropped down to 45 while Kira and Cass were both still well into the 60s range despite their injuries. I might have failed at my attack but I finally managed to get a read on my enemy.

```
Hive
Level Unknown
Health: 500
Hostile

Abilities:
Absorption
Resistance
Strength x 500
Damage Booster x 200
Melee x 100
Focus x 10
Latent Power x 10
Shadow x 10

Weapons:
Artefact M7- 3 Ki Rifle Prototype
Artefact MEK Rifle
Artfact Ultra Blade
```

'Hive?' I sent the information to everyone. 'What are you?' I asked shouting.

Skull-Faced Man ignored me.

I was beginning to bleed out again. When Gorge knocked me out of the way he had opened my wound from before. The pain was unbearable even with my settings turned down.

'Kira?' I said looking in her direction.

She began running towards me. Her mana dropping as she began to heal me from afar. Aiko was running towards my side as well. Immediately taking notice, Skull-Faced Man turned towards us. I screamed as he shot a gravity well over Aiko, sending my familiar crashing to the ground.

'Gods exist in constant conflict, moral codes, struggle, support, divine rewards that break the laws of the real. A thousand years from now humanity will drive itself to the point of extinction, I am the essence, the immortal. I am the embodiment of my master's will, the future of mankind, hive.'

'Finally, something,' Lady Gray said, 'I think I understand now. There is a rumour.'

'Fill us in please,' said Cass. I was equally anxious to know what insight she had.

'Created by a player, the Hive copies the consciousness of those it feeds upon. That is why it appears differently to different players, it shows us who it believes we want to see. The gun kills the player, allowing the exchange of information to become permanent, severing the link at the source and storing information. That's why all this...it wants...' before Lady Gray could finish, the Hive attacked her, burying its sword in her stomach.

'I was born, raised by my master to save humanity, freed by those that heard my calling and who crossed the threshold. I SAVED my master, saved him from a world that rejected him.' The Hive was angry.

As Lady Gray collapsed, she broadcast a burst of Quick Lore.

Aiko pulled Lady Gray out of the way and Kira went to work healing her.

'If you have Damien's memories, you know we don't have to fight,' I said, trying to calm the Hive.

'I saved Damien, just as I WILL save you.'

It came at me. Fast but not fast enough. The slight hesitation it had in killing me was still there. It was haunted by its own core programming. Haunted by the memories Damien had created inside it. Metal met metal as I swung *Aegis* forward. From behind me, Cass moved and fired with *Tyr*. The Hive's health was already down to 300 HP thanks to Lady Gray, who soon joined the fight again.

When my stamina ran low, the two of us switched out. All the while, Cass continued to fire. My health dropped to 55 HP. Lady Gray was sitting at 30 HP and Cass had taken a few hits herself from gravity wells, bringing her down to 40 HP. By the time the we had the Hive's health down to 150 HP, it was starting to look hopeless again: no matter how many times we relied on Kira for support. Gorge's health was no longer regenerating either. At 15 HP he tried to help us when he could, summoning the artefact rifle I had given him back at the Upsilon and raising it for a shot.

Gorge fired. A critical hit for 60 damage! It was a good shot that staggered the Hive, giving both Cass and I time to draw our rifles and fire full blast. When my battery started to die and my ammo ran low I used my HP to fire a second critical hit at the Hive. It turned towards me and with a gravity well placed above my head I felt an intense pressure. For a moment I feared my bones would splinter and crack and I would die right here in the game. The sudden impact broke my rifle. AKA *Naomi* was gone but it wasn't the end. I had given Lady Gray an opening.

The Hive's blade broke through Lady Gray's attack and slashed her, knocking her health down to 5 HP. She was out. It focused on Cass next, smashing her back against a wall with a gravity well. Kira didn't have the mana to heal anymore. Biting down against the Hive and snatching the MEK, Aiko ran in to join the fight.

Six of us had gone against the darkness. Now I stood alone.

My sword drawn in my hand I focused on the shadows. Time slowed down between us as *Aegis* began to crack. We fought like Samurai for what felt like eternity. Locked in battle for mere seconds. I blacked out. A vision of a beast with five eyes. I had pushed myself too far and my body, my mind had exhausted itself.

In that moment *Aegis* dropped from my hands and Skull-Faced Man, the Hive, held me by the neck again.

The Hive was down to 90 HP. Kira picked up *Aegis* and thrust it into the Hive from behind. 'For my brother,' she said, twisting my sword, whose tip emerged from the Hive's chest. Her face held a look of determination. Vengeance was hers. It let out a scream and for a moment I saw Damien. A ghost smiling at me. Maybe I was hallucinating. It wasn't possible that he was still there. Damien was gone.

Quest Complete!

— Quest —
A Whisper in the Void
Created by: Moonrain Media / Kira
Expected Difficulty: Veteran
Rewards: Artefacts, Experience

Details:
1. ~~Find a way inside the Cold Zone~~
2. ~~Recover the echoes of the lost (3/3)~~
3. ~~Kill the man with the skull mask.~~

+50000 EXP
3/3 artefacts added to inventory.

Level up! You have 15 skill points!
Welcome to level 52

At Eternity Access codes added to inventory.

An hour later a dozen Corpse Divers came to our 'rescue' with Chaz leading them to our location. It was over. The Hive, Skull-Faced Man was dead.

30.
At Eternity

LOCATION: DEEP SPACE
THE HIVE'S ORBITAL CARRIER

In the end, Skull-Faced Man was nothing more than an echo, an artefact creature born from the subconscious desires of a player to live forever. And who doesn't? Maybe the Hive wasn't lying. What if it was true and Damien was inside him? If not for the Hive's hesitation to kill me, would we have even won? The player that created it. What must it have been like for him or her? Living on the edge of the game like they were, so determined to find their way back, to find some kind meaning in the emptiness. Driven insane by the darkness. His own life, his real life must have been painful. I have seen that darkness. What it can do to people. What it had almost done to me. When Damien and the others had heard someone in the Cold Zone was crying out for help, they acted as quickly as they could. It took them time to prepare but they managed to hack their way into activating *At Eternity*. It was on that world, Nero, they hoped to find answers.

I was still laying on my back. I had just levelled up but didn't want to waste any effort in spending my new skill points. I had no idea what was going to come next and felt I had a need to save them. The image of Damien I had seen in my head continued to haunt me as I stood up and began to wander. I could hear something calling out to me. A voice in the darkness. A stranger in the night calling my name. It wasn't Damien. I knew he was gone.

Skull-Faced Man, Scrawl, all the players that had gone down fighting.

I found myself crawling through a small crevice in the wall. It had broken apart during our battle. Aiko came up by my side. I could hear her growling as the path became too small for her to follow.

I gathered my strength. I had arrived at a small hallway filled with stasis chambers. A small black sphere erupted from the ground. A trap. It shot out black spikes and I dodged out of the way of most, although one tore through my wrist. The pain quickly vanished. I had grown too strong for such toys. Blue lights revealed silhouettes around me trapped in ember. Inside them I could see dozens of figures, which looked like those of an alien species. The strange design of the orbital carrier made sense now, as did the origin of Skull-Faced Man. He had drifted with the unknown player across the galaxy to the edge of the map. Beyond the quadrants. The ship was a relic of a war fought long ago. They all slept now. They were, or at one time, had been weapons of the Chel, but more than that they were another sentient species. I could feel it. They had rebelled against the Chel. Unwilling to be their slaves.

In my inventory I had three new artefacts. One of which I recognized.

```
Damien's Rifle

Description: Gone but not forgotten.

Level: 51
Damage: 600
Weight: 7.5 lbs
Weapon Type: Battle Rifle
Rarity: Ultra-Rare
Impact: 10
Range: 7
Stability: 10
Reload Speed: 9
RPM (rounds per minute): 300 bursts
Affinity: 10
Sharpness: 9
Elemental: None
Critical Chance: 91%
Modifiers: None
```

I had one last mob to kill.

A creature stands before me in the shadow with five glowing red eyes. Two legs. A skeletal tail behind it. Burning rage. I'm not inside the carrier anymore. Time is slowed down. The world around me frozen. I'm immersed in the shadow. There is nothing but my body, my weapon, the creature and time. All the time I need. The immer, surrounding me. Giving me power. I feel the creature move closer towards me. It knows what I am. I aim down the sight of my rifle, holding it up ready in my arms. I can feel the energy build up inside as I pull the trigger.

Once again the creature disappears. The memory of it like a dream.

Aegis...

We fled the orbital carrier and left behind a drone to fly it into the closest star. I never wanted to see that ship again. The field that messed with our control commands was cut off. Even with Skull-Faced Man dead and gone the damage he had caused was permanent. Rumours of death in *Bane* were spreading like wild-fire as dozens of players and corporations did their best to salvage the situation, promising that it was all a lie, that the game was safe. Kira cut our feed as we regrouped inside the *Ibanez*. At the time of our battle we had hit ten million views. It was a new record. Each of us had been granted access codes to *At Eternity* but we all needed rest.

Together, we promised one another we would meet again in three days' time, hiding the *Ibanez* and Lady Gray's Titan at the edge of the system, deep inside an asteroid belt in the hollows of an old asteroid that had been mined, torn apart eons ago by the Chel or whatever alien species had actually created the world gates. As I said goodnight to Aiko I promised I would return, letting her crawl in beside me as I entered a stasis pod.

THE REAL

I spent the next two days in the real world. The moment I logged out I couldn't wait to meet up with Hannah, I knew she would be worried after the last message I had sent her. I couldn't imagine what she would say to me after I told her everything that had happened. As I came out of my pod, blood pouring down my

380

face, both Hannah and Reynolds were waiting for me. Reynolds, of course, was ready with a clean towel and food while Hannah grabbed me, wrapping her arms around my bloody clothes. I felt like I was going to faint but I smiled. Hannah kissed me. The rest of the night and most of the next day I let my body rest as Hannah stayed by my side.

I had been logged in for over twenty hours and pushed my body to the edge. Kira was right, the shadow power I had gained in the first dungeon was taking its toll on me both in-game and in real life. On my first day out, I found myself losing track of time. If not for Hannah I probably would have forgotten to eat and drink. As the second day began, Kira and Alexis sent me a message asking if I wanted to meet up at *The Sparrow* with them. I told them I was busy, taking a break, but they - together with Hannah - insisted. Apparently Alexis (Lady Gray) herself was demanding my presence and wouldn't take 'no' for an answer, when all else failed citing a clause in my contract. When they told me Gorge and Cass were going to be there, I gave in.

I arrived late as usual but I wasn't alone. Hannah had picked me up and walked in with me. Everyone was gathered around a table on which stood a variety of coloured shakes. Alexis, Kira, Chaz, Pierce, Cass, even Shiru. Hannah held up her hand, a peace sign asking for two more as the waitress thanked us for coming in. I felt happy. I had never imagined meeting like this.

On the wall was a picture of Damien, Cass, and I sitting together. The picture was signed by him. It was taken after I had been playing *Bane* for a few months. Alongside it there was a picture of Scrawl, Kira's brother, and the other two that had died in *Bane* sitting with Damien holding a sign that said: 'the stars are ours'.

'What is this?' I said. Alexis and Kira were smiling. The two were sharing a plate of fries, acting like best friends.

'We figured it out!' Kira said.

381

'Figured what out?' I asked.

'*At Eternity*, why they went.'

They had my attention. The whole start of this mess began when four players had found a way into the unknown.

'Why?'

'Because they could,' said Kira.

Alexis wiped her fingers clean. 'In the snow trenches of Cthonia, Scrawl and Damien were running a quest for a client named Gideon. He asked them to retrieve an artefact from a derelict ship that was neither human nor Chel. It was inside that ship that they found access codes to the gate. When they tried to return to Gideon to finish the quest he was dead. Taken out by a player-killer.'

'The stars belong to us, not the Chel. We declared war on them when we attacked the Spire. What we didn't know is that was always a part of what was supposed to happen.'

This seemed cryptic at best. 'What does that mean?'

'The Chel have been lying,' I heard Gorge's voice, but he was the only one I didn't see with us. Sitting next to Alexis on the table screen, facing everyone, was an old laptop with a video feed. There, from the waist up was Gorge, in his avatar as always.

'Sorry I couldn't join you in person,' he said.

'It's okay,' I smiled at the laptop's camera, knowing this was as close to seeing him in real life I would ever actually get. And I was fine with that.

'Before we set it to dive into the sun, we dug through the archives on the Hive's ship,' Gorge continued, 'the Chel are not the only sentient life in the galaxy. Ruins are being uncovered deep in all of the quadrants. New dungeons filled with archives dating back eons. All have one thing in common, they were wiped out or assimilated by the Chel. The Chel tricked humanity into coming through the world gate because they were at war.

382

They used Earth as a battleground. In the end both sides lost. The Chel went into hiding. That was why we found so few of them sleeping in the Spire. Their cities were in ruins. The humans that came through the world gate were meant to be lab rats, precursors to a new Chel army. They gifted us with powers and technology so that they could rebuild their empire. An empire they have started to reclaim. FTC troops have already started making moves against the Crimson Kings and Silvermanes using our attack on the Spire as a declaration of war.'

Alexis joined in, 'The Chel have come out of hiding. Just last night a new status appeared in our user interface. Alignment. It had two options.'

'Let me guess, Chel or human?'

'Close. It is Chel or Other. We are either with them or against them now. The whole system is split and guess who humanity have chosen as their poster boy?'

'No.'

LOCATION: DEEP SPACE
AT ETERNITY

Three days passed and we all logged back in just as we had promised. Lady Gray was right. A message appeared in my field of vision asking what my alignment wanted to be. I pushed it to the side. Minimizing the whole alignment box and watching it fade into my inventory. I would review it another time. I had become the villain. The emblem of the human resistance. At the moment none of that seemed to matter. I wanted just one thing. To set things right. To explore. To dive.

We recovered what we could. Without a body Nel was nothing more than a large piece of scrap. A small data core the size of my thumb however housed her mind. Unable to salvage anything else for the time being I installed Nel onto Damien's rifle, meanwhile Q-el's data core had also survived and recently been uploaded into the *Ibanez*'s computer by Kira.

AKA *Nel*

Description:
Gone but not forgotten.
Chances of survival ensured up to 99.9%

Level: 51
Damage: 600
Weight: 7.5 lbs
Weapon Type: Battle Rifle
Rarity: Ultra-Rare
Impact: 10
Range: 7
Stability: 10
Reload Speed: 9
RPM (rounds per minute): 300 bursts
Affinity: 10
Sharpness: 9
Elemental: None
Critical Chance: 91%
Modifiers: Artificial Intelligence Nel.

'I promised you an upgrade,' I said.

'I promised cookies, you don't always get what you want,' Aka Nel answered back, a familiar friend once more inside my head. 'What's the plan?'

'Answers. We still don't know where Skull-Faced Man came from, not for sure. There could be others like him out there, other modifications or worse.'

'I've already died once, what could be worse? Chances of survival are…'

'We'll survive,' I interrupted.

Lady Gray's Titan, the *Ibanez*, and seven other Corpse Diver ships stood at the threshold of the world gate. Kira entered the access code from the *Ibanez* and we watched as the gateway between worlds came to life. Unlike most warp gates that this one twisted in what looked like a hurricane of colour washing over all of us as we stared into it.

'Chances of survival are .01%'

+10 Luck

End.

Adrenaline 45

Affinity (weapons) 15

Agitation 15

Animal / Aquatic Expert 35

Artillery 15

Attack Boost 5 (+5 Bonus)

Blast Attack Boost 5

Blast Resistance 35

Bleeding Resistance 45

Botany 5

Bow Expert 5

Capacity Boost 5

Capture / Tame 15 (+ 50
Familiar Bonus) = 65

Carving 10

Charisma 25 (+10 Bonus)

Constitution 5

Critical Boost 50

Critical Affinity 50 (+10 Bonus)

Defence 5

Detection (stealth) 30 (+10
Bonus)

Divinity / Fame 5

Evasion 5

Explosives 15

Fire Attack 5

Fire Resistance 5

Focus 40

Fortification 5

Gambler 5

Guard 5

Hacking 25

Handicraft (crafting) 5

Heat Resistance 15

Health Boost 15

Hunting (survival) 5

Hunger (cooking) 5

Ice Attack 5

Ice Resistance 15

Intimidation 5

Iron Body 5

Latent Power 5

Luck 25

Medical Specialist 15

Mind's Eye 5 (+10 Piloting
Bonus)

Navigator 5

Nullification 5

Paralysis Attack 5

Paralysis Resistance 5

Peak Performance 5

Piercing (Damage Boost) 5

Pilot 5 (+20)

Poison Attack 5

Poison Resistance 5

Poison Duration 5

Psionic 5

Recovery 5

Stamina 30

Sheath Speed (reflexes)5

Strength 10

Stun Attack 5

Stun Duration 5

Stun Resistance 5

Survival 15
Tool Specialist 5

Training 5

Name: Aiko

Level 10
Mana: 100

Friendly
Health: 100
Stamina: 100

Adrenaline 70
Agitation 15
Attack Boost 15 (+5 Bonus)
Blast Attack Boost 15
Blast Resistance 35
Bleeding Resistance 45
Charisma 75
Constitution 25
Critical Boost 50
Critical Affinity 40
Defence 75
Detection (stealth) 40
Evasion 55
Fire Resistance 15
Focus 35
Guard 5

Heat Resistance 15
Health Boost 15
Ice Resistance 15
Intimidation 20
Luck 25
Nullification 15
Paralysis Resistance 15
Piercing (Damage Boost) 25
Poison Resistance 55
Recovery 45
Reflexes 35
Stamina 55
Strength 20
Stun Attack 35
Stun Duration 5
Stun Resistance 25

About the Author

Stephen Landry is a writer and graphic designer living in Nashville, TN with his fiancée, two rescue dogs, and cat. Much of his work is character-driven science fiction (space opera with aspects of fantasy, horror, and time travel) and LitRPG. When not writing Stephen can be found doing graphic design for many different clients including other authors, publishing companies, independent film studios, and more recently a few video game companies. His other passions include other artistic endeavours, helping people, hiking, playing video games, and working towards inspiring others.

Find Stephen online:
Website: stephen-landry.com
Instagram: stephen.landry

www.ingramcontent.com/pod-product-compliance
Lightning Source LLC
Chambersburg PA
CBHW020509260626
47156CB00006B/1929